P9-ARA-977

PENGUIN BOOKS

THREE DOG NIGHT

Peter Goldsworthy was born in Minlaton, South Australia, grew up in various country towns, and completed his schooling in Darwin. He graduated in medicine from the University of Adelaide in 1974 and has since divided his time equally between writing and medicine. His novels have sold over a quarter of a million copies in Australia alone, and have been translated into several European and Asian languages, as have his short stories and poetry. He has won numerous awards for his writing, including the Commonwealth Poetry Prize, an Australian Bicentennial Literary Award, and, jointly with composer Richard Mills, the 2002 Helpmann Award for Best New Australian Work for the opera *Batavia*.

Further information about the author
can be found at www.petergoldsworthy.com

'Goldsworthy combines deft social observation with stylish prose'

CHRISTOPHER BANTICK, *Sunday Tasmanian*

'*Three Dog Night* evokes a wonderful sense of Australianness . . . Goldsworthy is one of Australia's finest storytellers'

SUE STEVENSON, *Launceston Examiner*

'A powerful, emotional and intensely readable study of love, of life and of death'

DAVID CHRISTIE, *Newcastle Herald*

'Evocative prose carries the intensity of this book's dark journey . . . The novel pushes the reader almost as far as its characters'

JUDGES' REPORT, FAW CHRISTINA STEAD AWARD

'All Goldsworthy's skills as a poet and librettist are deployed in his most recent fiction. *Three Dog Night* is a novel of the here and now, at once lyrical and confronting'

JUDGES' REPORT, MILES FRANKLIN LITERARY AWARD

Also by Peter Goldsworthy

POETRY

Readings From Ecclesiastes
This Goes With This
This Goes With That: Selected Poems, 1970–1990
If, Then
New Selected Poems

SHORT FICTION

Archipelagoes
Zooing
Bleak Rooms
Little Deaths
The List of All Answers

NOVELS

Maestro
Magpie (with Brian Matthews)
Honk if You Are Jesus
Wish
Keep It Simple, Stupid
Jesus Wants Me for a Sunbeam

LIBRETTI

Summer of the Seventeenth Doll
Batavia

NON-FICTION

Navel Gazing

PETER GOLDSWORTHY

THREE DOG NIGHT

PENGUIN BOOKS

PENGUIN BOOKS

Published by the Penguin Group
Penguin Group (Australia)
250 Camberwell Road, Camberwell, Victoria 3124, Australia
(a division of Pearson Australia Group Pty Ltd)
Penguin Group (USA)
375 Hudson Street, New York, New York 10014, USA
Penguin Group (Canada)
90 Eglinton Avenue East, Suite 700, Toronto, ON M4P 2Y3, Canada
(a division of Pearson Canada Inc.)
Penguin Books Ltd
80 Strand, London WC2R 0RL, England
Penguin Ireland
25 St Stephen's Green, Dublin 2, Ireland
(a division of Penguin Books Ltd)
Penguin Group (India)
11, Community Centre, Panchsheel Park, New Delhi – 110 017, India
Penguin Group (NZ)
Cnr Airborne and Rosedale Roads, Albany, Auckland, New Zealand
(a division of Pearson New Zealand Ltd)
Penguin Group (South Africa) (Pty) Ltd
24 Sturdee Avenue, Rosebank, Johannesburg 2196, South Africa

Penguin Books Ltd, Registered Offices: 80 Strand, London, WC2R 0RL, England

First published by Penguin Books Australia Ltd, 2003
This edition published by Penguin Group (Australia),
a division of Pearson Australia Group Pty Ltd, 2004

3 5 7 9 10 8 6 4

Text copyright © Peter Goldsworthy 2003

The moral right of the author has been asserted

Cover design by Jo Hunt © Penguin Group (Australia)
Text design by David Altheim © Penguin Group (Australia)
Typeset in 12/19.5 pt Fairfield light by Post Pre-Press Group, Brisbane, Queensland
Printed and bound in Australia by McPherson's Printing Group, Maryborough, Victoria

National Library of Australia
Cataloguing-in-Publication data:

Goldsworthy, Peter, 1951– .

Three dog night.

ISBN 0140 28103 7.

I. Title.

A823.3

www.penguin.com.au

CONTENTS

PART I   Parsley, Sage, Rosemary
and Parrots

1

If love is an obsessive-compulsive disorder – same driven behaviour, same altered brain state, same chemistry – then I have been ill for years. But never as sick with bliss, as *diseased*, as now.

Sunday, mid-morning, early summer. My tenth day back in Australia after ten years of work and study overseas, ten years' hard mental labour in London. I am driving Lucy – my compulsion, my obsession – up into the Adelaide Hills for the first time. The day has taken its name to heart: a Sunday from the glory box of Sundays, a luminous morning saturated with sunlight and parrots. Happiness rises in my throat, thick as cud; the world outside the car, wholly blue and gold, seems almost too much for my senses, too tight a squeeze.

'Paradise,' Lucy murmurs, smitten.

Her voice, our common thought. There might be higher mountains on the planet than the Adelaide Hills, but they are no closer to heaven. Each valley is a little deeper and greener than the last, and each ridge, a little higher and bluer, seems another step in some sort of ascension. Even the names of the steps have a heavenly sound; Lucy speaks the words softly as the freeway exits slide past, big-print, white on green. Littlehampton. Oakbank. Aldgate. Bridgewater.

Music to my ears. I might be hearing these familiar place names for the first time, the imported words back where they belong, melting on an English tongue.

With the new sounds come new sights, as if I am seeing the hills for the first time also, through her fresh eyes. Our week-old red hatchback carries us steadily upwards. Each valley cups a single small town in its palm: a church spire, sometimes two, an old stone school, a single aisle of craft shops and Devonshire tea-rooms and petrol pumps.

Village is the better word for these untypical Australian towns, perhaps even hamlet; wanting to hear more English music, I wish the words into Lucy's mouth. She is straining forward against her seatbelt, peering out through the wind-screen, neck extended, face lifted, a pair of fine, wire-rimmed glasses perched on the bridge of her nose.

An extra rush of pleasure: her nearness, as always, makes me, simply, happy. So happy I sometimes feel I am drowning, strug-gling in the waters of a happiness far beyond my depth.

'They used to have ugly names,' I say perversely.

She glances at me, puzzled.

'Germans settled these areas. The church spires are all Lutheran. The names were changed after the war. Anglicised.'

Another exit catches her eye. 'Hahndorf kept its name?'

'Changed back again. For the tourist trade.'

'Don't spoil it for me, Marty. It reminds me of home. It's not at all what I expected Australia to be like.'

'You expected desert?'

'I didn't expect an English country garden.'

The names of imported trees replace the names of towns as she points out examples, their different, richer greens scattered among the dusty khaki of the eucalypts. Silver birch, golden elm, copper beech, golden poplar, weeping willow. More music to my ears; she could be singing those words, setting them to some common ancestral melody. *Parsley, sage, rosemary and thyme* . . .

Again I try to restrain my happiness, feeling dangerously loosened by it, made reckless. 'Some of us don't like the intro-duced species, Luce.'

She turns to me, surprised.

'Especially the pines. When I was a boy there was a kind of terrorist cell up here. GROAP.'

'Grope?'

'An acronym. Get Rid Of All Pines.'

'Is this another tease, Marty?'

'I kid you not. They actually used to bomb trees.'

Her full upper lip, a flautist's protruding lip, is flattened by a stifled laugh. '*Bomb* them?'

'With dynamite. But only pine trees – introduced pines.'

'Why pick on pines?'

'Nothing can grow under them. Native birds can't live in them.'

'You seem well informed. I don't suppose you were a member?'

'Not card-carrying. But sympathetic. A fellow traveller. I used to do a little birdwatching.'

A pair of brilliantly coloured parrots appears, flying parallel to the freeway, as if to test my credentials. The road *is* nearing heaven surely; such a gift is beyond coincidence. The birds veer in front of the speeding car for a time, bright-painted dolphins surfing the bow wave of a small red ship, then swerve away again, bored with the game.

'Rainbow lorikeet,' I tell her.

'Latin name?'

'*Trichoglossus haematodus.*'

She laughs, gratified. 'I can just see you as a birdwatcher.'

'Oh? And what exactly can you see?'

'A serious little boy. Not so much living in the world as studying it. Swotting it.'

I sneak a side glance at her, and then again; two short, safe bursts of attention. The larger-than-life eyes, the high, wide cheekbones, the strong nose, the upper lip forever about to press itself against some invisible mouthpiece. An arresting face, the kind that turns heads – not always pretty at close quarters, but utterly striking at a certain distance, the sum much greater than the parts.

'What happened to the original inhabitants, Marty?'

'The Germans?'

'The Aborigines. I've read things . . .'

'Then you already know. Died of the pox, mostly. Herded into missions. The usual sad stories. But it was a long time ago.'

I speak lightly, trying not to spoil the mood of the morning, but a shadow crosses her face and for a few minutes her thoughts are elsewhere. Another ridge, another valley bowl, more thickly wooded. Mostly native trees now: wattle scrub carpeting the slopes, giant gums along the creek beds.

Rousing, she half turns to me. 'No pines?'

'Spotted gums. *Eucalyptus maculata.*'

Self-parody is something else I have studied. Swotted. She smiles, returned to the pleasures of the present. Our eyes lock; for a long moment the car seems to guide itself along the sweeping curve and camber of the freeway, impossible to derail. This time I surrender to the swell of happiness; it fills me like a kind of liquid, moistens my eyes as if overspilling the brim of me.

Another big-print name flashes overhead, interrupting the trance. Lucy adds it to her list: 'Woodcroft.'

The exit skims past. I brake too late and too heavily, the wheels lock, the unfamiliar car veers, skidding slightly, into the safety lane of the freeway.

Lucy's grip on my arm, her startled hiss in my ear. 'Shit!'

But the car has stopped safely and the word carries no venom. I think to myself, In her mouth, here, today, shit might be nothing more than the name of another leafy hills town or imported English tree.

Or even a new kind of intimacy, a sweet nothing belonging to the moment just passed, a word from the same song.

2

I catch my first glimpse of Felix through trees. He is squatting in the grass at the back of the farmhouse, his jeans around his ankles, his buttocks exposed. He hasn't noticed our arrival. What is he doing? The house and its sanitary plumbing is no more than a few steps away.

'*Homo sapiens*?' Lucy whispers in my ear, amused.

'I wouldn't swear to the *sapiens*.'

He lifts his head at the sound of our voices. As he rises and unhurriedly shakes his penis, I realise he has been urinating, not defecating, but for some reason squatting to do so, like a woman.

His first words after ten years: 'You took your time.'

I want to shout his name, wrap my arms around him; his coolness deters me. A cigarette is jammed into a corner of his mouth; he doesn't bother removing it.

'We missed the exit,' I say, but he has already turned to Lucy.

'So this is the English bride?'

He reaches for her hand; she surrenders it reluctantly, trying – she tells me later – to remember which of his has been holding his cock.

She says brightly, 'I feel I know you already. Martin has told me everything about you.'

The stock phrase is met with a stock innuendo. 'Everything?'

His smile is mocking, lopsided, handicapped by the cigarette; his eyes linger on her, teasingly. I think, Not quite everything. Not the gaunt, shaven head, nor the leathery face. And not the weight loss. An athlete at school, full-bodied and muscular, he has shrunk to skin and bone. But his manner shocks me most of all – this air of cool mockery, so unlike the Felix of old.

I slip the wine bag from my shoulder. 'We've brought something for the occasion.'

'I'll try to find some glasses.' He turns on his heel and walks away to the house.

Lucy's eyes find mine. 'Well?' I ask.

She chooses her words carefully. 'Not quite what I expected.'

A rough wooden table sits on the terrace, ringed by canvas-backed chairs. She sits, easing the weight from her hip. She has been limping a little, favouring her left leg. Shorter than the right, malformed at the hip since childhood, it has not yet fully recovered from the plane trip.

Felix reappears before more need be said. I uncork and pour the champagne as he unscrews a water bottle for himself. Another surprise: is he on the wagon?

'To the return of the native,' he says, raising his water. 'And to his trophy wife.'

Lucy's eyes meet mine, startled. Where to look? It seems best to hide in formalities.

I raise my own glass. 'To the two people I love most in the world. Together at last.' To hell with coolness – time to say what I feel, or what I have been feeling for months, anticipating this moment. That my letters have been largely unanswered, that my oldest friend has changed beyond recognition, is forgotten in the rush of feeling. 'I'm sure you're going to be great friends,' I add.

Felix tilts his glass towards Lucy. 'Any wife of Martin's.'

Another sleazy, out-of-character joke. Lucy buries her face in her wineglass, sipping. She has never trusted in her looks, let alone felt at ease within them. A childhood spent in hospital beds hasn't helped. In public she is often gawkily awkward, carrying her beauty as she carries her left leg, as if it is yet another impediment. She knows she is beautiful – she has been told often enough – but has found only one use for beauty: as a filter. Those who are caught at the surface, who fail to pass through, are ignored.

He turns his attention to me. 'So, Herr Doktor Professor, you return wreathed in glory. An associate chair, no less.'

'Right place at the right time. I was lucky it became vacant.'

'What I want to know is, who sat the interview for you?' He glances towards Lucy, inviting her collusion; her smile is politely lukewarm, giving nothing away.

He looks back to me. 'And what on earth put the idea of psychiatry into your head? You might as well read entrails for a living.'

I think, unsettled, Has he read *any* of my letters? Lucy also has specialised in psychiatry; is he deliberately treading on two sets of toes?

'At least we *talk* to our patients. I couldn't believe my ears when I heard you'd gone into surgery. Speaking of reading entrails.'

'Believe. Sticking knives in people was one of the few things that gave me pleasure.' His smile has a knife edge itself.

Something in his emphasis alerts me. 'Was?'

'You haven't heard?'

'Heard what?'

'I thought my retirement would be a hot topic on the dinner-party circuit.'

'We've only been here a few days,' Lucy puts in.

Neither of us has a clue what he is talking about. 'You've given up surgery?'

He stubs out his cigarette and changes the subject. 'When do you start at the factory, Herr Doktor Professor?'

I want to ask the questions, not provide the answers, but it seems best to bide my time. 'Officially the new year. But I've been in to the department once or twice. Had a look round.'

'There must be a few ruffled feathers in Cloud Cuckoo Land. You getting a chair over the time-servers.'

'They know I can deliver the research grants.'

He opens the tobacco pouch at his elbow, plucks a cigarette paper from the pack. 'Ah, so you *bought* yourself a chair, Herr Doktor Professor!'

The mock title is beginning to grate. 'A half-chair. A stool. But it's a nice office. I get two windows. The senior lecturers only have one.'

A brief snort. 'What do you get when you make full professor?'

'Basil has a corner office. Four windows.'

He turns to Lucy. 'How many windows is the pain clinic giving you, Frau Doktor?'

So he has read my last letter.

'It's a part-time position,' she says. 'I'll be happy with a desk lamp.'

Again, the knife-twist smile. 'Ah, the sacrifices we make for lerv.'

I feel the need to defend her – to defend us. 'Lucy's position is senior consultant. With the right to private practice.'

'A psychiatrist running a pain clinic? What's the subtext there? It's all in the mind?'

She looks him in the eyes and says calmly, 'It *is* all in the mind. Where do you think we feel pain, Doctor?'

He lights his cigarette and takes a long suck, staring back at her, silenced. But only momentarily. 'Was it your own illness that made you interested in pain?'

Her turn to be silenced. She says eventually, 'Are you always this direct?'

'You were favouring one leg. What's the story? Perthe's? Osteomyelitis?' He looks to me without waiting for an answer. 'It adds something, don't you think? The real beauties are always ugly in some way. Flawed. How did Bacon put it? There is no excellent beauty that hath not some strangeness in the proportions?'

I sit frozen. This time he has gone too far, surely. But if Lucy feels shock, or anger, she hides it well. Professional habit: she, like me, is trained to use her reactions as a lens, less distorting than magnifying.

'What are you trying to say? You think my limp is sexy?'

He smiles. That bent mouth again; that hooded, supercilious gaze. A Latin tag comes back to me from the dissecting room. *Corrugator supercilii*, the bundle of tiny muscles that crinkles the forehead, lifts – cocks – the eyebrow.

'Tell us about the desert,' I say, changing the subject. 'You must have had some wonderful experiences.'

'I was a pig in shit.' Another long drag at his cigarette. When he speaks again, it is with a certain relish. 'Beatings, clubbings. Spearings. Open cranial cavities. Sucking chest wounds . . .'

He holds Lucy's gaze, less interested in sharing his experiences than trying to shock her, it seems. Unfazed, she stares back. She too has a medical degree, and has served time in the blood-splashed trenches of an emergency department.

'You sound disenchanted,' she says, fishing.

'On the contrary – it was a surgical goldmine.' He is still speaking through his cigarette. 'You see pathology walking around the communities that you just don't see down here, except in bottles. Leprosy. Yaws. Tertiary syphilis. When was the last time you saw a high-stepping gait?'

She interrupts. 'Wouldn't it make more sense to treat the causes?'

A loud snort, a puff of smoke. 'You've been in the country five minutes. What would you suggest, Frau Doktor?'

I use the German spelling deliberately; he has a way of hardening the consonant, making a mockery of the word and its entitlements. Lucy glances at me uncertainly, but presses on. 'I understand that their lands were taken from them. They live in squalor. Their life expectancies are Third World levels –'

'As I said, what exactly would you suggest?'

She looks out across the valley, seeking respite. We are far from the desert here. We might be sitting in some high dress circle, or opera box. The best seats in the house. The crooked creek below runs a crooked mile or so down towards the town; the slopes each side are sprinkled with new cream-brick houses on farmlet lots.

'You subdivided?' I say.

'Hobby farmers.' A snort of contempt. 'But they help pay the rent.'

My eyes meet Lucy's again: utter frustration. He is impossible to talk to.

A door bangs behind us; we turn together as a thin young woman in dark glasses emerges from the house. Her black T-shirt and jeans are crumpled, her thatch of short red hair dishevelled; she looks as if she has just fallen out of bed.

'God, it's so fucking *bright* out here.'

Felix offers no introductions; Lucy steps into the breach. 'Hello. I'm Lucy Blackman.– this is my husband Martin.'

Does she fail to notice Lucy's outstretched hand or ignore it? It's difficult to know what her eyes are doing behind those opaque black lenses.

'Have I missed breakfast?' The voice is husky – a smoker's voice, a night-owl's voice, much older than the smooth girl-skin of her arms and shoulders and face. She runs a handful of fingers through a tangle of hair. 'You guys old friends of Felix?'

'Long lost,' I say, surprised that she needs to ask, that she has apparently spent the night with Felix but knows nothing of the important visitors he has been expecting.

She is peering at her watch, not listening. 'Shit! Is that the time? Can someone run me home?'

Felix: 'You want me to abandon my guests?'

She turns to the guests for support. 'Can you believe this? He fucks the arse off me all night and won't even drive me home!'

More eye language between Lucy and me; her thoughts are carefully masked.

'I'll phone you a cab,' Felix offers.

'There's no *time*. Jesus, Felix, I'm working a late. And you know what matron's like.'

'I'll write you a sick note.'

'I took a sickie last Sunday. Remember?'

He rises to his feet, resigned amusement on his face. Left and right *Corrugator supercilii* raised in unison. The still nameless woman is already walking towards the house; she turns back momentarily, as if at last remembering the basic courtesies. 'Cool to meet you guys.'

'And you,' Lucy says.

'I could be a while.' Felix stubs out his cigarette.

He grins, and for the first time I see the gap in his teeth – the missing upper incisor, a black space in a wall of nicotine-yellow enamel. I can't take my eyes from it. Is camouflage the reason for the crooked smile, the cigarette permanently clamped between his lips?

He adds, oddly, 'Feel free to stay if you like,' then picks up his tobacco pouch and walks away.

We remain sitting, staring at each other, stunned.

'How are the mighty fallen,' I murmur.

I fill my glass, in need of another drink, even flat champagne. The muffled clunk of a car door carries down from the shed above the trees, then a second clunk; an engine coughs into life and a battered, early-model Toyota Landcruiser pulls out onto the creek road and bounces down towards the town.

'A penny for your thoughts, Herr Doktor Professor,' Lucy says.

Her appropriation of the title cancels Felix's mockery, mocks him instead.

'I thought, What a lovely young couple.'

She splutters, amused, and in that shared amusement we begin to be ourselves again.

'A penny for *your* thoughts.'

'You've talked so much about him, Marty. I'd built up this picture in my head. A sort of mental identikit.'

'You wouldn't pick Felix from the line-up?'

'With difficulty.' A wry smile. 'It's like seeing the film of a favourite book and the actors are nothing like you've imagined.'

'It's hard to believe he's the same man. All those sour jokes. Do you think he's depressed?'

She touches my arm lightly. 'Let's not put him on the couch just yet.'

'All the signs are there. And what about the little scene when we arrived? Squatting on his haunches to piss. What on earth was that about?'

'Perhaps he likes the tickle of grass.'

We chuckle softly together again; she lifts her glass and sips.

The wine catches the light and glows, a low-wattage bulb, golden, easy on the eye; she might be holding a lamp to her face.

'Let's just enjoy the day, Marty. We can worry about Felix later.'

Her nearness reassures me, her words calm me: fixed points in a mutating world. We sit for a time in silence, gazing out over the valley. The view, also, is calming: a geometric patchwork of orchard groves and vine rows and plush carpet-squares of lucerne and clover. Dairy cattle graze in the rich pastures, heads down: black and white Friesians, big-uddered Jerseys, the occasional brown horse a neck above them. Parrots feed noisily in the giant river gums along the creek: crimson rosellas, blue and yellow lorikeets.

A jacaranda – *Jacaranda mimosifolia* – is in late, last flower, a carpet of dusty purple at its feet. An apricot tree is so heavy with fruit that its limbs, bent concave, might be mistaken at a distance for a weeping willow. The sun pours its honey over our heads, bees sizzle among the ripening fruit, magpies roll marbles about their mouths in the high trees.

I think, Here, surely, is the last step in today's ascension, the actual bridge that connects heaven to earth.

'It reminds me of Tuscany,' Lucy says.

'Tuscany with parrots.'

The shocks of the last half-hour are fading. The Felix of old must still be hiding in this familiar landscape somewhere, and it can be only a matter of time before we find him.

'I loved to come here as a kid,' I tell her. 'I'd stay with Felix on exeat weekends. We'd help with the milking. The cherry-picking. But mostly we ran wild.'

'This was after his mother died?'

'I never knew her. His dad was always down in the butter factory, or the pub. We had the place to ourselves. The wine cellar. His old man's cigars. Fruit falling off the trees, blackberries all along the creek. We'd eat and drink and talk ourselves sick. For a boy from the western suburbs it was the Garden of Eden.'

'No apples?'

'Plenty of apricots.'

She rises. 'Speaking of which – all this wine on an empty stomach. Do you think . . . ?'

'I'm sure he can spare a few.'

I rise and follow her through the small orchard to the apricot tree. As she reaches in among the branches the fruit seem to pluck themselves into her hand, detaching at the slightest touch. I watch, stilled and silent, finding something deeply pleasurable in the sight of my wife gathering food.

'Are you just going to stand there and watch, Herr Professor?'

'I do the hunting. You do the gathering. It's an ancient contract.'

'It must have been in the fine print.'

She steps out from between the branches, kneels at the foot of the jacaranda tree and spills her bounty among the fallen blooms.

I kneel at her side. 'In fact,' I say, 'it *was* an apricot tree in the Garden of Eden. Apples are strictly cold-climate fruit.'

She presses an apricot into my mouth to silence me; the ripe fruit explodes at first bite. I shut my eyes; I would seal my ears also, if possible, losing myself in the singularity of the pleasure.

I mumble, 'Apple is a mistranslation from the Hebrew. Or maybe the Latin *pomum*, a general term for all fruit.'

'Pomme de terre,' she mumbles through her own mouthful. 'Apple of the earth.'

I laugh, a small splutter of fruit fibre. 'The forbidden potato? Doesn't quite have the same ring.'

We feast on, gorging ourselves.

'Perhaps it was a pomegranate.'

'I wasn't inviting debate, I was stating a fact. It was an apricot. Or maybe peach – *Prunus persica*, the Persian apple.'

Another bite, or explosion; my eyes close again, narrowing the focus of my senses. Lucy, speaking somewhere: 'Surely it's a Babylonian myth, originally, not Hebrew. Maybe it was a fig tree. Otherwise where did the fig leaves come from?'

I open my eyes to find that our faces are no more than an inch or two apart. 'The neighbours' fig tree?'

She laughs softly, and such is the rush of desire in me that we might have kissed already; the kiss, when it happens, is a rubber-stamp formality. But the softest of rubber stamps, and immediately much more than that, for the moment of the kiss, its expanding here and now, traps and holds us, insists that we continue. And so we continue as we always continue, opening windows through our clothing onto each other's bodies, then doorways into those bodies, ever-widening doorways.

The larger world about us – the summer glare and sizzling bees and parrot-screech – fades, the world of Lucy fills my mouth and eyes and hands, her small bird-cries of pleasure fill my ears.

It is some time before our attention can turn to subjects – objects – other than ourselves and our bodies; a mere half-hour as the clock flies, perhaps, but we are time-travelling in a less direct fashion.

'He's back,' Lucy murmurs, as a car crawls up the creek road in low gear.

But she makes no move to rise and the car drives on. Her hand plays idly in my groin, stirring the rich sexual scents which cling there; I brush the confetti of jacaranda blossom from her hair.

'I don't think he's coming back,' I say, and the realisation seems more amusing than disturbing, at least for the moment, in the afterglow of sex.

She says, 'Or else he's waiting down in the town for us to leave.'

A joke, but we have readmitted Felix to our world and he insists on a further hearing.

'Perhaps the signs were always there. Perhaps I just didn't notice them at school – the way he patronised me.'

'Academically?'

'We were pretty even. The two scholarship boys. Of course there was always the unspoken put-down: I needed to study all night, he breezed through on talent.' I chuckle, contented enough in the present to find amusement in the past. 'He used to write poetry,' I suddenly remember, surprised.

'We all used to write poetry at that age, Marty.'

'He used to perform his. Political poems, mostly. Protest poems. He was always in a hurry to change the world. South Africa. Palestine. Aboriginal rights. Which is why he headed out into the desert, of course. To save our corner of the Third World.'

'You weren't in such a hurry?'

'He always seemed a jump ahead of me. Discovering the Stones while I was still listening to the Beatles. Reading *Greek*, for Christ's sake, while I was struggling with Latin.'

She lifts her head, a please-explain look on her face.

'Our classics master at school – old Waldo. We were his pets, his chosen ephebes. Waldo liked to hold Sunday night soirées in his study after lights out. Sweet sherry. Toast with lashings of Gentlemen's Relish. Just the three of us.'

'He never . . . touched you?'

'If he wanted to it was displaced. He liked to read Catullus to me. Filthy postcards in beautiful Latin. But with Felix – with Felix he read Greek.'

'You resented it?'

'Felix never rubbed my face in it. But it was the tip of an iceberg. He always knew more. About *every*thing.'

Her lips are pressed against my neck; I can feel rather than see the slow spreading of her smile.

'You know more than anyone I've ever met, Herr Doktor Professor.'

3

I'm setting this down as if I am still back there, telling my story as it happens, live, in the freshness of the present. I want to break with professional habit. Psychiatry is nothing if not the habit of hindsight, and to write in the past tense – *we went, I thought, she said* – is to smother events with hindsight, to know too much already. To get a bit previous, as old Waldo liked to say. In short, I want to *be* there again, living that golden morning as if for the first time, innocently.

Of course, nothing is innocent.

London, last summer, my final psychotherapy case. Mr Paul J is a single white male, a twenty-something invalid pensioner. Presenting complaint? Much of his right frontal lobe had been torn from his brain by a steering column, years before. Clinical picture? The usual constellation of frontal lobe signs: disinhibition, inappropriate affect, shallow, labile moods. Plus – another textbook term – 'lack of reverence for social conventions'.

I quote chapter and verse from the *DSM-IV: Diagnostic and Statistical Manual of Mental Disorders*, fourth edition.

Complicating the picture are frequent epileptic seizures, during which he speaks in tongues. To me it sounds like Ancient Babylonian might have sounded: clashy, discordant mouthfuls of words like *ishtar* and *vashti* and *Gilgamesh* and *Baal*.

Lucy urges me to record his gibberish and run it through a computer, through some mix-and-match software that might seek out unconscious patterns. There might be a language in there after all, she suggests. We are lying in bed, sharing the day's news after lovemaking, a time and place when pillow-talk merges seamlessly with shoptalk. If the latest news from the linguists is correct, she continues, we can't help speaking in tongues. They are part of our nature. They *are* our nature.

Freud said something similar, I remind her in turn. There is always a deeper story, always an agenda.

Nothing, in short, is gibberish. Nothing is innocent, and nothing is gibberish. Including here, today, my little version of paradise in the hills.

More Latin, Virgil, this time, from the *Eclogues: Latet anguis in herba*. To which he might have added *semper*.

There's *always* a snake in the grass.

4

Another week, another Sunday, another ascension through those same towns and valleys, all green and blue and dusted with early-morning gold. I am alone this time, a man on a mission, inviting myself to lunch on the strength of an oblique voicemail apology from Felix.

About last Sunday – something came up. And I didn't have your mobile number. Hope you made yourselves comfortable . . .

I am ready for him today, better prepared. Summer is doing its best to help. The beauty of the day has a physicality that compels a physical, visceral response. As I park above the farmhouse my exhilaration seems less an internal state of mind than a sensation in its own right, as direct and unmediated as the sights and sounds that fill my eyes and ears.

Enamel skies, lush pastures, rainbow-painted parrots. Walking down through the cherry trees it strikes me that the world of Australia is less matter than mood – a mood worn on the outside of the body, like a garment. A summer garment.

Felix is wearing little else but summer. He is sitting in the sun on the back terrace, naked from the waist up, bent over the barbecue table, absorbed in some kind of card game. A large white bird is perched on an arm of the chair opposite, facing him like an opponent. Sulphur-crested cockatoo? Corella? I pause among the trees, spying. A pink cockatoo, its right wing skewed outwards in some kind of bandage or splint. *Cacatua leadbeateri.* Major Mitchell cockatoo. The usual cigarette is clamped between Felix's lips, a tray of butts sits on the table at his elbow. As I step out from the trees I notice the scars for the first time: parallel stripes of keloid criss-cross his shoulders and chest, thick as rope. My first thought: he has been flogged. But of course these must be tribal scars of some kind. Initiation scars, perhaps – scars of manhood.

'Early this week, Professor?' he says, and reaches for a T-shirt and tugs it over his head and shoulders. The message is clear: discussion of his scars is not on the agenda.

The cockatoo eyes me out of the side of its head, fluffing powder-pink breast feathers. A bottle of water sits among the scattered playing cards on the tabletop, a glass in front of Felix, a tiny shot glass in front of the bird. The effect is absurdly comical: all the Major Mitchell needs is a pile of poker chips and a cigarette stuck in its beak.

'Who's winning?'

'I can't even beat myself, Herr Doktor.' His gaze is past me, searching among the trees. 'But where's the trophy wife? Took the first flight back to London?'

'She sends her apologies. Unpacking.'

'Couldn't you send her instead? And you stay at home and unpack?'

The crooked smile is more familiar now, less unsettling. I tell myself again that I have spent too much time in the milder social weather of London, that I've forgotten how to read this harsh Australian teasing.

'Truth is I wanted to talk to you alone today. Chew the fat.'

'I think I feel an analysis coming on.'

He coughs suddenly, paroxysmally; a cough that doesn't stop, that reddens his face, bulges his eyes and raises the veins of his neck as thickly as the scars on his chest. He is left bent double in his chair, gasping for air.

'You okay?'

'Just a tickle.'

He straightens, shrugs off my arm, and is already reaching for his cigarette. He inhales deeply and almost immediately begins to breathe more easily, as if the noxious smoke is paradoxically soothing, a medicinal aerosol.

'Are you going to stand there all day, Herr Professor?'

'The chair's already taken.'

He gives a short, terse whistle; the cockatoo jumps awkwardly from the chair, flaps across the table and hops up onto his shoulder. It silently ruffles its head feathers, watching me sideways from one eye as I seat myself.

'Broken wing?'

'Humerus. Or the parrot equivalent. I tried to thread a Küchner wire through it.'

'You what?'

A quarter-grin, the dark gap in his teeth again drawing my gaze. 'Stupid idea in retrospect. Half killed him. Should have used Superglue first up.'

'You *glued* the wing-bones?'

'They still let me operate on birds.'

I allow this to pass. 'He's someone's pet?'

He shakes his head. 'Found him flapping about on my doorstep a week or two back. Lucky I got to him before the crows.'

I think, If Lucy were here she might warm to him a little this week. Lucy, earth-mother of all suffering creatures, great and small, who in our first week in Australia has already twice stopped the car at road-kill to offer palliative care.

The rescued bird edges closer to the side of Felix's head and nuzzles his ear with its small squid-beak.

'*Cacatua leadbeateri*,' I say. 'You don't often see them this far south.'

'Kakalyalya, the Warlpiri call him.' He pauses, thinking. '*Cacatua*. Kakalyalya. Oddly similar.'

A slight dropping of his guard; an opening. 'You learnt the language?'

'Enough to get by.' He sucks again at his cigarette, then adds, as if deciding to make conversation after all, 'You'll be fascinated to know, Prof, the desert languages are a bit like Latin. Case inflexions. Any number of suffixes.' He stubs out his cigarette, reaches for his tobacco pouch and begins to roll another.

Things are going well. I am encouraged to ask, 'How did you get the scars?'

Absorbed in the craft of cigarette-making, has he heard my question?

'Some sort of tribal initiation?' I prompt. Half-remembered Aboriginal lore comes back to me. 'They knock out the front tooth, don't they?'

Still no answer.

'May I?' I ask when he has finished, and reach for the tobacco pouch and begin to roll my own lumpy, misshapen tube.

'What's this, Herr Professor? Chapter one in the textbook: Establishing Rapport With the Patient?'

'Chapter two. The Difficult Patient.'

He snorts, but more good-naturedly. His latest cigarette is already half consumed, a fast-burning magnesium flare. My own roosts quietly between my fingers. How many years since I last smoked? School days, with Felix, sitting in our shared study, the windows flung open to release the incriminating fumes. Or later, at medical school, solving the world's problems

27

over a flagon of red, out-drinking each other, out-smoking each other, out-talking. Everything was a contest back then.

'Remember that first day at school? The two scholarship boys vying to see who could write down the most States of America?'

'Small things amuse small minds,' he murmurs.

'Mine was the smallest. I could never remember Nebraska. I still can't remember its name.'

The joke is less over his head than beneath his notice. He leans back in his chair and shuts his eyes, and I can study him again at leisure. His face is lined as deeply as the palm of a hand, and I have professional qualifications in the reading of such palms. *Is* he depressed? There seems – psych-speak, *DSM*-speak – a definite flatness of affect.

'Are you happy, Felix?'

'Fuck off,' he says matter-of-factly.

'You don't want to talk about it?'

More silence. At length he open his eyes and asks, 'Who was it who said that the secret of happiness is to love a good woman and kill a bad man?'

I hazard a guess: 'Catullus?'

'No doubt you can quote the Latin, Professor.'

He exhales smoothly; the smoke hangs between us in the still air. I have been breathing more of his smoke than mine, but passive smoking is the least of my problems. His relentless passive aggression – how to survive it? An appeal to nostalgia?

'Remember those nights reading Catullus in old Waldo's study after lights out?'

The glimmer of a smile. Is he remembering what I am remembering? The two of us sunk in Waldo's antique sofa, being plied with sweet sherry and sour poetry. Filthy poetry. Virgil by day, in the classroom; Catullus, in secret, at night.

'I remember reading Plato,' Felix says. 'Something about it being a teacher's task to pollute the minds of the sons of the bourgeoisie.' He grins again. 'I forget the Greek.'

'Waldo would have been sacked on the spot if word had got out.'

'You haven't heard then, Prof?'

'Heard what?'

'There was a . . . misunderstanding involving one of his favourites. One of the ephebes. The school managed to keep the police out of it, but the old bugger was sent home to New Zealand in disgrace.' The pleasure he takes in dowsing my nostalgia is obvious.

'He never touched *us*,' I say. Except with words, those Greek and Latin words. The old man had a mannered, seductive way of reading – longwinded but sensuous, rolling the big, ten-dollar words about his mouth. *Sesquipedalia verba*: words a foot and a half long.

'Are *you* happy, Herr Professor?'

I relocate into the present, startled.

He continues, 'For someone who has everything he wants – a trophy wife, an office with two windows – you seem to spend a lot of time in the past.'

I gesture out over the valley, refusing to be provoked. 'Your office has more windows than mine.'

He closes his eyes again, uninterested in the view through that big, figurative window.

After a promising start I'm getting nowhere. I've sat through most varieties of human silence: phobic shyness, silent protest, catatonic muteness, paranoid suspicion – even plain, pursed-lipped malingering. An old trick is to sit in silence myself, my only words at the end of the allotted hour ('Time's up this week') usually triggering some response ('How stupid is this?' or 'I thought you were supposed to *help* me!'), and in the very last minute of the consultation, the consultation proper begins. At other times I'm more active. 'Since I know you are only pre-tending not to listen I'll tell you why . . .'

Apples and oranges. But Felix is all onion. 'Tell me about the desert,' I say.

No answer. I watch him for a time, less frustrated than bewil-dered. His mouth is slightly ajar, his breathing regular; surely he hasn't fallen asleep in his chair? A snoozing pirate with a pink parrot perched on his shoulder.

I roll another cigarette, a more practised, shapely cylinder, and sit smoking in that high opera box above the valley. The jacaranda has shed its blue rinse completely, the ground about the apricot tree is carpeted with fallen fruit. *Prunus armeniaca*, the Armenian apple – I have looked it up during the week. Martin-lore, Felix liked to call such facts. My role in our friendship was less court jester than court scholar. Court encyclopaedist. Speaker of the foot-and-a-half-long words. More lore: apricot derives from the Latin *praecoqua*, early ripe. The precocious apple? These are well past their prime. I inhale, exhale, finding it calming. A bell tolls faintly in the town below; I can make out various ant-figures on the church steps. Ants in their Sunday best. Other ants scamper about on the town tennis courts, clad in their own Sunday best of crisply pressed whites. I shut my eyes; the sun is a hot blunt knife buttering my face and shoulders.

'Tell *me* about the trophy wife.'

Felix's voice jars me back into the world. His narrowed eyes are watching me again, a new cigarette dangling from his lip.

'I'd eat her shit,' I say, then turn away, uncertain where the words have come from. Accumulated frustration? A desire to hear something true spoken, something from the heart, even if I have to speak it myself, from my heart?

'No doubt you're the expert on that,' he says.

'I'm sorry?'

'Isn't that your field now? Perversions. Fetishes. I hear you spend a lot of time on the Net, downloading porn.'

'Who told you that?'

'A little bird.'

The Major Mitchell is nuzzling his ear again; I force a laugh. 'I'd forgotten what a small town this is.'

He takes in another lungful of smoke, saying nothing, waiting to hear more.

'The Net is only part of the story,' I say. 'I'm interested in all popular culture, its effects on mental illness.'

'Sounds like an excuse to watch a lot of cheap porn.'

'And listen to a lot of bad hip-hop.'

A faint smile. 'Nice work if you can get it.'

In the face of his mockery I feel a need to explain further. 'There's a useful German word, *Maskenfreiheit*. The freedom we have when we wear masks.'

A smoke-ring floats from his rounded mouth, or less a smoke-ring than a smoke-signal: *boring*.

'I'm interested in the masks we wear on the Net. In what those masks reveal of us when we don't have to look anyone directly in the eye. When we're hiding behind some chatline persona . . .'

His eyes have closed again. Is he listening? I press on. 'I have a notion – this is a long shot – that Jung's collective unconscious is being made manifest on the Web. Every instinct, every wild fantasy is there, acted out – but acted out with others. Shared.'

He opens his eyes and looks at me, mildly interested.

'The World Wide Id,' I say.

He sits up a little straighter. I have surprised him, and for the first time he has fully engaged with what I am saying.

'Nice phrase. A little glib, but I like it.'

A crumb from his table. Encouraged, I babble on. 'Of course I've never liked the use of the Latin *id* in English. Freud's *es* is better translated as "it". Something raw, ungendered –'

He interrupts. 'What you're saying about the Net, the unconscious becoming conscious –'

'Jung's *collective* unconscious.'

'Surely Freud is more your man than Jung, Professor. The Net is driven by sex.'

'Freud hardly invented sex.'

'But sex invented Freud.' A gap-toothed smile. 'And sex invented the Net. The e-porn industry supplies all the money, all the energy. Where did Amazon-dot-com come from? Porn merchants showed the way. Net business is ninety percent porn business.'

'I'm more interested in effects than causes.'

'Can you separate the two? Porn drove the development of scanner technology. Video cassettes. Colour printers. We owe it all to the thirst for porn.' A pause. 'Necessity is the mother-fucker of invention,' he adds in a small explosion of mirth and smoke.

What can I say? My cigarette is still alight on the edge of the table – just. I reach for it and suck deeply. A handful of smoky fingers feel their way into the wet gloves of my lungs – still a good fit, even after all these years.

'What *is* the story of the limp?' He changes the subject again.

'Perhaps you should ask Lucy.'

'Don't be coy, Herr Professor. We're all doctors here. Road trauma?'

Usually I love talking of her; today I am more guarded. 'Fractured pelvis. Hip.'

'Must have been more than that. The surgeons fuck up?'

'There were complications. She spent half her childhood in hospital. And the other half in a plaster spica, sliding about on her belly on a skateboard.'

'How did she manage school?'

'Home tutors, mostly. She had a lot of time on her hands. She likes to say she read the British Library – in bed.'

'So sickness was good for her?'

'That's not what I'm saying. No-one should have to go through that.' I pause, slowing things down, choosing my words more carefully. 'But I think it gave her a special sensitivity. Made her find things in herself. Depths.'

This time he says nothing. I reach across and take a too-large mouthful of water from his glass; a liquid rope of coldness descends at speed through my chest. I have come to interrogate Felix, not to be interrogated. Especially about Lucy.

'Your friend's not here today?'

'Which friend?'

'The nurse with the hangover.'

A derisory snort. 'The lovely Jenna. God, no.'

'It's not serious then?'

'Let's just say I'm not about to eat her shit.' He laughs more loudly at this. 'You know, I'm immensely reassured, Herr Doktor Professor. What worried me about this psychiatry racket was how someone as rational as you could make a living dealing every day with the irrational. But now the truth is out. You're just as loopy as the rest of us.'

And he laughs again, a laugh that ends in another paroxysm of coughing. The cockatoo, alarmed, hops from his shoulder to the safety of the table, where it promptly releases a large splash of thick white paint.

'Have you seen someone about that cough?'

He reaches for his water and sips. 'Campfire lung. Too many five-dog nights out in the desert.'

'I'm sorry?'

'Desert expression. It gets so cold out there you need dogs to keep warm. Three dogs, four, five – like degrees on a thermometer.'

Another chance to fish. 'You must have had some wonderful experiences.'

'It was just a job, Prof.'

'That wasn't your attitude when you went out there.'

His guarded eyes on mine, sceptical. 'Is that so? Your memories are obviously more reliable than mine.'

'I think you went out there for the same reason you took pity on the cockatoo.'

A harsh laugh. 'Shall I tell you about my relationship with my father now, Professor?'

'You can tell me about your scars.'

But he is on his feet and stepping away from the table. His body language is inviting me to rise also – inviting me, I realise, to leave. My time is up, as clearly as if a bell has rung to indicate the end of a consultation, but for the moment I choose to remain seated.

'Were you adopted into the tribe?'

'You never let up, do you, Prof?'

'Well?'

'Adoption is no big deal. They adopt you in the desert so that you exist. They adopt everyone, give everyone a skin name. So they can think about you, place you in the world.'

'What's your name?'

'Japaljarri,' he says. 'Felix Johnson Japaljarri.'

He walks away into the trees, loosens his belt and squats on his haunches, tugging the crotch of his jeans back between his legs, out of the way. A gush of piss runs out into the bracken.

The mystery again, but it is pushed to the back of my mind as my own bladder makes its presence felt in sympathy. I walk to the nearest tree and unzip. An odd thought strikes me as I stand there. My second visit to Felix, like the first, has taken place entirely outdoors. Even urination has taken place outdoors. Perhaps this is not so odd, perhaps it is merely some essence of summer and Australia, but it also seems the essence of the new, changed Felix. Once again he has told me nothing of himself. I have talked of my work, of Lucy, of London, of school, but I have been allowed inside none of his houses, none of his rooms.

'Give my regards to the English rose,' he says as he rises, and tugs his jeans up.

I recycle his own joke, trying to keep him standing there, talking. 'If she hasn't caught the first flight back to London.'

But he is already walking rapidly away towards the house, pausing only to collect his cockatoo from the table. Tethered to the bracken by a seemingly endless rope of piss, I can only stand and watch.

'She's far too good for you, you know,' he calls back. And then again, his parting shot, 'I don't know what she sees in you.'

A door bangs, and when I finally break free of the liquid thread there is no sign of him.

5

What does she see in me?

She entered my office and my life for the first time five years ago.

St Bartholomew's Hospital, London, mid-winter. Time? Mid-afternoon in theory, but the sun has already set, the last light curtained by thick cloud and dense rain.

'Doctor Blackman? I'm Doctor Piper. The new trainee.'

Her eyes are lowered; her chin-length hair, rain-damp, flops forward, obscuring her face.

'Martin,' I offer, but am offered nothing in return.

She sits opposite and opens the patient file she is carrying. 'I have a case I thought might be suitable.'

We are to spend fifty hours together – an hour of case supervision for every hour she spends with her patient. A hand strays to her cheek and remains there, as if hiding some birthmark or deformity; she is still avoiding my eyes. Shyness? I ask her to walk me through the file.

'Mrs Jennifer P,' she states. 'Age fifty-four, Caucasian, legal secretary, twice widowed.'

Businesslike, straight to the point. Both husbands have died in Jennifer P's arms, she tells me, during coitus – the quaint Latin term uttered without falter. Since the death of the second, on their actual wedding night, Jennifer P has become increasingly reclusive and solitary. In particular she avoids men, or places where men gather. She has come to believe, not unreasonably, that she is jinxed.

'The kiss of death,' I say.

Doctor Piper lifts her eyes to mine, unamused, and I see that she has nothing to hide but her beauty.

'I believe I have established good rapport,' she says. 'I believe she would respond well to insight-orientated psychotherapy.'

Shyness is not the word; there is something too self-contained in her manner, something politely reticent rather than shy – something at any rate impenetrable. She is quietly firm in her opinions. Too firm for a student? Unsettled, I begin to interrogate her, gently, testing other options. Is the patient depressed, biologically? Would drug treatment be more beneficial? I tug the *DSM-IV* from my shelves. We talk through criterion A, Delusional Disorder: non-bizarre delusions of at least one month's duration. We talk through the finer points of non-bizarre delusions (situations that might conceivably occur in real life, such as being followed) versus the bizarre (such as being abducted by aliens).

'Feeling that you are jinxed,' I suggest, 'might qualify as bizarre.'

She disagrees, mildly. 'Surely it is merely an extreme case of magical thinking.'

We swap these first sentences as cautiously as if they are hostages at a border crossing. Still unable to find her eyes, I talk at her mouth instead, the full upper lip, the smaller lower lip which she gnaws from time to time as she chooses her next words.

I say, 'Without the possibility of patient insight, psychotherapy will get nowhere.'

She demurs again. She would like the chance to free up Mrs P's guilt, to assist in its dispersal.

I like her eccentric, bookish vocabulary, her use of unfamiliar words in new contexts: catalyse, aerate. She doesn't like my preoccupation with the *DSM-IV*, its strict pigeonholes and black-and-white definitions.

'You seem more interested in classification than cure,' she says, the mildness of her tone not quite disarming the seriousness of the accusation.

'No cure without classification,' I say – a self-parody, but not without substance.

Her hand hides her face again, her reaction escapes me. Psychiatry is in the middle of a bloodless coup, I tell her. We are making a science out of an art: standardising the diagnostic criteria. The days of the talking cure – self-knowledge as the means of liberation – are numbered.

'You don't want to talk to your patients?'

'I want to listen to them. I believe in careful history-taking. I'm just not sure the talking does much good. The new generation of psychotropic drugs has changed everything, forever.'

Was that a wince? 'With respect, Doctor, you start drugging people when you tire of understanding them.'

She is me, five years back. Five years younger. Five years less rigid? I talk more generally, more philosophically. As the power of science to manipulate the world grows, I tell her, it seems clear that words can no longer compete with numbers; talking, in short, with counting. Statistics – probabilities, epidemiology, measurable quality-of-life outcomes – now rule the world of general medicine.

She watches me without expression. What is she thinking? That for someone with no time for talking, I won't shut up? Her lack of response goads me further; I babble on, digging myself an even deeper hole. Or if not deeper at least wider – an absurdly wide hole, ranging over areas of human knowledge far beyond me. There are strange developments everywhere, I lecture her. Physics is mounting a hostile takeover of metaphysics. Computers are teaching us more than we need to know about consciousness, and all we need to know about epistemology, about how we know the things we know. Evolutionary biology – mathematical game-playing – is fast providing the default settings for morality, love, murder, family loyalties, marriage . . .

'And our small pond, Doctor?'

'I'm sorry?'

'Psychiatry.'

Here, I tell her – especially here – the blowtorch of neurochemistry is fast reducing the art of psychoanalysis to a vapour trail of hot air.

'You sound disenchanted.'

'I served time on the couch myself,' I say, before adding hastily, 'as part of my training, of course.'

A quarter-smile on her lips? I stumble on, undeterred. 'It was great fun at first, being the star of my own psychodrama. Sixty minutes of fame a day, five matinée performances a week. On a narrow, upholstered Freudian stage.'

A half-smile now, quickly suppressed.

'After six months I decided if I could bear talking about myself this much, my diagnosis was clear and untreatable: Narcissistic Personality Disorder, *DSM-IV* code 301.81.'

'This is all very interesting, Doctor. But is it relevant to my patient?'

Back to earth with a thud. I reach behind and tug a case-file from my filing cabinet, two thick volumes, a *War and Peace*. 'This might be relevant.'

'An old case of yours?'

'An old disillusionment.'

'I thought we were here to discuss my patient, but I'm more than happy to help you with yours.'

Neutral tone, just a hint of sarcasm in her eyes. I bury my face in the notes. 'Mr Barry J. A thirty-something white male referred from the surgical unit after attempting to sever his own leg with a circular saw.'

'Suicide attempt?'

'Body Dysmorphic Syndrome. He just wanted his leg removed. Had been trying to have it removed surgically, legally, for years.'

'There was something wrong with it?'

'Nothing physical. He felt he *needed* it removed.' I quote from my notes. '"I've never felt this leg belonged to me, Doctor . . . I've never felt myself fully expressed in a body with two legs."'

She is all ears now, hooked on the human detail.

'An intelligent man. Loving parents. Good school. Ten years

married, holding down a highly paid professional job. Witty, well read. I enjoyed talking to him.' I smile at the memory. '"Speak wise polysyllables at me, Doc," he would say, settling back into the couch each week, hands behind his head.'

'Did polysyllables help?'

'Nothing helped. We talked till we were blue in the face. Blue in both faces. He knew he was a danger to himself. He also knew that he would never be happy attached to that length of foreign leg.' I glance up and offer the moral of the story. 'So much for self-knowledge. The head hath no dominion over the loony heart.'

She remains unimpressed. 'So *you* became disillusioned. But what happened to him?'

I seek refuge in my notes again. 'He'd done so much damage to his leg that the surgeons felt compelled to complete the amputation. From me they wanted to know, would obliging his fantasy harm him? Would colluding in his madness, even necessarily, upset some delicate mental balance?'

'Your answer?'

I tap my fingers on the thick case-notes. 'My answer was a book, but it was too thick a book for the surgeons. They needed practical, immediate answers.'

She can't help smiling. 'Does your book have a title?'

'*Body Dysmorphic Syndrome: Apotemnophiliac Type.*'

Her smile broadens, she realises that I am sending myself up again. 'A wise polysyllable?'

'The best I could offer. Perhaps it even helped him a little, naming his compulsion.'

'In what sense?'

'There are others like you, I was telling him. You're not alone.'

'This is the name of your club?'

'Exactly. And here is your life membership.'

Our eyes hold for a moment. A beep on my intercom from the department secretary; our time is up. In fact it has been up for some while and I have failed to notice. For next week's session, I suggest, we might concentrate on Mrs P's premorbid personality.

Puzzlement in her eyes. 'Then you still want to supervise me?'

'Let's take it a week at a time.'

She hesitates, averts her eyes. 'You don't think we might be . . . temperamentally unsuited?'

'I'm sure that is exactly why the training committee has recommended me to you.'

'Or you to me?'

What does she see in me? In the long week that follows I replay that hour of conversation endlessly, editing my side, wincing at what is beyond repair. My world has flipped upside down; I see myself through her eyes and wonder, What *could* she see in me? Condescension, glibness, stiffness of mind? A mouth crammed with foot-and-a-half-long words? A man five years older but no more than five minutes wiser?

I am wrong. She enters my office a week later as she left it, with a quarter-smile and a mild tease. 'Shall we discuss your case or mine this week, Doctor?'

I am in love with Doctor Piper – Lucy, she allows – by the

end of this second hour together. I accept that I am in love with her after the fourth hour, always a slow learner when it comes to my own mental state. By the end of the sixth or seventh hour I know I must disqualify myself as her supervisor, but still we talk on and around the standard psychobiographical chapter headings: Mrs P's Mother, Father, Early Childhood. First Day At School, First Sexual Experience, Recurrent Dreams.

Case supervision is real-time supervision: an hour for an hour. But refracted through the warped lens of Mrs P's biography, fragments of our own life stories can be glimpsed, largely under the same standard chapter headings, First Sexual Experience excluded. Excluded also are details of Lucy's injury, although she mentions in passing that she has spent much of her childhood in hospital. Food for thought as I try to peer beneath that carefully arranged surface beauty. How does Felix put it, years later: her illness was good for her? Not for him to say, and not yet for me to think. But I wonder then, as I wonder now, if her beauty has been a greater handicap than her ruined hip. I cannot ignore that beauty – it shines through her self-consciousness, her gawky awkwardness, her thick cladding of face paint – but without her illness, might she have too easily succumbed to it? Am I also caught at her surface, unable to see beneath? I am certainly struck by how thick beauty is. Skin-deep, perhaps, but such a deep, tough skin; such an armour. Difficult to break through, but even more difficult to break out of.

An hour for an hour becomes two hours for an hour. I move our discussions to the end of the day; we can talk each afternoon until we are emptied. Lacking sweet sherry and Gentlemen's Relish, I offer bag-tea and hospital-issue biscuits. In lieu of Catullus, a reading list: pharmacology, neurology, brain chemistry. She offers her own list in turn: new psychotherapy models, cognitive-therapy studies. Who is supervising whom? The atmosphere has thickened between us, become statically charged, electric. Are we losing sight of her patient? Yes, but I tell myself that the increasing voltage in the air is creative, that the sense of play in our gentle disagreements might make new connections, throw up new approaches.

I defend myself to myself by quoting Waldo. Who was quoting Plato quoting Socrates. The necessary Eros of the teacher–student relationship.

We are both vulnerable, she more than I – but Mrs Jennifer P most of all.

The eleventh session: May Day in England, or near enough. Lukewarm light teasing the cloud cover apart, splashes of pallid colour in the window-boxes and corner parks. Mayday inside, definitely. I must scuttle the small professional ship we have shared for three months.

'Before we start, Doctor Piper . . . Lucy. There's something I must say.'

She glances away. I sense that she has been waiting for this moment, but through hierarchical etiquette has left it to me to name the problem.

'I feel I must disqualify myself as your supervisor.'

'And my patient?'

'The training committee will assign another supervisor. I will hand on a full report.'

'And my hours with you?'

'They will be credited.'

She takes a deep breath, but rapidly, like a singer, as if what she is about to say, or sing, requires extra wind. But the words, when they come, are brief and softly spoken.

'I'm glad that you no longer want to work with me, Martin.'

Our eyes lock. My heart hammers against the bars of its cage. Standard boy-meets-girl disruptions to physiology, but I have never felt them so powerfully. I feel unstable inside, as if all my organs have shaken loose from their bony shelves and leapt out into the unknown.

A flush creeps above the collar of her blouse onto her exposed throat: a disruption in her own physiology.

Somehow I find the necessary words. 'Perhaps we could meet for a meal later tonight?'

'I'm on duty at Guy's.'

'What time do you finish?'

The glimmer of a smile. 'Three a.m.'

Silence. Without the safety net of a professional relationship and its default conversational structures, we are floundering a little.

'Are you on duty tomorrow?'

'No.' She glances up again. 'We could meet for lunch.'

I scribble a time and place in my diary, but after she has left, that time and that place both seem impossibly, painfully distant.

I can neither work nor sleep. Fuelled by coffee and adrenaline, I am waiting in the entrance lobby at Guy's at three a.m., heart pounding. Out-of-character behaviour? Utterly. I am *driven* out of character by new feelings. Or perhaps old feelings – for I have been infatuated before – but of new magnitude.

No sign of surprise on her face as she emerges from the lobby lift, a slight smile only, and the now familiar flush creeping up a chalk-white neck. I sense that she half expects me. We are both exhausted – we yawn contagiously – but there is no talk of sleep as we hurry outside. A chill in the night air; the night roar of London above, the seismic rumbling of the Jubilee Line below. I cannot keep my hands from her; I must touch her, immediately. Who is this strange, passionate man who pulls her into an alley, shoves her against a damp wall a stone's throw from the river and presses his cold lips against hers until they part and give up the warmth inside?

We move on, arm in arm now, fingers entwined. What do we talk about? Nothing of substance. Where are we going? Her place or mine, clearly, but precisely which remains unspoken as we glide through those streets, steered like a pair of upturned wineglasses on a séance table by some shared, half-conscious purpose.

Her place, finally. As if by accident. Two flights of narrow, curved steps, a narrow door, a narrow sofa-bed quickly unclasped. Shaken free of clothing, she abandons all camouflage and all reserve. She kisses me open-faced, open-mouthed, uncovering herself to me with a hunger that only momentarily surprises me. For almost immediately I am lost to such thoughts, stepping out of her narrow bedsitter into nowhere, into a free-falling weightlessness that carries me downwards and further down, heels over head.

Where am I when I take notice again? Suspended in a long, sweet after-glide, a drift towards the wider world. Where is Lucy? I can barely see her in the darkened room, but I can hear her shallow breaths, feel her still-trembling body. My fingers find the wetness on her cheeks.

'Did I hurt you?'

'Of course not.'

I wrap her tightly in my arms as her trembling eases. She has long sensed this part of herself, she finally confesses in a whisper. Has half imagined, half dreaded it. As she speaks, her words become more steady.

'My illness was my chaperone. My sickbed protected me, keeping me from other beds.'

'More dangerous beds?'

'Some, perhaps. I *thought* about sex a lot.'

Silence, while I take this in. 'You must have been aware of the, ah, interest of men.'

Warm feathers of breath tickle my face; she has turned to me, invisibly. 'I was very naïve. The world seemed full of nice, kind men. Men were always so helpful. So interested in my . . . wellbeing.'

'I'm interested in your wellbeing.'

And she in mine. Seamless the day and night that follow: the four corners of her flimsy, pull-down bed become a world without end; a curved, fitted universe of which all is now part. Where tongue ends, lip begins; where finger finishes there is skin. Hers? Mine? It no longer matters. Time passes outside that infolded universe – perhaps. Clocks tick, calendars flip – possibly. Inside, even the light of day that filters through the slatted blind cannot be told from night, and soon no separate thing can be told from any other thing. Bed, Floor, Pillow, Quilt, Her, Me – all names are subsumed in one name, Us, as the rhythmic sewing-machinery of sex stitches us together, seamlessly, irreversibly.

Several times in the narrow tidal-wash of consciousness between sex and sleep and sex she murmurs, each time with less embarrassment, 'I've never done *that* before.'

Nor I. Was Freud the first to claim that personality is fully formed in early childhood? That infancy is destiny, and whoever or whatever we are at five – angel or devil, bully or slave – we must remain for the terms of our natural lives? I think otherwise. I prefer to believe that what follows in her room changes me, moves me beyond childhood, beyond the life-term of myself, the jail of my own personality, in ways I hadn't thought possible.

Memo, Herr Doktor Freud: forget infantile sexuality, the adult variety is formative.

Towards the end of that second night, as the dawn light filters through the blinds, her beeper beeps; she is required. She rises from the bed with extreme slowness, through languor or reluctance to leave, or both: a nude ascending, but in frozen time. The sweat of our lovemaking still varnishes her, she is all soft focus in the dim light, an idealised film goddess of the fifties seen through a butter-blurred lens. *Et vera incessu patuit dea.* Virgil: In her movement she truly shows herself a goddess. A steaming shower softens her further, but as I watch her towel herself dry she deliberately turns her back.

'Let me look at you.'

'I don't want you to look at me.'

'It's more than that.'

For as she pulls on her clothes this is what I see: only those clothes are in proper focus, as if her body itself has not yet arrived in the present. She stands in front of the mirror, applying makeup, bringing her face at least into clearer focus. There is something at once innocent and worldly in her actions that further mesmerises me; some mix of sensuality – the soft pressure of lipstick against an open mouth, the smoothing of creams onto cheek and throat, the heightening of eye contour – with an awkwardness of technique. Several times she corrects mistakes – dabs away a stray speck of eyeliner, wipes a rim of misapplied lipstick. Is it my presence that unsettles her? Like her clothes, these tiny jars and coloured bottles and delicate brushes are things of the here and now, but her hands and lips and lashes are still out of focus in the present, preferring to live in the past, a breath behind, a heartbeat back, as if reluctant to leave the hours and the bed we have shared together.

6

Of that first month back in Australia I remember the Sundays above all: a month of Sundays, each of which meets the promise of its name for the first time in years.

Sunday, summer day, blue day.

Felix day? There are other, lesser friendships to resume and other, lower-altitude paradises to visit. December is a month of holidays also, for our work has not yet officially begun. Most weeknights and weekend days the diary offers a choice of Christmas drinks or cocktail parties or barbecues or dinners. We leapfrog into new friendships on the backs of old; we trade phone numbers with colleagues and social promises with old school friends and email addresses with strangers.

Incomplete strangers. Even after ten years away there are no complete strangers. Two degrees of separation is still the norm. A new friend will always connect with an old friend, multiply.

Odd then that in the thick-ply folds of this city, doubled and redoubled upon itself, no-one has much recent news of Felix. I hear the occasional grudging admiration for his decision to head into the desert after completing his surgical training. I hear numerous third- or fourth-hand stories of work difficulties on his return – theatre tantrums, surgical instruments dashed onto floors, nursing staff abused – but in a world accustomed to surgeons behaving badly this is small beer. Smallish beer even to a professor of psychiatry keen for clues to his best friend's current mental state.

The range of more recent intelligence is near zero: a narrow-band spectrum somewhere between haven't-seen-him-for-months and where-in-the-Third-World-is-he?

Sunday. Today. I wake late, reluctant to leave a bed steeped in the familiar sex-musks of the night before. Lucy, as always, is up already. A childhood spent marooned on sickbeds has left her with little love of sleeping in. Nor has marriage overcome this aversion; she might be learning to love bed for the company it keeps but not yet for itself. Her eyes spring open at first light; her body, clasped fast to mine, unclasps and rights itself; she is thankful merely to be on two working feet.

Even in England the sun would wake her, daily, at dawn, the milder milk-and-water light somehow finding her bedroom through the thickest cloud cover, the narrowest London alleys. Here, our bedroom opens onto an east-facing balcony. The shutters offer little defence against the glare of an Australian summer morning.

I throw open those shutters. *Fiat lux*: let there be light! *Fiat musica*, also: the strains of a clarinet are rising from the stairwell. Still naked, I descend the flight of narrow steps to the kitchen, a compact submarine galley of zinc and chrome and stainless steel. Mozart surrounds me, stereophonically. Köchel number 433, Martin-lore number in the high millions. The light that floods the kitchen is also in stereo, a high-fidelity radiance that enters through two widely spaced courtyard doors as if through balanced speakers.

Lucy is sitting in a canvas chair at the table outside, writing on a notepad, vanilla-naked in the morning light. She lifts her face, smiling to herself; I sense that she is writing a letter to her mother. I prepare two coffees, a light-industrial process involving the machine she insisted accompany us to Australia – 'Marry me, marry my addictions' – then ease my way backwards out through the door, cups in hand.

She lifts her mouth to be kissed, her lips cool at first press with the freshness of the morning, then body-warm.

'A coffee for your thoughts.'

'Not a thought in my head. Just feelings.'

'Homesick?'

'A little. But I know I'll be very happy here, Marty.'

I sit opposite and sip my coffee, savouring the internal trickle-down of warmth; she resumes writing. Mozart flows out through the open doors, a soft blast of sound in a small, privileged ghetto. Familiar happiness engulfs me like the music; I am lost in yet another of those moments during each of which, forgetting all others, I believe I have never been happier. Lucy-moments, present-tense moments, the overwhelming pressure of the here and now.

'Homesickness was once a classified illness,' I tell her.

No reaction.

'It's recorded in Cullen.'

She glances up. I press on, encouraged. 'First seen in Swiss mercenaries in Italy. In the sixteenth century. *Mal du pays*. I made a bit of a study of it in England.'

'You were homesick?'

'At first.'

'You thought you could study it into submission?'

'If I didn't die of it first. It *was* regarded as fatal. Epidemic in the European armies on long campaigns. Extreme melancholy accompanied by extravagant delusions about home.'

'How did they treat it?'

'Drills. Military exercises. Martial music.'

She smiles. 'I'll take Mozart.'

Blue day, fresh day, gold day. We sit nursing our doll's-house espresso cups in the high-walled courtyard. The Sunday morning traffic beyond those walls is sparse and erratic, a vague aural horizon. A few early birds are up and about, jumping jerkily from high branch to low branch to paving tile, full of nervous, staccato energy. I name the species aloud. Piping shrike. Yellow-faced honeyeater, *Meliphaga chrysops*. The cooing of a dove – peaceful dove? Brush bronzewing? – carries from somewhere, a soothing, repetitive throbbing.

'Turtle-dove?' from Lucy.

She is teasing me, reminding me of an outbreak of Martin-lore the night before. She had been reading to me in bed from the Song of Solomon, an old favourite. '"Thy name is as oil poured out . . . Thou art fair, my love, thou hast doves' eyes."' Then, weirdly: '"The voice of the turtle is heard in the land."'

'Mistranslation,' I interrupted. 'Turtle-dove, in later versions.'

This morning, what is mostly heard in the land is the voice of the honeybee, a background continuo. Various other small life forms are also up and about, on the move early. Lines of ants

explore the paving at our feet, solar-powered nanomachines energised by the early sun. When I rise to fetch fresh coffee I find
that a forward party of honey ants has already entered the house
through the open doors. I leave them to their work, untrodden.

'It's a wonder you didn't die of homesickness,' Lucy says on
my return. 'Away from this.'

As ants stream in and out of the door it strikes me how seamlessly in Australia the interior world merges with the exterior, as
if the great outdoors is merely, after all, another wing of each
suburban home, and here, today, the blue world of morning is
merely the largest room of our home, if also something of a
common room.

'Any plans for the day?' I ask.

'No news from Felix?'

'Not a peep.'

'Then you still haven't shown me where you grew up. Your old
neighbourhood. Your school.'

'Early Childhood Experiences,' I mock.

'You do seem to be avoiding them.'

'Shall I tell you about my relationship with my father now,
Frau Doktor?' I say, quoting Felix.

She laughs, but only briefly. 'You never talk of it. His death,
I mean.'

'There's not much to tell. It happened suddenly. A heart
attack. At work.'

'You were . . . thirteen?

'Fourteen.'

Old news this. We have in fact talked of it many times, but today she wants to talk again, if less to place those events in some sort of geographical locale, to tag them with place names and dates, than to use that locale to coax more information from me.

'You cried?'

'Of course I cried. But I was in the middle of scholarship exams. I had to stay focused.'

She finds this significant. A formative childhood experience, definitely. I step back into the kitchen and reactivate the espresso machine, a toytown refinery, all zinc piping and miniature storage tanks. The toytown espresso cups are soon half filled. Three peaches – Persian apples – sit in a silver bowl; I choose two, place them with a knife and the coffees on a tray and carry them outside.

'Mum believed you coped by doing things,' I defend myself. 'You didn't dwell on things. You got on with it. Dad was the same.'

'Perhaps you should dwell more.'

'I prefer to dwell less.'

But it is Sunday, and a rare afternoon empty of other commitments. I dawdle and filibuster, but all too soon we are breakfasted and dressed and ready for time-travelling. A Sunday visit to the past.

'Where to first, Lucy?'

'First Day at School?'

'Then we can walk,' I say, relieved that she hasn't suggested we visit my father's grave, or perhaps the various car-assembly plants in the western suburbs where he spent his working life.

Hand in hand we step out into the street. Early afternoon now, the air hazy with dust and pollens, air plankton stirred from the bottom of the deep, blue sky. The light is all reddish honey, a golden glow that invites nostalgia as we stroll eastwards through the inner-city streets.

'It must have been difficult,' she fishes. 'The death of your father, then off to boarding school. Losing both your parents, in effect.'

'Boarding school was a distraction. It took my mind off Dad. I had no idea what to expect. It was another world.'

'You were bullied?'

'There were the usual initiations. Camel bites. Chinese burns.'

'Because you were a nerd?'

'The word didn't exist. I was . . . a Brain.'

She smiles. 'I can just see you. With a pocket full of coloured pens and a pair of birdwatching binoculars around your neck.'

'Brain was a term of praise back then. Or at least an accommodation. And I had Felix to hold my hand.'

Lost a father, but gained a brother? I chew a little on the gristle of this thought as we stroll on. Sunday, and the human common room is packed. Crowded lunch tables clutter the footpaths, family groups and young lovers fill the cafés and boutiques and galleries. The Athens of the south? Waldo always ridiculed the term – the Detroit of the south, he preferred to sneer – but within an hour we are walking through the high gates of its main Academy, beneath a school motto wrought in iron: *Veritas vos liberabit*.

'Work makes free,' I mistranslate.

Lucy laughs. 'You sound ambivalent.'

'I was the scholarship boy. I didn't fit in.'

Inside the gates we find ourselves in a different, greener dimension where the city no longer exists.

'More Eton than Eton,' Lucy murmurs.

Eton in the afternoon flush of an Australian summer. Eton with parrots. The trees and playing-fields and old stone buildings appear sprinkled with gold, if here a softer gold, an unmetallic dust, lacking the hard edges of summer proper. More invitations to nostalgia? But if Adelaide Grammar School is another local franchise of paradise, it is a complex paradise, part purgatory. Chinese burns on my first day, and the mild burn of mixed memories ever since, the friction burn of past against present. Old scholars' newsletters – 'Dear Old Blue' – tracked me down in London, relentlessly, even though I had never subscribed. They tugged me back, offering schedules for Old Blue golf days or wine-tastings, or invitations to 'put together a table' for the farewell dinner for this or that much-loved master of boats, or coach of the first eighteen.

Always the same cocktail of feelings on reading this babble: sentimentality and scorn, gratitude and resentment. Nostalgia and bitters. I loved the place. I'd arrived with an empty mind, it filled that mind to overflowing. I hated the place. It kept me in *my* place.

'Felix made it easier for me. He straddled both worlds. Like me, he was one of old Waldo's elect. But he was also captain of the football team.'

'A centre-half who spoke Latin?'

'Greek,' I say, amused. 'He got away with murder in class. He always had an answer, a come-back line.'

'In Greek?'

This time I laugh aloud. 'Pearls cast before swine.'

A favourite insult at the time. One of many. *Procul, O procul este, profani!* Keep your distance, uninitiated ones! I think, I might have flown back from London for Waldo's farewell, of which there was no mention in 'Dear Old Blue'. Cloaked in classical lore and intellectual arrogance, we quoted him endlessly at our classmates. My excuse was the wrong-side-of-the-tracks chip on my shoulder, less real than imagined. Felix had no excuse but intellectual snobbery.

'He liked to say that Grammar's exorbitant fees were a tax levied on the rich and stupid to provide scholarships for the poor and clever.'

'No contradiction that he was rich and clever?'

'An accident of history. From Waldo he stole the notion that the main purpose of Grammar was the education of the elect: the Nobel Prize-winners, the prime ministers, the jurists and thinkers and writers. Those,' another phrase comes back to me, 'who leave more than a semen stain on the world.'

Waldo speaking, or Catullus? Whichever, I am boasting now, obliquely: absurdly proud of my old school while pretending to mock it. Nostalgia's sweet syrup is threatening to drown the bitters.

Her hand slips easily into mine; we stroll by the boarding

house. I point out the high, second-floor window of the study and bedroom I shared with Felix through our senior years.

'Why would you choose to board? You only lived a few suburbs away.'

'The scholarship covered boarding fees. It took the financial load off Mum.'

'She must have missed you.'

'I was fifteen. Half my classmates had left school at that age. Assembling Chryslers. Digging up roads. Squeezing out babies . . .'

We stroll on among cricket nets and tennis courts, through beds of English summer flowers: roses, hollyhocks, lavender.

'And Felix? Why did he board?'

I press a finger to my lips. 'Ssh.'

She looks askance as I turn, guiltily, to see if a master is watching. We have entered the soldiers' memorial garden, a strict zone of silence where conversation was always forbidden. No masters in sight; the school is deserted for the summer holidays. Absurdly relieved, I laugh out loud. How easily and automatically the old habits return; how tenacious their grip.

'Family tradition. His father had boarded at Grammar, his grandfather before him – back when it was a couple of days' ride on horseback.'

We turn a corner and walk on. Water sprinklers chutter on a cricket ground; a groundsman wades through green shallows of lawn.

'I loved him more than anyone back then. More than I loved any girl.'

She squeezes my hand, unperturbed. Encouraged, I add something I have never confessed before. 'I once told him that if he'd been a woman I would have wanted to marry him. We were drunk, of course.'

'What a beautiful thing to say, Marty.' She pauses, then adds, 'He said yes, of course.'

We laugh together, quietly. She asks, 'Was there ever anything, ah, erotic in the relationship?'

'God, no – we would have been horrified!'

'You don't think that's strange?'

'Innocent, perhaps. Unthinkable, at the time.'

The slow *thock-thock* of tennis balls being struck reaches us, an occasional 'Well played,' or 'Shot.'

'No,' I say, 'that's not quite true. *He* might have been willing to experiment.'

'You were the innocent.'

'It wouldn't have occurred to me. But he was always so restless. So inquisitive. Always had to be on the move, physically, intellectually. He dragged me along in his wake.'

'Sexually?'

'Crumbs fell from his table.'

She chuckles and we stroll on again, arm in arm, across the sun-flooded quadrangle.

'I missed him in England. And then out of the blue he wrote me a curious letter. About our lives taking different directions.'

'You never mentioned that before.'

I pause, struck by this – another unintended secret. Secret, also, from myself; I had forgotten the letter until now. It was something else that had been unthinkable at the time.

'It was the last letter he wrote to me – seven, maybe eight years back.'

'Before he headed off into the desert?'

'Yes, but that wasn't what the letter was about. It was odd. Over my head in many ways. Do you know what it sounded like?'

'A Dear John letter?'

Always half a thought ahead. 'Exactly. Although I couldn't see it at the time. I wrote back another of my cheerful, standard-issue chatty newsletters.'

'And he never wrote again.'

'Worse. I kept on writing for years.'

Finding that last letter – its tone, its tact – incomprehensible, I had ignored it. It slipped from memory as easily as a joke, or a dream, which it almost might have been.

'What made him go out there? Into the desert, I mean. It seems surprising, given his background.'

'He was always on the side of the underdog. Sensitive to injustice.'

'Of course. But where did that come from?'

'You don't think people are born sensitive?'

'Not the privileged. Not without some kind of sensitisation.'

She is talking also of herself, I realise. Talking of, or from, her disability. And it strikes me how little I have thought about Felix over the years in a professional sense. As a case study, he has somehow remained just below the window-ledge of analysis. Or perhaps loomed too large to be considered. He was a childhood given; his presence in my life long preceded the development of analytical habits of mind.

'His mother's death?' she suggests.

'We never talked of that. His mother's or my father's.'

'You don't think that's odd?'

'Not at that age.'

'Or that gender.' She smiles. 'The widow and the widower never hit it off?'

'Chalk and cheese.'

She is silent for a time, mulling things over. Eventually she murmurs, 'I was thinking, back in the soldiers' garden, how easily we slip into old mental habits. How powerful the past is.'

As always, our thoughts are running parallel; I know she is thinking again of that initial meeting with Felix in the hills. 'That first day,' I say. 'I let him overwhelm me. I should have protected you more from him.'

'Perhaps you were a little deferential.'

'Were you disappointed in me?'

Her face turns up towards me, concerned. 'Never. I love you.'

'But?'

'You sometimes seem . . . different in Australia. Not much different, just a little.' She is treading carefully, surrounding each phrase with hedge-words. *Perhaps, sometimes, a little.*

'Perhaps you see me with different eyes,' I suggest.

'Perhaps. But the past tugs at you here. Both the good and the bad.'

'Felix is bad?'

She ignores this attempt at lightness. 'What first struck me in London – there seemed something free about you.' She finds the word inadequate, tries to straighten the thought in her mind, give it a better setting in words. 'What I loved was your separation from the world, your immunity to it. Your *aboveness*.'

'I've lost that here?'

Her eyes lock onto mine, reassuring. 'Of course not. But there are old patterns of response. With Felix especially. And here, at your old school. On the one hand you proudly show me around, on the other you seem to despise the place.'

I repeat an old, much-cherished belief. 'I never quite fitted in.'

Or did I fit the niche I was given too well, a Brain-sized niche of predetermined shape and size and expectation? And another, more troubling thought now struggles to be heard: is it possible that if we remain here, in Australia, Lucy might find it more difficult to love me? That I might be diminished in my own country, diminished *by* it, compressed back into the smaller spaces that old habits demand?

'Seen enough?' I ask.

'For now.'

The paradox preoccupies me as we stroll back across the playing-fields to the main gate: that this enormous, empty land might be oddly constricting. For the first time since my return I wonder, seriously, if I might have had more room to be myself in the cramped bedsitters and crowded streets of London.

7

Sunday again, blue day, birthday: Lucy's. Another day off the rack: cloudless, fresh of breath, the trees so bright in the morning light that each separate leaf appears incandescent, lit from within.

We breakfast late on the balcony, at leaf level. Lucy unwraps my gifts: an expensive Italian watch, a slim volume of love poems. The poems lead us straight back to bed; after following their implied logic to its conclusion I leave her propped amid pillows, rereading the book, and step into the shower. Time presses; a birthday lunch for eleven – five couples made odd-numbered by Felix, invited at the last minute on Lucy's insistence.

'He *is* your best friend.'

'Second-best. And falling.'

'Well, he needs friends.'

'You're feeling sorry for him? He acted like a pig towards you.'

'I'm a big girl, I can handle Felix.'

'I don't want anything to spoil the day.'

'He probably won't come, Marty. But I think we should at least invite him.'

Downstairs, I step out into the courtyard and erect a long trestle table in the shade of the Japanese maple. Also Japanese, more or less, the table-setting ritual that follows: the spreading and smoothing of white linen; the precise arrangement of cutlery, plates, napkins, wineglasses tall and short, water tumblers, flowers. I find immense pleasure in this ceremonial place-setting – its promise of pleasures to come, its geometric representation of those pleasures, but also the pleasure of itself, the odd nourishment it offers even before the food.

Cooking preparations next. The laying open of thick cookbooks at suitable texts for the day; the setting out of gleaming tools in precise, surgical array; the roll call of herbs and spices and vegetables marked present and correct. Peeling, chopping, food-machining. After showering, the birthday girl wanders down in jeans and T-shirt to offer more coffee and advice; I continue to insist, sternly, that she lift not a finger to help. Or tongue.

I love cooking with her; today I cook for her.

She peeps on tiptoes across my shoulder at the cookbook propped open on the bench. 'Looks delicious.'

'Gastro-porn,' I say, flipping over another high-gloss, mouth-watering photograph.

'Is that the soup of the day or the playmate of the month?'

'I wouldn't know. I only read cookbooks for the articles.'

She laughs obligingly. This type of banter is new between us, an extension of sexual play; I am still learning to revel in it. Before Lucy I have too much been, in Felix's mocking words, a 'single entendre sort of guy'.

She glances out into the courtyard and its gleaming table settings. 'You've set a place for Felix?'

'Yes, but I'm not holding my breath.'

The doorbell interrupts. Lucy returns shortly with Felix surprisingly in tow, even more surprisingly early, and still more surprisingly brushed and combed and wearing freshly pressed clothes. He hands her a long cardboard tube and a child's bright-coloured birthday card. *Happy Birthday 5 Years Old*.

'You've erred a little on the downside,' she says.

'Woman years are the opposite of dog years. You divide by seven.'

So far, so good. He seems happy enough to be here, or determined to make an effort to be happy. Why the change? I try to read his face, but he is giving nothing away except the birthday gift. Lucy eases a rolled canvas out of the tube and spreads it carefully across the kitchen bench. An Aboriginal dot painting, thick daubs of acrylic paint in the usual desert colours: ochre-red, rust-brown, burnt umber, off-white.

'Warlpiri?' she asks.

He nods. *'Ngatijirri Jukurrpa.'*

'Was he a friend of yours?'

The first note of impatience in his voice. 'That's the name of the painting, not the artist.'

'What's it mean?'

'Budgerigar Dreaming.'

She studies the spread canvas and its geometric patterns, half bevelled cuneiform, half exotic paw-print, its white margins smudged by thumbprints.

'It's very beautiful,' she says. 'Tell me about it.'

'There's not much to tell. It's just a painting.'

She holds down the upcurling ends, waiting patiently. At length Felix shrugs and taps his finger on a small painted circle. 'Warlpiri iconography is pretty simple. This might be a person, an animal, a place. In this case it's a hole in the ground – a waterhole. The place where the Dreamtime budgie comes out.'

'Budgies live in the desert?'

'Budgies belong in the desert. Ngatijirri, in desert Latin.' He turns to me. 'Which is what in Roman Latin, Prof?'

'*Melopsittacus undulatus.*'

Nothing on that canvas of squiggles resembles a bird of any kind. Felix points to a bent-stick figure. 'This little bird is Japaljarri skin. My mob. He travels all over the place. Has all the usual adventures, usual trials.' He leans back on his stool, his tone bored. 'It's a bit like Nintendo.'

'Does he get to the next level?' Lucy says.

He smiles, momentarily. Another tap of his finger. 'He goes back into the ground here. Ngarlpa.'

'It's a real place?'

'Of course. The Dreaming places are always real. Ngarlpa is a waterhole.'

'An oasis?'

'That might be stretching it. A sinkhole.'

'You've been there?'

'No-one's been there for fifty years.' He plucks his tobacco pouch from some denim crevice and begins to roll a cigarette. 'Blackfeller or white. No-one's even sure it's still there!'

We wait patiently. He is talking at his own pace, but at least, today, he is still talking.

'The rains failed a few years in a row and the people walked out of the desert. Back in the thirties. They got a taste for tea

68

and damper on the cattle stations and never went back.' He pauses to lick his cigarette into shape. 'But the artist grew up there. An old Jungarrayi.'

Rapid arithmetic in my head. '*Very* old.'

Lucy catches my eye, her expression uneasy. 'It's a very generous gift.'

'Didn't cost me a cent. We were camped out in the bush one night and the old man got sick. Luckily I had my bag of tools with me. Useful Western doctor-magic. In return he gave me that.'

'Then I can't accept it,' Lucy says immediately. 'It was a gift to you.'

'Plenty more where that came from.' He strikes a match and leans forward to apply his cigarette to the flame. 'He's not a well man.'

'But it has special meaning for you.'

'It's just decoration, for Christ's sake. The old man whipped it up in a couple of hours. It's like jazz – visual jazz. Let's not get sentimental about it.'

'But it's a work of art. And you earned it.'

An irritated wave of his cigarette. 'I was just doing my job. The painting was a payment.'

'I don't believe you,' she says abruptly.

He looks at her, surprised, silenced.

'I don't believe that's all there is to it. I don't just mean the painting, I mean everything. Why you went out there. You speak so carelessly about it all, but I think you had . . .' she pauses, searching for the right words, 'better motives. Once.'

'Anything the Herr Professor might have told you I'd take with a grain of salt.'

His smile is opaque again, encrypted. She holds his gaze for a second, then gives a small, resigned shrug and turns back to the painting. 'I think it's beautiful, Felix. Extraordinarily beautiful. Thank you. I'm flattered. And I don't want to appear ungrateful. But I'm only taking it on loan. I insist.'

'Whatever,' he says, tired of the subject. 'What birthday gifts has the Herr Professor showered on you? A *Field Guide to Australian Waterbirds*? A new translation of Virgil?'

She stretches her left arm across the bench; he bends to inspect the watch.

'But it's broken. The minute-hand has fallen off. You'll have to take it back.'

She takes back her wrist instead. I bought the watch at first glance, entranced by the stylish minimalism: a pure silver face, framed in black, a single tiny hour-hand, bright crimson. There is neither minute nor second hand.

I say, 'I couldn't resist it. Time reduced to a kind of essence.'

Lucy rises from her stool. 'Which reminds me – time is *of* the essence. You'll have to excuse me, I need to make myself presentable.'

And she is gone, a single sandal slapping on her left foot, one shoe on, one shoe off balancing her unequal legs better than the most expensive orthotics.

Felix watches her leave. 'Was I too rough on her?'

'I think she held her own.'

He turns to me, smiling minimally, conceding the point. 'You've done well,' he says. His tone of voice is mocking, but something else has leaked out, some measure of genuine feeling. I feel an absurd, irrational shiver of apprehension.

'I'm glad you think so.'

As if aware he has revealed too much, he turns away. 'You should take your princess out into the desert some time. Show her the real world.'

An opening. 'What happened out there?'

'Nothing you can help me with, Herr Doktor Freud.'

The shutters are up again, but we have travelled some distance and I must be patient. The life so short, the craft so long to learn, Hippocrates wrote, and for a moment I'm tempted to ask Felix for the Greek. *Ars longa, vita brevis*, in Seneca's translation, although Hippocrates was writing about medicine, not art. But psychiatry is at least half art, the art of biography, and half of that half is the ability to coax, to prise the crucial biograffiti out from between clenched teeth. Felix's teeth are clamped tightly about his cigarette, but for now I have other work to do.

'There's an ashtray on the table outside,' I say.

He glances into the courtyard and its table glittering with silver and crystal and dazzling white linen.

'You didn't mention on the phone that it was a fucking state dinner, Professor. Who's coming?'

I reel off a string of names; he interrupts to snort contemptuously, 'Frank Boyd? You invited Frank Boyd to Lucy's birthday?

After two drinks he'll be all over her. Does he still wear that ridiculous fez?'

'I haven't seen him for ten years.'

The doorbell rings; he escapes into the courtyard, whether to smoke or to jump the wall and flee I can't tell. Of course it is Frank and Poppy Boyd at the door, bearing flowers, rare wines, and an elegantly wrapped birthday gift.

'Martin Blackman, boon companion of my youth! Long time no see!'

Of all my former schoolmates, the new State President of the College of Surgeons has changed least of all. If anything, he has changed in reverse, become *more* himself. The puffy boy-face is more boyish, the smile more self-satisfied, the braying laughter more intrusive. Life-of-the-party Frank, and yes, still wearing the battered, red-tasselled fez.

'You remember the lovely Poppy?'

Not in this shape and size. One of the vivacious beauties of her nursing year, Poppy seems diminished in every way – even somehow physically shrunken, as if she is inches shorter. I can only wonder what is tugging at the drawstrings of her tight smile, her pinched face.

Lucy is still upstairs, Felix outside in the courtyard, his head shrouded in smoke. I hand the new arrivals champagne, and with a 'For this relief much thanks,' Frank is out the door, all hail-fellow-well-met, silent wife in tow.

'What ho, Felix Johnson, boon companion of my youth! You remember the lovely Poppy?'

The doorbell is ringing serially now; I admit more couples bearing gifts and wines and flowers. Short of vases, I stash bouquets in wine decanters, empty bottles and even the odd jam jar. Frank reappears in the kitchen, his 'Something is rotten in the State of Felix' more a declaration than a question, requiring no answer. As of old, Frank has all the answers himself, a self-appointed auxiliary host, an Official Greeter pouring drinks and reintroducing friends. He has a gift for this, and for the moment, as I prepare canapés, I am grateful. Perhaps even the absurd fez, braying laughter and repertoire of stock Shakespeare are harmless-enough social lubricants.

'So,' he says, 'where *is* the Queen of Hearts I've heard so much about?'

Lucy, at last, descending. White, geisha-thick face paint, simple black dress and black stockings, single strand of white pearls. Not fully comfortable as guest of honour among strangers, she has spent extra time on her appearance. Her armour. Her clothes neither flatter her slim figure nor draw attention to it, but her larger-than-life beauty, unable to be hidden or completely stylised, still sets her apart.

As does her limp: her trailing foot catches on the last step; she stumbles slightly.

'I think I'm in love,' Frank whispers loudly in my ear.

Private dancer, public gawk. Illness cost her a normal adolescence; not just the standard, middle-Kent, middle-class ballet and deportment lessons, but more importantly the shared girlfriend world of trying on clothes and postures and endlessly practising dance steps in front of mirrors, the teenage muscular habituation so necessary in coming to grips with an enlarging body. In public, she sometimes still seems twenty years younger, an awkward adolescent unbalanced by elongating legs and arms and burgeoning breasts and widening pelvic base. Birthday greetings drown her apologies for lateness; gifts are proffered, air kisses exchanged with the women, the attempted full-frontal kiss of Frank evaded.

'Why are we all crowded inside?' she asks.

Frank immediately leads a general exit. 'Once more into the courtyard, dear friends!'

I follow, carrying platters of seafood. 'Alas, poor oyster,' from Frank as he directs the seating arrangements – Lucy at the head of the table, himself planted at her right hand. She finds my eyes with an unspoken, Help! But my place is at the opposite end, close to the kitchen. Poppy is on my left; Jill Perlman, a GP and an old friend from medical school, on my right. Jill's partner Stella, butch half of the couple and another friend from student days, is seated on Lucy's left. In the predictable boy-girl-boy-girl of Frank's seating plan, Stella, in her mannish suit and short-cropped hair, is an honorary boy.

'We're fully booked today,' Frank says to Felix, odd boy out. 'Perhaps you could come back next week.'

Felix inserts himself mid-table, but angled slightly away from the others. More gifts are unwrapped: books, CDs, stylish glass-ware. The big *Budgerigar Dreaming* is unrolled on the tile paving and much examined and much admired. Stella, a weekend painter herself, gasps as she reads the artist's name, printed in thick felt-tip in a child's large hand on a back corner of the canvas.

'Doctor Jerry Jungarrayi? *My* birthday's in three weeks, Felix. Please take note.'

'You know his paintings?' Lucy asks.

'This isn't a painting, darling. It's your superannuation.'

Lucy's eyes meet mine, troubled. 'It's just on loan,' she insists.

'He's a medical doctor?' someone else is asking.

'A witch doctor,' Frank suggests.

'I love those desert colours,' Jill says. 'But what's it mean? Is it a map?'

Felix is still saying nothing. Stella fills the vacuum. 'I imagine it's a kind of quest story. A journey. Like many of the Dreamings.'

'Looks like a board game,' Frank says. He kneels and lifts another corner of the canvas and reads the inscription on the back. '*Ngatijirri Jukurrpa*. What's that in Swahili, Bwana? Do not pass go? Do not collect $200?'

His bray of laughter sounds funnier than the joke; a few other guests join in, infected, but Felix remains aloof.

'*Nam risu inepto res ineptior nulla est,*' he mutters.

Over Frank's head, but I remember my Catullus: Nothing is more foolish than a foolish laugh.

'Ancient Roman toast,' I dissemble, and lift my glass. 'To laughter.' There is a general, happy clinking.

Frank, irrepressible, raises his glass again, remembering one phrase at least from Waldo's Latin 1A. '*Carpe diem.*'

The day seizes us back, seizes us first. Bright sunlight finds us through a thousand leafy skylights, a thousand miniature translucent green windows. Several of the women are wearing fashionable animal-print tops, perfect camouflage in the sun-speckled courtyard. The whole world today might be a warm animal print, all mottled leopard pelt and tiger stripe, a world upholstered in fur.

Felix still sits slightly apart. Wilfully apart? The psychiatrist in me wants to know more, but the husband in me has other concerns. At the far end of the long table Frank continues to monopolise Lucy's attention with dog Shakespeare ('The rest is silence,' 'To eat or not to eat,' 'You are the very pink of courtesy') and general life-of-the-party repertoire ('Ta muchly,' 'Trap for younger players'). Even once, after a mild joke, 'Boom, boom,' followed by the braying laugh. Her eyes meet mine and roll upwards, discreetly. I smile back, reading the message: another kindly, generous man interested in her wellbeing.

'Someone needs to rescue Lucy,' Poppy says.

My concern has been for my wife; for the first time I realise how much Frank's behaviour must humiliate his. I rise and move towards the far end of the table, under pretence of uncorking more wine.

'What's that lovely fragrance you're wearing?' he is murmuring in her ear as I pass behind.

'Garlic,' she says.

Felix laughs derisively. 'Nice to see you haven't lost your touch, Frank.'

A grin dimples Frank's puffy face. 'If the lines work, Bwana, why change them?'

'That was working? What comes next? "Do you come here often?" "Haven't we met somewhere before?"'

His voice is a little too loud, silencing the table.

'Now, now, children,' I say, pouring wine.

Frank is unfazed. He turns his amiable grin on Felix. 'So your objection to my lines isn't moral, it's aesthetic?'

Lucy stifles a laugh, partly won over by this first sign of non-formulaic intelligence in Frank. One reason I have a soft spot for him: his occasional left-field unpredictability, his brain that can surprise with something more intelligent than itself.

Conversation resumes, in neutral gear. Phatic noise, in Plato's phase. Small talk with big designs: social grease, pecking-order placement, flirtation with a view. Normally I would watch and listen intently, an avid student of unconscious purpose, but today, while sports and wine commentaries, hospital talk, gossipy footnotes and second-hand Internet jokes eddy about, I have work to do. I fetch out the main-course adjuncts: cute bonsai potatoes, baked baby beetroot, big bowls of various designer greens.

'Shall I be mother?' from Frank, standing and reaching for a serving spoon.

'Mother of all fuckwits,' Felix says.

I carry out the fish – one baked trout per guest – but on most plates they grow cold, unable to fight their way upstream and into mouths against the strong current of talk. Conversation jumps about the big white and silver board of the table like a shared chesspiece – a knight – less free association than loose connection.

'If cooking is *the* artform of the twentieth century,' Stella is saying, 'then what about movies? Where does that leave movies?'

John Fisk, bow-tied lawyer and former first speaker in the Grammar debating team (I always spoke second, Felix third), argues back. 'Apples and oranges. You can't compare them. Cooking is an abstract art – like music, like the paintings of Jackson Pollock. It aims to be nothing other than itself.'

My turn to get in a word of rebuttal. 'Films are mimetic art. To quote Aristotle.'

'Aristotle went to the movies?'

'Plato went to the movies. In the *Republic*. Aristotle just read about it. Black and white movies, of course – shadows on the cave wall. The Greeks didn't have technicolour.'

'The Romans invented technicolour,' Lucy puts in. 'In *Ben Hur*.'

Laughter all around. Things are going well; even Felix takes part, the odd pungent sarcasm leaking from his bent mouth. From time to time he rises from the table, fast-burns another cigarette in a corner of the courtyard, and returns to his place.

Ceremony time: I fetch out the cake I have cooked – blitztorte, my mother's recipe – and light five candles. Felix's dog-years joke revisited. I rise to my feet and wait for the hubbub of conversation to die; I am in no hurry, I have been waiting for this moment for days.

Metal dings against glass in Frank's hands. 'Friends, countrymen, lend him your ears . . .'

'Welcome everyone on this, this *luminous* day. And welcome to this luminous occasion – a celebration of Lucy's birthday. It took great courage and great love for her to leave her country and her family, and follow me back here –'

'You come to bury her or praise her?' from Frank, followed by a general shushing from the rest of the table.

'And I want to thank you all for making her welcome. One of the reasons I wanted to come home was because of you – all of you.'

'Violins, please,' Frank says, and the world does its best to respond; the light is as close to music as light can be, a sudden power surge of radiance, a golden downburst as I talk on.

'So charge your glasses. To my darling Lucy.'

'To Lucy.'

The chorus of 'Happy Birthday' segues – led by Frank – into 'For She's A Jolly Good Fellow'. Lucy bends and blows out the candles as various voices urge, 'Speech! Speech!'

She stands before us, smiling, slightly unbalanced. I think, I have never been happier, never been so much in love.

'Thank you, darling – and thank you, all of you, for making me feel so at home. It's wonderful to be here. Here in Australia, and here, today, among so many new friends . . .'

She soon escapes the limelight under the pretext of preparing coffee. Late afternoon now, the sun below the city skyline. The light has gone out in the leaves; enclosed by the high courtyard walls, we are in a premature twilight. Lucy, her arms and face pale alabaster against the blackness of her dress, carries out a tray of coffees; I follow with plates of cheeses, grapes, figs. Talk continues its knight's-jump around the table: films, music, books,

79

food. Cricket, tennis. Lucy slaps one pale, exposed arm, then Jill slaps hers; the mosquitoes are starting to bite. I realise that Frank's seat has been empty for some time; when he returns he is carrying a black doctor's bag which he sets on the table and tugs open.

'What now, Frank?' from Poppy. She turns to the rest of us. 'Can't take him anywhere.'

He plucks a tourniquet and blood-taking syringe from the jaws of his bag. 'Lucy is being eaten alive. I thought we could set up a little, ah, decoy.'

A groan from Stella. 'You're not planning what I think you're planning?'

'A saucer of blood.' He is swaying slightly, half drunk, half high on his own inspiration. 'A sort of blood offering.'

More groans from around the table – but tolerant groans, willing to be entertained further.

'It's not the scent of blood that attracts them,' I remember from somewhere. 'It's the scent of sweat.'

But Frank is unstoppable. 'It's the scent of blood that attracts *me.*' He fits a needle to the syringe and waves it mock-threateningly. Any volunteers?' He looks around the table. 'Felix excepted of course.'

'Frank!'

Poppy's sharp warning silences him, but only momentarily. He turns his flushed face to her, puzzled. 'Well, I'm not about to stick a needle in *him,* am I?'

'That's enough, Frank.'

Her tone is horrified. My bewilderment is mirrored in Lucy's eyes; what on earth is going on? Frank continues to wave his exposed needle dangerously about. He won't be silenced easily.

'It's hardly a state secret –'

'It's privileged information, Frank! So please – shut *up*!'

Everything is changed, abruptly. In trying to silence her husband she has inadvertently blurted out much more.

'Shut up yourself. We're all doctors here. Who gives a fuck if Felix –'

'*Some* of us are lawyers,' John Fisk interrupts, firmly but quietly. 'So perhaps you'd better sit down before you dig yourself an even deeper hole, Frank.'

Maintaining an idiot grin, Frank appeals to Felix. 'Have I said something I shouldn't have said, Bwana? I thought it was common knowledge.'

Silence around the table; Poppy's head is in her hands.

'I suppose it's reassuring that you managed to keep your mouth shut this long,' Felix says at last. He turns to Lucy. 'What Frank is dying to tell you – I'm contagious.'

He is talking to her quietly, intimately, as if no-one else is present, but it is her birthday and perhaps she is owed the largest share of the explanation. 'I'm hepatitis C-positive.'

Frank's bumbling idiocy is forgotten; the murmurs about the table are all of concern for Felix. 'I had no idea.' 'I'm so sorry, Felix.' 'What a tough call.'

He waves away the sympathy. 'The disease itself was nothing. But I'm still shedding the virus.'

Lucy realises first. 'Which is the reason you've had to give up surgery.'

'It was just a needle-stick,' Frank puts in helpfully. 'It could happen to any of us.'

'Can't you do any surgery at all?' John Fisk asks.

'Nothing invasive.' Frank is speaking for Felix again, deluded enough to think he can make amends. 'I offered him an endoscopy clinic. Outpatients. Administration work –'

Felix turns to him abruptly, turns *on* him. 'You disgust me.'

Frank's jokey smile freezes on his face. Felix's eyes are narrowed, and for the first time this afternoon he has removed the cigarette from his mouth to speak, as if needing to spit the words out with more force. 'You sit there pawing Lucy all afternoon. Isn't fucking three shifts of nurses a day enough for you?'

Poppy is suddenly her husband's staunchest ally. 'Felix, how could you say such a thing?'

Lucy, trying to hide her distress: 'It's my birthday, Felix.' Upper-case Scenes are her professional bread and butter, but usually in the privacy of a consulting room, with strict protocols of management.

Frank finds his tongue. 'It's the green-eyed monster which doth mock the meat it feeds on.'

'What do you mean by that, you sleazebag?'

'I mean this – you've known her for fifteen minutes and you give her a painting worth, what, twenty thousand bucks?' He glances from face to face, seeking support. None is forthcoming; he ploughs on nevertheless. 'Now, there's a Dreamtime story.

82

Why don't you just tie a ribbon around your cock and give her *that*?'

Lucy's eyes find mine, anguished, but I am speechless. Others at least can find their voices. 'Take it easy, Frank.' 'That's a bit out of order.'

'He started it,' Frank says, and the words, a five-year-old's, sound so absurdly comical they ease the tension. Eye contact is made around the table again; there are a few nervous, relieved titters, and for a moment it seems possible to move on, to pretend that the Scene need not be taken seriously, or no more seriously than any children's party ending in tears.

Until Felix rises abruptly. 'I think our revels now are ended.' He moves towards the house but pauses at the door and turns to Lucy. 'I'm sorry, Frau Doktor. I should have kept my mouth shut. I hope you can enjoy the rest of your birthday.' She half rises and he insists, 'No – please. I'll see myself out.'

I rise instead and follow him through the house, brimming with questions. The noise of the quarrel has obscured its cause, but I need to know more. He is moving at speed, trailing cigarette smoke, eager to escape; he jerks open the front door before I can reach it, then suddenly half turns and removes his cigarette again from his mouth to speak.

'You used to loathe that cunt at school, Professor.'

'And you used to defend him. He was your friend, not mine.'

'A friend who became an acquaintance. I outgrew him. What's your excuse?'

'It's not important. What's important is you. Are you okay?'

He jams the cigarette back between his lips. 'Of course I'm okay. It was nothing. Subclinical infection.' He speaks quickly and irritably, the rapid-fire sentences punctuated by a chain of puffs, like smoke signals. 'I didn't even know I'd been infected till that shithead organised a medical.'

And he steps out into the street and slams the door shut in my face. Before I have time to follow, the house behind me is full of departing guests, talking over-cheerfully of babysitter deadlines, forgotten engagements, urgent hospital calls.

Poppy, to anyone who cares to listen: 'Felix *did* provoke him.'

Frank, calmer now, setting his fez straight. 'Sorry, gang. Looks like I touched a nerve.'

He drapes an over-familiar arm across my shoulders and whispers in my ear, with exaggerated confidentiality. 'Apologise to him, Marty. For me. Please. I want to help. If he can swallow his pride, I'll throw a little work his way.'

'He doesn't want charity.'

His smile stiffens. 'Then that's his problem. And I'd keep my eye on him if I were you. He wants to get into your wife's pants.'

I shrug his arm from my shoulder. 'I think you're projecting your own fantasies.'

'Is that so, Prof? Then maybe I'm the one you'd better watch!'

And with a bray of laughter he is off into the street, restored to full power, immune to criticism, invulnerable to shame, his harried, thinned-down wife close on his heels.

They vanish from our thoughts as soon as they vanish from our sight, along with the other guests. As I clear away the wreckage of lunch, Felix's plight is all I can think of. Lucy fetches a textbook of general medicine, unread for years, from the upstairs study. Sitting at the kitchen bench, she flips through the rice-paper-thin pages as I cork the undrunk wine, cling-wrap the various odd-shaped polygons of cheese.

'. . . long-term risk of cirrhosis,' she reads, 'and hepatoma . . .'

I listen with one ear only. Putative physical complications seem trivial compared to the psychological. For the first time since my return I feel I am beginning to comprehend the changes in my friend.

'Maybe it's for the best,' I say. 'He was wasted in surgery.'

She glances up from the book. 'Marty, that's a bit glib.'

'He said himself he was weary of it.'

A moment of silence; neither of us believes for a moment that he meant it.

I say, 'He can't just sit around feeling sorry for himself. There are areas of medicine he can still work in. Non-contact specialties. Pathology. Radiology. Research.'

'Psychiatry,' Lucy states the obvious last.

Odd that I have failed to think of it. 'Herr Doktor Professor Felix Johnson,' I say.

Lucy's compassion is more focused; irony plays no part. 'He needs to see someone. He needs to talk it through. *You* need to talk to him, Marty.'

'It's like talking to a brick wall.'

'He might talk to me,' she says.

The Aboriginal painting sits half rolled on the table outside, amid the smeared glasses and plates; she is staring at it thought-fully. I feel again that slight shiver of apprehension, but quickly suppress it.

She adds, 'And I can return the gift.'

There is something restless in her body language, some sense of movement or anticipation of movement, even though she is still sitting on her stool.

'Tonight?' I say. 'You want to drive up into the hills now?'

'It's important, Marty. He needs help.'

She holds my gaze, pleading with her eyes. Pointless to suggest that he might not want our help; she cannot be happy till she has done her best.

I turn away and reach for the kitchen phone. 'We should ring first. After today he might not even let us in the door.'

She slips from her stool and covers my hand gently with hers. 'That's why we shouldn't ring.' I replace the receiver reluctantly. 'If you don't want to come that's fine, Marty. But I think we should drive up together. Talk to him together. I wouldn't be . . .' her eyes slide from mine, 'comfortable alone.'

I am comfortable with nothing about this proposed visit, hers or ours, but my own body is now also in motion, infected by her urgency. The ruins of our lunch party still cover the kitchen and courtyard like the debris of some explosion, but I am already searching for my car keys among that debris.

For now, all else must wait.

8

Night is approaching as we crest the saddle of the Woodcroft valley, the sun gone, the sky fast fading, denim-blue to grey.

'We should have rung,' I say. And a few minutes later, 'He's probably not even home.'

But a light gleams in the farmhouse window, and as we turn in off the creek road we find the battered Landcruiser parked in the shed. We pick our way carefully down through the dark trees to the front door. No answer to our knock. We walk around the corner of the house to the terrace. Still no sign of Felix. I rap hard on the back door, and again. Eventually, a slight vibration of footsteps inside, the door opens. Felix, still wet from the shower apparently, wears nothing but a white towel wrapped sarong-fashion around his hips. The raised lines of his scars stand out across shoulders and chest, thick as fingers. I have told Lucy of them but still I sense her sharp intake of breath.

'The Frau Doktor and Herr Professor! Don't tell me, you just happened to be in the neighbourhood?'

'Don't play games, Felix. You know why we're here.'

My bluntness doesn't faze him. His eyes find the rolled canvas tucked under my arm. 'I invited you up for Monopoly?'

Lucy's fingers rest lightly on my arm, restraining me. 'We came because we're worried about you. Because we care about you.'

His eyes linger on hers with no change of expression. 'How very Californian of you.' He makes no attempt to stand aside.

'You're not going to invite us in?'

He opens his mouth to snarl some further sarcasm – instead he coughs convulsively, the deep, dry cough that has been present, subtly, for weeks.

'Have you seen someone about that cough?'

'Is this a house call, Herr Professor?'

The face-off continues. Lucy slaps at her exposed arm as if swatting a mosquito. I can see none; the thought occurs to me that this is a ruse, an out-of-character stratagem. When she slaps again I am certain of it.

'Oh, Christ,' Felix says. 'Come in. Before someone calls Frank Boyd Pest Control.'

And so a literal threshold is crossed: we enter his house, his home, for the first time. Inside, he has already turned away, presumably to find clothes.

'Make yourselves comfortable.'

Not much has changed in the big, dark room that faces out onto the terrace. A study-cum-library, it has the same clubbish feel I remember from childhood: worn leather Chesterfields, leather-topped desk, Persian rugs. Books everywhere: toppled stacks on the floor, and tightly squeezed into the highest of the shelves that line three walls of the room, floor to ceiling. A few names jump at me from the volumes scattered on the desk. Plato – the *Phaedo*. Marcus Aurelius. A thick Holy Bible, open, face-down. I turn it over. The Book of Job.

'No wonder he's depressed,' I murmur to Lucy, but fail to raise a smile.

I flip rapidly backwards through the pages, locate the Song of

Solomon, then carefully replace the big book on the desk, in the same position, face down. *Thou art beautiful, my love. Thy name is as oil poured out* . . . Subtle, anonymous psychotherapy.

A saucer of birdseed sits in one corner, splashes of white bird-paint decorate the furnishings here and there, but there is no sign of the Major Mitchell. Perhaps a dozen furled canvases, some as thick as carpet rolls, lean against the bookshelves; I place the birthday gift back among them. The lower book-shelves are crammed with other Aboriginal artefacts: painted stones, bone fragments, weavings of string and feather. Warlpiri? Stooping to examine one specimen, Lucy starts back with a look of disgust.

'Is that what I think it is?'

I look closer; a leathery, mummified human hand sits on the shelf attached to a woven string cord. 'Next year's birthday present,' I suggest.

Still no smile as Lucy explores the shelves, captivated. None of the standard tourist-kitsch is here: no varnished boomerangs or didjeridus, no clapsticks or dinner plates handpainted with cartoon piccaninny heads. The function of these pieces is not at all obvious; they manage to seem somehow both domestic and sinister. The slivers of bone attached to lengths of plaited hair are clearly anything but needle and thread. The shrunken human hand sits incongruously next to a pair of what seem to be slippers, woven from fine feathers.

The further dissonance of these artefacts with the surrounding library strikes me with some force: the great books of the Western world on the higher shelves, but at a lower altitude, a darker, more ancient stratum. Deliberate? A pilgrimage I made some years ago to Jung's house on the Upper Lakes above Zurich comes back to me, and the different rooms designed to house the old man's different selves: the 'maternal-womb' (his term) of the central hearth, the upper-storey designated as ego space, the 'spiritual' tower. I was open to such claptrap then.

Felix's division is more natural, less self-conscious: an ego-sphere of the written word above; a lower realm of human nature in its older, more savage forms. I pluck a bone sliver from a nest of feathers and try to place it anatomically. Human rib? Metatarsal?

'Careful which way you point that.' Felix is in the doorway behind us, in T-shirt and shorts, licking a cigarette into shape. 'It's loaded. You wouldn't want it to go off.'

A joke, but I replace the bone needle in its nest. 'You have quite a collection.'

A shrug. He seems calmer, more resigned to our presence. 'I picked up a few bits and pieces over the years.'

'Because you were initiated?' I prod.

'Like joining the Masons?' He laughs. 'No. Even the old sorcerers don't keep this stuff lying around. Far too dangerous.'

'The slippers are beautiful,' Lucy says. 'What are they made of?'

'Emu feathers.'

'They're very delicate. Are they worn by women?'

An amused snort. 'Men only. Kadaitcha men. Ritual

murderers. The feathers are glued together with human blood.' He watches her reaction. 'The killer wears them to hide his tracks.'

There is pleasure to be had, it seems, in telling her such harsh things, in sticking conversational pins into her. A stray memory comes back to me, passes through my mind as briefly as a shiver. I am six again, besotted with the seven-year-old girl next door – a besotment that is beyond words and, therefore, unbearable. I tease her, pinch her, tug her plaits till she cries. I follow her home from school, a stone's throw behind. She seems so perfect, such a fragile doll, I can only think I want to damage her, to *break* her.

'Are you permitted to own these slippers?' Lucy is saying.

'Finders keepers.'

'You found them?' I ask.

'You might say they fell off the back of a truck.' He watches me for a moment, amusing himself, perhaps deciding whether to reveal more. 'A wreck in the middle of nowhere – an old Bedford. The shoes were under the bonnet. The Warlpiri are great prag-matists. They make use of anything. Car wrecks are good cupboards. One of the lessons of life in the desert: make do.'

'Then you *stole* them?'

'Let's just say I removed them from harm's way.'

'But they weren't yours to take,' Lucy protests. 'They're sacred objects, surely.'

He turns to her disdainfully. 'They're murder objects. Tools of the murder trade.' He stubs his butt into an overfull ashtray on the desk. 'Of course all death is murder in the desert.'

He sinks into a Chesterfield and reaches for his tobacco pouch. We seat ourselves opposite and wait.

'No such thing as death from natural causes,' he says, licking another cigarette into shape. 'It's always due to magic. Sorcery.' Match flame licks at cigarette tip, ignites it. 'Part of the funeral rites out there – the sorry business – involves a formal inquest. A kind of whodunnit. The old men put their heads together and look for clues.' He gives a brief, cynical laugh. 'Funny how it usually turns out to be an enemy.'

'What happens then?' Lucy asks.

'Kunka.'

'Meaning?'

'Payback.'

'Always?'

'One way or another. If a posse doesn't head off and spear the villain, some clever-man will sing him to death. Point one of these little beauties at him . . . ' He picks up another sharpened bone-splinter and dangles it from its length of string. He is exaggerating, surely, pointing his own version of a bone – sharpened sentences – at Lucy for the fun of it. Part of me – the part that is still six years old, perhaps – is all too alert to the pleasure he takes in unsettling her.

'You're exaggerating,' I tell him.

'Maybe a little. Sometimes a beating is enough. Or the villain turns out to be dead already, so face is saved all round. All very convenient.'

'I don't believe you,' I say.

92

Lucy: 'Surely things have changed these days?'

'Whitefeller law has forced it underground. And the new generation is not so interested.' He fixes another sardonic smile on her. 'Isn't it a shame how the traditional culture is being destroyed?'

I think, The Felix of ten years past would never have joked so brutally, or handled these priceless objects so carelessly. He tosses the death-pointer back onto the shelf.

'Did you steal that too?' I ask.

'I was given it to destroy.'

I will not let him off so easily. 'Then why didn't you? Should it be on display? Aren't there conditions for owning such things?'

He turns to Lucy. 'What the Herr Professor is trying *not* to tell you – this is secret men's business. You're not allowed to see any of this. So now we have to kill you.' And he laughs, loudly – a spluttery, smoke-signally laugh which contracts into a cough.

When he finds his breath again: 'Luckily, as I said, the Warlpiri are a pragmatic mob. The rules can be bent. They don't seem to apply to white women. But I'd be careful crossing any busy roads for a time.'

'People must have thought highly of you,' she says. 'To give you such gifts.'

His face has turned opaque, his eyes masked. 'There were all kinds of gifts. Good Fairy gifts and Bad Fairy gifts.'

More riddles; what is he talking about? He watches us impassively, indifferent to our puzzlement.

Lucy says suddenly, 'Did you get hepatitis from the initiation scars?'

Less a question than a conclusion, it strikes me as obvious once she has said it. Why hasn't the connection occurred to me? If Felix is surprised, he tries not to show it, examining his cigarette tip with narrowed eyes.

'Nice try,' he says. 'But as a matter of fact, no.'

'Then how?' I prompt. 'Frank mentioned a needle-stick. Was it during surgery?'

He glances up impatiently. 'Of course it was during surgery. I was careless. You might even say I deserved it.'

Lucy again: 'You can't say that. Accidents can happen to anybody.'

'No. It was a gift I deserved.'

Silence. We wait through another smoke cycle: inhalation, exhalation. At length he adds, 'Fair payment for services rendered.'

Another riddle, but no further clues are offered.

I say, as sympathetically as I can, 'I understand you feel hard-done-by. But a lot of people have to change careers.'

The tone of his reply is less angry than weary. 'It's been a long day. I think I've told you what you wanted to know. So if there's nothing more . . .'

'Of course there's more. We want to know about *you*. How this has affected you. How you feel. And what about the scars? You were adopted into the tribe. Given a tribal name –'

'A skin name. I told you, it's no big deal. The Warlpiri are great imperialists. They'll adopt anything that moves.'

'It was more than that. You were initiated.'

A small, sour smile. 'Don't know what came over me. A few whitefellers had tried it before – hippie anthropologists with a death wish, mostly. They were lucky to survive. I should have listened.'

'I imagine it must have been agony.'

A harsh snort. 'You couldn't *begin* to imagine.'

Lucy says quietly, 'You did it because you thought it would help with your medical work.' Again her tone is less a question than a pronouncement. He looks up at her, silenced; she has clearly touched a nerve. 'You thought it would give you some authority,' she adds.

He is suddenly on his feet, pulling open the front of his shorts.

Lucy's eyes meet mine, startled. 'What are you doing?' I ask.

He is moving towards us, tugging out his penis. 'Since you have to know every fucking thing – here, look at this.'

We can look at nothing else; he is literally thrusting his cock in our faces. He holds it pinched between thumb and fingers, as if by the scruff of its thick neck, half male organ, half some finned, winged thing. Reared up, turned inside out, it looks like nothing so much as a pink, filleted fish.

'Subincision,' I remember from somewhere. 'I didn't think it was still practised.'

'You learn something new every day, Prof.' He turns to Lucy. 'The old men use a razor these days instead of a stone knife, but it still needed four of them to hold me down.'

She turns her head away, horrified, but he will not let her

escape. 'One good thing. Women love it. Opens out like a great butterfly.'

Averting her head has not been escape enough. She rises and moves towards the door. 'I'll wait in the car, Martin,' she says quietly, and steps outside.

An explosion of smoke and laughter follows her out. He turns back to me. 'One down, one to go.'

I should follow immediately, but I have to know more. 'Why did you go through with it? Did you *want* to mutilate yourself?'

'What's this – penis envy? You want to see it again, Prof? You want to touch it?'

'Not without a rubber glove.'

He is silenced momentarily, his gaze still mocking but with a glimmer of amused respect. 'You're a hard man to provoke, Herr Professor.'

'*That* provokes me. Could you stop calling me that? Psychiatry outgrew Freud years ago.'

'Really? Seems to me you've learnt the main lesson well – everything means something else.'

'You keep trying to drive me away. That must mean something.'

'It doesn't mean I want you to stay.' And with that he is at the door, holding it open. 'Confidentially though, Sigmund, if I have to be on someone's couch, I'd much rather be on your wife's.'

This, also, provokes me, but I bite my tongue as I step outside into the night. I pause at the edge of the terrace and turn back one last time. Felix has followed me out, a dark figure with a glowing cigarette between his lips.

'I'm sorry we intruded,' I force myself to say.

The tip traces a tiny arc, down and up, a nod of acknowledgement. I am encouraged enough to ask, 'What are your Christmas plans?'

'When's Christmas?'

Tell me your jokes and I will tell you your worst fears, I want to say to him. 'We're lunching at Mum's,' I say instead. 'She'd love to see you. She often asks after you.'

The ember of his cigarette glows fiercely and fades, glows and fades.

'Or just join us for a Christmas drink. Anytime in the morning.'

Now the glowing tip describes a larger loop, an arc disappearing out over the lip of the terrace into darkness. 'I just want to be left in peace, Prof.'

I walk away through the trees, climb into the car and sit, stunned. Lucy's eyes are smudged with tears, her cheeks with ruined eyeliner. She reaches over and squeezes my hand.

'I'm sorry, Marty. It was my idea to come.'

'He's been drinking,' I say, without evidence.

'He's insufferable. I thought this morning he seemed changed. Willing to make an effort.'

'Until Frank and the others arrived.'

'Then tonight, I thought his illness – he needs us. But now . . .'

I finally remember to start the car. 'Well, we've tried. We've done our best.'

As we turn into the creek road and drive past the house, he is still standing on the edge of the terrace, a silhouette backlit against the light of the doorway. I beep, automatically, but he gives no acknowledgement of our passing. We might still be in the valley, his valley, but we have left his universe. He stands motionless, impassive; a stone monument planted on a ridge to warn off intruders.

The Greeks have a word for it, I remember: *ataraxia*. The inscrutable stare of the gods. The thousand-yard stare. And a line from Aristotle comes back to me, another crumb from Waldo's late-night supper-table: He who has no need for society is either a beast or a god.

9

Sunday, Christmas Day, and a morning already hotter than any Christmas in memory. A February morning, perhaps, that has jumped the squares of the wall calendar like a boardgame counter and shoved in weeks ahead of its proper midsummer place.

We unwrap our gifts in bed while a hot, sandpapery north wind scratches at the balcony doors; we make sticky, sweaty love amid the scattering of wrapping paper and CDs and books and household utensils. Afterwards, Lucy rises to open the doors onto the balcony, seeking relief in the movement of air; she immediately shoulders them shut again against the buffeting, pressing heat.

'You should have a name for this wind.'

'We do. It's called the north wind.'

'Very funny. I was thinking of something more poetic. Like the mistral.'

'The mistral is a cold wind. A northerly, yes, and it drives people mad. But it's a cold wind. This is more like the sirocco.'

'You'll drive *me* mad,' she smiles, and escapes into the bathroom.

I love her so much I want to bury her in lore. 'The sirocco blows across the Mediterranean from North Africa,' I call after her. 'Hot and dusty. Comes off the desert, like our northerly. The only difference, it's a southerly.'

'We should coin a new name,' she says, but the sudden gush of the shower prevents any chance of her hearing my reply. I rise, follow her into the bathroom and pull open the glass door of the shower cubicle. She is showering in cold water; drops spatter off her body onto my face and chest, deliciously.

'The Arsonist?' I suggest.

'The Blowtorch?'

'The Wasp.'

'The desert people probably have a name for it. We should ask Felix.'

I step into the shower with her, the full shock of the cold water making me gasp. 'The Dog Breath,' I say eventually.

Face upturned, her answer gurgles against the downrush. 'Dog Breath is good. But we must use the name as often as possible. In phrases like, As my grandmother used to say, the Dog Breath . . .'

'As we say in Adelaide, the Dog Breath . . .'

We towel each other dry amid continued wordfoolery, then I make my way downstairs to prepare coffee and fruit: a mango, thickly cubed, in cold yoghurt. She is brushing her hair when I return; the usual huge pleasure floods through me at the sight of her, as if we have been apart five years instead of five minutes.

'We should ring Felix,' she says.

'He won't come.'

'We should at least leave a reminder. Just in case.'

Of course we have discussed him endlessly in the previous seven days. Obsessively? The to-and-fro of talk has at least sanded smooth the sharp edges of our indignation. This morning, forgiveness almost seems possible. Refreshed by sleep, nourished by love, sated by sex, Lucy especially is once again able to reach out to Felix.

'Ring him now,' she suggests. 'He might be more reasonable. Things always look better in the morning.'

I dial his number, only to be answered by his machine. Is he sitting there reading Marcus Aurelius or the Book of Job, ignoring the call? I leave a friendly message, a further open-ended invitation to Christmas dinner or drinks.

Midday, Sunday, Christmas Day. Roast turkey for three at my mother's. The Dog Breath buffets the car as we cross the city to her beach suburb, but at least the car is air-conditioned. The uninsulated roof and walls of our destination are a heat trap, porous to the summer bake outside while paradoxically retaining and magnifying the various cooking heats and body heats within.

Lucy finds the heat exhausting, but I have no trouble producing enough conversation for both of us, at home again in a summer Christmas, a red crêpe-paper Christmas hat jammed on my head like a jaunty fez. My mother seems to have hoarded ten years of turkey dinners in my absence. Third and fourth helpings cannot be refused; we eat till bursting point, till our stomachs are so bloated the food is wedged tight beneath our lungs, restricting their movement. We can barely breathe the stifling air.

'Seafood should be the national Christmas dish,' I tell Lucy as my mother fusses in her kitchen, out of earshot.

Has she heard? She seems stunned by the heat and the food.

'Oysters,' I say. 'Cold lobster. Followed by cold summer pudding.'

'Say that word again.'

'Pudding?'

'No – cold.'

'Cold.'

'It makes me feel colder just to hear it.'

'Cold,' I repeat. 'Cold. Cold. Cold . . .'

The mantra works temporarily, as if each chanted syllable is the swish of a little hand-held fan, lowering the temperature a degree or two. The champagne is also cold, but repeated mouthfuls, like the repeated word, offer diminishing returns. Greeting cards line every shelf and mantelpiece in the room, a snowfall of scenes from the other, colder hemisphere: fir trees, snow-capped cottages, carrot-nosed snowmen, thickly clad Santas. Like small winter windows, these also offer respite, a blizzard of cold-climate images that are at least psychologically cooling.

Their familiarity must tug at Lucy, sweating through her first midsummer Christmas. She phones her mother late in the afternoon – early morning Greenwich Mean Time – and sheds a few tears, which in the heat might be a type of sweat themselves. What is the tear duct but a more evolved sweat gland?

My turn on the phone. 'Nancy? Yes, I'm taking good care of her . . . Settled in well . . . She's made a terrific impression on everyone . . .'

My mother's turn. 'It's nice to talk to you at last, Mrs Piper . . . You must miss her terribly . . . I always wanted a daughter, but I couldn't ask for a nicer daughter-in-law . . . We're getting on famously . . .' Her voice drops conspiratorially. 'No, I think she still plans to establish her career first . . . Yes, I hope they don't leave it *too* long . . .'

Lucy rolls her eyes at me and smiles, her tears already subsumed in sweat. The delusions of *mal du pays* cured by the first reality check.

'Put on some martial music,' she says.

My mother turns on the television instead, and the rest of the afternoon is spent in front of Christmas TV specials, predictably banal. Finally, even the cold flicker of the screen feels too warm, too psychologically radiant, and we escape home to our cool, deep house and a supper of iced tea and cold turkey leftovers.

No messages on the phone. I dial Felix's number and leave a last Christmas greeting. Still no answer. Nor is there an answer to several further messages in the week that follows, calls spanning a spectrum from hearty seasonal greetings to concerned pleadings for contact, the tone depending on my frustration threshold, blood-sugar level, weariness, the time of day, and a dozen other variables.

Another surprise visit is out of the question, and although we still talk about him often, we have come to an unspoken decision: the ball is in his court.

10

We spend New Year's Day, and the month of Sundays which follows, driving in other directions than Felix's. And in other directions than back into my formative past. For the moment, that dossier is closed; Lucy has seen enough.

If the Adelaide Hills are paradise, then the city is its anteroom, and the winemaking valleys of Barossa and McLaren Vale its north and south wings, decorated in the same sky-blue and leaf-green colour scheme, and stylishly furnished with the same colonial stone buildings and vine rows and olive groves and giant river gums.

I am introducing Lucy to my larger neighbourhood, but I am also reintroducing myself. Much has changed in ten years, if more in quantity than quality. More of the same? Grown larger, the city seems to have become merely more familiar – an exaggeration of herself. A parody? Her thousand cafés and restaurants have become two thousand; her vineyards now have the suburbs besieged on three sides like the rank and file of a vast, green-uniformed army. On the fourth side lies the sea. We lunch in wineries listening to string quartets and counter-lunch in pubs listening to poets. We fish-and-chip in coastal cafés and browse in bookshops; we escape the midsummer heat in the cool of cinemas; we pore over competing portraits of the city displayed in her libraries and galleries. Athens or Detroit? Retirement Heaven or Serial Murder City? Clochemerle or Wine Capital of the World?

Opportunities for lore abound. 'Eighteen ninety-four was the year we gave women the vote. The first place in the world.'

'Thank you. I'll try to be grateful.'

A small flare of panic. Are our sightseeing excursions boring her? I remember all too well the interminable Sunday drives of childhood, my parents' preferred weekend relaxation. The route varied with the seasons. In winter, with the weekend real-estate pages her travel guide, my mother would drag a reluctant child – me – and a semi-reluctant husband from open inspection to open inspection, though more as a free entertainment – a window into other lives, an actual doorway into other lives – than through any desire to move house. In spring and autumn the chosen routes were less staccato: long, meandering loops through the surrounding hills and vales. Summer meant a perfectly linear route: the endless beach esplanade that rules the western boundary of the city. From southernmost Marino to the northern tip of Outer Harbour our small Morris would chug, then back again. We seldom stopped; proximity to those miles of dazzling beach, packed with tens of thousands of bathers, was sufficient to cool my parents' sweating bodies. Even within a beachball's throw of water, Sunday drives were less a means than an end.

As I Sunday-drive Lucy up and down that same ruler-straight coast, or march her in and out of cafés and wineries and galleries, I worry that I am willing my hometown too much upon her. Military drills, martial music? She teases me endlessly, but gently. Her happiness is palpable, and the final destination of every Sunday drive is always its beginning: our home. And within that home, its powerfully beating heart, our bed.

'You were the *second* place in the world to give women the vote. Not the first.' Pillow-talk, one Sunday night.

'And the first?'

'New Zealand. I looked it up on the Net.'

'Do you always check up on me?'

'Only when I'm suspicious.'

Monday to Saturday our hospital work has begun. The pain clinic fills Lucy's days; a small alp of journals and textbooks occupies her nights. The new, much-vaunted multidisciplinary approach means that she must specialise at speed in any number of multiplying disciplines: anaesthetics, biomedical engineering, and above all pharmacology: the interface of brain chemistry and pain chemistry, mind chemistry and medical chemistry. Her particular brief: neuropathic pain. She has travelled some distance from the London of couches and talking cures into this concrete world of pain measurement and kinase-blocking drugs. But there is room for new ideas.

'Chronic pain is a kind of memory,' she tells me. 'Sensitisation to pain is a remembered state of mind.'

'Or at least a state of brain.'

Our pillow-talk can even encompass recent advances in neurochemistry. Memory, she informs me, evolved in primitive organisms as a response to pain, and those primitive responses are still hardwired inside us. Why else would the new generation of drugs that improve memory also increase the response to pain? In every nursing-home in the West, she claims, demented codgers are suddenly remembering their aches and pains.

'You're not suggesting what I think you're suggesting?'

'It's hard to avoid the obvious – why shouldn't drugs that diminish memory also diminish pain?'

'You would choose to deliberately give your patients amnesia?'

'Given the choice, some might jump at it. A *degree* of forgetfulness.'

'Dangerous territory,' I warn.

Was it predictable that our research interests might cross in passing, travelling in opposite directions? Of course our enthusiasms infect each other, even to some extent cancel each other's out. I have strayed some distance from textbook psychiatry into the wide world of Internet porn, but each step of the journey seems invincibly necessary, even if I would like to forget much of it. My early work in London proposed (proved, I think, but that is not for me to say) a link between certain kinds of music and depression.

'If you're depressed, perhaps heavy metal is the kind of music you choose to listen to, Marty.' Lucy, softly spoken Devil's advocate, probing my flaws from her side of the bed, goading me into thoroughness. 'Which is the chicken and which the egg?'

'Both are both. It's called a vicious circle.'

New directions, old arguments. In Australia I have research funds to study links between the Internet and mental disorders. My chosen corner of the World Wide Id? The paraphilias. The gospel according to the *DSM-IV*: 'recurrent, intense sexually arousing fantasies, sexual urges, or sexual behaviours involving a) nonhuman objects b) the suffering or humiliation of oneself or one's partner and c) children or other nonconsenting persons'.

That cool-temperature definition covers much overheated cyberspace: every website and chat-room and blog-cellar from 302.4 Exhibitionism and 302.89 Frotteurism through to 302.81 Fetishism, 302.83 Sexual Masochism and all the way down (up?) to 302.9 Paraphilia Not Otherwise Specified. Not yet specified in the *DSM-IV*, perhaps, but exact specifications abound on the Net, where Freud's *Three Essays on the Theory of Sexuality* have become three billion. Chickens or eggs? Talking cure or chat-room contagion? Searching for answers, I restrict myself to criterion (a), inanimate objects of affection. Narrow-spectrum website turn-ons are everywhere I look. Virtual clubs of foot fetishists and food-fuckers and mannequin-lovers and necrophiles and tribes of plushies who live only for sex with plush, stuffed animals.

Variety is the spice of life? For harmless soft-toy fanciers, perhaps, with nothing more to obsess about than how to keep the fur of their chosen sex partners from getting sticky. But for life-threatening self-amputees? I am more the pragmatist than the moralist, and more utilitarian than both – these questions are therefore beyond my research brief. I am seeking merely to verify or falsify cause and effect. Of course I know where my funding is coming from: a community obsessed with Net porn. My working hypothesis might even feed that obsession: a hunch that the most obscure paraphilias – the left-field fetishes – are multiplying; that the World Wide Id (I use the term more and more freely) is providing less a dark alley of kooky cats begging to be copied than a vocabulary, a way of thinking and seeing, onto which more general anxieties can be specifically mapped, blamed, given new names.

Log on and multiply, plushies.

Lucy whispers her useful doubts in my ear during breaks from her own work. *Cart or horse? Chicken or egg?* And interrogates my methods with polite tough-mindedness as the answers to various cyber-questionnaires flood in from the chat-rooms.

'It's a self-selected sample, Marty. How representative do you think this material is? How honest?'

'Possibly more honest than you think. People love to be the star of their own questionnaire. Their own fifteen seconds of fame.'

'But if they wear masks on the Net, why wouldn't they wear masks in your interviews?'

'The questions are structured to catch inconsistencies. There are subtle repetitions. You know the drill.'

'And where are your control groups?'

'Ah, I'm working on that.'

Through January and February, between blocks of such talking and thinking – shop-thinking, pillow-talking – the weekday routines of our working lives firm up. Monday to Saturday we rise early and walk together through the cool of the morning to the hospital. Fiat Lux! The Dog Breath is in abeyance, the summer sun not yet high enough to hurt our northern-winter skin. We pause for eggs and headlines at any of the various East End cafés, wide-windowed annexes of the larger morning room all. Hospital duties carry us through the heat of the day as effortlessly as a siesta; we walk home hand in hand through the fading after-burn of each summer evening, although even these seem cooler than I remember as a child, as if this summer has burnt its annual ration of calories too early, squandered them in the unseasonal Christmas heat.

No word still from Felix, and no-one at home when we contrive a Sunday drive-by after a long lunch with Jill and Stella in a vineyard restaurant in the hills. Lucy's birthday is now two months-of-Sundays past, and while we have forgiven Felix, it seems we are not forgiven in turn.

Late in February, after some debate, we accept an invitation to Frank Boyd's fortieth birthday dinner. A scorcher of a day at last, mutating with no loss of heat into the hottest night of the century, or at least of the previous fortnight. Seven-thirty p.m. for eight, but Frank and Poppy's big, eastern-suburbs bluestone home still glows with the stored heat of afternoon. A white marquee has been erected on the tennis court; a long Tuscan table meticulously set for twenty or thirty. Flowers everywhere; gold napkins, silver service. Gold helium-filled balloons strain upwards against taut silver ribbon leashes fixed by extravagant bow ties to the backs of the chairs. I have been home three months, but it is the first I have seen of many former classmates since returning. *En blob* I am struck by the generic sameness of them, their names and faces and wardrobes so interchangeable. Four Johns, three Peters, two Franks and a Paul all sweating inside identical dress shirts and formal dinner suits. A flock of penguins stranded far from their Antarctic habitat? Their mobile phones and pagers chirp from time to time identically, but size and carriage identify the variant subspecies: king penguin, erect-crested penguin, thick-billed penguin, a pair of fairy penguins, in matching floral cummerbunds.

The women are more individually named, or nicknamed – two Poppys, one Pip, one Fliss, one Flick, one Boo – and encased in a greater variety of filmy summer frocks, but the various isthmuses of their bodies – necks, wrists, waists, ankles, fingers – are uniformly gilded or gem-encrusted or empearled. Their mobile phones also seem more jewel-like, smaller and more elegantly feminine; the bird-chirpings of these designer phones are more highly pitched, more musical, more varied. Bach, Bacharach, Bob Dylan.

'The collective weight has increased a ton or two,' I whisper to Lucy, 'but not much else has changed.'

Are we also interchangeable? I am wearing what Lucy calls

my 'London black' – the black shirt, black tie and black suit which is the uniform of another, different conformity. More raven than penguin, but equally unsuited to the heat of an Australian summer night. Lucy is also clad in generic black: black LBD and black stockings, but, as always, her limp and larger-than-life beauty set her apart, turning heads as we move among the various clumps of pre-dinner drinkers. Several plumpish penguins are reluctant to leave her side after introductions; she rests her hand lightly inside my arm, a gentle but unambiguous tether.

We are seated by place-card, each lovingly handlettered by Poppy in gilt ink. Lucy finds herself, inevitably, at Frank's side: a penguin distinguished from the black and white flock by his fez. The rare red-crested penguin? From that end of the table come snatches of his mating call. 'For this relief much thanks' – twice within minutes of arrival. 'Get thee to a nunnery.' The peculiar tang of 'You are the very pink of courtesy', if growing less peculiar each time I hear it.

Occasionally Lucy laughs with him – the flow of the predictable and the rehearsed still redeemed by the odd flash of inspiration. More often her eyes seek mine out, not so much needing help as stoically amused at her predicament, but as his arm begins to drape itself about her shoulders I feel the need to mount another rescue operation. After the main course I abandon my end of the table for hers; she rises, I slip onto her chair, she reseats herself in my lap.

'For this relief much thanks,' whispered in my ear.

'Martin, sirrah!' Frank is saying. 'So pleased you and the Queen of Hearts could make it.' His arm transferred to my shoulders now; perhaps I have read too much into his Lucy-attentions. 'Could always rely on Marty at school,' he is telling her, 'Marty and Felix. We had some times! S'pose he's told you all about it. The Three Musketeers . . .'

This is news to me, but it's Frank's party and if he wants to shed sentimental tears he can.

He continues, 'Pity that D'Artagnan didn't condescend to join us tonight.'

D'Artagnan was the fourth musketeer, I want to correct him. The Three Stooges might be a more accurate description. But Poppy is clapping her hands, summoning us to the lawns behind the marquee. In lieu of a cake and candles, professional fire-works have been arranged. Champagne flutes in hand, the assembled guests ooh and aah in chorus as a procession of sky-rockets scream upwards and explode incandescently.

'Shouldn't Frank try to blow them out?' I murmur to Lucy, and the mild malice in the thought makes her splutter a mouthful of wine.

As the guests count each ascension aloud, 'Thirty-seven . . . thirty-eight . . .' the oohs and aahs become more prolonged, more ironic. As the fortieth rocket detonates, Frank himself leads a chorus of 'Happy Birthday To Me', 'For I'm A Jolly Good Fellow', and finally three cheers.

'How long before we can decently leave, Marty?'

'We shouldn't be the first couple. Perhaps the second.'

'*Droit de seigneur*,' Frank is shouting somewhere as he moves among the women, demanding birthday kisses. His speech is slurred, his gait unsteady, his face as beet-red as his fez, but twice he glances over a shoulder towards Lucy, checking her location, planning his approach with more sober cunning. Drunk or not, he knows exactly where she is; he is, in some sense, stalking her.

'I'll just say goodbye to Poppy,' she says, and slips from my side, timing-perfect, an instant before he arrives.

'Don't run away,' Frank calls after her. And then, more loudly, 'I only kissed the others so that I could kiss you.'

For one long practised in seduction it seems an innocent sexual tithe: to steal a birthday kiss, his own, from another man's wife.

'You'll have to kiss Martin instead,' she calls back.

'He's already got a boyfriend!' Frank brays, finding himself again. He turns to me. 'Speaking of whom, I was hoping you might tell me what's really wrong. He must have told you.'

'Told me what?'

A mocking laugh. 'O brave new world that hath such people in't! Come on, Marty, this is Frank. You can tell me – just between us musketeers. Is his liver packing up? I bumped into him in Outpatients last week. Not a pretty sight. He took one look at me and ran for cover.'

'He's working in Outpatients?'

He gives me a long-suffering look. 'Marty, he was there as a patient. What's going on? He looked like death warmed up.'

Out of the mouths of fools. No bray of laughter this time, but it's a fool's voice that drunkenly spits out the last, most important words of the day. Not the foolishness I might have expected – another absurd variation on your-best-friend-wants-to-bed-your-wife, or, less indirectly, I-want-to-bed-your-wife – but something from the other side of Frank's brain, not so much the left side or the right side, but the dark side, that strange connecting machine in his head that is occasionally more inspired than the rest of him.

PART II   The World Wide Id

11

Is writing in the present tense now as much beyond me as living in the present was beyond me then? How did *this* fool manage to miss the obvious? I notice – noticed – nothing.

I like to think I'm a good clinician still, if only by reflex. I served out the usual medical apprenticeship: six years in the hands of teacher-princelings speaking loudly and also carrying big sticks. Reading human bodies was once second nature to me, was drilled into me. The sixteen types of cough, each as specific as a birdcall. The spectrum of skin tints – a dull rainbow of pallors and flushes, black-and-blues, greens and jaundice-yellows. The swellings and finger-clubbings and muscle-wastings. These clues and a hundred more once rang subliminal alarm bells long before the actual laying on of gloved hands.

So what went wrong?

'You don't know for certain, Marty.'

'No – it's obvious. I should have seen it immediately.'

Midnight; we lie together in bed, two disembodied voices in the darkness. I have rung Felix's number several times to find his phone engaged or off the hook. I'm unable even to leave a message.

'It was probably nothing, Marty. A yearly check-up. Routine liver-enzyme screens.'

'Lucy, use your eyes. He *does* look like death warmed up.'

'You're jumping to conclusions.'

'I should have jumped that first day in the hills.'

I slip out of bed and grope about in the darkness. A sudden glare of light; Lucy's reading lamp switched on. 'What are you doing?'

'Looking for my clothes.'

'You're getting dressed?'

'I can't sleep. I thought I might go for a walk.'

'At this hour?'

'I need to think.'

'Then I'll come with you.'

'There's no sense in both of us losing sleep.'

'Then come back to bed. I'll help you sleep.'

The infallible Lucy Blackman insomnia cure. I bend and kiss her forehead, grateful for the offer, but for once I have other plans. 'You go back to sleep. I'll be fine.'

Her eyes are screwed against the light, examining me suspiciously. 'Marty, I've never seen you like this. So agitated. Where are you going?'

'Nowhere. Anywhere. I just need some exercise.'

She will not allow me off the hook so easily. 'You're not driving up to the hills? Tell me. I know you're hatching some plan.' She reaches out her hand; I take it and allow myself to be drawn back to bed, and to candour.

'I thought I'd walk into the hospital. Check his case records.'

'Now? Can't it wait till morning?'

'I won't sleep till I know for certain.'

'Then you're doing it for yourself, not for Felix.'

'Perhaps. But I have to know, Luce.'

'There's also the small matter of privileged information. He's your friend, not your patient.'

My eyes slide from hers. 'It wouldn't be the first time.'

'You've looked at the case-notes of other friends? Marty? How often have you done this?'

A deep breath. Time to tell her something I have never before admitted. 'Only once. In London . . .'

Her lips part slightly, a voiceless 'Oh' as awareness dawns.

'It was just after we'd met. You were so . . . private. I wanted to know more. *Had* to know more. So I did a little detective work.'

'I don't know that I want to hear this.'

'I don't know that I want to confess it.'

London, midnight, five years past. I am standing in the records department of the Royal Children's Infirmary, Cheltenham, heart in mouth. I have known Lucy for four weeks, four brief *hours*, and all I know of her – a single clue let slip through the cracks of our clinical discussions – is that she spent much of her childhood in hospital. Exactly which hospital she hasn't said. There are other children's hospitals, other children's wards – I begin with the most likely.

'It was after our fourth session together. I couldn't get you out of my head. I couldn't eat that night, couldn't sleep. I kept thinking about your limp. It looked like an old injury.'

'Why didn't you just ask?'

'At three a.m.? I couldn't wait till morning.' I laugh briefly at the memory, or at the relief of the confession. 'I knew I wouldn't sleep till I'd worked it out of my system.'

'You were obsessed.'

'I was in love. I caught the Tube over to the Royal Children's. Fronted up to the medical records department and pulled your notes.'

'At that hour? No-one was suspicious?'

'The night clerk was some moonlighting student. I flashed my ID from Bart's – no problem.'

'You would have been in all sorts of trouble if anyone found out.'

'I knew that. I knew it was wrong but I couldn't help myself. I was driven.'

'I suppose I should be flattered.' She settles back into her pillows and joins her hands behind her head, beginning to find the idea less surprising and more amusing, even charming. The hint of a smile plays about her lips. 'You were in a bad way.'

'Love hurts. I sat in a cubicle for the rest of the night reading those two thick volumes. Swotting them. Birth date, address, phone number – of course. But I wanted much more . . .'

A broad smile now. 'Obsessive-Compulsive Disorder, Marty. Criterion B: the person recognises that their behaviour is excessive or unreasonable.'

'Recognition was no help at all.'

Two obsessions – two passions – joined forces in me that night, feeding off each other, amplifying each other: my thirst for facts and my infatuation with Lucy. I flipped on through her thick medical biography, heart pounding, shallow-breathing. But at the same time exulting – thrilled. *Presenting Complaint, Past History, Family History* – I could have fallen on my knees to Galen or Hippocrates or William Osler in gratitude for the tradition of thorough history-taking. *Psychosocial History*. Standard entries here: *only child, living at home. Both parents well. Father teacher, mother part-time nursing sister. Scholarship student*. Me too! *Hobbies* . . . One only was listed, but it filled my bookish, lore-crammed heart with joy: *reading*.

'I felt an idiotic closeness to you just reading about you. Your blood films, your X-ray reports. Even phrases from letters written between various specialists. I still remember the wording – *this delightful eleven-year old . . . intelligent lass . . . brave through so much . . .* I loved reading those words.'

'This is all very kinky,' she says, but she is more moved than amused. My crime is long past, I have not been struck off, and love has won out.

'I've never done anything like it, before or since. Till now.'

Confessing has calmed me, bled away the heat of my earlier restlessness. Lucy peels back the quilt; a gust of her warm woman-smell engulfs me. I slide in next to her, her mouth finds mine. Its night-strangeness absorbs me, distracts me – a small-hours bed mouth, dry-lipped and as oddly tasteless as a sip of water in the night. I kiss her again; we make economical, sweaty, rapidly concluding love. Sleep follows even more rapidly, as if it is a drug administered intravenously, as if I am counting to ten and fail to reach three.

I wake to find the first light squeezing through the shutters and Lucy, fully dressed, setting a doll-sized espresso on my bedside table.

'You don't need to go to Medical Records in person, Marty.'

'I'm sorry?'

'You don't need to be quite so invasive.'

Sluggish thoughts stirring in a thick head. What is she talking about? She sits on the edge of the bed and reaches for the phone. A familiar eight-tone melody, two bars of a quick-time march – the hospital switchboard number.

'Switch? Doctor Lucy Blackman – could you put me through to Radiology please.'

I prop myself on pillows and reach for the coffee, but fully alert now, needing no caffeine.

'Radiology? Lucy Blackman. From the pain clinic. I'm chasing some recent scan reports on a Felix Johnson . . . No, I don't have a case-record number on hand . . . J-o-h-n-s-o-n . . . Yes, I'll wait.'

Her eyes find mine, guarded, slightly embarrassed.

'What scan?' I ask.

'Any scan,' she says. 'If you're right, he must have had some sort of scan.' She begins speaking again to the phone. 'Sorry? . . . No, I'm not sure of the dates. Can you tell me the most recent reports you have? . . . No, this is Doctor Blackman.' Her eyes glance back to mine. 'The reports have already gone to whom? . . . Yes. Thank you.'

She replaces the phone and turns to me. 'Doctor Sally Need?'

I set down the coffee, half shocked, half weirdly energised. My suspicions – second-hand or not – have been confirmed. To Lucy I say simply, 'Staff oncologist.'

Her brow furrows, she gnaws at her upper lip. 'Oh, no,' she whispers. 'Poor Felix.'

I rise from the bed and pace excitedly about, naked. Much of his strangeness over the past few months – the mockery, the bitterness, the personality change – now makes even more sense. 'He must have been ill for months.'

She looks up at me through moist eyes, bewildered. 'I don't understand where you're coming from, Marty. You're behaving as if it's good news. You seem almost elated.'

Seldom in five years has she found fault with me beyond the trivial. An occasional bad shave. Mismatched socks, once or twice. Philosophical disputes over the direction of my work, or hers. But of course she is right; she has seen me clearly, seen clear through me.

'He must feel terribly alone,' she says.

I defend myself lamely. 'He seems to want it that way.'

But I am chastened, and that flare of elation is already fading. No fool is on hand to pre-think the obvious for me this morning, but it has been necessary for my wife to do the obvious pre-feeling.

Sunday morning, an hour later, driving eastwards up into the hills. A hot Dog Breath pummels the car, the light is harsh in our eyes. Waves of heat shimmer vertically from the freeway, transformed by some miracle of perception or optics into their opposite: waves of cool water, a river rapid running backwards, uphill, against gravity. No human life can be glimpsed on the streets of the towns; their quaint English names – Bridgewater, Woodcroft – might be a kind of mirage themselves, a verbal illusion promising coolness and shade that can never be delivered.

The wind bullies us as we climb from the car, kicks grit in our eyes, snaps at our clothes. But Felix's battered Landcruiser is parked in the shed; our gamble of arriving unannounced has paid off.

We walk, sweating, down through the trees to the house and knock at the front door.

'I don't think we should tell him we've been digging around in his records, Marty.'

'*Who's* been digging?' I remind her, and she manages a small, tight smile.

The vibration of approaching footsteps inside; the door opens.

'One mad dog and one Englishwoman!'

He is wearing a loose caftan, but it fails to hide the weight loss. Skin and bone, yes – the skin shrink-wrapped even more tightly about the bone.

'Don't you ever phone first?' he says, but without anger.

'Don't you ever check your messages?'

His mouth is clamped about the inevitable cigarette; his expression gives nothing away as he scrutinises our faces.

'May we come in, Felix?' Lucy asks. 'Please. Out of the heat.'

'You might find it even hotter in here.'

But he stands aside and allows us to enter. Stale tobacco

smoke pervades the air, but it is a cool staleness, welcome after the sandpaper rasp of the Dog Breath. We follow him through a darkened passage to the study. The doors opening onto the terrace are shuttered, the curtains drawn. Saucers of birdseed and water still sit on the desk; here and there the white paint-splash of cockatoo droppings lightens the smoky gloom. The Holy Bible still lies open and face-down, its black covers spread like the wings of some heavy, flightless bird. Song of Solomon? Somehow I doubt it.

A sudden beating of wings: attracted by our presence the cockatoo flies in from another room and after some threshing of the air alights on Felix's shoulder. We turn gratefully towards it – a pink-and-white beacon, a conversation-starter.

'You took the splint off?'

A cursory nod. 'Now I can't seem to get rid of him. Drove over to the next valley and tossed him out the window. He flew straight back in.'

'He likes your company.'

'He likes a free lunch.'

Felix makes no move to sit, so we stand awkwardly in the middle of the darkened room, needing to find more conversation.

'It's odd that he found his way to your door,' Lucy says. 'Don't you think? A chance in a million.'

'Maybe he knew where to come. He's a relative of mine, that Major Mitchell. My skin have a share of his Dreaming.'

Mockery in his eyes, but the bird takes things more seriously, watching us through its left eye, head sideways.

'Maybe he was sent to keep an eye on you?' I suggest.

'My family and other animals?' He grunts disparagingly. 'Saw another relative down at the creek yesterday. Panungkurla. Brown snake. He didn't seem all that pleased to see me.'

'Has anyone written the Dreaming stories down?' Lucy asks. 'They sound wonderfully poetic.'

'Perhaps you should write them down,' I say to Felix. 'Before it's too –'

I stop myself mid-sentence; he finishes it for me. 'Before it's too late?'

Lucy, quickly: 'Before the stories are forgotten.'

Momentary relief, but his illness is the reason we have come, after all, and the matter must be raised sooner or later. I am about to speak when he says simply, 'Who told you?'

'Who told us what?'

He sits, finally, and grinds out his butt in a heaped ashtray on the desk. 'Let me guess. A little bird wearing a fez?'

'Why didn't *you* tell us?' Lucy asks mildly.

'Because it's none of your fucking business.' His tone is more weary than angry, the obscenity more force of habit than forceful. 'You're interested in Dreamtime stories, Frau Doktor? Sit down and I'll tell you a story.' He laughs, softly and sourly. 'A story about another little, ah, animal that I own.'

We sink uncertainly into the deep leather of the nearest Chesterfield, sitting close together.

'It's a whitefeller Dreaming,' he says. 'The Yellow Virus Dreaming.' Another sour laugh. 'That cranky liver virus.'

He lights up his cigarette, inhales; we wait in the gloom. We might be characters in a Victorian novel, sitting in some smoke-filled adventurer's club, surrounded by trophies from darkest Australia.

'I killed a child up there,' he says suddenly. A pause, an amendment. 'Let's rephrase that. A child died because I sat on him too long. Burst appendix. Septicaemic by the time I opened him up.'

Lucy feels the need to defend him, if only against himself. 'A judgement call, surely. We've all made those mistakes.'

He isn't looking for sympathy. 'Shit happens, Frau Doktor? True enough. Especially when the surgeon's been drinking.'

'You operated drunk?'

'I waited till I sobered up. That was the problem. I should have got the air ambulance in. Airlifted the kid to Alice Springs.'

Lucy's eyes slide to mine, and back to Felix; her next question is more tentative. 'Should you have been drinking on call?'

'I was always on call. I was never not on call.'

'Couldn't someone else have operated?'

'Who? The magic man? The clever-doctor feller?' He laughs again, harshly. 'Funny, isn't it? Pay day in town – Thirsty Thursday – and it was the drunk whitefeller who caused all the problems.'

He is pacing about the room now, sucking at his cigarette, the most agitated I have seen him. But also, fuelled by that agitation, the most talkative.

'There was a coroner's inquest in Alice. Medical Defence

flew John Fisk up from Adelaide. No-one could prove I was drunk. And a percentage of appendices do perforate, of course.'

'You were exonerated?'

'Whitefeller law. Whitefeller technicalities. But the family weren't happy. And I'd left a lot of . . . footprints.' My eyes shift briefly to the emu-feather slippers on the shelf behind him. 'Nursing aides were talking around the community. Aboriginal Legal Aid was making noises. And of course I was an initiated man. There was talk of tribal punishment.'

Lucy's hand has found mine as the drama of the story builds. She glances over her shoulder at the dark shelves, at their hoard of ancient, blackly magical objects. 'I hope you got the hell out of there.'

'I wasn't allowed to leave the Territory till after the release of the coroner's report.'

I shiver involuntarily. The surrounding shelves seem to be crowding in on us, like a room with shrinking walls.

'Payback law is very simple,' Felix says. 'I kill your child, you kill mine – or me. Unless we can negotiate some kind of settlement.'

'An eye for an eye,' Lucy says.

'To quote another desert tribe.' He manages a fleeting smile at the thought. 'Up there it's sometimes two eyes for an eye. Or a nose for an eye – exchange rate on application. You could, for instance, adopt my child as a replacement. If I had one. And bring it up as your own. That might satisfy the rules.' He is talking rapidly now, under some pressure of speech. 'The Lands

Council people set up negotiations. I had plenty of friends – the old Jungarrayi. The senior men from my mob. People I'd helped. Payback was being negotiated with the family, privately.'

'Money?'

'I didn't have a son to swap.'

Lucy winces at this brutal way of speaking.

'You paid up?' I ask.

'I paid nothing. The men on the other side couldn't agree on compensation. My initiation was a factor. If I was a member of the tribe, I had to submit to tribal law.'

'Which meant?'

'Ritual spearing. And I'd seen too many of those. The moment the coroner handed down his report I got out of there fast.'

'Best thing you could do.'

He shakes his head. 'Worst thing I could do.' He lifts his eyes and looks from one to the other of us, a faint smile on his lips. 'You still don't get it, do you?'

I glance at Lucy; what is he talking about?

'You were looking for coincidences,' he says, and pauses to suck at his cigarette. Watching us. Playing with us.

Eventually, slightly exasperated: 'Christ! Do I have to spell it out? They got me anyway. They got me with my own spear.'

Lucy's eyes widen; she almost gasps, 'You caught hepatitis from the child you operated on!'

'The child I killed.' He stubs out his butt and reaches again for his tobacco pouch. 'Now, *that's* spooky. Talk about payback. Enough to make you believe in voodoo.'

Silence. The cockatoo is shifting restlessly on his shoulder, as if it, too, finds the story difficult to bear.

'You were stressed,' I say eventually. 'Your hand slipped. You don't need to look for supernatural explanations.'

'On the contrary. I think I might need all the supernatural explanations I can get.' Another pause; his speech has slowed again, the pressure relieved. A bent grin. 'Pascal's wager, Herr Professor – you've got nothing to lose by believing in magic, and everything to gain.'

Lucy says, 'Pascal was talking about accepting the last rites on your deathbed.'

He tugs a bulky X-ray envelope from beneath a stack of books on the desk and tosses it onto the coffee table before us, then slumps back onto the sofa opposite. Lucy and I stare for a moment at the big yellow envelope, each waiting for the other to make a move. My friend, my duty? I slip out a thick, flexible sheet of film, turn on a desk lamp and hold it against the light. Chest shot, anteroposterior view. Years now since I last examined a radiograph, but the opacity in the left lower lobe of the lung can't be missed, even by an academic psychiatrist – an opacity which largely *is* the left lower lobe, a fuzzy-edged, many-clawed crab.

Felix gives a new cigarette a lick. 'Diagnosis, doctors?'

I can't bring myself to put a name to the obvious. Lucy, leaning over my shoulder, her tone carefully neutral: 'Could be infective. Old scar tissue. Sarcoid –'

He laughs derisively, bending his face to the flare of a match. 'Or maybe it's all in my mind.'

He might be ill – dying – but enough is enough. My weeks of frustration with him suddenly find a focus. I do something utterly out of character. I reach over, rip the cigarette from his fingers and stub it out in the ashtray, grind it *into* the ashtray, among dozens of other butts. Lucy's lips part in astonishment, but Felix is already calmly unfolding his tobacco pouch for a replacement.

'Wrong guess,' he tells me.

'What do you mean?'

'Look at the film again. The tumour's not in the lung.'

Lucy holds the X-ray to the light a second time. 'Pleural?' Her diagnosis is tentative. 'A secondary?'

His next coffin nail alight, he inhales deeply. 'No wonder the two of you went into psychiatry.'

'Where's the primary?'

A pause, an exhalation. 'First principles, doctors. Note the raised right hemidiaphragm.'

'Hepatoma?' Lucy states the obvious, belatedly.

'Caused by the hepatitis,' I add.

'Caused by magic,' he says. 'And I pointed the fucking bone at myself.'

Silence once more. Conversation, never easy, has become impossible.

'Of course you want to know the bottom line,' he says eventually.

Lucy and I look askance at each other; of course we do and of course we don't.

'Six months. If I'm lucky.' His tone is matter-of-fact, unemotional. *Quem di diligunt adolescens moritur.* How's my conjugation, Prof?'

Whom the gods love die young.

Lucy's hand tightens on mine. 'Surely something can be done? Chemotherapy?'

The tenderness in her voice only seems to goad him. He turns to her, turns on her, speaking with particular harshness. 'Someone sticks a needle between my ribs from time to time. Sucks out the fluid. Western voodoo. There's talk about ripping out the pleural lining.'

Rip, suck, stick; she flinches as each brutal verb strikes home. Even now he still wants to hurt her, lash out at her.

'Liver transplant?' I suggest.

A snort. 'Keep to reading entrails, Prof.'

Rebuked, I sit in silence as he draws deeply and repeatedly at his cigarette. He can't seem to get enough of the smoke, but it does at least appear to soothe him, or perhaps it is the act of rolling the cigarette itself that soothes him. Brief occupational therapy.

He says, more calmly, 'A line from one of Waldo's Greeks came back to me the other day: The central task of philosophy is learning how to die.'

'Socrates,' I tell him.

Lucy says, 'He meant, surely, learning how to live.'

Felix's eyes fix on her, hooded, predatory. 'If you had six months to live how would *you* spend it?'

She looks to me for help. 'With each other,' I immediately say.

He turns my way, irritably. 'You're already with each other. What else?'

Silence.

'I suppose I'd want to travel. See some of the places I haven't seen. Rome. Athens. Delphi –'

'Disneyland?' he sneers.

'I'd want to hear some of the great orchestras of the world. With Lucy, of course. Eat in some of the great restaurants –'

'The life of the senses. Now we're talking.'

'Not completely.' I pause, thinking. 'I'd also try to set a few things right, mistakes I've made. Make amends –'

'Lucy?' he interrupts, bored with my answers, finding them too pat, too predictable.

She answers more slowly, hesitantly, placing the words carefully heel to toe. 'I think . . . I'd want to get much . . . *closer* to the world that I was leaving. I think I'd like to . . . *be* in that world much more . . . intensely.'

A slight softening of his face; her words have touched something in him. 'Live every moment as if it were an unexpected gift,' he murmurs. 'Perform every act as if it were your last.'

Marcus Aurelius. His hawk eyes are still on her, but less fiercely. A predator thinking about why his prey attracts him? A predator asking questions about his own nature?

Aware of how her words have disturbed him, she retreats into more mundane wishes. 'Of course I'd go back to England. Spend some time with my mother.'

'With or without the Herr Professor?'

She reaches out her hand and grips mine again, tightly. 'I wouldn't spend a minute away from him. I would want Martin to share that . . . that *being*, that intensity, absolutely.'

'True love,' he says. 'How sweet.'

But there is more in her grip than love; there is also desperation. I search for some halfway tone, half serious, half jokey. 'Remember Chapel at school? Father Brian?'

He waits, wreathed in smoke, willing enough to see where I might be heading.

I turn to Lucy. 'The school chaplain, Father Brian. Must have been ninety not out. He had a book of sermons he read from each week in a dead monotone. When he got to the end he turned back to the beginning and began again. Word for word, year in, year out. He'd preach for an hour and you'd look at your watch and it had only been five minutes. You can't imagine the boredom.'

A tentative smile. 'Oh, I can imagine.'

'We used to joke that *that* was the secret of eternal life. Spend your last hours listening to Father Brian preaching and make them last forever.'

Felix laughs briefly. 'Who says religion doesn't have the answers?'

Encouraged, I press on. 'Wasn't there some Mayan civilisation that chose someone to be king for a year? He feasts, drinks, has all the women he wants. Then at the end of the year they sacrifice him on top of the pyramid.'

Lucy turns to me, appalled, but Felix laughs again. 'Where can I sign up?'

I blurt out unthinkingly, 'You want all the women you can have?'

His eyes slide to Lucy, then away, and I immediately regret my words. In that instant, that expanding moment of time – as long as any sermon – my heart stops beating.

As, surely, does hers. The flush is rising on her neck.

Felix's eyes remain averted. He hasn't noticed our reactions and perhaps still believes that he alone is privy to his inner thoughts. He covers his tracks further by airing those thoughts in joke form, as if they are absurd and unserious. 'I suppose a night with the Frau Doktor is out of the question?'

Lucy's grip tightens again. There is nowhere to hide except in forced, canned laughter. And almost immediately Felix is on his feet again, his body language telling us clearly that enough is enough, that it is time to leave. Is there more tact in this abrupt act than meets the eye? Is he offering Lucy, or me, or perhaps all of us, himself included, an escape?

'So how *do* you plan to spend your time, Socrates?' I ask lightly as Lucy and I rise from the sofa.

The eyes are masked again, the smile as crooked as ever. 'Sex, drugs and rock'n'roll?'

Lucy will not be dismissed quite so easily. Her eyes move to the black book sitting face-down on his desk. 'Where does the Bible come in?'

'Cramming for my finals,' he says, and opens the door onto the terrace, and the fan-forced oven of a hellish February day.

12

A Thursday night, early to bed, and the sweet free-fall into sex has begun again. Do I dwell on sex too much? Of course I cling to those memories, now more than ever, but sex has structured our days since that first night together. Our shared bed is a book-end at each end of our working days, and on Sundays a long shelf between. I often feel as if we are falling back towards bed all day, every day, from the moment we rise; returning, if obliquely, down some force-field or gravitational gradient to our starting point, our separation each morning creating a latent energy that must be realised, made kinetic, sooner or later.

Yet after our visit to Felix there is something more low-key, even hesitant in that nightly realisation. Preoccupied with his predicament, it is as if we wish to be less conspicuous in our consumption of each other, unwilling to flaunt our happiness – absurdly, since the only witnesses to any given night's happiness are each other.

Until tonight, when we are interrupted mid-fall by the phone. 'Herr Professor?'

'Felix? I've been trying to ring you.' Daily since our last visit, with no answer. I cover the receiver with my hand and whisper unnecessarily, 'It's Felix.'

'It's about the College of Surgeons dinner tomorrow night,' he is saying in my ear. 'I'm in need of moral support.'

The oddness of this takes a moment to sink in. 'You're think-ing of going to the College dinner? I thought you detested those people?'

'I agreed last year. Just after I came back. It seemed like a good idea at the time. Reconnecting.'

'I'm sure you could cancel. Frank would understand. Under the . . . ah . . .'

'Circumstances?' A small laugh. 'Stations of the Cross, Herr Professor. I thought I might turn my speech into a sermon. Make it last forever.'

'You're the after-dinner speaker?'

'Aboriginal health issues in Central Australia.'

'Are you, ah, well enough for this?'

He ignores my concern. 'It's short notice, I know. But I have an invitation for two.'

I'd be delighted, I'm about to say, but he speaks first. 'I'd like to borrow your wife.'

Silence while I readjust my thinking. Lucy lifts her head from my chest and examines my face. 'She's right here,' I tell him. 'You can ask her yourself.'

I muffle the receiver again. 'Felix wants to take you to dinner tomorrow night. The College of Surgeons.'

A hissed whisper: 'He's giving a speech?'

'A sermon on Aboriginal health.'

Her brow furrows. 'I can't very well refuse. What do you think?'

Her ambivalence mirrors mine, but that mirror allows me to see myself as mean-spirited. 'I think, in the circumstances, it's the least we can do.'

'It's odd, don't you think, Marty?'

137

'That he would ask you?'

'That he would want to go.'

'It's a beginning. And we did want him to open up.'

She composes herself and reluctantly takes the receiver. 'Felix? . . . Yes . . . I'd love to . . . What should I wear?' She forces out a laugh. 'Black tie, then . . . Yes, of course. Seven-thirty . . . I'll look forward to it.' She hangs up and rises from the bed, clearly troubled. She opens the balcony doors and I follow her out into the heat of the night.

'Well?' I ask.

'It's hard to put into words. My instinct tells me not to go. But I feel I have no choice.'

Seeing my own fears mirrored in hers again, I am better able to quell them. 'Lucy, he's dying. You said yourself he's lonely. Let's not read too much into it. He just wants a dinner companion.'

'But why me? What about his woman friend? Or you? Why not you?'

'I'd rather take you than me any day.'

A joke, but if she manages to find a smile I cannot see it. The balcony is in darkness; I can barely make out the pale moon of her face.

'It's more than the dinner, Marty. I feel uneasy. I haven't thought it through, I know, but his dying gives him some sort of power.' She hesitates. 'I'm sorry – this sounds terrible. Is it too selfish of me to think that?'

'A little.'

I am judging my own selfishness as much as hers, yet my

agreement hurts; her face remains invisible, but I sense the tears that spring into her eyes as clearly as if I can hear them.

I also hear the catch in her throat when she speaks again. 'You don't feel uneasy about me being alone with him? After what he said on Sunday?'

'A night with the Frau Doktor? It was just a joke. Tasteless, but still a joke.'

I tug her towards me and hold her closely. We are both uncomfortably sticky, sweating in the heat.

'I've found him difficult, Marty. Unbearable at times. Partly I've stuck it out because of you.'

'I wish you could have known him before.'

She squeezes me into silence. 'And because I feel sorry for him. And of course I'll go. But that's the problem – I *must* go.'

I don't want to think about this; it suddenly seems too baffling.

'And what about you? Aren't you jealous?'

'Of course I'm jealous,' I say. 'I wanted him to ask me.'

We both laugh, and although my laugh is louder than Lucy's, I know that talking has provided a partial cure, a palliative, for her also, and that her tears have dried and we can safely return to bed. If now for no other purpose than to sleep.

The following morning, refreshed by that sleep, we walk hand in hand to the hospital. The fierce northerly of recent days has shrunk to a breeze, a mild pup's breath that barely ruffles the pelt of the city, its green fur of trees and bushes, its yellowing grass-ways, its scurf of litter. In the full light of day the apprehension that overwhelmed us the night before seems less significant. Stop-gap rationalisations have become convincing reasons, self-deception has become self-evident truth. Palliation, in short, has become cure. What harm in a little platonic male–female companionship? Lucy's company will be good for Felix, will bring him out of himself.

Held back by certification assessments – a rush of psychotic admissions – I arrive home late.

Friday night. Yesterday's tomorrow night already. Speech night at the College of Surgeons. Lucy is upstairs in the bathroom, hair-dryer roaring. I hesitate at the foot of the stairs; I have entered unnoticed and don't wish to startle her. When the noise stops I call up, 'Luce?'

'Marty?'

She meets me on the landing, naked and still warm from the shower. She clings to me a little longer than usual.

'You're still worried?'

'More how to act with him. With someone in his . . . predicament.'

'You see people in his predicament every day.'

She releases me, surprised by my tone. 'It's hardly the same thing.'

I attempt a saving joke. 'Because you don't date your patients?'

'Because this is your best friend!' She turns back to the bathroom. 'Thank you for being so understanding.'

Chastened, I appropriate a chair from the study and sit straddling it in the doorway as she resumes her preparations. 'I'm sorry. That was a stupid thing to say.'

'No, I'm sorry. You were just trying to jolly me along.' Hairbrush in hand, she stoops to kiss me briefly but warmly on the mouth.

'Just be yourself,' I suggest. 'This is a public dinner, not a tête-à-tête. Everyone will want to talk with Felix. And he will want you to enjoy yourself.'

Is it the reassurance of my words or her daily ceremony of skin-cleansing and hair-brushing and face-painting – localised, partial massages – that calms her? Her routines have evolved and grown over our years together, become a ritual. I have always loved watching the process, taking a sensual pleasure from it. At times, besotted by this strange other-world of feminine self-pampering – besotted at least by her femininity – I have even asked to help. Once or twice, tolerantly amused, she has permitted me to sketch lipstick onto her mouth, or brush dark, sticky powder into the lashes of her eyes.

Today I merely watch. And talk, quietly and calmly. Palliation with a view to cure. But as Lucy relaxes, my own uneasiness inversely grows. Never before have we prepared for a night of entertainment separately. As I watch her from my chair – her re-emphasised face, her woman's body, still pink and full-nippled from the shower – I can't stop thinking how tonight these preparations are for someone else.

I immediately crush the absurd thought. How can I be jealous of a dying man?

Slowed by soothing talk, Lucy is only half painted when the doorbell rings. I descend and open the door to find Felix, cigarette in mouth. His gaunt frame is well disguised in a formal dinner suit, cummerbund, black tie; his brow is corrugated, his smile bent. *Eudyptes supercilii*? The mocking penguin. A taxi sits at the kerb, cabin light on, the driver reading a newspaper propped on the wheel.

'Is the prom queen ready?'

'Not quite. Come in for a coffee.'

He raises his cigarette questioningly.

'You can smoke inside.'

A knowing smile. 'Special dispensation, Herr Professor?'

I have ignored my own advice to Lucy: act naturally. I have made allowances, out of pity, and of course he will allow no unexamined pity.

'Keep the meter running,' he says to the cab driver, and tosses his butt out into the road and follows me in.

His shoes are scuffed, but otherwise he is transformed by his formal suit. Mounted on the base of a starched collar and black bow tie, his head now seems a separate thing, like the bronze busts of famous Old Blues in the school hall. Less gaunt than lived in; a tough, stoic face, carved from marble. Marcus Aurelius on Rhine frontier rations.

'How's the speech shaping up?'

'I thought I'd wing it.'

He seats himself on a stool as I busy myself in coffee-manufacturing. I hear a match strike behind me; I turn and push a saucer across.

'How are things on the World Wide Id?' he asks, as close as he has come to making idle conversation for months.

I hand him an espresso. 'Are you online? I could send you some sites to check out.'

'Anything I can't live without?'

'The usual human comedy. Lesbian Barbie Dolls in bubble baths. People with Webcams behaving badly . . .'

Footsteps on the stairs, Lucy descending. The usual black cocktail dress, slightly larger than little, black stockings, black shoes with asymmetric soles. Her favourite single-strand pearl necklace matched by pearl earrings, one of which she is still fastening.

'You've scrubbed up well,' Felix says.

'Thank you.'

Her eyes are on mine, avoiding his. She looks pale, or is it just the stark contrast of vanilla skin and black clothing? I am pierced as always by her perfected geisha beauty, and pierced even more tonight by its apparent fragility.

'I hope you didn't go to any trouble on my account.'

She finally looks at him directly. 'Nothing out of the ordinary.'

And nothing fragile either; she can handle Felix, I think.

'I'm looking forward to your speech,' she says.

'I was hoping you might help me write it over dinner.'

He drains his coffee, rises and offers her his arm with exaggerated gallantry; she takes it and I follow my friend and my wife outside to the cab. Felix opens the rear door and waits, chauffeur-like, as she turns back and kisses me on the mouth, smudging her lipstick.

'You'll need to fix your mouth,' I say, holding her tightly, suddenly reluctant to let go.

'I won't be late,' she whispers in my ear.

I will my fingers to unclasp her; she slips into the cab.

'I'll wait up,' I call after her. 'I have some work to catch up on.'

'Does it involve a bubble bath?' from Felix as he climbs in after her.

'You young people have fun now,' I say, and all too quickly they are driving away, Lucy's pale face looking back through the rear window.

The world other than Felix and Lucy reclaims me. A band is playing somewhere, a deep seismic throb of music, heard as much through the soles of the feet as through the ears. Friday night in the city: people in the streets, walking, laughing, shouting. I suddenly find the idea of work unappealing while everyone else is having fun. On impulse I lock the house and follow my ears to a nearby pub. The band is upstairs, the balconies packed with drinkers forced out by the pressure of amplified white noise or unable to hear themselves talk inside. Downstairs I wedge myself against the bar between two groups of drinkers, two smallish pods of humped-backed business types. I order a counter meal of fish and chips as conversations roar on about me and the deep bass thumps against the ceiling upstairs. Friday night football fills the wide overhead screens, a spectacle usually of no interest, but tonight as I occupy my mouth with beer and fish I am grateful also for anything that occupies my eyes. Staring into football offers a kind of meditation, a losing of the self. Quick-time yoga-at-a-distance in which the bodies of others do the contorting.

Halftime in the football, the last fish flake swallowed, and no place to hide from my thoughts. Lucy's concerns flood back through me, more forcefully in her absence, when I no longer need to deny them to her. Is it true that illness gives Felix a kind of power, permitting him to make demands that must always be met? I trust Lucy completely, but not for the first time allow myself to wonder if Felix's true intentions are clear, especially to himself. Flutterings in my stomach, as if the swallowed fish has come alive. I have no idea how to quash the flurry of emotions – restlessness, anxiety – that stirs in the deep silt of me. Cognitive therapy? The heart is subject to the brain, according to that fashionable school. Feelings can be reasoned to a standstill, imprisoned inside the bars of their own illogic.

I have left the pub and am walking at thinking pace. Cognitive pace, *tempo andante*. One criticism of the cognitive method: it denies the sheer power of emotion. The primacy of emotion, some argue. Surely I should trust my feelings – jealousy above all, a reliable early-warning instinct I have studied so often in others. I pass a soup kitchen on the far side of the square and a hand plucks at my sleeve, startling me from my reverie. An upturned palm is offered; a gaunt, unkempt face grins toothlessly. A face not unlike Felix's.

'Good evening, sir. My name is Harris. I'll be your beggar for today.'

Normally worth a laugh, and a fiver. Even the beggars are polite in Adelaide. But tonight I brush past, thinking only this: Even the men who want to fuck your wife arrive in tuxes wearing smiles on their faces in Adelaide.

An absurd, unworthy thought, and as I walk on I know I must kill it quickly. The doors of other pubs tempt me with light and warmth and music, distractions from turbulent feelings. The Saracen's Head, the Rob Roy, the King's Head: I might pub-crawl as a way of passing the time, or at least dividing it into smaller, more manageable chunks.

Can the body know a thing before the mind does? Or before the mind admits it? Do I believe that my walk is aimless, my route accidental? All the way to the Hyatt on North Terrace? The highest of all the pubs of Adelaide is perhaps the logical endpoint of any crawl, but self-deception can take me no further than the lobby. COLLEGE OF SURGEONS DINNER: MEZZANINE. What now? Walk on in? Part of me must know everything, as usual. Less usual is the added goading of jealousy.

But standing in the glittering, gilded foyer – late-Vegas decor, high-gangster decor – I feel ridiculous. What am I doing here? What will Lucy think if I walk into the mezzanine? What will Felix *say*?

This, finally, is the emotion that saves me from myself: the shame that overpowers jealousy. Shame therapy? One thing at least is clear to my cognitive processes: the heart can best save itself, with no help from the head.

The shame cure holds all the way home. Felix's tobacco pouch sits on the kitchen bench, forgotten. A last stab of jealousy – was he so overwhelmed by the vision of Lucy that all else vanished from his mind? I carry the pouch upstairs and roll myself a cigarette and sit outside smoking on the balcony. My new-found calm lasts no further than the second cigarette. The Town Hall clock strikes midnight and each toll of the bell seems to further stir the discontent inside me.

A siren wails in the distance; I am instantly on my feet, straining out over the balcony. Could Lucy have been in an accident? An ambulance races by, heading south, away from the city and the Hyatt, but I feel no relief. Where *is* she? I pace the wrought-iron cage of the narrow balcony, half in mind to head back to the Hyatt. But surely they are not still there.

Half-past midnight. I can take no more. I toss the last cigarette out into the night, hurry back inside the house and descend the stairs, two at a time. Stepping out through the front door, I collide with Lucy, large as life, key in hand, about to step in.

Startled, I burst instantly, ridiculously, into tears.

'Marty? What's happened? Tell me.'

As quickly as the tears have come, embarrassment follows. 'It was just the shock. Seeing you there. I didn't expect . . .'

She knows me better than this. *We* know me better than this. 'An ambulance went past. It's irrational – but I was worried sick.'

She presses her cheek to mine and eases past me into the house, less relieved than distracted. She clearly has other things on her mind. I follow her into the kitchen and sit waiting as she prepares two large cups of weak milky coffee, her standard 'homeopathic' sleeping draught.

'Well?' I prompt. 'How was it?'

She keeps her eyes fixed on the coffee preparations. 'Surgeons. Surgeons' wives. The odd surgeon's husband.'

'Frank was there?'

'Frank was running the show. We were seated at his table.'

'With you on his right hand, no doubt?'

She manages a weary smile. 'On his left. Felix was on his right.'

'How was the speech?'

'I thought it . . . cynical. No, contemptuous. And even sad. He wanted to shock them, of course. Stories of spearings. Clubbings. Wife-beating, glue-sniffing. Ethnoporn – is that what he calls it? For a moment I thought he was going to pull his penis out.'

'He talked of his initiation?'

'Obliquely. What he was really telling them was, You haven't a clue. You whitefellers can't even imagine what life is like out there.'

'The sermon lasted forever then.'

Another small smile. 'It lasted no time at all. Raised hackles all around. You could have cut the air with a knife. Frank's face was as red as his fez. He even stopped pawing me.' Her smile widens, vanishes. 'We left early. Went to some bar across the road.'

'Felix drank?'

'Soda and bitters.' She looks directly at me for the first time. '*Plenty* of bitters. I heard the rest of the speech alone. An audience of one.'

'I'm sorry, darling. That you had to go through this.'

Her eyes slide away again. 'It's not going to be easy, Marty. I mean, it's impossible for him. But I think it's going to be very difficult for . . . us.'

She gnaws at her lip as if to prevent herself from saying more.

'He said something to you, didn't he?'

She hands me my coffee, again avoiding my eyes.

'What did he say? Lucy?'

'It's late, Marty. Come to bed. We can talk in bed.'

I follow her up the narrow stairs, alarmed by this evasiveness. She shuts herself in the bathroom briefly, then emerges and climbs immediately into bed.

'You're wearing makeup to bed?'

'I'm exhausted, Marty.'

'What are you hiding?'

'I'm sorry?'

'You won't look at me. You're wearing a mask to bed. Tell me. What happened?'

'*Nothing* happened. It was just a dinner.'

'Followed by a tête-à-tête in some cosy bar.'

'This isn't you, Marty. You're being irrational.'

She turns the bed lamp off and we lie in silence, mere inches apart but invisible to each other in the blackness. My body is restless again; small, anxious movements stir in my muscles, small urgencies that slowly become larger movements, coalescing finally, as if finding common cause, seeking common release, in a growing sexual insistency. Absurd, given the circumstances? It's less Lucy's presence that arouses me – the warm tickle of her breath in my face, her soft breasts pressed against my chest – than her resistance. I want her to open herself to me, but a sexual opening is the least of it. I need to *know*.

'Did he touch you?'

'Of course not!'

'You were so late. I didn't know what to think.'

'I walked home.'

A safer focus for my anxiety. 'Alone? Through the city? At this hour?'

'Marty – please. I needed to clear my head. Think things through.'

More significance. I give her time, sensing she is still finding the wording for that thinking.

'It's his birthday next week,' she says finally. 'The last thing he asked me, before I left – he wants to cook a birthday dinner. Something special.'

Relieved to be given a fact at last, something solid for my anxieties to chew on, I say, 'Is he up to it? It might be better for him to come down here, for us to cook, rather than for us to go there.'

No answer. Nothing but the sound of her swallowing, a small sound expanding to fill a vast available silence.

'Talk to me, Luce.'

'You're not invited,' she murmurs eventually.

'I'm sorry?'

'He wants to cook dinner for me. Just the two of us.'

Now the pounding of my heart is filling the silence. Can she also feel it, hear it? The darkness of the room masks our faces like thieves' stockings; if I can control my thumping heart it might be possible to dissemble without giving myself away.

'I guess it's not so much to ask,' I say. 'It's just another dinner.'

'Is it?' Her voice is suddenly small and vulnerable. If invisibility allows me to lie, it allows her to be honest; I know that there are tears in her eyes again. And somehow, weirdly, our roles have reversed; I am arguing for Felix, Lucy against.

'He needs someone to talk to. Who better than you?'

'He doesn't want to *talk*, Marty.'

'But he needs to.'

'He doesn't know what he needs. It's all jokes and sneers. There were a lot of people there tonight who cared about him. Old friends. Even Frank, given half a chance. But he was having none of it. He didn't make the slightest effort to hide his contempt.'

'He's a proud man.'

'He refuses to accept pity – without realising that pity is exactly what he's asking for. Pity in other forms.'

'Love,' I blurt out, although I mean something more, or less, than love.

Silence again.

'He's never going to admit that either,' she says.

'Perhaps it's best that way. If you act as if it's innocent, perhaps it is innocent.'

Another, longer silence. A silence that soon becomes too large to end unobtrusively, too difficult. Her head rests on my chest, her tears are a sticky film between us. Emptied of those tears, and now of words, she manages to drift slowly, with two or three small starts awake, into exhausted sleep.

I am not yet emptied and cannot follow. Her tears have strengthened me, oddly, but as her body loosens itself from mine, and my reassurances are no longer needed, much of that strength departs with her. I have an urge, briefly, to hold this against her. How can she sleep? Does her – *our* – predicament mean nothing to her? But as her breathing slows and deepens I accept that sleep she must, either through weariness or in self-defence, or both.

My anger soon finds a clearer target: Felix. Again I must remind myself that he is dying.

I lie flat on my back. Various night noises marble the smooth darkness; the to and fro of Lucy's breathing, the random creak of cooling floorboards, the pigeons rearranging themselves in the eaves. I close my eyes, open them. A different marbling: faint light through shutter cracks, the noise of early birds in the square. I must have slept, for time has surely passed. As the light increases, Lucy's sleeping face reveals itself by increments, her mascara smeared by last night's tears.

A wave of panic washes through me. Has Felix known all along that I would put his case to her, however unintentionally? I have been trying to make things easier for her, not for him, but perhaps he has even foreseen this – that I might inadvertently speak for him while not, at least at this particular moment, giving a fuck for him and his dying?

I slip from bed and pull on the minimum clothes. For once Lucy sleeps on, utterly spent, as I tiptoe downstairs, collect my car keys from the hall table, and step outside.

13

First light. A cold southern front has washed across the city, unnoticed, during the night, and passed on, leaving a cooler world behind. I drive out of the city with the windows wound down, hoping the flow of air over my face and arms might refresh me, invigorate me. My mind seeks similar refreshment, or escape. Outside the urban speed limit, I perversely slow the car, feeling a need to dawdle through this cool morning, to derail my small red locomotive and play among the buttercups.

And especially to delay the confrontation; to think about Felix more calmly.

The sun is not yet up, the ceiling of the world less blue than silver-grey. Cockatoos everywhere on the stubbled slopes, white corellas and powder-pink galahs. *Cacatua sanguinea. Cacatua roseicapilla.* Two smaller green-and-yellow parrots, feeding on grass seeds among their larger cousins, catch my eye. Budgerigars? Surely not this far south. Lorikeets, perhaps. Or elegant parrots. *Neophema elegans.*

I am still dawdling in low gear as I crest the Woodcroft ridge, drive down through the valley and up the narrow creek road.

Felix is sitting outside on the terrace, still wearing his dress shirt and trousers from the night before. His feet are on the tabletop, his dinner jacket hangs on the back of the chair, his bow tie is loose about his neck. Has he been sitting here all night?

'You took your time,' he says.

'You were expecting me?'

'I saw you coming from the other side of the valley. You seem to be confusing the speed limit with your IQ.'

Slightly more warmth than usual allowed to peep through the mask. The mandatory cigarette is jammed between his lips, a pot of coffee sits at his elbow. Two cups – he *has* been expecting me.

'Caffeine?'

'No. Thank you.' Formal, stilted, already on the back foot and wondering where to begin.

'At least sit down, Martin.'

Is it the first time he has uttered my name, without irony, since my return? There is something disturbing in this, something ominously benevolent. I sit reluctantly; he stubs out his cigarette and fills the second cup with coffee anyway.

'I've come about Lucy.'

The smile quiescent now, the eyes deadpan. 'Do tell.'

A deep breath; a forced calm. 'She was very upset last night. You need to understand that. You need to understand what you might be putting her through.'

'Her or you?' No mockery in this, but little sympathy either.

I say, 'I think she is in the more difficult position.'

'I beg to differ. I believe that I am in the more difficult position.'

There is, again, no easy answer to this.

He reaches for his tobacco pouch and begins the rolling process. 'One thing about dying, Marty. As they say in the classics, it concentrates the mind. You tend to . . .' A pause while he licks. 'Review your priorities.'

The edges of his cigarette paper fail to stick; he licks again. I realise, surprised, that his mouth is dry; that beneath the cool exterior he, too, is finding conversation difficult. This small sign of nervousness in him, of human fallibility, is even more disturbing than his sympathy.

I say bluntly, 'Is Lucy a priority?'

He sets the cigarette down on the table. 'Let's just say I was less unhappy last night than I'd been for some time.'

A single lazy fly, sluggish in the fresh morning air, bumps at my face. I brush it irritably away, the least of my concerns.

'You're talking about my wife,' I remind him.

'I know that, Prof. What I am about to say is tentative. I don't want you to feel threatened.'

'But?'

'You asked me last Sunday how I'd like to spend my last months. Part of the answer became clear to me last night.' A small, corrective smile. 'No, this morning, sitting here. Thinking about last night.'

His worn face has relaxed into something thoughtful, even rueful – something resembling the face of the friend I left behind ten years ago. A month back I would have welcomed and cherished it; now it just creates more anxiety. Sensing what is coming next, I shiver involuntarily. Involuntary, also, the sugar which I have stirred, unnoticed, into my coffee, as if as an antidote for the sourness to come. I haven't taken sugar with coffee for years.

'What are you trying to tell me?'

No answer.

'Are you telling me that you love my wife?'

He plucks another cigarette paper from his pack and begins, carefully, to roll more tobacco. Is he so distracted or nervous that he has forgotten the cigarette at his elbow?

'I don't think love is a useful word. I don't want to put a label on it – just tell you what I feel. What I think I feel. I like being near her. She makes me feel . . . alive.' He lights up. 'Relatively speaking, of course.'

The glimmer of a smile, a black joke at his own expense. I reach for the first, forgotten cigarette and the matches, giving myself some thinking space.

'I know you're dying, Felix. I'll do everything I can to help. *We'll* do everything. But have you thought of Lucy? You put her in an impossible position.'

'That's why I'm talking to you first.'

A surge of anger; again I have to remind myself that he is a dying man. 'You want me to do your procuring? I'm her fucking husband – and I mean fucking!'

'Martin.' That patient, disturbingly reassuring tone. 'I don't want to fuck her. I won't be capable of fucking her much longer. And even if I could I don't think she would –'

'Of *course* she wouldn't!'

A look in his eyes – sceptical amusement – as if he thinks I don't fully understand my wife.

'If she did, it would be out of pity,' I say, infuriated further.

'I'll take pity. I'd rather lust, but I'll take pity.' A wry smile. 'All I want you to consider is this: you have the rest of your life with her. I just want a loan. It may be selfish, but I think I'm entitled to a little selfishness.'

That calm, unnatural gentleness again. I'm reminded of an early psychotherapy patient, my first therapeutic disaster. Ms Jane W, a twenty-something single mother suffering post-partum depression. Our sessions together had been tumultuous, full of tears and guilt and even anguished suicide threats over her inability to care for her baby. The last session couldn't have been more different. She arrived in an altered state, calm and reasonable, her face relaxed, her body language at ease. Even her surprising gesture at the end, kissing me lightly on the cheek and thanking me – 'You're a lovely man' – failed to ring alarm bells. I felt satisfied for the first time, convinced that we had turned some therapeutic corner, that at last we were making progress.

The police fished her body out of the Thames the next day, her drowned baby strapped to her back. That last, terrible calmness on her face stayed with me for years, haunted me: the calm of someone who is no longer helpless, who in making a final decision has found a kind of peace, or a deluded foretaste of the greater peace to come.

I shiver again, a small convulsion. Felix's newfound calm is less chilling, but no less ominous. The thought might be unfair, but I cannot avoid it: his decision is not to harm himself – he is beyond further harm – but to harm others.

'I don't think I'm asking for much.'

'Not yet.'

'You're afraid of what might develop?'

I try to match his calm with my own, to keep my tone measured. 'Lucy's a very giving person. And you might be demanding. Given the . . . circumstances.'

'If she gave more than I asked, would that be too wrong? In the . . . circumstances.' Heavy irony again on the last word.

I say, 'Isn't there something in one of those books you've been reading about not coveting thy neighbour's wife?'

Silence. We inhale together, exhale.

He says, 'I've been reading a lot of old books. I think I prefer the Greeks.'

'Then you will know that this is how wars get started.'

'Marty, keep calm. This is not about sex.'

'Not *yet*,' I repeat.

'I want nothing more than to spend some time with her. To get to know her better.'

'You *need* to get to know her better! You don't know her at all if you think asking me first is going to help your case! What is she, a side of beef?'

Another silence; more silences now than talk.

'I think I have asked her,' he says, 'if not explicitly.'

'And what was her answer? Explicitly.'

He looks directly at me. 'Troubled. Distressed. But more ambiguous than you want to believe.'

'Bullshit,' I spit out, and rise and stalk across to the other side of the terrace, unable to sit and listen any more.

His words follow me, softly spoken but carrying clearly. 'Difficult times require difficult decisions, Marty.'

'What the fuck does that mean?'

'My speech last night was about the desert people. About how things used to be done, before whitefeller law.'

'I might have come and listened if you'd asked me.'

He ignores this. 'It wasn't an easy life. Warfare between the tribes. Wife-stealing. Punishments were brutal, but the conditions demanded certain behaviours from people. Certain moralities.'

I want to block my ears against what I sense is coming, but continue to listen.

'They learnt to share their property. Food. Tools. Fire.'

I interrupt, 'Since when are wives property?'

'Since about a million years ago.'

'Then thank God for whitefeller law!'

'For someone taking the moral high ground you're hardly consistent,' he says.

'What's that mean?'

'You act as if she's *your* property.'

'She *is* my property. And I'm hers. It's called a marriage.'

He continues, 'The Warlpiri have marriage. But the law permits acts of, shall we say, generosity outside marriage. Acts of comfort. Mostly between relatives who hunt together. Between brothers especially.'

'And the wives? They don't get a say?'

'Right of veto. But they usually agree.' He exhales, and laughs softly. '*Plus ça change*, as we say in Warlpiri.'

The joke gives me a new focus for my indignation. 'What we are doing would disgust Lucy. This . . . *bargaining*!'

I pace about the terrace, agitated. Stripped as emotionally naked, it occurs to me, as any jealous desert husband.

'Martin, don't misunderstand me. I don't think that dying gives me the right to have whatever I want. But I think it gives me the right to be honest.' He adds, almost as an aside, 'One thing I did like about the desert. It was free of bullshit.'

'We live in the city, Felix. And you're full of it.'

'I'm doing my best not to be.' He holds my eyes. 'Allow me this last small adventure. Please. This last,' and here he allows himself a small, half-mocking smile, 'adventure of the feelings.'

A line from something else he has been reading? The Greeks? Not the Bible, certainly, unless in a cautionary text: *Thou shalt not have adventures of the feelings.*

I say, 'It's not up to me.'

The first sign of impatience in his voice. 'Of course it's up to you, to both of you. Lucy would never do anything you didn't want.'

'And I would never veto anything she did want.'

Another silence; a mingling of smokes between us in the cool, still air.

'You like to quote the Greeks,' I continue. 'Didn't Socrates say somewhere that it's better to suffer evil than to do it?'

'Oh, I'm suffering, Prof. Don't you worry about that.' His gaze still upon me, difficult to meet but impossible to avoid. 'I just want to cook dinner for her. Something special. Is that so evil? I don't eat myself, and I haven't cooked properly for months.'

And now there is something else in his face, something neither calm nor mocking. It's there also in the tone of his voice, a tone I haven't heard for ten years. Hope. And I see again, more definitely, the source of that hope. He might deny the word, or smother it with cool-temperature euphemisms, but without question he loves Lucy.

He stubs out his cigarette. 'She shouldn't feel she is under any pressure.'

'You don't think she might just feel that anyway?'

'Under any unreasonable pressure.'

The sun pokes its head above the house behind him; the single housefly has been joined by several sisters, warming to their pesky work. The flies and the sun in my eyes are a final irritation. I rise, toss away my cigarette and gather my car keys.

'You're leaving?'

'I need to talk to Lucy. This is about her, not us.'

A last, brief eye contact. The bent smile is back, the twist of bitters. 'She would make a dying man very happy,' he says.

'We're *all* dying,' I spit out as I turn and walk away. But I am speaking more to myself than to him, and as soon as I have uttered the words I almost hope that he hasn't heard them.

14

She takes time preparing herself. More time than usual?

Saturday night, one week later. Dinner in the hills, an invitation for one. I sit on our made bed, the current issue of *Psychiatry* propped open on my chest, watching her through the bathroom door. I have been here before, too recently, watching her prepare for dinner with another man. The same other man. Small details distract me. The skin of her cheeks yields slightly to her fingers as she smooths in a moisturising cream. She seems too deft at this tonight, too practised – where is her adolescent awkwardness? Her head turns towards me, my eyes evade hers by a split second. Of course the paper, 'Olanzapine and Tardive Dyskinesia: A Horizontal Study', has no chance of holding my interest. I spy on her again as soon as she turns back to her own face.

Cognitive wrestlings, the head trying to pinfall the loopy heart. Her heart as much as mine. I understand her seesawing feelings even less than my own. I tell myself she would take identical pains for a girls' night out, for a clinical dinner – for work. I tell myself she is masking herself, fitting on a layer of armour, a protective helmet.

'It's just a dinner, Marty.'

'Not to Felix.'

'You don't trust me?'

'I don't trust Felix.'

'I can handle Felix. '

'He can be very persuasive.'

The same banal arguments have been revisited many times during the previous week, without advancing further. How can they? The same anxieties might occupy different arrangements of words, but everything that can be said has already been said.

Dressed, she sits beside me on the bed. Her war paint is thicker than I have ever seen it. Close up, her face remains oddly uncharacteristic, as if out of focus, or seen from a distance – half cartoon beauty, half perfected essence. I feel a slight reassurance. She is dressed more as geisha than comfort woman, less made-up than made-over into something non-specific. This straw I can at least grasp at: if she ever gives herself to him, it will be a generic Woman that is given, not this particular woman.

'It's not easy for me either, Marty.'

I pull her mask gently to mine to kiss; she averts her painted lips but offers her cheek.

'I have to go. I love you very much.'

I rise and follow her downstairs, and outside to the car. 'Do some work,' she urges. 'I won't be late.'

'Be careful,' I can't help calling after her, one last time.

I climb the stairs to the study and force myself to work for a time, surfing exotic websites, nose to screen. The more exotic, the better. I spend an hour on a chat-line among men who can only excite themselves by licking a partner's muddy gym shoes. The specificity of the fetish distracts me. I follow links to those dedicated to licking clean gym shoes, or muddy hiking boots, or ballet slippers dunked in vanilla custard – and only custard, and only vanilla flavoured. www.fetish.com: the weird wired web. Surfing these cybershores of bizarre sexual imagery, fuelled by jealousy, is it any surprise that a fierce riptide carries me far out of my depth? Images of Felix's mutilated penis pop into my head with hallucinatory power. Absurd fears plague me, adolescent insecurities that I cannot exorcise. What might his cock look like erect? *Does* it give greater pleasure? Google-searching under 'subincision, penis',

I ride my mouse into the whitewater of a Victims of Male Circumcision Trauma Support Group. Infantile trauma, repressed memories, foreskin envy: I find myself gazing into a warped mirror of Freudian psychobabble. Here is a tribe of men who blame every problem ever suffered – failed marriages, failing health, lost loves, bankruptcies – on the trauma of circumcision as an infant. Links are offered to therapists who promise hypnotic recovery of that surgical abuse. Physical cures are demonstrated: before-and-after jpg-images of weights taped to foreskin remnants, aiming to stretch them back into existence.

Enough material for a conference, but not to get me through the night. I am glancing at the computer clock more frequently. How long till she arrives home? How long, for that matter, till she arrives at Felix's? Time seems jammed, even its digital representations frozen. The cursor is winking through the seconds; I can *see* that time is passing, but the numerals that count out the minutes might be taking no notice.

Sensitised by that dinner a week ago, and under even fewer illusions, I am far more agitated this time round. Of course the same solution offers itself. The sole solution? To calm my fears I must know the facts, must know everything. All the bird names and Latin mottoes, the capitals of South American republics and states of the USA that begin with N or H or P now seem a mere apprenticeship for this new addiction. The bowels of my brain are in desperate need of something solid to chew on, some rough fibre of fact. Nothing can be left to my too-fertile imagination.

Better, almost, to discover the worst than to fear the worst –

certainty of any kind would be a relief from uncertainty.

Lucy has taken the car; I cannot easily follow. Yet as I stare at a becalmed Netscape Navigator, the cursor winking inexorably centre screen, follow I must. I fight the urge for some time, but am soon compelled to step out into the night and hail a cab.

'Woodcroft, please.'

A woman driver, middle-aged; a tough, seen-it-all face softened a little at the edges by the chub of fat. 'Hard to get a fare back from the hills at this time of night.'

'It's a return trip.'

She turns and runs her eyes over me, a brief psychiatric examination. What does she see? A face flushed more with anxiety than booze. A coat and tie unstained by spilled beer or vomit. She turns on the meter. 'It's your money.'

We U-turn and head south. I am in no mood for talk. Sensing this, she turns up the radio: commercial-infested easy listening. Or perhaps not so easy. 'I Heard It Through The Grapevine', 'Always Something There To Remind Me'. A clear night above the hills, a low full moon. Bright moonlight on the stubbled ridges, but shadows filling the bowls of the valleys like a heavy black soup. Here and there the twinkle of lights: fireflies stuck in that soup, one of them perhaps Felix. TURN BACK. YOU ARE GOING THE WRONG WAY. The words flash by on a feeder road, jolting me. What am I doing here? Having my own adventure of the feelings?

'Next exit, driver.'

An unwanted adventure. But how to end it?

'Drive straight through the town. And if you could turn your lights off.'

The cabbie brakes in the well-lit main street and turns to examine me again, a supplementary consultation, or assessment of mental state. 'I think it's time I saw some ID.'

I tug my wallet from an inside coat pocket and hand it over. She flips it open, inspects it briefly, shrugs and hands it back.

'You're paying, Professor.'

She turns off the headlights and drives on through the town and up the creek road, carefully now, navigating by the light of the full moon. We are well past Felix's farmhouse, almost to the end of the road, before I ask her to stop.

'Wait for me here.'

'How do I know you'll come back?'

I toss my wallet onto the front passenger seat. 'Feel free to keep the meter ticking.'

Silence outside the car; the air still, the creek dry. The moonlit road is as bright as salt, my shadow precedes me as I follow its steep descent. An owl speaks somewhere, distant but startling, its call amplified by the great bowl of the valley. 'Mopoke. Mopoke.' *Ninox boobook*, the boobook owl. I turn in at Felix's drive, the farmhouse below, the terrace visible now between the trees. A figure is sitting at the barbecue table. Lucy? I take half a dozen steps closer: yes, Lucy. And Felix? I stop in my tracks, heart pounding. Felix is kneeling on the paving before her.

An ancient configuration: a man on his knees before a woman. Is he begging? Worshipping? The tiny flare of a match;

now he bends to light something. A candle? I step closer and see that Lucy is surrounded by half a dozen flickering pinpoints of light. Glimpsed imperfectly through the trees, she might be a victim in a circle of enchantment.

Even closer now, and a prickle in my nostrils: the sharp scent of citronella. I almost laugh out loud with relief; Felix is doing nothing more satanic than surrounding my tender-skinned darling with burning mosquito coils.

Somewhere the owl begins speaking versions of its name again. 'Mopoke. Boobook.' I feel a surge of shame, a monstrous owl myself, all eyes in the darkness, spying. *Ninox clandestinus, Ninox suspiciosus*. The snoopy owl, the green-eyed owl. *Ninox furtivus*. What *am* I doing here? TURN BACK. YOU ARE GOING THE WRONG WAY.

I pull my mobile phone from my pocket and punch Lucy's number. The melody of her phone carries clearly through the still night air; I watch as she reaches for her bag and checks the tiny screen. A moment's hesitation before she answers.

'Marty?'

What to say? I am almost close enough to speak without a phone.

'Marty? Are you there?'

'I'm here.'

'You sound strange.'

'I'm fine. Working hard.'

She indicates something to Felix with her head. A need for privacy? He rises and enters the house.

'Why are you whispering?'

'Am I? No reason. How are things?'

'We're sitting outside on the terrace. Lots of company – of the biting variety.'

'No blood offerings?'

She laughs softly. 'Felix offered.'

'Is he behaving himself?'

'A perfect gentleman. You mustn't worry.'

'I'm not worrying.' Not here, now, with a clear view. 'How long will you be?'

'I've had a few drinks. I shouldn't drive just yet. I don't want you to wait up, Marty. There's no sense two of us losing sleep over this. I might be late.'

'Wake me when you get in?'

'If you promise to finish your work and go to bed.'

'I promise.'

My work here is finished, but bed is an hour away. As I turn and walk back up the road to the waiting cab, it's less shame therapy than a sense of the absurd that saves me from myself. Spying on my wife while talking to her on a mobile phone? A scene from a slapstick movie, surely. In which I have been the stooge. The One Stooge. The Lone Stooge.

The cabin light is on, the driver reading a thick paperback. She hands over my wallet as I climb in.

'Happy, Prof?'

'Not unhappy.'

'Want to talk about it?'

Brief psychotherapy with the meter running? Taking a talking cure with any sympathetic listener is as effective as with a trained psychiatrist, according to one famous study.

'There's nothing to talk about.'

We drive back down to the city as we drove up, without speaking. The radio does its best to disturb my newfound calm. 'Suspicious Minds'. 'Don't Explain'. 'What Becomes Of The Brokenhearted'. 'Run Around Sue'. Are there no other subjects for song?

'Could you turn the radio off, please driver?'

At home I swallow two 10mg Temazepam and climb into bed, intending to time-travel straight to morning. The song lyrics at last stop repeating like stuck records in my head. Lucy is safe. She is – we are – doing the right thing. Companionship, within limits. Platonic compassion, if not Socratic.

I sleep, but porously, the noises of the night leaking through the thick wall of drugs and dreams. Three a.m. A palpitating heart wakes me; I am sweating and nauseous as if after a night of drinking. Where is she? Drug-dulled, my mind is still relatively calm; my body alone is agitated. I recognise my state as one I have often observed in others: inner pain finding outward release. Psychic pain, somatic release. Or is it merely a somatic representation of inner pain? The aches and restless muscles offer no actual release from anxiety. I lie naked in a bath of sweat, my face a clammy mask, my armpits soaked. If you can't weep, your skin weeps for you? Freud's cartoon formulation comes to me peripherally, uselessly.

Psychiatrist, shrink thyself. I free myself from the tangle of bedclothes, step through into the shower, and twist the hot tap. A gush of scalding water engulfs me; eyes closed, I surrender to its comforting pressure.

When the water runs cold I step out of the cubicle, overcome again by nausea. Three-thirty a.m. I dial Lucy's mobile. Just before the phone rings out, her sleepy voice: 'Martin?'

'Lucy, where *are* you? It's almost four in the morning.'

'You're still awake?'

'I was worried.'

'It was too late to ring. I thought you'd be asleep.'

'You didn't think I'd be worried *sick*? That I would *want* you to wake me?'

Silence. Eventually, 'I'm sorry, darling. There's nothing to worry about. I drank a little too much and fell asleep.'

'Where?'

Puzzlement in her voice. 'Here, of course. At Felix's house.'

'*Where* in Felix's house?' Why must I ask these stupid questions? Once begun, there is no thwarting them.

'In the study. On the couch. I'm fine, Marty. But I need to sleep it off.'

'Where's Felix?'

My need will not be denied, the need to see everything, to turn the images this way and that in my head as if on a computer screen, trying to get behind them, or above them, to visualise them from all possible angles.

'He's asleep, Marty. And I want you to go back to sleep.

I love you, darling. I'll be home in the morning. Before you know it.'

I pace the house, heart pounding, upstairs and downstairs, wearing nothing but a film of sweat – a nightgown of sweat. London, five years past. Lucy's second psychotherapy case. Mr John A, a young accountant, pathologically jealous of his wife. We often discuss him at night in bed, less unofficial case supervision than Lucy seeking a second opinion. The more she tells me, the more I am struck by the sheer energy of John A's obsession. I am struck even more by the inventiveness fuelled by that energy. Suspicious minds? Paranoia powers the search engines of his brain into finding solutions to non-existent problems. He steams open his wife's mail. He checks phone records. He rings friends, using foreign accents to track down her whereabouts. Towards the end he even follows her about the streets in absurd disguises. A few joules of that creative energy diverted into his profession, into any profession, might have made him millions.

Treatment? Lucy talks to John A of trigger situations; they endlessly rehearse more rational responses. But when he tries to put those responses into practice – to resist his jealousy, to not reach for the phone, not open the mail, not check her underwear for semen stains – anxiety overwhelms him. He can't fight it. He becomes ill: nausea, palpitations, diarrhoea. Breathlessness, chest pain. The full somatic catastrophe. He finds he can only relieve his agony by following his first impulses.

'How is his wife coping?' I ask Lucy some weeks into his therapy.

'She left him last week. And moved in with the man he had always suspected.'

'So he was right all along? She was unfaithful?'

'No. Completely faithful – till last week.'

'What are you saying? Her husband's jealousy drove her into another man's arms?'

'Perhaps. But why that man? Why the one he suspected all along?'

We lie safely in each other's arms, thinking it through.

'He detected traces of a potential attraction?' I suggest. 'An attraction that only later blossomed.'

She laughs softly. 'Jealousy is clairvoyant? A psychic sixth sense? Sounds like heresy, Doctor.'

'There must be some rational explanation. Perhaps his jealousy made him super-sensitive to non-verbal cues. Unacknowledged attractions.'

'Unacknowledged by her also?'

'Of course. Perhaps, ironically, his obsession first brought them to the surface. Made her conscious of her own unconscious desires.'

As I replay this exchange in my head now, years later, sleep is impossible. I too have been that man, stalking my wife. I am following in his footsteps therapeutically also – self-knowledge provides no cure. Remaining in the house is again impossible; I simply have to know more.

The *DSM-IV*, chapter 297, verse 1:

Delusional Disorder, Jealous Subtype: the central theme of the person's (non-bizarre) delusion is that his or her spouse or lover is unfaithful. This belief is arrived at without due cause and is based on incorrect inferences supported by small bits of 'evidence' (e.g. disarrayed clothing or spots on sheets), which are collected and used to justify the delusion. The individual with the delusion usually confronts the spouse or lover and attempts to intervene in the imagined infidelity (e.g. restricting spouse's autonomy, secretly following the spouse . . .)

Spouse? That gender-neutral term is over-generous to jealous husbands, of whom I am king as I phone for a taxi and dress hurriedly. I am outside in the square, pacing back and forth, fully awake now, as the cab rounds the corner. Against mathematical odds (how many hundred taxis work the graveyard shift?) but true to some deeper psychological probability, it is the same driver.

'Don't tell me,' she says, deadpan.

'It's one-way this time.'

'I'll have to charge for the return.'

'You take Visa?'

Her nod is our last communication until she turns in at Felix's driveway an hour later.

'You want a business receipt?'

'It's personal.'

'Hope you can sort it out, Professor.'

More resolved now, I walk rapidly down to the house through

the trees. The full moon is directly above, bright enough to flush a little dull colour into the leaves; the path is easy to follow.

The terrace is empty. Smeared food plates on the barbecue table, a single lipsticked wineglass, scrunched paper napkins. A bottle of Scotch and a shot glass. No lipstick there; is Felix drinking again? At the door into the study I stop in my tracks, frozen. Only the desk lamp is on, but its intimate glow heightens rather than softens the impact of the scene. Lucy sits on a Chesterfield, her head lolled on the backrest, sleeping. Felix also sleeps, stretched out on the same Chesterfield, his knees tucked into his chest, his head on Lucy's lap. Her left hand rests lightly, tenderly, on his neck. Innocent enough on the surface? I feel the surge of nausea again, the prickle of cold sweat on my brow, the thump of a clairvoyant Othello-heart.

Her eyes suddenly open; she is staring straight at me. Time unfreezes and she straightens herself as I step in through the door, her expression puzzled, but happy enough to see me.

'Marty?' she whispers. 'How did you get here?'

My answer is louder than intended. 'I think we have more important things to talk about than how I got here.'

She raises a finger to her lips. 'Ssh.' Her other hand remains on Felix's shoulders as he sleeps on, undisturbed.

But I cannot keep my voice down, the words burst out of me. 'This is wrong, Luce. I can't – I *won't* – go along with this any more.'

'Marty, we've been talking. That's all.'

'Well, we haven't talked it through anywhere near enough. The three of us.'

Pain now on her face. She removes her hand from Felix's neck and moves it to the back of the sofa, self-consciously. More clairvoyant feelings: the talking has been done in my absence, by the two of them, and the decisions have already been taken.

'What have you been talking about?'

Her eyes slip from mine. A deep breath, then she looks back. 'Felix wants me to go away with him.'

'He wants to *what*?'

'Go on a trip. With me.'

'And where does he plan this little honeymoon? Disney-fucking-land?' A night's pent-up feelings – an emotional white noise of possessiveness, anger, frustration, shame – find release. I spit the words out in an ecstasy of contempt.

'Hush,' she urges again. 'You'll wake him.'

'I asked you a question. Where, for Christ's sake?'

Again she averts her eyes. 'I don't think the destination is the issue, do you?'

Silence. She is the destination, she is reminding me. Lucyland. Male-Fantasyland. Her face paint cannot hide her feelings; if anything it exaggerates her anguish, makes of her features a tragedian's cartoon mask.

'What did you tell him?'

'I said I'd have to think about it.'

'For about three seconds!'

She is still whispering, as if to negate, or at least average down, the volume of my ranting. 'I said I'd have to talk to you.'

'Do you want to go?'

Barely audibly, 'Of *course* I don't want to go.'

I am silenced, momentarily. But in her hushed vehemence I can already hear a different, deeper answer. She is saying that she must go. That I must agree with a decision that has already been taken.

'Look on the bright side, Herr Professor. It probably won't be a long trip.'

Felix's voice startles us. Has he been feigning sleep, eavesdropping all along? He eases himself into a sitting position, massaging his stringy neck muscles with one hand.

'I really don't think I'm asking for much,' he says.

'So you keep saying. But you want to take my wife away on some bizarre comfort trip.'

Lucy's face is averted; I sense the pain I am causing her but cannot stop myself.

'Calm down, Prof,' Felix says. 'If this was about sex I'd ring an escort agency.'

'Then what is it about? True love?'

He lets this pass. 'I just want to get to know her a little better. I'll book separate bedrooms if it's the sex that bothers you. But why you should get in such a state about sex is beyond me.' He yawns and stretches and looks about for his tobacco pouch.

I force myself to speak more calmly; it must be possible to reason with him. 'You might as well be holding her hostage. Don't you see that?'

'So that's what you're worried about? The Stockholm syndrome? She might get to like it?'

'Dying gives you an odd kind of immunity, doesn't it?' I say, infuriated. 'It makes you fucking invulnerable.'

'Marty!' from Lucy, but I will not be stopped.

'Have you thought about afterwards? About *her*? When you're six feet under the fucking ground?' The brutality of my own words stops me momentarily, the pleasure of uttering them catching me by surprise. 'Have you thought how this might leave *us*?'

'I'm sure you can workshop yourselves through it. It's what you do for a living, for Christ's sake.'

Lucy stares up at me through tear-reddened eyes. She has said nothing for some time. I realise, suddenly, that she has no need to, that everything I have said has surely been said, or at least thought, by her already.

Felix lights his cigarette and takes several deep inhalations; as always the smoke seems to soothe him, calming whatever bee-swarm of emotions is seething inside him. 'I'm sorry,' he says. 'That was glib. I have, you may be surprised to know, thought about this a great deal. I've even tried to see it from your side. But one thing seems clear: I'd rather experience a grief reaction than experience being a grief object.'

He inhales again, exhales smoothly. Smoke also seems to help him think, if only by slowing his mouth down, allowing him to pace his thoughts. I feel the urge to roll a cigarette myself as he continues. 'You can talk about these things too much. I've been sitting up here trying to work out how to spend my last months. I've wasted so much time thinking about it, I haven't left enough to actually live those months.'

He smiles crookedly and I feel my own maddened bees begin to settle.

'Sit down, for Christ's sake,' he says. 'I'm getting a crick neck looking up at you.'

I sit on the sofa, facing him across Lucy: two ridiculous males, our weapons less tooth and claw – or club and spear – than tongues. The sharp spear of the human tongue.

'I want to show her some of the country,' he says.

'The desert,' I realise, struck by what should have been obvious. Silence. His eyes move to Lucy, and back to me. 'There's a bush track into the desert north of One Shoe Creek, the so-called Warlpiri Highway.'

'People *die* out there, Felix.'

'The Toyota has satellite navigation,' Lucy says. 'And radio.'

I glance her way, surprised by an attack from that flank. 'It's already been decided, then? A dying man and an Englishwoman are going to drive out into the desert –'

'It's been raining up there, Prof. There's plenty of water. Plenty to eat.'

I have lost sight of my argument, displaced my anxiety onto physical rather than emotional dangers. 'I haven't seen the desert either.' I make one last, lame attempt to derail his plans.

Lucy rests her hand on my arm; I pull away, refusing contact.

'Why would you want to go back? After everything you've told us?'

'I like it there.'

'And if someone sticks a spear in you?'

178

'Someone already did.' A small smile. 'It's hard to explain if you haven't lived there, Professor. Who was it who said the desert is where the gods go to think?'

I neither know nor care. I've heard enough tags from the Greek and Latin in recent weeks. Another realisation strikes me, more obvious even as I speak it. 'You want to die there.'

A shrug. 'It's on the cards.'

I watch as he rolls himself another smoke.

'Could I have a cigarette?' Lucy asks, if not for the first time in her life, for the first time in mine.

He gives the cigarette a final tweak, lights it, passes it across, and begins to prepare another.

'Or else you want to be saved,' I say, thinking aloud.

'Maybe he just wants to do some thinking,' Lucy suggests.

'No, it's more than that. The coincidence has got to you. The child's death, your illness. Part of you wants to believe in voodoo.'

'Marty,' Lucy repeats. 'Please.'

But this is my final blinding insight, and my most inspired. I won't easily give it up. 'No, you joke about it. You joke about Pascal's wager, but some part of you believes in it. Believes the magic can be reversed. The cancer can be somehow paid off, paid back.'

'Who knows?' A bent grin. 'There are worse odds on offer. Staying here, for one. And there are still some clever-men left in the desert. Magic men. Jarnpa.' He gestures towards the canvases rolled against the wall. 'The old doctor for one.' A pause, a grin. 'But somehow I don't think so.'

He rises and steps out through the door onto the terrace. Unnoticed, light has begun to infiltrate the outside world; dawn is not far off. He walks to the barbecue table, picks up the bottle of Scotch from among the wreckage of last night's meal, and fills the shot glass. The state of his liver is clearly no longer a concern.

'I'll need a lift home,' I say to Lucy.

She takes a novice's shallow puff at the remains of her cigarette.

I repeat the request, more specifically. 'Are you coming home with me?'

She stubs out the cigarette and reaches for my hand. Squeezes it. 'Of course I'm coming home with you.'

I grip her hand tightly in return, barely able to speak. 'Then I think it's time we left.'

Unable to say more, I rise and tug her gently to her feet; we step hand in hand through the door onto the terrace.

'Breakfast of champions,' Felix says, draining his Scotch.

'We're leaving,' Lucy tells him. 'I'll ring you later.'

She slips her hand from mine and hugs him; he embraces her awkwardly with his elbows, still clutching his bottle and glass. A nod to me and we leave him standing there, pouring himself another.

Tacit agreement limits us to small talk as we drive home. Large talk and even larger thoughts await us further down the road, but to put those thoughts into yet more words would for the moment be too exhausting.

'Rosy-fingered dawn,' I murmur as we crest the far side of the valley and the full flood of morning light fills our eyes. The sun sets behind the ridge as we descend into the next valley, rises again at the next hill, and again sets, as if the car is a type of time-machine, and several days, or even years, have contracted into a single morning. I feel numbed, drained, as if I have not slept for several days. I – we – have spent much of the night in some unrecognisable future; now at least we are returning to the familiar present.

'You're very quiet, Marty.'

'Talked out.'

We drive on: another saddle, another valley, another dawn, another day. Stands of feral trees – maples, elms, poplars – blaze in the morning light among the khaki eucalypts on the slopes, incandescent red or gold. A numb thought: In autumn the valleys resemble not so much England as those parts of North America that have taken the verb fall and made it a noun.

Fall, with cockatoos.

Foothills, suburbs, home, almost without noticing. Lucy slips from her clothes and enters the shower; I climb into bed, fully clothed, and close my eyes. Eight a.m. An entire Sunday stretches before us, as blue and gold as ever, but I want only to hide from its light, to sleep through it.

'Marty?' She stands in the doorway, still dripping. Her face, cleansed of makeup, looks years older. 'I need you inside me. Please.'

The whispered urgency of her words is sufficient foreplay. I am already hard as she straddles me on the bed and tugs open my trousers, easing herself onto me immediately. She comes almost as quickly, shuddering, but then abruptly the shudders become sobs. She has shed tears of pleasure before, but whatever comfort our brief coupling has offered is already forgotten. I can do nothing but hold her as her body shakes convulsively, waiting until she is emptied of tears and talk is again possible.

'I'm sorry I got you into this,' I say. 'I feel I abandoned you to him.'

She inhales unevenly, a slipping cogwheel of small, jerked breaths. Her tears reassure me, oddly. She still needs me at least as much as Felix needs her.

'I can't refuse him and look myself in the mirror, Marty. But I can't accept him and look you in the face.'

I reveal my own welling tears. 'You can always look me in the face.'

'Look *us* in the face, then.'

'I love you, Luce. I will love you whatever you choose to do.'

The slight jolt of another sob. Hers or mine? We lie in the haven of our bed, the breaking heart of our home, holding each other but unable to talk further. The necessary words do not exist, and their makeshift stand-ins have proven imprecise, ambiguous, even duplicitous. I turn away briefly to shake the last four sleeping capsules from their phial into my palm. We share them equally between us, as carefully as addicts.

PART III   Palliative Love

15

Thursday night. I sit at my desk, a vast playing-field of cedar and leather, unable to take my eyes from Lucy's delicate walnut escritoire across the room. The contrast between our workspaces irritates me the more I think about it. Why is the furniture we wear as gender-specific as our clothes? It seems particularly pointless given that my work is mostly done on a compact laptop, while she is always elbow-deep in pain-clinic files and in-trays of snailmail.

She has been gone a day. She. Her. Small words, but resonant. Even now – setting this down, months later – the pronouns kick and flutter in my head, skitter my pen when they speak of her, and of this.

Somehow I tear my attention from her empty desk. I log onto the Web, seeking the usual distractions. www.alt.sex.fetish.robots. Chat-rooms abound; I knock softly at the nearest virtual door and enter. My presence is false, even devious. *Ninox furtivus, ninox clandestinus.* The sub-tribe of robot-lovers is a private club, cyber-owls are not invited. And here is the great paradox of the cyberworld: its north and south poles of extreme honesty and extreme dishonesty. Sexual honesty at one end, the honesty of raw, procreative energy. At the opposite end, infinite opportunities for *Maskenfreiheit*.

Owl-eyed behind my own cybermask, I am struck by this: the key to robot-fetishism is the restrictive/repetitive nature of mechanical movement. Passivity, immobility and helplessness are the turn-ons, literally – the power to incapacitate or energise the chosen loved one at the flick of a switch. Chat-talk tonight has turned to robot movies. I lose myself in the frisson of details for a time. Mad scientists, female zombies, pleasure units, evil organisations seeking world domination. I type in a reference to the ballet *Coppelia*, in which a man falls in love with a mechanical doll. But clicking SEND activates nothing more than my own internal search engine. The laptop screen with its club of techno-fetishists swims from focus; Lucy is returned uppermost to my thoughts. I remember little of *Coppelia* except that I first watched the ballet with her, in Covent Garden. Her, she. A rush of longing; I wish overwhelmingly that she were here to share my travels through this bizarre, tragicomic world, instead of travelling – where?

The phone rings, improbably on cue.

'Marty?'

A small flare of joy at the sound of her voice. 'Lucy. Where are you?'

'Woomera. We've stopped for fuel. It was the first place that had a phone.'

'Don't you have your mobile?'

'There doesn't seem to be any coverage out here. How are you?'

'Surviving. Trying to work. How was the drive?'

'I slept much of the way. I needed to sleep.'

Neither of us slept the night before, her last at home.

'It's good to hear your voice.'

'And yours.'

But both our voices are suddenly hesitant, my flare of happiness already fading, a pilot light extinguished at the first attempt to boost it.

'How's Felix?' I force myself to ask.

'Doing his best. I drove for a couple of hours while he slept.' When I can find nothing to say, she adds, 'There's not much daylight left. We're looking for a place to camp.'

'We should swap desks,' I say. 'This arrangement is irrational.'

'I'm sorry?'

'Our desks. It's ridiculous that I have the big desk.'

A moment's silence. 'Marty, if it's the idea of us camping together –'

'Of *course* it's the idea of you camping together. I can't help it, Luce. I feel mean-spirited saying it, but I don't trust him. I don't think even he knows what he wants.'

'But you trust me?'

'Of course.'

'Then it doesn't matter what Felix wants, consciously or unconsciously.'

Recurring questions, recurring answers. Like a liturgy, a chanted mantra, I want her reassurances to wear deep grooves in my brain, to become part of my brain.

'I love you very much, Lucy.'

The intensity of this silences her momentarily.

'I love you too, Marty. I don't want you to worry. This is something I have to do. *We* have to do. He has no-one else.'

'I know that.'

'And I don't want you to think about . . . that. It's not about that. I haven't been with him.'

Her coy euphemisms offer another clutch of straws that are easy to grasp. If she can't talk frankly about sex with Felix, she can hardly *do* it.

'How's the babysitting going, Marty?'

'I'll have to get a cage. He keeps banging into the window-panes, trying to get out.'

'Where is he now?'

'In the bathroom. No windows. And the birdshit is easier to hose down.'

We talk on, less consequentially, for a time. When I hang up I feel, if not exactly happy, at least less disturbed. She has talked me through another outburst of madness. Ineffectual at giving, perhaps I am at least able to take the talking cure.

I walk into the bedroom and lie down on the bed. *Our* bed, still chaotic from last night's insomnia. Lucy's wardrobe door is half open; her clothes, even empty of her body, seem all too human. Humanoid? I rise and open the door fully. The presence of Lucy is unmistakable, her clothes still holding her shape, still marinated in the delicious scent of her. Functional clothes mostly, black and minimal; one or two filmy, frivolous things. I reach in and cup a black silk dress in my hands. I press my face to it, but the slippery fabric runs away through my fingers like liquid. A weird urge: to step in among these garments and pull the door shut after me; to stand there in the darkness wrapped in her textures and perfumes; to bask in these scented ghosts of her, her various black-linen and black-silk shadows.

On the floor of the wardrobe are a dozen asymmetric pairs of shoes, a dozen raised left soles. An image comes to me of her dragging her bung leg around some desert oasis, gathering firewood while Felix erects a snug, two-person tent.

I escape into the bathroom, but even in this harder-edged world – all glass and chrome and porcelain and cruel light – her soft presence pursues me. Felix's cockatoo eyes me from the shower rail, but I will not be distracted. The mirror-fronted cabinet is a museum case of Lucy-remnants and Lucy-fragments; reminders of her lie in every phial and jar and bottle. I unscrew the lid of a wide-mouthed pot of face cream and smear a little on my left cheek. I select a lipstick and screw out the elegant red blade.

A vacant space on the second shelf: her pack of contraceptive pills is gone. Cognitive wrestlings: I tell myself that of course she would take it with her, of course she must complete each month's course once begun. But the missing pack gives my mind something to fasten upon, allows certain distressing possibilities an easier re-entry into a resistant head.

That rush of mixed feelings again, the multi-stopped organ-swell of my own love for her contaminated by the dread of another's. How could any man not love her? Not make demands of her? If I were dying, might I not expect that right, make that demand? Last meal, last cigarette, last fuck. Or less last fuck (for I am still making Felix's case for him, if only to myself) than last 'adventure of the feelings'.

I reach for the phone and rapidly punch her mobile number, a familiar arpeggio of tone-bleeps. Followed by a familiar answer: *The mobile you are attempting to call is either switched off or out of range.* A surge of frustration: why couldn't she have recorded the message herself, and left me the comfort of her voice?

I hang up and dial again, trying to find some comfort at least in the music of the bleeps, a simple melody that I have played a hundred times on this unlikely instrument and could almost set words to. I am behaving absurdly, but how to think my way out of such behaviour? A favourite Waldo line comes back to me: The mind is proof against enchantment. The *Odyssey*? Homer is speaking of love, but surely jealousy is another version of love's enchantment, and amenable to the same ancient cognitive therapies.

I return to the wide world of my desk and log again onto the Net, this time with a different purpose. After searching various virtual atlases, I download a selection of outback maps and begin to plot the progress of Felix's Toyota across them. I open a bottle of Scotch as I work and gulp down several shots of the strong spirit. Breakfast of champions? The forty-proof whisky offers zero proof against the enchantment of obsessive worry.

Well after midnight. I dial Lucy's mobile once more; once more the same musical sequence of tones is followed by the flat bleep-bleep of nothingness. I check my email, an absurd hope – nothing but spam. YOUNG SLUTS WHO SUCK COCK. MAKE A MILLION EASY. FUCK MY FACE, BIG BOY. CONGRATU-LATIONS!!! YOU WON!!! I LIKE IT IN THE ARSE.

The World Wide Id might never sleep, but I am in desperate need of unconsciousness. I take a small handful of Temazepam caps, climb into bed – and suddenly the sun is up, blazing through balcony doors that I have forgotten to shutter.

Seven-thirty on the clock-radio. I reach for the bedside phone: no messages. She has not rung. I dial her mobile with the same result as the night before. I remind myself she has spent the night in the desert, under the stars. Of course she cannot ring.

I shower and dress and fill a saucer in the bathroom with fresh, large-calibre birdseed. Bright light outside but cool air, the common-room thermostat at last recalibrated to autumn settings. Visions of campfires under moonlight and two single sleeping-bags zipped together for body heat fade from my head – the world this morning is too brightly lit to allow me to visualise anything but itself. I walk to the hospital safe in the knowledge that I can immerse myself in the structures of a working Friday: ward round, department meeting, research committee, journal club. Afternoon outpatients offer further, extended distraction – the latest instalment of various continuing psychodramas.

First up: Mary C, an unmarried staff midwife who for nine months refused to admit that she was pregnant. *I must get more exercise, I need to lose weight. How could I be pregnant?* So far, ho-hum. But with the birth of her son, her denial became epic, even majestic. She felt purged, cleaned out – of exactly what she didn't want to know, for she kept her eyes averted throughout the delivery.

She still keeps her mind averted through our sessions; our weekly conversations achieve little beyond exciting my own curiosity. Today we talk of her mother, who cares for an infant who, Mary C decides, must be another sister.

At ten minutes to the hour I see her to the door. A familiar undertow tugs at my thoughts: how I would love to share her story with Lucy.

'Your wife rang, Martin. She wanted to let you know she's arrived in Alice Springs.'

The department secretary is normally a more than competent mind-reader. I say angrily, 'Why didn't you put her through?'

'You were with a patient.'

'But this is an exception.'

'I'm sorry, Martin. I didn't realise.'

'If she rings again, I want her on the line. Immediately. I don't care what I've told you before.'

Difficult to concentrate on the next case, or the next; my attention keeps drifting to the phone. And to the clock.

Ten to five. 'I think our time is up this week.'

I punch Lucy's mobile number even before the last patient has left my office. No answer.

Restless and fidgety, I decide on impulse to join the trainees for their usual Friday happy hour in the front bar of the Botanic, across the road. Two quick Scotches and I am the life of the party, lacking only a fez. Two more and I am depressed enough to sense that I am an intruder, that this is a different generation, that my presence makes the students uneasy. I will, after all, be their judge and, for some, executioner, come the final exams. But as I catch sight in the bar mirror of the rolled eyes and winks and nudges that pass between them behind my back, I also begin to see myself mirrored in their eyes. *Hypomanic Episode, criterion B: more talkative than usual. Pressure of speech, increase in psychomotor agitation* . . .

I excuse myself and set off homewards. Sunset, the still time of evening, but I am anything but still. I walk rapidly, pushing myself, half jogging until breathlessness and physical discomfort leave little time for thinking.

A phone message at home, but not the one I hoped for. Frank Boyd's hearty voice: 'Long time no hear, doctors. We are convening a small tennis party on the morrow and crave your company . . . One-ish?'

My heart sinks. Has he heard something on the grapevine? Is he fishing? Physical exhaustion is forgotten; obsession has another bone to gnaw on. Has someone in the medical loop spotted Felix and Lucy in transit together? The possible humiliation of this, gossip's death by a thousand cuts, occupies my neural search-engines for some time. There is no enchantment like obsession, but slowly, word by word, I try to reason it to a standstill, to proof my mind against it. Or at least relegate it to the second tier of anxieties. The reality of the desert trip is more than enough to worry about. What I feel overwhelms whatever others might think about it.

I turn to my work and manage, efficiently enough, to lose myself. XXX DREAMS. REFINED WOMAN WITH BIG SHAVEN CUNT SEEKS FRIENDSHIP. MONSTER COCKS, TIGHT PUSSIES. I NEVER THOUGHT MY HUSBAND WOULD GET OFF ON CARTOONS.

Lucy rings at ten. 'Martin? Darling?'

'Lucy. At last. How are you?'

'Missing you. You got my message?'

'I'm sorry. I was with a patient. How was the night?'

'It was fine.' Deliberate restraint in her choice of words, for my sake? 'I've never slept under the stars before.'

'I would have loved to have been there with you.'

'I wish you had been.'

'Did he pressure you?'

'Of course not. Marty, you mustn't worry. I can handle Felix.'

'Where are you now?'

'Alice Springs. I spent the day sightseeing. It was very enjoyable.'

Her stilted tone is difficult to read. Is she cautious because she doesn't want me to misinterpret her words, or because she has something to hide?

'Felix found me a guide. An Aboriginal driver. That's his name – Driver. Bedford Driver.'

These details are of no interest. 'Felix wasn't with you?'

'He had business at the Lands Council. A permit for me to enter the tribal lands. But Bedford took me out to some gorges. It's such beautiful country, Marty. Have you been here?'

'Where are you now?'

'The Centralia Motel.'

'And Felix?'

'Gone to bed. He's very tired. He wants to get an early start.'

Mean-spirited pleasure floods through me. That she has enjoyed herself in Felix's absence. That if she can't share the sights with me, at least she is not sharing them with him. Suddenly I can't hear enough of her day, where she went, what she saw, who she met. It's some time before I can bring myself to release her, after a last, filibustering expression of love.

I climb into bed feeling calmer, but, without a drug, sleep fitfully. Dreams are vivid, and frequent. I am a famous analyst walking in the Vienna Woods. My name is Fred, Herr Professor Sigmund Fred. I wake and fall asleep and dream again. I am trapped in a mangrove tree by a giant crocodile waiting among the roots below. I begin to spit on it, angrily. I spit again and again, spit until the croc is covered with a glistening varnish – and still keep spitting, finding each gobbet of spittle immensely satisfying, a catharsis, a sweet release.

Then the croc climbs the tree as effortlessly as a goanna and I wake, in a cold sweat, heart pounding. Four a.m. on the bedside clock. I rise and type what I remember of those fast-fading dreams into my laptop. An old habit this, continued long past the use-by date of Freudian dream interpretation, if only because my dreams occasionally amuse me, aesthetically. Dreams are wish fulfilment, Sigmund Freud claimed. Sigmund Fred claims nothing more than this: dreams are program clearance, their clunky storylines improvised from whatever random noise screens across a waking mind.

Which doesn't prevent me telling Lucy the third and last dream of the night when she rings first thing in the morning.

'I was in a strange land. I was very hungry, but it was a poor land.'

'England?'

I ignore the quip. 'A desert land. The Sahara, maybe, but there were cactuses everywhere, like Arizona. It was the local custom to take strangers in, to feed and shelter them.'

'You knew this?'

'A dream premise. I was taken to the tent of a family who had no food, who were hungry themselves.'

'That's it?'

'There's more. Their custom when hungry was to warm a smooth stone in the campfire and place it on the stomach. They brought a hot stone to me and I lay on my swag, letting its warmth spread through me.'

'You found the stone comforting?'

'I forgot my hunger.'

'You could microwave a brick for breakfast,' she says, and this time we laugh together.

Calmed again by her voice, I shower and dress and prepare a leisurely Saturday breakfast: poached eggs, fried bacon, toast, fruit, coffee. No hot stones or microwaved bricks this morning. I eat outside in the courtyard, with further nourishment coming from above, a warm sun spreading golden marmalade across the world. I feel the best I have felt since Lucy left: well loved, well fed, well warmed. And, blessed with such riches, big-hearted.

My oldest friend is dying; how could I *think* of denying him the company of my wife for a few days?

And nights.

Remembering the nights casts a small shadow over the brightness of the morning. Two down, how many to go?

The jaunty, repetitive music of a computer game starts up abruptly in the next courtyard, have-a-nice-day elevator music punctuated by mechanical-sounding death screams and explosions. A call to work? Roused, I enter the house and rapidly climb the stairs. Work comes more easily; I have data to collate, a collective cyber-id to sift, and enough energy to carry me through the morning. PISSBABES.COM. VIOLET WANDS FOR EROTIC ELECTRICAL PLAY. KAMA SUTRA KRAZY KUNTS . . .

Saturday afternoon. Is it my optimistic mood that urges me to risk tennis at Frank's? Or a growing muscular restlessness? I starch and iron my ancient tennis whites, toothbrush the grimy crevices of my sneakers. Despite ritual preparations and an hour's walk out into the dress-circle suburbs, I am the first to arrive. The garden pavilion is empty; on the tennis court a small lone figure, a boy of six or seven, repeatedly bounces a ball and swats at it with a racquet as large as his body.

'Are your mummy and daddy home?'

No answer as he bounces the ball and swats at it again with his unwieldy sports-cello – or double bass – and again misses it completely.

'What ho, sirrah! Good morrow!' Frank, emerging from the house in tennis whites and red fez, bearing a tray of drinks.

'Have you met our Ben? Say hello to Nuncle Martin, Benjamin.'

The boy, his snow-capped head dazzlingly bright in the sun, continues to ignore me. Endlessly patient, spun this way and that by the heavy torque of his racquet, its equal and opposite momentum, he continues to miss the ball. He might be practising to perfect that miss-hit, to achieve the quintessential mistake.

Setting down his tray, Frank tugs the ring-pull from a fresh can of balls and spills them, bouncing, out onto the shaved grass. Stilled by gravity, they gather at his son's feet like a cute species of rodent, compact and green-furred. Hamsters, perhaps.

'White or red turpentine, Prof? And where is the English rose? Got herself to a nunnery?' His smile is encrypted, impossible to read.

'White, please. Lucy sends her apologies. She's tied up elsewhere.'

'I'll tie her up anytime she wants,' he says, and his bray of laughter does nothing to allay the suspicion that I have, after all, been invited for interrogation.

'Seen Felix lately?' he asks nonchalantly.

'Not for a few days.'

I haven't come to talk, I have come to lose myself in tennis. As if sensing my mood, he reaches for his racquet. 'What say you, Sir Knight? Racquets at ten paces?'

I follow him out onto the court, windmilling my arms, loosening the forgotten muscles.

'I should warn you,' he calls across the net, 'I have new weaponry. Carbon-fibre.'

'Is that permitted? Under the terms of the arms-limitation treaty?'

'I'm not a signatory.'

Ritual humour, but its mechanical nature offers an escape from thinking. As does the tennis. I have missed these contests in the other, colder hemisphere, this national summer pastime of scampering about on a patch of lawn swatting little balls across a length of fishnet. We begin trading warm-up strokes. I haven't played since university, and I was never Frank's equal in ability – but he was always careless of his abilities. For tennis, read life. My approach is to keep the ball in play using spin and guile, letting him make mistakes; his game is more muscular and more staccato – stop/start bursts of male athleticism punctuated by insults and Elizabethan quotes. The words that cross the net, at least from his side, have more sting than the tennis balls for a time, but soon he begins to find his range. As does my serve. Ingrained muscle memory: the arm deformed into a sprung corkscrew, the racquet twisted behind the head, the top-spun ball biting hard into the grass and rearing up, fizzing and unpredictable, into Frank's face.

Guests are drifting in, milling courtside. Frank welcomes them between rallies, invites them to pour their own drinks, but stays on the court, playing now to a gallery, stepping up the tempo. Even conserving energy, using cunning rather than power, I am soon too breathless for talk, too breathless even for irritation. After a last, extended rally I find myself at the net, bent double, gasping for breath.

'You okay?'

I shake off his arm. 'Fine.'

'No, I mean are you *okay*? You're not your usual self.'

'What do you mean?'

'I mean, do you want to talk about it?'

'Fuck off.'

Louder than intended, but the small talk flows on about us, undisturbed. Other guests take my place on the court as I seek refuge in phatic noise: cricket scores, wine comparisons, medical gossip. Was it a mistake to come? I have a lingering sense of an entire medical network gathering less for tennis than for gossip. But the wine helps to ease my paranoia, and crude inquiries about Lucy or Felix are easily deflected.

The lunch party is now in full swing, a crowd of healthy, muscular Australians of both sexes. Of all sexes: Jill and Stella, evenly tanned, athletic on the court, seem especially to glow. Dulled by wine, I bask a little in their company, their sweaty physicality, the caressive push and pull of their conversation. Pleasurable, too, is its unacknowledged erotic charge, low in voltage but steadily accumulative – although, without Lucy, such subliminal arousal has no use or meaning beyond itself.

'Think you're up to doubles?' Frank presses me.

'Depends whose side I'm on.'

'Boys against girls. Stella? Jill?'

This is lazier tennis, slowed by wine, ballasted by food. If I pace myself – walking pace – the supply of oxygen is adequate to meet the demands of tired muscles. The grass beneath my feet seems to have thickened over lunch, a rapid-growth mattress undersprung with tightly matted roots. I find it difficult to move quickly on the spongy surface; once or twice I even lose my balance.

'You sure you're okay?' Frank's interrogation continues between each rally. 'You can't say I didn't warn you about him, Marty.'

And again, changing ends a game later, 'You *sure* you don't want to talk about it?'

'You should get a job driving taxis.'

Each intrusion strikes a spark of irritation in me – irritation at him and irritation at Lucy, that she should expose me to him. This, too, is steadily accumulative, and soon anything but subliminal. Where *is* she? And will you, Frank, shut the fuck up!

I seem to be lying on my back, looking upwards. Stella's horrified face is bent over me.

'Martin? You okay?'

The left side of my face is sticky, a wet saltiness in the corner of my mouth. Frank's face appears somewhere in a blue-sky field, left of centre.

'What happened?' I mumble.

'You were chasing a wide backhand. You ran smack into the gate. Take your hand out of the way.'

I move my fingers aside; Stella examines me intently.

'I should have shut the gate.' Frank's voice, offscreen now.

'I was last one through,' I say. 'It's on my head.'

A wry smile from Stella. 'Literally.'

Poppy arrives with a wet towel, which Stella presses to the side of my face, beginning now to throb.

'Did I make the backhand?'

'Clear winner,' Frank says.

'Then it was worth it.'

'This will need some needlework,' Stella murmurs.

'I'd like a second opinion.'

Frank supplies it, looming over me again. 'Five or six stitches, Prof.'

Poppy has a mobile in her hand, pressing buttons. 'Is this your phone, Marty?'

'Maybe. Why?'

'I'm looking for Lucy's number.'

'Don't do that,' I say, a little too quickly. 'I mean, I don't want to worry her.'

'How many fingers?' Stella is asking me, holding up two.

'Including all three thumbs?'

'Very funny. Do you remember hitting the gate?'

'Nothing.'

'Lucy's not answering,' from Poppy, offstage.

'I asked you not to ring her.'

'You're concussed, Marty. She needs to know.'

Stella's voice again: 'We might need to admit you for observation.'

Too much throbbing in my head, too many voices speaking at once, too much happening. Is Poppy punching another number?

'What are you doing?'

'You said she was with Felix.'

I jerk up into a sitting position. 'I said no such thing!'

Or do I only mean to say the words as my head spins giddily? A wave of nausea engulfs me and I flop back onto the lawn. A pillow arrives from somewhere and is slipped beneath my head.

'I'll have to do it here,' Frank says.

'Do what?'

But he has vanished.

'No answer at Felix's house,' Poppy is saying.

John Fisk's head looms over me, silhouetted. 'As tournament director it is my duty to warn you, Martin. You're allowed fifteen minutes' injury time, then you have to forfeit.'

Has he been here all along? I can't remember him arriving. Which may be due to the concussion – retrograde amnesia. Now Frank is back, kneeling at my side, setting a sterile, green-wrapped surgical pack on the lawn.

Stella's voice: 'You sure about this, Frank?'

'We need to stop the bleeding.'

Genuine concern? Or playing again to the gallery, a command performance?

'How many drinks have you had?' I remember to ask.

'I've stitched more facial lacerations than you've had hot dinners, sunshine.'

'Does Felix have a mobile number?' Poppy is asking anyone who might listen.

I close my eyes against the hurt of the daylight, a fierce migrainous glitter. Stella places a cool flannel across my lids.

John Fisk again: 'If you're scarred for life you can always sue.'

'Think of it as a duelling scar,' Stella says. 'A Heidelberg scar.'

Frank's turn: 'It's such an ordinary face, it might add some romance.'

'Enjoying yourselves?' I mutter from somewhere within a vast, dull ache.

A sharp needle-prick, then the spreading sting of anaesthetic. I keep my eyes shut, feeling only the tug of numbed skin now, and the brushing of Frank's gloved knuckles against my face as he works. Perhaps my headache is the best anaesthetic, a wall no other pain can penetrate.

Stella, in the background: 'I'll book a bed at St Andrew's, Marty.'

'I'm *not* going to hospital.'

'All finished,' from Frank as he snaps off his gloves and presses a sticking plaster to my brow.

'If you won't go to hospital, you must stay here tonight,' Poppy says. 'You shouldn't be by yourself.'

'I won't be by myself,' I say, flaring up again. 'Why would you think I'll be by myself?'

'I'm sorry – I just thought. If we couldn't locate Lucy . . .'

What is the matter with these people? I lost consciousness for a few moments, not a few months. Nothing has changed in my life. Or nothing that need concern them. I elbow myself to a sitting position, and then, after a moment, stagger to my feet, only to immediately lean forward, hands on knees, waiting for the faintness to pass.

'Can someone drive me home?'

A few minutes more of argument and I am sitting in Frank's car, driving west into the city, into the setting sun, the hard pressure of light on my eyes almost unbearable. If I screw them shut, the motion of the car causes a giddiness which is even worse. I tilt the sun-visor, turn my head this way and that, but there is no escape.

The pressure against my ears is no better. 'You're a fucking mess, Marty. If you don't mind me saying.'

'I do mind.'

Frank examines me sideways, nods towards my wound. 'I mean, what is *that* about?'

'Watch the road,' I tell him.

He steers back into the centre of the lane before speaking again. 'Think about it, Doctor Freud. You can't hit her, so you hit yourself instead?'

I turn to him, angry again. 'Must everything have a deeper meaning? I left the fucking gate open. I wasn't watching where I was going. It's that simple.'

'Whatever you say. But I think Poppy's right. You shouldn't be on your own.'

'I *won't* be on my own.'

His smirk might be borrowed from Felix, a straight face-graft. 'You're sticking to your story?'

'Pull over.'

'I'm sorry?'

'Pull over, fuck you!'

'But we're almost there.'

'I'll walk the last block.'

'Have it your way.' He slews the car into the kerb and turns to me. 'Martin, why pretend? Everyone knows where she is.'

Except me. 'Fuck off,' I say, and am out of the car and walking away, his parting words – 'Stitches out in four days' – fading behind me, unacknowledged.

At home, my turn to call Lucy. Futile, of course. I try the motel number in One Shoe Creek that she has left stuck to the fridge; a polite voice informs me that she is not in. Upstairs, I check my email – a last, faint hope. ENLARGE YOUR COCK, BIG BOY. WANNA SEE ME NAKED? FREE VIAGRA.

I didn't know it was in jail, I mutter – a joke that offers zero relief. On impulse, I tug our photo album from its shelf by my desk and climb into bed. Unable to locate her in the present, I turn to the past. Lucy in Tuscany, T-shirt and jeans. The touching beauty of that single sandal on her left foot. Lucy in London, the College of Psychiatrists induction, radiantly happy in academic black. Lucy in bed, late morning, tangled in white sheets – a flat image, but holographic with resonances. I comfort myself, drowsy now, with memories of the first time we made love, of the way she stretched her body afterwards, anointed with our different oils, her throat and neck crimson with come-blushes, her breathing slowing into sleep . . .

Darkness when I wake, fur-tongued. My wound throbbing; 1:03 in small red numerals somewhere in the blackness. I switch on the bedlamp and dial the motel number again.

A male voice, thick with sleep, but cheery enough. 'Lucy Blackman? No-one registered in that name, matey.'

Cold sweat on my brow, proxy weeping. My dry tongue not wanting to ask the obvious. 'Do you have a Felix Johnson registered?'

'The Johnsons? Yeh, matey – room 12. You want me to put you through?'

I hang up. The Johnsons? The plural is a meaningless entity, a stupid void. A rush of nausea, legs of rubber somehow carrying me into the bathroom before giving way. I slump over the toilet bowl, leaning forward into my knees, an upright foetus nursing itself for comfort. My foetal stomach heaves, I eject a long thick stream of saffron vomit into the bowl. The stomach also weeps? Inadequately and insufficiently, for after the surrogate tears of cold sweat and warm vomit comes the real, unmetaphoric variety, hot and wet.

I sob drunkenly, convulsively, but still without release. The heat of those tears on my face and in my throat merely connects me with other hot emotions. Effortlessly I imagine them together in a motel bed, in *his* bed. Felix in Lucyland. How could this last wish of my friend, now explicit – to bed my wife – have seemed remotely a reasonable idea? Ever? How could I have given it even a moment's consideration? A stream of images downloading from Id World – I see again that odd, fish-headed cock, imagine it reared up, gaping and huge. I hear again the sounds of her pleasure.

A different kind of vomit rises in my throat and mouth. 'Shit!' I shout uncontrollably. 'Shit! Shit!'

My noise wakes the cockatoo, sleeping on the shower rail;

startled, it begins to squawk and beat its wings. I reach up and grab it roughly. Fury rages in me; I feel a weird, voodoo urge to stick the stupid bird – *his* relative, *his* skin – full of pins, to kill it with pins. Instead I stalk back through the bedroom, fling open the balcony door and cast it into the darkness.

A pale flickering of wings, going, gone.

After some minutes, breathing more easily, I return to the washbasin, rinse the taste of vomit from my mouth, then sit on the bed watching the phone. The Johnsons must be faced, somehow. *It* must be faced. As I reach for the receiver it rings, clairvoyantly, startling me.

'Marty?'

Fighting my anger. 'I just tried to ring *your* room.'

'We're sharing a room.' No hesitation, no shame, just urgency. 'I've had to spend the night with him, Marty. I didn't know what to do. As soon as we left Alice he began coughing blood –'

'You should have driven back to Alice. To hospital.'

'He won't. He refuses. I thought if I stayed with him –'

'With him?' Stupid, reactive words, far ahead of reasoned thought.

'Not *with* him.' A trace of impatience in her voice. 'I finally got him off to sleep.' I prevent myself from asking exactly how. 'But I'm worried, Marty. He should be in hospital. Instead he's still planning this crazy trip. He's too sick to travel. The desert will kill him.'

'It was always a stupid idea,' I say. 'Stupid. And utterly – selfish!' The words burst out of me like the last of the vomit.

'I can't do this alone, Marty. I can't leave him here. But I can't manage him alone.'

It takes me a moment to realise what she is saying. 'You want me to fly up?'

Clear relief in her voice. 'Please, Marty. I need you here. You might be able to talk some sense into him.'

'Of course.'

We talk on for some time, and with each word she grows calmer, less panicked. As each word of hers in turn eases my madness. She needs my help and I am gladdened beyond words.

Beyond words, also, a more terrible gladdening – but I do not shy from it. Felix is dying and I am glad. Psychiatrist, shrink thyself? Not this time. I relish this feeling; for a time I allow myself to luxuriate in the shock of it, wilfully.

Felix is dying and I am glad. Half numb perhaps, half dead from emotional exhaustion, but much, much more than half glad.

16

Business class is the only short-notice fare to Alice Springs, but at least I am first off the plane.

Sunday, midday. Blue skies; a high, warm autumn sun on my head. I pause at the top of the boarding ramp and scan the faces pressed to the terminal window. No sign of Lucy. Business people jostle past me down the ramp, impatient men and women in power suits, plucking mobile phones from designer scabbards, designer quivers.

Greeks spilling from an aluminium horse.

I follow in their wake. More disappointment: no sign of Lucy in the arrivals lounge. I crane my head above the crowd as the foot soldiers of economy class wash past. Holidaying family groups in shorts and slapping thongs, Japanese tour parties in uniform Hawaiian shirts, young Aborigines in football beanies and hip-hop ghetto gear. A pair of white twenty-somethings – inner-city nocturnal types in grunge twin-wear, black jeans and nose-studs – blink repeatedly, as if surprised to find themselves in daylight.

Still no Lucy. I wait anxiously. The last passenger off the plane passes me, a small boy hand in hand with a flight attendant. A holiday-access father in moleskin jeans and Akubra hat steps forward and claims him.

Part of me wants to reach for the attendant's hand myself and ask her to wait with me. Instead I flip open my mobile and dial, hear again the same synthetic recorded voice, snap the phone shut. Agitated, I follow the last stragglers down to baggage collection. Where is she? A red warning light flashes, the conveyor belt grumbles into life, the priority luggage begins to glide out. Expensive pieces with designer labels, mostly – Louis Vuitton, Fendi – riding their rubber canal like stately barges; a procession of handtooled leather interrupted by a battered khaki swag, an ancient, schoolboy's Outdoor Ed canvas roll with a business-class tag and my name attached.

The incongruity causes some commotion among the Japanese. My second bag follows: a more conventional carry-bag, if also a little world-weary. I pluck both from the belt and turn to the exit.

'Martin?' A hoarse voice, a rolled 'r', the 't' blurred into a 'd'. Marrdin. The face is black, the speaker short, thickset, pot-bellied. His words are aimed, like his gaze, slightly past me.

'Mr Driver?'

'Yah. Bedford.' The 'f' closer to a 'p'. Bedpid.

His check shirt is faded and dusty, the brim of his limp stock-man's hat less turned down than sagging, half obscuring his face. His eyes are still looking at my feet, at my bags, over my shoul-der – anywhere but directly into my eyes.

'Lucy isn't with you?'

'That Pillage. Pillage Johnson. He ask me to pick you up, eh?'

The edges of the word are bevelled smooth, difficult to hear. I repeat the name to myself: Pillage Johnson. If the name fits . . .

'Got that Toyota outside, Mardin. We go for drive, eh?'

He makes a subtle gesture with his chin towards the exit and turns in that direction. I follow, carrying my bags. His back is slightly bent – arthritic? – but it's difficult to guess his age. Tufts of white hair poke like stuffing from the black ears and the broad flat black nostrils. Sixty? Sixty-five?

'Where's Lucy?'

'Stay in Oneshoecreek.' The name telescoped, a single rapid, uninflected word. 'That Pillage bin sick little bit. She stay behind, look after 'im.'

We step out into sunshine less hot than bright; a brightness that seems to pour upwards from the flat plain as much as down from the sky. A wall of blood-orange mountains rises abruptly from that plain a few miles distant; a low, long range stretching in both directions as far as I can see. Felix's Toyota sits in the carpark, more worse for wear than usual. Red dust powders the sides and underbelly so finely and evenly that it might be a coat of spray paint.

Or the base acrylic for a dot painting. Someone has begun finger-painting the rear-door window: WASH ME. Bedford heaves open the door with difficulty and I toss in my bags.

'We're driving straight to One Shoe Creek?'

Another slight nod, another 'Yah.' Or rather, a yah that my ear can now tease apart. Yuwayi. Desert Latin?

'How long?'

'Six, seven hour maybe.'

My heart sinks. I glance back at the terminus, wondering if there might be a local flight instead.

'No aeroplane today, Mardin. Little aeroplane tomorrow. Mailplane.' Having read my mind, Bedford scrutinises me directly for the first time. 'Pintapinta we call him. Tree moth. You know – butterfly.'

His eyes slide away. Has he also read my emotional state? Is he trying to divert, or even entertain me? We climb into the dusty Toyota from opposite sides; he starts the engine, forces the difficult gearstick. His fingers are blunt black spades, the knuckles and joints thickened with arthritis. As he painstakingly backs out of the parking bay my heart sinks even further. This might take forever.

'Shall I drive?'

No answer.

Travel business sped me through the night and morning, stilling my anxieties, giving me something to do: haggling for a flight, packing luggage. A dawn trip to my mother's to dust off old boots, old hat, the battered business-class swag. A thrifty, Depression-bred Methodist, of course she has thrown nothing away. All the possessions once crammed into our family home are even more densely packed into the nooks and crannies of her tiny unit. The flight covered half a continent, but its sheer groundspeed soothed my impatience. From a window seat I watched the distance between Lucy and me, measured out in hills, paddocks, towns, desert dunes, shrink by many miles every minute.

Motion, I have learnt in recent weeks, consumes anxiety, burns mental as well as physical energy. Now, as the elderly Bedford steers the Toyota through the carpark with an invalid's slowness, anxiety returns.

I can at least keep my tongue in motion. 'You drove down alone?'

'My job, Mardin.' A throaty chuckle. 'My name, eh?'

'That's how you got your name?'

'Whitefeller name. I drive that old Bedford truck for mustering. And droving. Bullock. You know, Mardin? Stock plant. Before.'

The airport falls slowly behind; taxi after taxi passes us at

213

speed, the invading Danaans still shouting orders fiercely into their mobile phones. I reach for mine and punch the usual buttons. Still no useful answer.

Flat country crawls past, offering little distraction. A plain of red sand and white clay softened by mulga and spinifex. The occasional crooked line of paperbarks or coolibahs staking out the course of a dried creek bed. A breach in the orange hills appears; a gap enlarging as we approach, a great door opening. And suddenly we are through, driving along a wide river of sand lined by tall river gums. Alice Springs envelops us, a glitter of roofs and cars and motels and fast-food outlets in bright sunlight.

'Might be you wanna stop in Alice tonight, eh Mardin?'

'I'd prefer to keep going.'

A first intersection, a red light, a group of Bedford's countrymen sitting under a tree, drinking from flagons. Men in stockman's hats, barefoot women in long dusty dresses and football beanies. There is much talking and glancing our way as we wait for the green light. Two of the men rise and drift towards us, unsteady on their feet.

Bedford winds his window up, averts his face.

'Rubbish people,' he says. 'They eat you for meat.'

As he drives on he looks at me slyly, and I sense that he has said this outrageous thing for effect. And perhaps to elicit some response. To feel out my scruples? Or to test my appetite for the exotic, some common whitefeller appetite it might amuse him to titillate?

'Are you a Warlpiri man, Bedford?'

'My daddy was Warumungu. Mix-up country over that way, Mardin. Warlpiri, Warumungu, Kaidej. All boxed up. Multi-cultural, eh?' He chuckles softly. Muddy kulchur, he might be saying, in his blurred rumble. 'Warlpiri mob call me Jangala. You know – skin name. My daddy marry that old Napangardi, Betty Napangardi.'

'A Warlpiri woman?'

'Mmm.' Barely breathed, but a penetrative vibrato. 'My daddy pull that Warlpiri woman blackfeller way. You know, Mardin?'

He steals a sideways glance at me, measuring my interest again. I shake my head.

'You walk into the next country, pinch a wife from other mob. Steal her.'

My heart skids. Is he feeling me out in some subtle, complex way? What does he understand of the relationship between Felix and Lucy? And my sudden arrival? Things that cannot be asked directly, perhaps.

He chuckles again, as if to relieve my anxiety. 'Not like before though, eh? Might be have to spear her husband in the old days, Mardin. You know, early day time. Before whitefellers.'

An indirect interrogation, almost certainly, conducted according to some ancient forensic method.

'Sounds a bit harsh,' I venture.

He glances more directly from beneath his floppy hat brim. Yellow plaque in the white of each eye, encroaching on the blackness of the cornea. It's hard not to fix on that yellow:

215

bloodshot, capillarised, like fertilised yolks. Tiny quail yolks. Should I tell him they will need to be scraped clean?

'You been working hard in the city, eh Mardin?'

Another oblique question. 'I'm a doctor.'

'Same like Pillage, eh?'

Not remotely like Pillage, but how to explain it? Brain doctor? Doctor of the emotions?

'Psychiatrist.'

'Doctor for mad fellers, eh? Deaf fellers, we call 'em here.'

Madness as a kind of deafness? A notion worth talking through, but Lucy is uppermost in my mind, and my own madness makes me deaf again to Bedford. Why has she not rung? She must know that I have landed. I try her number once more, in vain.

Beyond the town limits now and crawling slowly northwards. Limited distraction in the passing scenery: stony downs covered with mulga clumps, crooked aisles of thin white ghost gums in the gullies. Behind us, the red hills becoming bluish with distance. The country looks less barren than I expected – thickly grassed, with plenty of medium-density scrub.

'Green grass time.' Bedford is reading my thoughts again.

'It's been raining?'

'One, two months back. Big rains from the north, from my country. Warumungu country. That way.' He gestures with his chin, ahead and slightly to the right. 'Ngapa we call him. Ngapa Jukurrpa. Rain Dreaming. He come straight through there, my place, all the way from the Gulf country. He finish up back that way.'

A kilometre or two of silence. A wedgetail eagle floats on the air no more than thirty metres up, watching for road-kill. Another, a kilometre further on. *Aquila audax*. Magnificent birds and magnificent hunters, waiting for the leftovers of an even better hunter. That bitumen hunter straightening now, leaving the stony downs behind. We still drive with painful slowness; I try to forget my impatience by immersing myself in the landscape. The plain now horizon to horizon, the highway running arrow-straight between red-dust shoulders as wide and smooth as the road itself, and probably no less driveable. Repetitive scrub and small anthills offer little to catch the eye. Lizard pizza here and there, a wedgetail stepping awkwardly about on the bloated body of a kangaroo, watched by two crows.

A manual on the dashboard catches my eye, a makeshift book of fifty-odd pages, stapled crudely together. 'Warlpiri–English Dictionary'. I flip through the well-thumbed pages, trying to get a feel for the odd-looking words, beginning with the few that I have already either heard or seen. Yuwayi – yes. Jukurrpa – Dreaming. Ngatijirri – budgerigar. Other bird names jump out at me, names that speak their own birdcalls, that *are* their own birdcalls. Kaarnka – crow. Kurlukuku – diamond dove.

Bedford's voice rumbles again. 'You know that place, Mardin?'

A turn-off to the left; a red dirt track vanishing into dense scrub. A signpost: CONISTON.

'Should I?'

'A whitefeller borrowed a blackfeller's woman over that way. Long time back. Before army time, you know?'

217

'Before the war?'

'Yuwayi. That whitefeller borrow two women, that Napurrula and her niece. Over that way, Coniston Station. Near the place we call Yurrkuru . . .'

He is telling me a story but it feels more like another interrogation. Paranoia? There is a mystery in my arrival that he cannot yet fathom. I might be back in Adelaide, the day before, being interrogated by a man in tennis whites and a red fez – but Bedford's methods are more subtle. Pre-Socratic.

'That's okay. The whitefeller pay for those women. He give the husband, that Japanangka, and his cousin Japaljarri tucker. Hatchets. Bacca. They work for him, mustering camel.' He speaks slowly, with frequent pauses, the pace of his storytelling as leisurely as his driving. 'But the wives don't come back. The two blackfellers think about it. You borrow woman, Mardin, but not too long. Borrow too long, big trouble eh? They spear that whitefeller. Blackfeller way, Mardin. Payback. He keep those women too long.'

He glances at me sideways. My turn to read his mind: where have I hidden my spear? Rolled up in my swag?

'True story, Mardin. My daddy was a little boy.'

He brakes and pulls to the shoulder of the road. I wonder, absurdly, Is he going to search my baggage? Confiscate any weapons? Instead he climbs down from the cabin and ambles off towards a clump of paperbarks. It still surprises me to see a grown man squat to piss. He stands for a moment afterwards, staring towards the west, then turns and strolls back to my window, plucking a tobacco pouch from his shirt pocket.

'Bacca, Mardin?'

'No thanks.'

His thick fingers are deft manipulators of paper and leaf. His palms flash pink within the blackness of the hands, like small animals freshly gutted, their bellies opened up.

'What happened then? What happened to the, ah, blackfellers?'

The cigarette is lit, the story resumes. 'Big trouble, Mardin. This policeman name of Murray went all over the country killing people.' He aims his lips back over his shoulder. 'That way. He kill a big mob of blackfellers. But them two men who did the spearing, the Japanangka and his cousin, they run away. Live to old age. In the spinifex country. That way.' And he chuckles, walks back around the Toyota and climbs in and starts the engine.

For a time the cigarette occupies his mouth.

'You brother to that Pillage, eh, Mardin?'

'No. Just friends.'

He ignores this. He nods his head and says, 'Yep. Reckon that Japaljarri your brother.' He seems pleased, having solved some riddle, and we drive on again in silence, and perhaps even a little less slowly.

Small hills each side of the road now; thicker scrub, better-watered. Fine, fish-boned ti-trees, witch-fingered mulga above a carpet of yellow grass and woollybutt. The odd claw of blood-wood or desert oak among red termite mounds, knee-high. The Latin names of the species are beyond me, but the English comes without difficulty, downloaded from some disused cache of botanical lore. Dead kangaroos every mile or two in this richer country, each with a staff of black-feathered undertakers going about their business.

A fork in the road, and Bedford turns the Toyota abruptly left off the highway onto a narrower bitumen road.

Consternation. 'I thought we were driving through to One Shoe Creek?'

'First we gotta fetch that old man, eh?'

'What old man?'

'That old Jungarrayi. That doctor. Father to Pillage. His camp along here. Widjuri way.'

'The artist? Why are we bringing him?'

'He knows that country out west. The spinifex country. That bin his country. Before army time, you know?' He aims his lips towards the north-west and the sinking afternoon sun. 'Sundown side. Might be Pillage make sick camp out that way.'

Pointless to argue further. I sit stewing in my own impatience as he steers the Toyota around something large and furred and dead in the middle of the road. Fresh kill? Old: a sudden stink in the nostrils, an eruption of flies as we pass. A pair of satin-black crows flap away unhurriedly. Everything out here is unhurried. I turn and watch them flap back in our wake. How much does Bedford know of Felix's illness? That the sick camp will become a death camp? A sorry camp – the phrase comes to me from somewhere.

'We won't be going into the desert,' I say. 'He's too sick.' If I can't prevent this detour, I can at least be firm on that.

His voice rumbles again, unperturbed. 'Might be that old man look out for Pillage in the desert. Bush medicine, you know? Lizard meat. That little yam.'

Pillage Johnson, clutching at yam stems? Is this the reason he's out here? Traditional medicine? Bush oncology?

'His daddy, that old Japaljarri, was a magic man. Before. You know? Clever-feller. One time I see that old jarnpa, that ngangkayi, pull a piece of bone right out of this gin. This Nangala, over Yuendumu side. That way.' Lips pursing to the west. 'That old man, that blackfeller doctor, reach inside her and pull it out. Right out of her heart. One minute she dying, nearly finish up – the next minute she walking. Eating. True story, Mardin. Knowledge, that one.'

The hills have risen higher about us; red and white sandstone ridges, ghost gums in shallow gullies. In my head each kilometre we travel is doubled already, a return trip that keeps me from One Shoe Creek and *my* knowledge. A dented signpost appears, peppered with bullet holes: ACCESS TO ABORIGINAL LAND PROHIBITED WITHOUT A PERMIT.

'Am I allowed here?'

'No worries, Mardin. Your country too. You brother to that Pillage.' A brief sideways glance. 'He's our countryman, that Pillage Japaljarri. Bin cut, you know. Properly, blackfeller way. Old way. Bring in the doctor butcher.' He makes a knife-slashing movement at his groin, and chuckles at my discomfort.

WIDJURI COMMUNITY. SLOW DOWN. Bedford speeds up a little as we enter the town. A squat, cement-block Community House inside a fenced enclosure on one side. A row of smaller cement-block buildings on the other side, roughly signposted: ART HOUSE, POST OFFICE, CLINIC. A water tank high on a steel lattice. We drive on into an older, more ramshackle part of the settlement: sheds and shacks of corrugated iron scattered among rusting car bodies. A wheel-less caravan, propped on bricks. Refuse everywhere on the baked earth: newspapers, bottles, tin cans, the mica-glitter of broken glass. Car tyres. A child's overturned trike. Apart from several whippet-thin dogs, the place seems deserted. A ghost town.

'Where is everybody?'

'Big football match today. Yuendumu side.'

The Toyota finally halts by a small tin shack of garden-shed dimensions. The first sign of human life: a finger of smoke rising from a smouldering fire, an old woman in a headscarf sitting cross-legged in the shade of a coolibah. Closer: she is squatting in the middle of a giant canvas, dabbing paint between her legs with a small stick or brush. The back of her faded red dress is furred with flies, a cluster as dense as a mink stole. A rusted iron bedstead stands beneath another tree; a plump, immobile buddha figure in a stockman's hat sits on the bare springs, staring across the fire. The back of his shirt is also black with flies, as if the flies normally shared among two or three hundred people have settled on two.

'That's Doctor Jerry?'

'Yuwayi. And his missus. Old Mary Nangala. You wait along the Toyota, eh?'

Bedford climbs out and ambles almost in a circle towards the couple. The woman looks up and mutters something, the buddha waves a languid arm. Flies rise, disperse, resettle. I sit in the cabin feeling a little giddy, a little disorientated. Red dust, bleached khaki vegetation, black figures. Where am I? Mars? There is something alien in these fierce, eroded faces, more rock-faces than human flesh and blood. Blackness is the least of it. They bear even less resemblance to the familiar black faces of London friends, the smooth-browed Jamaicans and high-cheeked, baby-faced Nigerians. A slight shiver passes through me, an ancient id-alarm. Are these the people who eat you for meat?

Bedford turns my way, gestures. 'Mardin. You come here now. Meet that old man.'

I climb down from the cabin and approach. An old man, certainly – a generation older than Bedford, and with health problems to match. He is wheezing heavily, his skin colour as much grey as black – or a blackness bleached by a lifetime of desert sun. A broad head, a brow even more protruding than the usual bony Aboriginal sun-visor. His face seems squashed beneath it: a dense, complex face, a face with enough features for two faces, or at least two lifetimes, compressed into one.

The old man looks past me. 'You brother to that Pillage?'

It seems I have no choice in the matter. 'Yuwayi,' I venture.

The word draws his eyes to mine momentarily, then he rises and shuffles off, wheezing, into the shed. Heart problems? Cattle-dust lung? His wife ignores me, dipping the tip of her twig in a small can of acrylic paint, then dabbing tiny perfect circles of canary yellow on the black canvas. Am I permitted to address her? What is the local protocol? We have not yet been introduced.

'What's she painting, Bedford?'

'Hey, Nangala. That painting might be sugarbag Dreaming, eh?'

'Bush plum,' she says, and glances a little past me. 'You buy it, Mister?'

'When will it be finished?'

A toothless smile. 'By and by.'

The sight of those coloured dots, their map of circles and half-moons, brings Felix back to mind, reminds me of more urgent matters. 'Shouldn't we get moving, Bedford?'

'Smoko first.'

A groan of rusted springs as he eases himself onto the iron bedstead. 'Sid down, Mardin.' He pats the rusted frame next to him and chuckles. 'Blackfeller's chair, we call him.'

I sit, gingerly, as he plucks a tobacco pouch from an unbuttoned shirt pocket.

'Bacca?'

I take a paper and wad of tobacco. Anything to keep the agitation at bay. The flies have found me, a little smoke might also keep them at bay.

'Yuwayi,' I murmur again, and he chuckles tolerantly.

The old woman patiently dabs her yellow dots; the smell of paint solvent mingles with the tobacco smoke and smouldering mulga scraps, not unpleasantly. Again I try to immerse myself in the moment and set aside whatever might lie ahead. Around us the background hum of the bush: a continuo of flies and bees. Birdcalls from the paperbarks: the soft trumpet of finches, the tinkle of honeyeaters. A blue flash of feathers in a nearby gidgee bush.

'Blue wren,' Bedford points with his chin. 'Jiwirljiwirljiri, we call him. You see his name in that book.'

The language lesson is cut short as Doctor Jerry emerges from the tin shanty with a battered kitbag and blanket roll. He shuffles over to the fire and kicks it apart, drops a flaked-enamel mug into the blackened billycan with a clang, and moves off towards the Toyota. A man of few words, clearly.

'We go, Mardin,' Bedford says, and heaves himself off the bedstead with another groaning of springs.

New seating arrangements in the Toyota: Bedford and Doctor Jerry in the front, me relegated to the back. The older man's stern presence has a quietening effect on Bedford; he becomes a man of fewer words himself. As we drive, his tone of voice also changes, coming, oddly, to resemble the doctor's, echoing his slower cadences and deeper smokiness. They rumble at each other in Warlpiri from time to time, pointing out some passing piece of landscape with a laconic gesture of chin or lips. I am not included in the conversation. No more tourist exotica is offered, nor does Bedford fish for further information.

There are no more jokes.

I would dial Lucy's number again but my phone is dead. Instead I immerse myself in the dictionary, in these odd desert words bristling with thorny 'k's and 't's and fishhook 'j's. Kartaku. Kurriji. Jingijingi. Turlkami. To my unpractised eye they bear little resemblance to the blurred, smooth-sanded sounds that reach my ear.

After many kilometres and not many pages, I lean back into my cabin corner and try to sleep. Is the sun lower when I open my eyes? The landscape has changed. Spinifex plains surround us now, eroded granite outcrops here and there, the pimento-red of the earth heightened by the last flush of the setting sun. Dust in the air; a faint mustiness, mixed, weirdly, with the smell of burnt hair.

A battered roadsign slides past. PETROL 2 KM.

'Eh, Jungarrayi,' Bedford murmurs.

The older man rouses from his own slumber; I follow their gazes to the west. A small flock of birds is moving parallel to the road, perhaps fifty metres off – dark, scissoring silhouettes against the red sun.

Our paths are converging on a small settlement ahead: a single house, a store of some kind with a single petrol pump out front, a windmill bore. AMBUSH FLAT ROADHOUSE. VACANCIES. A garden sprinkler scatters glittering diamonds across a patch of lawn outside the house – an impossible, expensive luxury in the desert, surely. Bedford pulls to the side of the road as the birds descend to drink, turning into the light, all luminous green and yellow, the brightest colours in the landscape.

'Ngatijirri,' I say.

The old man half turns to me momentarily, his broad face still totally impassive.

Bedford, surprised: 'You know that little bird?'

'*Melopsittacus.*' A different Latin.

He turns the ignition off. 'We stop longa here little bit, eh?'

My heart sinks. The birds, the strange desert sights, my exotic companions – they can offer no more than temporary distraction. 'It's nearly night,' I say. 'Is it much further?'

'We stop here,' Bedford repeats firmly. 'That little green bird make that old man happy. He own that little green bird, Mardin. His animal. His Dreaming, you know?'

No signs of happiness in the old man's face, but his lips are moving slightly, and when Bedford cuts the engine I realise he is singing, a soft chant that is barely audible beneath the excited twittering of the descending birds.

Bedford mutters, 'Peaceful bird, that one. Quiet one.'

I glance impatiently at my watch, and for the first time since the old man came aboard our desert ship Bedford feels comfortable enough to try a joke.

'Don't worry, Mardin, that Pillage lookin' after your missus. Might be he want me to drive slow, eh? Keep you longa here.'

He chuckles throatily, and when I fail to respond, shrugs and restarts the engine. Startled, the budgerigars whirr up into the air in unison, as if thrown by some invisible hand, and vanish rapidly into the blue.

'Fly home now, Mardin. Back to their camp.'

17

'He was staying here, matey. His missus took him to hospital. About two, three hours back.'

Six p.m. One Shoe Creek. The Flag Inn Motel. The proprietor, summoned from dinner by a push-bell, stands behind the reception desk: a paunchy fifty-something with a grubby napkin wedged into the V of his cowboy shirt.

'Friend of yours?' he asks.

'Brother.' Skin-brother, by about two hours.

'Didn't know he was poorly, matey. The housemaid said they hadn't been out of their room much. I thought, you know, lost weekend . . .' A grin cracks the leather of his face. Food particles are stuck between his teeth, bright yellow, momentarily distracting. Sweetcorn? He winks knowingly. 'Maybe his missus worked him a bit hard.'

I interrupt, 'Did his, ah, wife, leave a message?'

'No message, matey. They was in a hurry, but.' He wipes his fingers on his napkin and lifts a key from a row of hooks. 'In all the excitement they forgot their key. Room 16. I'll be closing up soon. If you see them . . . ?'

'I'll be needing a room for the night myself.'

He peers out through the window at the battered Toyota. Two impassive black faces stare back from beneath their hats. Easter Island heads behind a windscreen.

'Friends of yours?'

'Relatives.' Also by about two hours. Classificatory cousin and father, Japaljarri-Jungarrayi moiety – I have been studying my dictionary. 'They're just dropping me off.'

Relief on his face. 'Single room then, matey?'

'Double.'

Another knowing wink. 'You feeling lucky?'

'My wife will be joining me later.'

He lifts a second key from the rack. 'Room 6. Don't lose 'em. Or you'll be camping out with your relatives.' He chuckles and turns to the door behind him, and whatever bright-yellow food might be waiting beyond it.

'How do I get to the hospital?' I call after him.

'Turn right at the highway. Can't miss it.'

Mounting impatience now; Lucy only minutes away, but long minutes as Bedford drives at tortoise pace. At last he stops the Toyota at the steps of the base hospital, leaving the engine running.

'You're not coming in?'

He nods towards the sleeping doctor. 'That old man buggered, Mardin. Sleep time. I look out for you tomorrow.'

Standard hospital décor inside: merciless fluorescent lighting, scrubbed white surfaces. A single ward, a young Aboriginal woman writing on a clipboard in the nurses' station, her broad black face a softer version of the men's carved basalt, but still mildly shocking in its unfamiliarity.

'Felix was admitted an hour ago. Bay 5.' On first-name terms with her patient, but her tone is bored as she gestures up the corridor.

I see him before he sees me; he's propped on pillows, reading a bible-thick book. No sign of Lucy. A saline drip runs into his arm; a nasal oxygen spec sits across his top lip, a transparent plastic Dali-moustache curling upwards and backwards over his ears, fixed in place by an elastic band behind his head. The head itself is closely shaven – a flint axe-head.

Lost in his book, or deafened by the steady hiss of oxygen, he fails to hear my approach. What is he reading? Song of Solomon?

'Pillage Japaljarri,' I murmur from the foot of the bed.

He looks up, momentarily startled. 'Herr Professor Blackman!' His voice is a hoarse, oxygenated whisper. 'You sneaking about in emu-feather shoes?'

Has he seen that deeply into my mad heart? But he is less interested in looking through me than past me. 'Lucy isn't with you?'

'I thought she would be here with you.'

'She was walking back to the motel to wait for you. Must have stopped somewhere for a bite to eat.'

I want to turn on my heels immediately and search the town high and low. A minimal grin; he knows exactly what I am thinking. Feeling.

'Sit down, Prof. Give her a bit of time to herself. She's exhausted. It's been a long day. And I haven't exactly been the most co-operative of patients.'

I remain standing at the foot of the bed, torn.

A flicker of impatience on his face. 'You've got all night together. And we need to talk.'

I force myself to sit. 'So how are you? Lucy said you'd been bleeding.'

'I sprang a small leak. It seems to have stopped. How was the drive up?'

'Slow. But entertaining.'

A knowing grin. 'Bedford's full of stories.'

'He's full of something,' I say, trying for a lighthearted tone.

'Years of practice. He knows what whitefellers like to hear. Especially the juicy bits.' He coughs. 'Ethnoporn.'

'He told me one thing I wanted to hear – if you steal my wife I'm allowed to spear you.' My words begin jokily but end with some venom, sharpened spear-points themselves.

'Required, I would have thought. Tribal law is strict.' His grin sets into something fixed. 'You want to spear me?'

'Apparently it doesn't apply to brothers.'

'We're brothers?'

'According to Bedford. Though I don't think the old doctor has rubber-stamped the adoption papers yet.'

He manages a slight chuckle that turns into a cough. 'You mustn't make me laugh, Herr Professor. I might spring another leak.'

I am still struggling with my own leaks, a week's stored anger demanding release. I could spear him with jokes, I think. I could tickle him to death. *Have you heard the one about . . . ?*

'Don't tempt me,' I say.

The nurse enters without warning, jams an electronic thermometer in his ear and records the reading on her clipboard.

Felix says, 'Have you met my brother, Betty?'

She fiddles with the saline drip. 'Briefly.'

'Sister Betty Ross Napanangka. Professor Martin Blackman Japaljarri.'

'Welcome to the family,' she says, utterly uninterested.

Felix watches me from behind his bent grin. 'Napanangka skin makes Betty one of our mothers-in-law. So we're not even supposed to talk to her.'

'You shouldn't make fun of the old ways,' she rebukes him as she walks out, but even this is a bored monotone.

'I'd take her with us,' Felix says. 'A registered nurse might come in useful. But the old men wouldn't wear it. We're not even meant to be in the same room.'

Kinship taboos are suddenly the least of my concerns. 'Take her where?'

The oxygen hisses softly, his chest heaves. 'There's a place out there, Prof. Ngarlpa. A desert soak. Three, four days' drive –'

'The budgerigar Dreaming,' I say.

'Trust you to remember. No-one's seen it for sixty years. And no whitefeller ever.'

'No way, Felix! Not in your condition!'

'I think my condition is the point, Martin. I've got nothing to lose.'

Mixed feelings fizzing again inside me, emotional white noise. 'And what have you got to gain? Death in the wilderness? The lost oasis of the budgies? It's a bit self-indulgent, isn't it?'

'I can't see much indulgence. I think it will be rather difficult.'

232

I have no answer to this. My eyes slip from his, admonished, as he continues.

'But more and more it feels right. For a lot of reasons. None of them easy to explain.'

'Try me.'

'For one, I've always liked it out there. It's very . . . clean.' He pauses, distracted by the oddness of the word. 'It's especially clean of people. Driving up through the desert, one thing became clear to me: dying is a very private thing. I don't want people around.'

'You want Lucy around.'

'Let me rephrase that. I don't want anyone around . . .' he searches again for the precise phrase, 'wearing a fez.'

Even in my state of mind I can't suppress a smile. He returns it.

'And the old men? You want them around.'

'Doctor Jerry was born out there. His family walked out when he was a boy. In the thirties. He might not show it, but he's dying to go back.' A pause, a slight laugh. 'So to speak.' He unravels the plastic tubing from about his head. 'Turn the oxygen off, Featherfoot. I need a fag.'

'You're not going to smoke?'

But he is already searching for his tobacco pouch in a bedside drawer. I reach behind him and rotate the wall valve; the flow-ball drops inside its calibrated shaft, four litres per minute to zero.

'What if you start bleeding again out there? Or get into breathing difficulties?'

'You mean I might die!' He laughs again at my discomfort. 'One of the advantages of a medical degree – death holds no imagined terrors. All the terrors, and they are real enough, are known. I've seen them any number of times. *You've* seen them.'

'From the outside.'

A shrug. 'Maybe the outside is the worst of it. Maybe it's not so bad from the inside.'

'You can't be serious.'

'If I take the right drugs. And if that fails, there's always Doctor Jerry.'

'So you do want the best of both worlds. Blackfeller and whitefeller.'

'Pascal's wager, Herr Professor.' The cigarette he licks into shape is less finished than usual, a crooked cylinder. Exhaustion? Flagging concentration?

'What happens . . . afterwards?' I ask.

'You mean, when I'm dead?'

'Okay, when you're dead. What do we do with your, your *corpse* out in the middle of nowhere? Tie it to the roof-rack? Pack it in ice?'

Brutal words, knife-sharp, but he doesn't flinch. 'I don't plan on a return trip, Featherfoot.'

I'm not sure whether I prefer the new mock title or the old. 'So we bury you out there?'

Now he is searching for matches. 'Not exactly bury.'

'What then?'

'Bedford didn't tell you? He usually gets off on these details. Titillating the whitefellers.' Match flare, inhalation. 'Local custom was to expose the corpse on a tree-platform.'

'Leave it to rot?'

'Leave it to the crows and maggots.' I flinch; he has easily out-brutalised me. 'They don't do it much any more. The old ways are out of fashion. But I like the notion. Re-entering the food chain a bit lower down.'

His lumpy, crooked tube is alight now. Weirdly, his breathing seems more comfortable on four deep inhalations of tobacco smoke per minute than on four litres of oxygen. His smoking also gives me breathing space, time to regain composure, and even a little clinical detachment.

I say, 'You seem to get off on the details yourself. What did you call it? Ethnoporn?'

'Just telling it like it is, Herr Professor.'

'No, it's more than that.'

He sucks at his cigarette impassively, waiting.

'I think you're depressed. I think your behaviour is part of a depressive illness. Self-destructive. Self-*hating*. Listen to yourself – you relish these details. Your corpse being picked apart by crows. You're still trying to punish yourself in some way. The more brutally, the better.'

'The desert isn't brutal, Herr Professor. It's indifferent. It's especially indifferent to me.'

Silence; the ghost of a smile playing about his lips.

'I just want to look death in the eye. Allow me that. No euphemisms. No sentimentality.'

'No love?'

My sharpest spear-point yet, and perhaps for the first time a palpable hit. His grin fades, he becomes more watchful. Measuring me?

Eventually: 'I know it's been difficult for you, Prof. No. More than difficult. Impossible. But I want you to know something. I might not look it, but I've been . . . happy these past few days. Less *un*happy. With Lucy. I want you to know that I'm grateful.'

'I would have thought that Lucy was the one to thank.'

His eyes hold mine for a moment, resisting the chance to strike back. Too exhausted to fight? Or something else? He says quietly, 'I thank her a hundred times each day.'

I look away, pretend to examine the saline drip. He feels the need to hide in activity himself, pinching out his cigarette butt, wrapping it in a tissue, stuffing it in a waste-bag.

When he speaks again his tone is matter-of-fact. 'Tell Bedford enough food for a fortnight. He used to run a droving plant, he'll know how much. And no need for an early start. We can make Green Swamp by nightfall.'

'You're planning to leave tomorrow?'

'The sooner, the better.'

'I haven't said I'm coming yet.'

'If Lucy comes you'll come.' The mask is back in place, with its mocking grin. 'Besides, something tells me you wouldn't miss this for the world, Featherfoot.'

A bubble of anger in my throat again; I am not able to meet his eye. 'What are you reading?'

He raises the book. The *Phaedo*.

'Comforting?'

'More a cautionary tale.'

I wait for more; it is not forthcoming. I remember the book's closing passages all too well, in Waldo's sentimental, sweet-sherry translation. 'Where are you up to?'

A wry grin. 'Near the end.'

This time when I wait he deigns to continue. 'Shall I bring you up to speed, Prof? The sun hasn't yet set, you will recall. Crito urges Socrates to delay taking the poison. To enjoy a leisurely last meal.'

'And to spend a little quality time with his friends.'

'Point taken.' The grin widens slightly. 'Friends *and* lovers, I think Crito means.'

I walk to the door, then turn back one last time. 'I hate to spoil the ending,' I say. 'But Socrates takes the poison anyway.'

His grin remains fixed, unfazed. 'As I said, Prof. A cautionary tale.'

Nurse Betty is sitting in her station, writing, as I leave. As I pass I say on impulse, 'The patient in room 19 is smoking, Sister. Is that allowed?'

A subtle spearing by proxy? She doesn't even glance up from her clipboard, her records of successful bowel actions, spongings, shaves. But as I reach the door she calls, as an afterthought, 'You on foot?'

'Yes.'

'Staying at the Flag Inn?'

'Yes.'

'Maybe give the main street a miss.'

'Why?'

'Closing time.'

'I'm sorry?'

'A lot of cranky people out in the streets. Best to keep your distance.'

18

Closing time or not, the pub is still packed. Where is Lucy? White faces, mostly, inside; official last drinks being plonked down on the bar, several per patron, and the roar of conversation undiminished. No sign of her among the press of bodies. Mostly black faces outside; a bottleneck at the bottle shop, family groups stocking up with a night's supply of casks and flagons. Box wine. A single café further along the street is closed; a group of drinkers sits on the dry grass verge outside watching, vaguely interested, as two young men stand toe to toe in the middle of the road, taking turns to punch each other in the head. Both gladiators grip flagons in their left hands and strike alternately with their right fists. Some residual chivalry seems to prevent the use of the flagons as weapons, or perhaps it's some desert-bred husbandry of precious resources. The heavy flagons surely act as counterweights, or handicaps, reducing the force of the blows – but I can hear each land, sickeningly.

I cross the road to avoid trouble. A drunk, middle-aged woman in a long filthy dress staggers on spindle-legs after me.

'Ten shillings for fuck, Mister.'

The awesome, amnesic power of booze: to wipe away thirty years of dollar currency. To bring back the shilling. And what else besides? What has Lucy been teaching me? Pain also is a kind of memory? I recall something from Virgil: *Beyond words, my queen, the grief you would make me remember.*

'Not tonight, sister,' I say, and hurry on, refusing eye contact.

Back at the motel within minutes, safely. I walk past room 6 and knock at the door of 16. No answer.

I take her key – his key, their key – from my pocket, unlock the door and step into darkness. The cleaner has been through: over-deodorised air, nauseatingly sweet. I grope for the light switch and the sweetness fills my eyes as well as my nose. A pair of fresh towels and face washers sit on a kitsch, desert-pea bedspread. A pair of cute, foil-wrapped chocolates on the pillow. The sight of these intimate pigeon-pairings strikes me with some force: I am in a honeymoon suite. A pair of khaki swags – one brand new, one old and battered – stacked in a corner of the room completes the picture.

I jerk back the covers of the bed, sending the chocolates flying. What am I looking for? Used condoms? Sheets stiff with semen stains? Obsessive id-urges perhaps, but only after inspecting the bed linen do I feel any qualms about my behaviour.

I step through into the small bathroom. More paired objects, difficult to look at but impossible not to notice. Disturbingly sweet marriages of the inanimate: foreign shaving equipment nestled among familiar phials of cosmetics, two toothbrushes standing together in a glass tumbler, one wild-haired and punk-ish, one smooth-bristled – an unlikely marriage but as unsettling as a pair of statuettes planted on a wedding cake.

'Marty? Are you there?'

Lucy's voice, but who is this woman framed in the doorway? She wears a stockman's hat, her dusty jeans are tucked into elastic-sided boots. Dark glasses hide her eyes, although the sun has long gone.

'I didn't know you'd arrived,' she says. 'I kept ringing your phone. Leaving messages.'

'Flat battery.'

Habit draws us together but the embrace is awkwardly chaste. There is a new embarrassment between us, an embarrassment on both sides.

She says, 'I had a counter tea at the pub.'

'You shouldn't have been there alone.'

'It was fine. Have you eaten? They do a good fish and chips.'

'A thousand miles from the sea?'

Phatic noise, going nowhere, but I cannot see a way out. Fine details strike me: the desert sun has ripened a crop of freckles, previously near invisible, on her nose and cheeks. Still she keeps her sunglasses on. In London, dark glasses are nightwear, a badge of cool; in the fierce Australian summer they are a matter of survival, and never more so, perhaps, than here, now, tonight.

'How are you?' I ask.

'Exhausted.' She reaches up to my damaged cheek, her brow crinkling with concern. 'What's this?'

'Duelling scar. It's nothing.'

'What happened?'

'I had an argument with a steel gate. As I said, it's nothing.'

Rebuked, she steps away from me. Her attention turns to the bed I have torn apart. 'You had a nap?'

I say nothing. I need say nothing.

'It's been pretty intense, Marty,' she says.

'I can imagine.'

She looks sharply at me; was there sarcasm in my voice? Not consciously. Unconsciously? I'd be the last to know, by definition. She removes her sunglasses, if only to better study my expression.

'It was terrible, Marty. But I felt I couldn't leave him. He was too ill.'

'He keeps winning the sympathy vote,' I say, this time with enough conscious malice for all the world to hear.

'Martin, that's not worthy of you.'

'Maybe. But he seemed full of beans a few minutes back.'

'You've seen him already?' Her tone is suddenly less awkward than cautious. 'What did he tell you?'

Her eyes are on mine, searching, anxious, and the realisation is instant and terrible and certain: she *has* slept with him. *Fucked* him. The shock of it sends my heart skittering, bathes me with cold sweat. She rests a hand on my arm, I shrug it off. 'Don't!'

She slumps onto the bed and wraps the desert-pea bedspread about her, rolls onto her side, facing away.

'How could you?' I say. 'How *could* you?'

She takes a deep, weary breath. 'Do you think it was easy for me?'

'So you admit it!'

'How can *you* be so possessive? You know I love you.' She turns back to me. Red-rimmed eyes, but she seems more exhausted than tearful. I sense that she has expended so much energy on one sick man that she has little energy left for another.

'What about his hepatitis? Did you think of that? Do you know the risk! I hope you took precautions!'

'Is that what's worrying you? You don't want to *catch* something from me?'

'That's the least of my worries.'

She takes another deep breath, as if about to speak, then seems to change her mind. 'I can't talk about it now. Come to bed, Marty.'

'You think I'm going to sleep in this room?'

'Why not?'

Because you fucked him here, I want to shout at her, scream at her – but she is already answering her own question.

'It was just sex, Marty.'

'Sex is never just sex.'

'You don't think you might be overreacting? Felix will be gone soon. And we have the rest of our lives together.'

'*Do* we have the rest of our lives together?'

Silence. 'I imagine that's up to you.'

I know that every word I utter is lowering me in her estimation, digging a deeper ditch between us, but I cannot help myself. 'I'll be in room 6,' I say, and turn to leave.

'If you want to know the truth,' she says, 'we had sex before we went away. We had sex that night up at his house.'

Softly spoken words, but they stop me in my tracks, hold me within the doorframe as if in some kind of force-field. But a force-field in which I am able to turn and hiss back at her, 'But you came home that night and had sex with *me*!'

A pause the length of several dozen pounding heartbeats.

'Perhaps I was in need of some kind of . . . comfort myself. I thought you could see that. I thought there were certain things we didn't need to talk about.'

Another pause as her words drag a trail of implications through my brain, hooks on a long-line.

'How many times?'

'How many times what?'

'How many times did you fuck him in Adelaide?'

'That's hardly the issue, Marty.'

'What *is* the issue? The quality, not the quantity? His butter-fly cock?'

'Don't do this, Marty. Please.'

'No, I'm sorry. I have to do it. I need to know.'

'You *want* to know.'

'I want to know if you enjoyed it.'

A small explosion of exasperation. 'Fine – I enjoyed it. Of course I enjoyed it! Is that what you want to hear? What do you think, I lay there and thought of England?'

Those long-line hooks dragging the deepest id-trenches now, hauling everything that is ugly up and out. The sea monsters, the nightmare fish.

'It was clearly not just sex, because you are changed by it.' And not just changed, but removed from me; become almost physically smaller as I look at her now, giddily, down a lengthening tunnel. 'How did it happen?' I shout. 'How could you *do* that?'

'He kissed me and I liked it. Is that what you want to hear?'

'He kissed you and you *liked* it? *He* kissed *you*? What, you didn't have a say in it?'

'I'd had a few drinks. I thought, He's your closest friend. He's dying. He needs me. We're all grown-ups.'

'I feel I don't even know who you are any more.'

'No, Marty – it's *you* you don't know. And guess what? I'm afraid I haven't got time for your disgust. I've been pandering to one invalid. I can't take on another.'

She rolls away on the bed, her back to me again. I step outside, slamming the door after me, and walk across to room 6 and into the same deodorised sweetness, the same twin-pillowed, desert-pea bedspread, the same ridiculous chocolates.

I flop onto the floral cover, curled less like a foetus than some kind of worm or grub. Grubby emotions fill my head – jealous rage, jealous hatred. I try vainly to smother these feelings with reason, to think them to a standstill. An hour passes in which nothing stands still, not my thoughts, not my feelings, not my body, tossing on the bed, winding itself in linen. But slowly, incrementally, hatred becomes self-hatred. Anger turns to guilt. Why did I come back to Australia? Why did I stupidly try to revive a friendship that Felix clearly had no time for? Above all, why – stupid, stupid, *stupid*! – did I throw the two of them together?

Midnight. A tap at the door. A second, insistent tap. A muffled voice: 'Marty, I can't do this without you. I need your support.'

I open the door and she is in my arms and we both are sobbing, and now she is kissing me, and my cock, absurdly, astonishingly, is stirring. The unconscious body making itself conscious? If so, not fully. What is the attempted sex that follows about? Reclaiming territory on my part? Easing guilt? Mutual comfort? As Lucy, pressed back against the closed door, legs parting, responds in turn, I feel myself become flaccid. My body has led me into this solo – it now changes its independent mind. Conscious thought follows physiological thought within seconds: the noises and movements of her arousal, her whimpers and trembling knees, have been shared with another man. I cannot avoid hearing – seeing – them together.

Infandum, regine, iubes renovare dolorem. Unspeakable, O queen, the things you would have me remember.

We cling to each other for a time after my failure. The heat of our bodies is at least a comfort. The mere presence of our bodies. My last thought as we slump onto the bed and drag the quilt across us: the sexual comfort she offered me – offered both of us – is no different from the comfort she has offered Felix. A kind of palliative, a narcotic for those parts of me – of us – that are dying.

The irony of this fills my head, deafeningly, as I lie next to her in silence, pretending to sleep. Is she also pretending? Eventually, through being feigned for long enough, sleep arrives, a sleep so sound that I have no idea what time the ever-earlybird

Lucy takes flight. A knock at the door rouses me; waking, I find that I am alone in bed. Light squeezes past the floral curtains: day, certainly. A second knock, and the door opens to admit Lucy, fuzzily silhouetted against the glare of day.

'You're up?'

'I've been up for hours.'

'Why didn't you wake me?'

'You needed to sleep.'

'Where have you been?'

'Packing up the other room. Shopping. Can you fix the bill? I'll be back in half an hour. I'm going to pick up Felix.'

Still dull with sleep, I am unable to process information with any speed or thoroughness. 'He's been discharged?'

'He's discharged himself. See you soon.'

Brisk, minimal answers, avoiding implications. She hands me the key to room 16, kisses me lightly on the lips and is gone before I can ask more. I shower, pull on the same dusty clothes I wore the day before, walk across to reception and press the bell on the counter. A fresh napkin wedged into the V of a different cowboy shirt, bits and pieces of a different-coloured meal – fried tomato? – stuck between his teeth. But the same knowing grin.

'Sleep well, matey?'

I toss the two keys onto the counter. 'I'm paying for both rooms.'

'Your brother still in hospital, eh? Just saw his missus drive off. She's been coming and going all morning . . .'

I slide a credit card across, giving nothing away. He squints at the embossed gold lettering. 'Don't get many professors in these parts, matey. What you a professor of, exactly?'

'Latin.'

A tried and tested deterrent; the last thing I want is a stream of 'anyone who goes to a psychiatrist needs their head examined' jokes. He slips the card into his imprinter, covers it with a voucher, grinds the press forth and back.

'Your missus show up?' he says, still fishing.

'She left early.'

He is looking past me, over my shoulder. I turn in the direction of his gaze to see the Toyota pulling back into the drive with Lucy at the wheel. No sign of Felix or the old men.

'Here she is now. Or is that your sister-in-law? Can't quite tell from here.' He chuckles and hands me the receipt. 'I reckon *she* should be paying for both rooms.'

I snatch the receipt and stalk out past the shelves of video-tapes. *Debbie Does Dallas. Head Room Below. Sorority House Massacre III.* A stray, alarming thought: What are the odds he has video cameras hidden in his rooms? Peepholes in the black hearts of the wallpaper desert peas, secret viewing compartments behind the mirrors? Samizdat tapes? I can just picture our own contribution to the World Wide Id – threesome.com

Bright sunlight outside; I shield my eyes against the glare. 'Where's Felix?'

'Already at the meeting. Hurry. We're late.'

The rear compartment of the Toyota is a tight squeeze of

provisions and bedrolls. Boxes of tinned food, flour, tea, sugar. Two ice-chests. Two bulging plastic water kegs, a sack of potatoes. I stash my bags among them and climb into the front passenger seat.

'What meeting?'

'With the family.'

'What family?'

'Of the child who died. Felix didn't tell you last night?'

More brisk exchanges, their content slower to surface. The bright dazzle of the morning further obstructs my thinking. Where are my sunglasses?

'Felix has made an offer. He wants everything settled before we leave.'

Finally something to wrap my mind around. 'He's offering compensation? Isn't that an admission of guilt?'

'I think that's the point. It was his idea, not theirs.'

'He wants us there?'

'The old men want you there.'

'Me? Why me?'

'You're his brother.'

'His *classificatory* brother.'

'The more brothers, the better, Bedford says. There are a lot of brothers on the other side.'

'What's that mean? We're outnumbered? I need to bring a spear?'

'Don't be ridiculous, Marty. These are modern Aboriginal people.'

'One generation out of the desert.'

'Aren't we all?' she says, the nearest we have got to talking about ourselves, about the night just passed, and the various nights that preceded it.

I retreat again into the impersonal. 'Where's the meeting?'

She gestures with her chin. How contagious this body language is, the unconscious mimicry. Postural echoes.

A red-dust clearing among scrubby trees at the northern end of town. Aboriginal shack housing beyond, the usual scatter of rubbish and broken glass and rusted, stripped car bodies. The cars parked on the edge of the clearing are barely more road-worthy – dented Falcon and Commodore sedans, several missing fenders and windscreens, their popped bonnets and doors wired crudely shut. A single late-model Landcruiser stands high among them, gleaming, flawlessly intact: CENTRAL LANDS COUNCIL.

A couple of dozen people sit in the dust beyond the vehicles in a rough, broken horseshoe. The man who is fucking my wife sits cross-legged towards the end of one arm, a portable oxygen cylinder cradled in his lap, the plastic Dali-moustache still perched on his lip. An uncharitable thought: his legal advisers have advised him to wear breathing support as a strategy, a play for the sympathy vote. He is bare-chested beneath his brown Akubra, his initiation scars like thick ropes across his chest and back. Another strategy? A public statement, surely. Bedford and Doctor Jerry sit each side of him, two broad black heads dark-ened further by the shade of their own battered hats. A white man and white woman sit at the apex of the horseshoe, clip-boards and paperwork spread in the dust between their legs.

Lawyers, certainly. The man is reading from a document in English, pausing between phrases for his companion to translate into a Warlpiri which I find only slightly more incomprehensible than the legalese. 'In the aforementioned . . . In relation to . . . Full and final settlement thereof . . .'

A line of grim-faced Aboriginal men forms the other arm of the horseshoe – younger men, in brightly coloured cowboy shirts and stiff black hats, fresh off the rack. Their women sit behind them, talking among themselves, showing no interest in our arrival. A withered, crone-like woman in a well-dusted frock sits off to one side, striking something hard against her head. A stone? *Thock.* The noise again, shockingly: *thock.* Lucy kneels instantly at her side to offer help, but is brushed away.

'The family of the aforementioned deceased shall hereafter have no further claim . . . in relation to the assets or any monetary entitlements . . .'

Bedford's eyes find mine, a twitch of his lips summons me to his side.

'You late, Mardin,' he says, loudly enough for all to hear. 'You sit along here. This side.'

My immediate thought: *Which* side? With the man who seduced my wife, or with the family whose child he killed? Several times last night I sensed a capacity in myself to kill Felix, even if the impulse lasted no more than a second. And now I am expected to side with him, to support him? Me against my brother, my brother and me against our cousins, our cousins and us against the rest? My brother's face is pale and drawn. I can see the pain that is tugging at the tight drawstrings of that face and am momentarily glad. Giddiness again overwhelms me; fleeting, murderous thoughts; alien, dislocating surrounds. How did I get here? The escarpment of black faces opposite offers no relief. Enemy faces? Or the enemies of my enemy, and therefore my friends? My cousins? Their expressions are impassive, impossible to read. Monumental heads, Easter Island heads – more recently carved than those of the old men, and less time-worn, but still foreign to me. Cousins, perhaps, but cousins from a galaxy far, far away.

The configuration of the two arms of the horseshoe also alarms me. Why are we facing each other, adversarially? Where are the spears hidden?

'. . . that subject to the specific provisions of this order . . . the aforementioned parties do hereby release the other party from any liability . . .'

Slightly behind the front rank of men in their hats and lurid shirts sits a lone bareheaded man in white collar and tie, staring into his lap, taking no part. I lean towards Bedford. 'The child's father?'

'Yuwayi. His full brothers there.' A stab of the lips. 'Japangardis. His wife's brothers that side – Jampinjimpas.'

'The mother?'

'Not here that one, Mardin. Stay away. Hurt too much. Granny over there.' A gesture to the far side, where Lucy has found a bandage somewhere and is wrapping the bleeding head of the old woman.

'. . . furthermore, in acknowledgement of the hurt . . . and in all other respects . . . I bequeath to the mother and father of the aforementioned deceased and to their respective sub-sections or moieties, in trust to the Central Lands Council . . . to be administered . . .'

The female lawyer is thirtyish but dressed in an older, quainter style: a throat-brooch clasping the neck of a buttoned-up blouse. There is something Victorian about this, something that resembles, oddly, the missionary generation of a century before. The occasional word of her translation seems intelligible to me. *Junga . . . Yarlparu . . . kirda.* Her white companion is more casually dressed: moleskin trousers, check shirt, the mandatory whitefeller Akubra.

A soft hiss of oxygen reminds me of Felix's nearness. 'What are you offering?'

'My life-insurance payout.' The twist of his smile; the irony amuses him. 'Death insurance, in this case.'

One of the Japangardis says something; there is a slight hub-bub of voices among his brothers and brothers-in-law, angry, schooled English clear among them. Words meant for Doctor Jerry are aimed just past him. 'You shouldn't be here, Jungarrayi. With respect, this is not your business. Doctor Felix is a white-feller – we should settle it whitefeller way.'

'If he's dying he doesn't fucking need *any* money,' someone else says. 'He can pay more.' Various noises of assent, the older women among them.

'Wurdungu jarriyalu!' Whatever Doctor Jerry has said – shut up, fuck off, drop dead – the effect is instant silence. He draws his hand in a straight line through the dust before him and speaks, softly and rapidly, in Warlpiri.

Bedford leans to me. 'He tell 'em the Law, Mardin. The straight line. Jungarni – one way, true way.'

The most talkative of the young Japangardis tries again. 'This is not for the old way, Jungarrayi. This is about compo. Pamarrpa!'

'Wurdungu jarriyalu!' The command this time from Bedford, his hand raised, a stylised threat to strike. Again I feel at some physical risk. If it comes to blows – spears – we have nothing on our side but the authority of age. In a conflict which is now as much between generations as between skins, is the shield of age all we need?

No-one looks directly at old Doctor Jerry as he speaks, quietly and firmly. The eyes of the younger men are everywhere, but their ears are clearly on him. The primly buttoned female lawyer is translating into English now, phrase by stumbling phrase. 'Men are not as reliable or obedient to the Law . . . The sun still acts lawfully . . . That sun comes up each day, goes away to his camp each night . . . The rains come, according to the Law. Ngapa – that rain-snake. Your mothers know that Dreaming, Japangardi . . . The kangaroos breed, the lizards make children . . . But you men are not so obedient. You, our children in the towns, you want to forget the Law. You want to live whitefeller way. Wingkirli – crooked way . . .'

Bedford's hoarse voice is again loud in my ear, unconcerned that anyone might hear. 'These are young men, Mardin.

Jalanguwarnu we call them. Just-married men. Little bit knowledge, you know?' He chuckles. 'Little bit cheeky – too much
want money.'

'Shouldn't their fathers be here?'

A snort. 'These Japangardis think they their fathers already.'

'You want the old way, we spear him!' a young Japangardi
blurts out in angry English, but this time one of the old women
reaches forward and clouts him on the head, to the accompani-
ment of a torrent of bird-shrill advice.

'Granny patrol,' Bedford mutters in my ear, amused.

Doctor Jerry speaks on, rapidly and repetitively. Do I imagine
I can pick out the same phrases returning, re-emphasised, like
choruses in a song? As the lawyer struggles to translate, Bedford
loudly whispers his own version in my ear. 'Jungarrayi tell them
Pillage is dying anyway – you know, going in. Should be enough
for 'em. Proper kunka. Payback. He tell them that insurance
money is a gift.'

'Ngulajuku,' Doctor Jerry says suddenly, then adds in English,
'that is all.'

Silence. Side-sliding eyes as the younger men confer mutely
with each other. The old doctor waits, stone-faced, but soon it is
over, a poll of nodding stockman's hats. No-one asks the hatless
father in the white collar and tie for his vote, but he reaches
between his Japangardi brothers and takes a pen from the lawyer
and signs the document on its clipboard.

An obvious thought, but still potent: Here is the only spear in
the room, the terrible whitefeller spear, the spiller of ink, sharper

and more powerful than any shovel-nosed or flint-tipped weapon.

The father passes that small sharp spear across to Felix, who also signs. The Japangardi brothers each sign, Cousin Bedford scratches a cross, then finally, by some loose kinship logic, it is my turn. Or am I merely a witness?

The old men push themselves to their feet as I sign, and suddenly the whole gathering is moving through the dust of its own arising towards the battered vehicles. Felix alone remains stranded, until the dead child's father turns back, reaches down a hand and helps him to his feet.

'Japangardi,' Felix murmurs.

'Japaljarri.'

A nod of thanks and the father has turned away. A laconic redemption, perhaps, but with a feel of business back to normal. Business done with, ended, closed off. The Japangardi family might deny it, but perhaps the ceremony here has been more blackfeller than whitefeller after all – more about honour than money. A small legal spearing, a letting of ink and cash in lieu of blood, and face is saved, social life can safely continue.

Bright sunlight on my head, thick dust itching my nose. The granny patrol has Lucy surrounded, offering shrill advice as she tapes the final bandage into place. Felix is alone again, standing half stooped, breathing heavily, clutching his oxygen cylinder, too weak to walk unaided – but still I cannot bring myself to offer an arm.

Lucy offers hers instead and I am pierced by the sight of

them together. They are dressed as twins: faded denim jeans, T-shirts, sandals. Dark glasses, Akubra hats. Accidental choices? The implication of a bond, two peas in a pod, two chocolates on a kitsch bedspread, is almost too much to bear.

One small detail, at least, separates her from him, connects her to the past she shares with me: her one sandal on, one off. As they cross the road arm in arm I fix my attention on that, and all that it means to me.

PART IV   Three-Dog Nights

19

'Dinner stop, eh?' Bedford, leaning forward over the steering wheel, peering out through the windscreen. 'Find a shady tree, eh?'

Noon, two hours out of One Shoe Creek, one hour past the end of the bitumen. Spinifex and saltpan country as far as the eye can see, the plain a sandy monochrome. Nothing much has been said for some time. The old men sit in the front seats, Lucy is sandwiched between Felix and me on the back bench. Second-class, whitefeller-class. Mid-afternoon in the great common room outside, but inside the cabin of the Toyota we seem walled off, invisibly, into five even smaller cabins.

'Find a shady tree, eh?' Bedford repeats.

He turns off the dirt track and bumps across the tufts of spinifex. Felix grimaces with each jolt, clearly in pain, but Bedford's destination is not far off, a low clump of vegetation a kilometre to the north.

Closer quarters, higher resolution: the clump becomes a line of wattles. We halt at a dry creek bed, distinguishable from the ochre plain only by the washed whiteness of its sand. Doctor Jerry climbs down and plants himself cross-legged in that soft sand, his chipped enamel mug like an alms bowl before him. Lucy helps Felix to another small pool of shade as Bedford gathers scraps of firewood; I follow him in among the wattles to help.

The wider world is a relief after the hot glasshouse of the Toyota, but the flies find us immediately. Bedford drops a token armful of bark and wattle scraps into the creek bed and settles at the old doctor's side, rolling cigarettes for both of them. 'Light fire, eh Mardin?'

Automatic boy-scout routines; the small pile of bark and branches is soon alight, and soon thereafter a glow of coals. The sting of smoke in my nostrils mingles pleasantly with strong tobacco as I take a wire clamp-grill and bag of meat from the Toyota. Cooking duties are also apparently mine. And why not? Whitefeller tribe, western-suburbs skin, backyard barbecue ceremony. Men's business, definitely: the Steak Sandwich Dreaming. The Rissole Dreaming. All I lack is the proper ceremonial dress: a can of beer in a styrofoam jacket, an apron with a pair of giant women's breasts or some hearty-funny motto: A MAN NEEDS A WOMAN LIKE A BICYCLE NEEDS A FISH.

And perhaps a fez. To cap it off.

Small jokes for a mind seeking large relief.

The meat begins to sizzle, the maddened flies gather as close to the juices as heat allows.

'The old men will want it like charcoal,' Felix wheezes.

I roll the burnt sausages in slices of bright white bread, smother them in bright red sauce, and hand them about. Bedford slides a blackened billycan of water in among the coals with the sole of his boot.

Silent, sustained eating for some time, inside the same separate cabins which have somehow been removed, like invisible capsules, from the Toyota. Even Felix is eating, or nibbling. The food, or the activity of its preparation, begins to lift my spirits, dispel my numbness. Is this all it takes? For the moment at least, as I begin to look beyond our small, weird group, take a tentative step outside my cabin. Or am I merely seeking further refuge in details?

No biblical wilderness this. The signs of life are thinly spread but the desert is alive. Ants frantic everywhere. Quicksilver skinks rustling among the dried leaves. Birds, of course. Two grass wrens in a nearby bush. A single giant wedgetail riding the currents high above. And in the creek bed a familiar totem from the Suburban Patio Dreaming: a wagtail nervously twitching its long tail, twisting its head.

'Here, Willie,' Lucy calls, and tosses a crust of bread. 'Here, Willie.'

Cabin doors are opening everywhere. 'Jintipirri,' Felix tells her. 'No doubt the professor has told you the Latin name.'

'No, but he has mimicked their call.'

They both turn to me, waiting. It seems I have no choice. '*Sweet pretty creature*,' I chant, falsetto. '*Sweet pretty creature*.' The bird takes to the sky.

'Sounds like a mating call to me,' Felix says, and grins weakly, but it helps ease the awkwardness.

An opening for Bedford-lore. 'Same word for this wagtail inside, Mardin.' He crooks a finger and dangles it in front of his open mouth. 'Jintipirri. You know, tonsil.'

'Uvula?'

'Yuwayi. Little wagtail. His Dreaming comes through here.'

'The Tonsil Dreaming?'

He chuckles at the joke. 'Wagtail Dreaming. His camp that way.' He aims his lips southwards, across the sleeping torso of the old doctor, who has keeled over on his side to sleep. 'Rain-snake come through here too – Ngapa. My daddy's Dreaming. Warumungu mob bring that rain this far. Warlpiri mob take him over that way. Sundown side.'

The billy tea is ready; Bedford scoops out a mugful to which he adds a white avalanche from the sugar bag. 'We go that way. Find that waterhole.'

'You know where it is?'

He shakes his head. 'My mother's country. Long time back. Before army time. My job to keep an eye on it. Kurdungulu for that country, you know? But I never bin there.' He glances towards Doctor Jerry. 'That old man bin there. Father country for that old man.'

The old man sleeps on. Bedford smooths a small square of sand with the palm of his hand, a white page on which his fore-finger now draws a straight line, axis north–south. 'Here's the whitefeller road, Mardin. Stuart Highway.' He draws a second line, east to west, bisecting the first at right angles. 'Here's the sun's road.' He jabs the point of intersection of the two lines with that same broken-nailed finger. 'And here – middle of the world. One Shoe Creek, Warumungu country. My daddy's country.'

He laughs; another well-rehearsed performance. Now he draws a diagonal line just north of the east–west axis, running west-north-west. 'Here's the blackfeller track. We call him the Warlpiri Highway.' Another chuckle. 'Down here,' his finger moves southwards, into empty space, 'a week's walk in the old time. Wild time. That's where that little green bird goes. He goes in there. That hole in the ground.'

'Ngarlpa,' I say.

'Yuwayi. We drive there, Mardin.'

The older man still lies immobile, snoring softly with his back to us. Bedford grins his lazy, gap-toothed grin. 'Might be he forget, eh Mardin? Might be we get lost!'

Doctor Jerry suddenly rights himself, rises with some difficulty, and climbs with even more difficulty up into the Toyota. Time to leave, clearly. No change in the seating arrangements as we drive off: the whitefellers less chauffeur-driven than relegated to the seats without a view.

'How are you managing, Felix?' Lucy asks as we lurch on.

'Fine.'

But he is not fine. The slightest jolt of the road is recorded on his face as if on some amplifying instrument, an ultra-sensitive seismograph.

'We can still go back. We don't have to do this.'

'I said I'm fine.'

Surely he must know he has bitten off more than he can chew? The told-you-so satisfaction of this thought is faint only, a distant satisfaction. More immediate is his continuing pain, which even I can feel. This journey will kill him. Kill him off, at any rate.

263

'You need some morphine.'

'It can wait.' He winds down his window and irritably tries to shoo out the flies which have followed him in. 'Wait your turn, fuck you. You'll have me soon enough.'

After such jokes, what possible conversation? We drive at walking speed now, bumping over wheel-ruts and saltbush clumps and sand-drifts, not so much navigating the Warlpiri Highway as inventing it. The day has not been hot but there seems plenty of fight left in the late afternoon sun, its heat amplified by the lens of the windscreen and the slowness of our progress. The movement of the air is negligible.

I spy on my companions in the back seat. Despite the dark glasses and identical clothes, they are no longer remotely twins. Lucy glows, the torch of her fair hair magnifying the late light, giving it back. Felix might be in shadow. An odd, spooky thing: the light seems to vanish into him, absorbed into the black hole of his clothes, certainly – the dark T-shirt and jeans – but also into the leather of that gaunt face.

His eyes catch mine.

'How are you doing?' I ask automatically.

'So far so good.' The glimmer of a smile. 'As the man falling from the top of the Empire State Building kept shouting into windows on the way down.'

Sandhill country now. Bluebush, saltbush. Handfuls of cane grass on the slopes and ridges of the small dunes. Dogwood? I have no idea. Correct or not, names keep popping into my head.

A stand of scrappy, bonsai eucalypts rises out of the plain, enlarges; we stop without warning. Doctor Jerry climbs down and walks a few yards off the track, lowers his trousers and squats.

Lucy touches her hand to mine. 'You okay?'

'So far so good.'

She manages a smile, as does Felix. 'You taking the mickey out of me, Professor?'

My own full bladder is tweaking at me; I climb down and walk away from the Toyota and its glasshouse heat. A slight, cooling breeze on my face now, keeping away the flies. The shadows of the trees have lengthened, venturing out into the cool of the evening from beneath their daytime shelter. The sun is almost gone, but the retained warmth of the planet still glows upwards from the desert floor, as if the molten core of the earth, no more than a few kilometres below, were the true source of heat.

As I walk back, the thin, baked-clay crust gives a little beneath my feet. Felix's gaunt face watches me impassively from the Toyota. I think, This narrow rind we inhabit, this crust of life, is so thin that I too could step through it at any moment.

20

The wave of night slowly rises in the eastern sky behind us, catches and overspills us, crowding the remains of the day into a narrowing afterglow ahead. A distant tree-line, ink-scratched against that last red glow, takes shape as we approach; soon we drive into a crooked aisle of coolibah trees staking out the margins of another narrow sand river.

My spirits rise. Picture-postcard Central Australia, a perfect campsite. 'Shouldn't we find a place to camp?'

Felix, chest heaving: 'Leave it to the experts, Herr Professor.'

The experts are in fact conferring, Bedford mumbling suggestions, the old doctor, as impassive as ever, making no acknowledgement. More suggestions, more indifference. The light is almost gone when he finally aims his chin, minimally, out beyond the trees into the open desert, and the Toyota turns in that direction. Bedford drives with his head stuck out the side window, examining the lie of the land by high-beam headlight. Another near-invisible cue from the doctor and we halt at the edge of a bare claypan. A campsite expertly chosen no doubt, but for reasons that escape me. Correct sand texture? Absence of ant nests? There are no trees – no firewood – within a long stone's throw.

Bedford the mind-reader: 'You can see him coming long way off out here, Mardin.'

'See who coming?'

'That red-ochre man, you know?' He half turns, grins. 'He sneak up on you at night. Wearing those emu-feather shoes.'

Felix snorts. 'Don't get him started, Prof. You'll be looking over your shoulder all night.'

Doctor Jerry has already climbed down and found himself a

bed of soft sand; Felix shakes off my offered hand and clambers down by himself.

'We get that firewood, Mardin,' Bedford says, and I follow him back towards the coolibahs. Last light now, not a breath of movement in the air. 'Still time, Mardin. Kangaroo time.'

There are none to be seen. When we return with our armfuls, Felix is lying on his back in the sand next to Doctor Jerry, utterly spent. His tobacco pouch lies open in his hand, a cigarette paper is stuck to his lip, but he doesn't even have the energy to complete this smallest of physical tasks. Lucy kneels at his side, drawing up a syringe.

'A pain patch would do,' he is saying.

'Too slow. You should have agreed to have something earlier.'

Her tone is direct, matter-of-fact, even a little impatient, but I find it more disturbingly intimate than any sweet-talk. She wraps his wasted upper arm in a tourniquet. Blue ropes rise in the crook of his elbow; she deftly slips in a needle, releases the tourniquet, injects. The morphine rush is rapid; the clenched tightness of his face melts away as if pain is nothing more than a facial expression after all, its torments as skin-deep as ugliness.

Gratitude in his eyes as Lucy bandaids the puncture site. And something more than gratitude. Love? A lover's gaze? Less a lover's than a dog's, licking the hand that comforts. Or so I tell myself.

I unfold his swag and we roll his pliant, drug-loosened body onto it. How much younger he looks dosed to the gills with narcotics, as if age is also as skin-deep as pain. Or perhaps a type of pain itself, an accumulation of remembered pains. Lucy's specialty of course – the kinship of pain and memory. Is she thinking what I am thinking? Memory also is skin-deep? I suddenly long to talk to her of this, as of old. By washing away our memories, I want to ask, might the years also be washed away? Might we forget ourselves back into childhood? But she bends over her patient with more pressing matters on her mind. Our clinical pillow-talks are just another painful memory.

'Sleep for a while,' she murmurs to him, although he is asleep already and surely cannot feel the kiss she places on his sweating brow. 'We'll wake you when the food is ready.'

He sleeps on through the food – steaks, fried onions, a thick-crusted damper baked by Bedford in a pit of coals and ash. Traditional tucker? Only to a point – he first wraps the loaf in aluminium foil. The old pragmatist and his even older companion crawl inside their blanket-swags after eating and fall instantly asleep; Lucy and I sit by the fire, too exhausted to move.

A moonless, near-noiseless night, the faint snoring of Doctor Jerry the only sound. The last warmth of the day has evaporated outwards and upwards; we find ourselves huddled together over the glowing remnants of the coals, the chill of night pressing against our backs, pressing us closer together, physically closer than we have been for some time.

I spill more hot tea from the billy into our big enamel mugs.

'Central heating,' Lucy says, sipping.

The small clouds of vapour that emerge with every breath

vanish instantly in the night air. Our talk is almost as ephemeral, less small talk than shoptalk. Middle-sized talk, trying to find safe ways to enlarge further.

'We can put a patch on him while he sleeps,' Lucy says.

The thinnest straw of intimacy in that inclusive 'we', but I clutch at it gratefully. 'What sort of patch?'

'Slow-release opiate.'

She talks drugs for some time, listing their names, their properties. Haloperidol, sodium midazolam. Fentanyl citrate. Drugs to counteract the effects of other drugs: metoclopramide, benztropine. Dexamphetamine to keep the mind clear. We are far from the Adelaide Hills – very far – but I remember our first drive up there, months before, the names of English villages and English trees melting in her mouth. The music of her voice nourishes me again tonight, in the middle of the desert, even listing the drugs of palliative care. Clinical pillow-talk, of sorts.

'Coloxyl, of course. Psyllium.'

I am many years past prescribing such drugs. 'Which are?'

'Laxatives. The narcotics will bind him up.'

A hoarse croak from behind us. 'Sex, drugs and rock'n'roll, Professor.'

How long has he been listening? He still looks ten years younger, waking into some pain-free littoral between the end of sleep and the return of pain. Lucy shifts on her buttocks, subtly but surely breaking physical contact with me. Is she aware that she is doing this in front of him? It's not the first time.

'How do you feel?' she asks.

'Floating.' His parched tongue sticks to his palate, retarding his words. 'Wasn't Morpheus the Greek god of sleep, Prof?'

'God of dreams.'

'I dreamt I'd died and gone to heaven. But there was nothing to eat. Any hot stones?'

The shock that floods through me is almost electric. Lucy has been telling him my dreams!

'Fentanyl patch first,' she says, avoiding my eyes.

'I don't need it.'

'You will when the morphine wears off.'

That straight-talking intimacy again, proxy wife to husband. She rummages in her black bag, unpeels the narcotic patch and applies it to his upper arm.

'Slow-Release Dreaming,' he says.

I pass him the plate of leftovers we have kept aside. Invigorated by sleep and still a little high on morphine, he is more interested in talking than eating.

'Narcotics are a foretaste, don't you think?'

'Of what?'

'Little deaths that portend the big one.'

Uncomfortable with this direction, Lucy busies herself, noisily, with packing away her medical tools.

'Don't be coy, doctors. You know what I'm talking about.'

It's left to me to co-operate in the conversation. 'Near-death experiences?'

'Celestial light at the end of the tunnel. Overwhelming

euphoria.' He is panting a little, but too euphoric himself to notice. 'Suspension of time.'

'The terminally ill often find spiritual comfort in those stories,' I say.

He snorts. 'It's all basic physiology, Prof.' A pause for breath. We wait, captive; he has suspended time himself and will continue when he is good and ready. 'What happens when brain cells start dying? A flood of natural opiates – no wonder you feel good.'

'And the light at the end of the tunnel?'

'Random sparking of the visual nerve cells. Produces a white-out.' A slight grimace, the first sign of the return of pain. 'The brain dies from the outside in. Think about it. The cells of the central visual cortex, more densely packed, better supplied with blood, die last. You lose the edges first, leaving the tunnel effect.' Pain tweaks again at the corner of his mouth. The last of the morphine is finally wearing off, but he manages to hide it in a crooked grin. 'Would the last brain cell to die please turn out the light.'

Lucy: 'You won't allow yourself the consolation of other possibilities?'

'I prefer my consolations in quantifiable form.' He shifts uncomfortably. 'Speaking of which, when is that patch supposed to clock in?'

'I'll give you another shot to tide you over. But you must eat.'

Soon he is sleeping again, the food largely untouched. I take a spade and toilet-roll and walk out into the night; when I return

Lucy is already inside her swag. I slip into mine and lie facing her, trying to read her shadowy face. A much brighter face peeps over her shoulder, a yellow three-quarter moon, rising.

'You awake?'

A reluctant whisper: 'Just.'

'Can I ask you something?'

'Mmm.'

'Why do you always move away from me when Felix is around?'

'Do I? I hadn't noticed.' Pause. 'Perhaps I don't like to flaunt our closeness in front of him.'

'You flaunt your closeness with him to me.'

'Can this conversation wait, Martin?'

She rolls over, turning her back. Why did you tell him my dreams? I want to also ask, but of course it too can wait. *Must* wait. I feel ashamed of myself, but, as so often in recent weeks, that sense of shame has been slower to arrive than jealousy. A tortoise-emotion, lagging far behind. As compassion seems to lag behind anger. Forgiveness behind spite. Slow and steady wins the race? At least the tortoise of sleep also finally arrives tonight, a sleep of utter exhaustion that for once outpaces my agitation and fills my brain or my mind or both not so much with celestial light as with comforting nothingness. A nothing that is neither light nor dark.

21

Fire-stokings and billy-clankings at the edge of consciousness. The soft, percussive shock of footsteps transmitted through sand. A scent universe of frying bacon – restorative no matter how thick-headed I feel.

'Tea, Marty?'

I open my eyes to find Lucy kneeling at my side, haloed by the bright morning glare.

'Breakfast's ready.'

The old men are sitting in the sand, already eating. Felix sits to one side, hunched forward, picking at his food. Despite the oxygen catheter hissing in his nose, he is breathing more heavily than the night before. Lucy passes me a plate.

'What are these?'

'Wild onions.'

More stalk than bulb, the so-called onions sit between the eggs and bacon like a mess of stir-fried weeds.

Bedford, through a mouthful: 'We call him janmarra, Mardin. Little brown onion. The doctor find them.'

The old doctor makes one of his rare, terse comments. 'Good medicine for sick.'

The sick man is still poking at his medicine as we pack up the campsite around him half an hour later. He leaves the eggs and bacon largely untouched but forces himself to finish the onions. Pascal's wager? His eyes find mine as I take his plate; he winks, ambiguously.

We are soon jolting along the track. Granite outcrops to the south, claypans to the north. The monochrome sand-yellow of yesterday has become more a three-coloured map: salt-white, ochre-red, clay-brown. Dot-painted country. Scarecrow eucalypts of various species stand waist-deep in mulga scrub. Stringy-barks, coolibahs, bloodwoods – the names again are somehow known to me. I look up their desert-Latin names in the diction-ary, seeking distraction. The termite mounds – mingkirri – are also larger. Lucy dozes with her head on my shoulder as I read. I sense she has slept little overnight. Bedford for once has nothing to say; not a morning person, it seems. Five separate cap-sules inside the cabin again, with Felix especially silent in his, staring hollow-eyed out the window, chest heaving.

'Should you turn up the oxygen?'

'Stick to birdwatching, Prof. I'm fine.'

I escape back into the dictionary for a time. Karrawari: coolibah tree. Kurrkara: desert oak. Walawurru: wedgetail eagle. But sustained reading is impossible, and soon I toss the book aside. The car lurches on at tortoise speed, its jolting rhythms like the ticking of a harsh, irregular clock. But measuring what? Time might be standing still. No wonder the gods went into the desert to think – there is nothing else to do. My own thinking tosses this up: Might boredom in the end prove a stronger emotion than anger, or jealousy? Or at least provide an inner desert, a great emptiness into which my raging obsessions of recent weeks might pour themselves, and vanish, like inland rivers sucked into sand?

Felix is almost gasping for breath now, making no protest

when Lucy, rousing, reaches for the portable oxygen cylinder on the seat between them and turns up the flow rate.

'We should stop.'

'Not yet,' he gasps.

An urgent whisper from the doctor: 'Jangala. Yakarra!'

The Toyota brakes and Bedford jumps down from the cabin with unprecedented speed. A pair of fat lizards lie basking on the track ahead; he is upon them before they can move, whipping them up by the tails and clubbing their heads against a large stone.

He presents his spoils at the old doctor's window. Blood clings to the smashed blunt snouts, already attended by half a dozen flies. The old man inspects the offerings, rolls one stubby tail between thumb and forefinger.

'Only skinny one that one.'

Bedford isn't fazed. 'Dinner time,' he announces, then looks to me. 'Fire time, Mardin.'

'I'm not feeling particularly hungry,' from Lucy as I climb down from the cabin.

Bedford sits in the sand sawing at the bellies of the lizards with a blunt clasp-knife as I gather wood. 'Lungkarda,' he says. 'Blue-tongue lizard, you know, Mardin?' And, as I nurse the fire to life, 'Number one good tucker, Mardin.'

'If you say so.'

The gutted lizards are soon roasting in the flames, their innards for some reason set aside on a plate. Hors-d'oeuvres? Doctor Jerry, back from a piss, stirs at the slop of guts with thick, blunt fingers. Absorbed in his task, he might be reading entrails. In fact, he is teasing out the grapelets of yellow, glistening fat.

After some time he hands his harvest to Felix. 'Good medicine for sick, Japaljarri. Lizard-belly fat.'

The longest English sentence he has spoken in two days is clearly of some import.

'You listen up, Pillage,' Bedford urges. 'Clever-doctor, that one.'

Felix tosses the half-handful of fat into his mouth without argument. Lucy offers a mug of water to wash it down, but he waves it away.

'Feeling better already.'

The reptiles sizzle in the ovens of their own armour, their juices bubbling noisily through various wounds and orifices. Bedford flips them, inspects them. 'Old man first,' he says.

Is he talking of Doctor Jerry, or the larger lizard as he scoops it onto the plate?

'Someone once said if you swallow a toad each morning nothing more disgusting can happen all day,' Lucy murmurs.

Felix accepts a chunky segment of tail from Jerry and sucks the flesh from its pouch of toad-leather. No doubt he has feasted on blackened lizard flesh many times before, but a notion for a research paper half forms in my head: the palliative uses of exotic distractions.

Bedford is busy sawing at the smaller lizard. 'You sitting without meat, Sister?'

'I'm not hungry.'

'You too skinny, Sister. You eat this.'

'I'll share with Martin.'

I brush the flies from my portion, a rough-torn hindquarter, and chew. White meat, slightly rubbery, but not at all tough. Squid texture, although more bird than fish in taste. 'Not bad.'

Doctor Jerry licks the lizard grease from his lips and mumbles something in Warlpiri. Bedford turns towards me, tapping a forefinger on his left shoulder.

'Jungarrayi say you have that little lizard, Mardin. Lives in your left shoulder. Here.'

'Blue-tongue?'

'Nah. Magic lizard. We call him Nguwa. Spirit lizard. He sometime step out, look around. He can see things coming, you know? Tomorrow, next day. He can warn you.' With a meal of lizard meat inside him, he is his talkative self again, restored to full power.

My eyes find Lucy's. 'He's not doing much of a job,' I say.

But the old men have paused in their eating and are staring out into the desert, as stilled and attentive as cats. More blue-tongues to stalk? No, a pair of birds in the distance, approaching fast. The sun catches them, a flash of greens and yellows, as they settle in a nearby coolibah.

Ngatijirri. Budgerigars.

The old doctor begins singing immediately, a song so low and barely voiced it is little more than a hum.

Bedford grins. 'He coming into his father country, Mardin. His dirt, you know?'

'What's he singing?' Lucy asks.

'Trying to remember that Dreaming, Sister. Bring back the country. That little green bird come from down there.' A south-pointing chin. 'Pawurrinji. Five day walk.' He pauses, listening to the words of the song. 'That bird, that little Japaljarri, he come out and go all over this country. He travelling with his friend.'

The actual bird and his friend are twittering at high speed and high frequency in their tree, drowning the old man's monotone.

A sly grin on Bedford's face. 'Good meat that bird meat.'

Lucy, shocked: 'You eat budgies?'

'Yuwayi. Number one good tucker.'

'You're allowed to eat your Dreaming animals?'

'Not our animal, Sister. You and me. Good meat for us.' A nod in my direction. 'He belong you, Mardin. You and Pillage. The old doctor. You proper hungry, nothing else to eat, might be you eat him up. But you have to tell him sorry. You know?' He chuckles. 'You tell him, Sorry, little father. What a pity I eat you up.'

As if overhearing his words, the two birds take to the air alarmed and flee rapidly towards the south-west. Bedford cups his hand to his mouth and calls after them. 'Don't go long that way, little bird. Pintupi mob that way. Proper wild mob, them blackfellers.' He turns back to Lucy, enjoying himself. 'Pintupi mob eat him raw, Sister. Chew that little bird up whole, spit out his bones, his feathers.' He chuckles again as she screws up her nose. 'I like him little bit cooked. Burn his fluff off. You know, kirlka. Clean skin, eh?'

'There's an old whitefeller recipe for cooking cockatoo,' I remember.·

Bedford turns to me, interested.

'You boil the bird in a pot of water with a couple of stones.'
I pause, trying to get the punchline right. 'When the stones are
soft, you throw out the cockatoo and eat the stones.'

Bedford chuckles more hoarsely. 'Might be you own that
cockatoo, Mardin,' he says. 'That pink cockatoo. Major Mitchell.
Might be you *have* to eat those stones!'

Doctor Jerry has walked out beyond the Toyota in the direction in which the budgerigars have vanished. No afternoon nap
today; the sight of the birds has animated the old man. Does he
take them as some sort of sign? Is their flight a compass bearing?
He stands there for a time, his face as immobile and impassive
as the surrounding mingkirri. Ataraxia, the thousand-yard stare.
Abruptly he turns back and climbs into the front passenger seat.

Bedford, rising: 'Drive time.'

We have been bumping across the claypan for some minutes
before I realise we have left the track behind. A terse command
from Doctor Jerry – 'Kurlirra!' – and Bedford swings the Toyota
even further southwards. I look back and the track – our tether,
our lifeline, our highway – has vanished.

Felix grins. 'Can't get lost, Prof. Satellite navigation.'

The Toyota jolts on over saltbush and spinifex clumps. At least
the narcotic patch is doing its job; he seems in less pain today.

'You okay?'

'Nothing like a second helping of reptile fat.'

No sign of our guide-birds, but the old man seems to have his
own internal navigation system. Trackless country, the odd distant

hillock or rocky outcrop the only landmarks I can make out. I think, How wilfully the eye seeks altitude, makes mountains out of anthills, elevates a line of bushes on the flat horizon into a crest of trees. Tricks of illusion, or self-deception? We drive on. Rapid progress across the claypans alternates with slow lurching through dunes and tussocky undergrowth, or between the rock-hard mingkirri that stud the plain like a baked-terracotta army. Several times Bedford engages the four-wheel drive to reverse out of a sand-drift. Perhaps we average ten or fifteen kilometres an hour. Concentration is difficult. I manage a little birdwatching, binoculars in hand, but language-spotting has become impossible, the dictionary jumping about in my hands with each lurch of the Toyota. Short bursts of singing from time to time from the old man, broken chants, repeated again and again, their meaning beyond me.

'He singing up this country, Mardin. No-one bin looking after it. No-one bin out here since army time.'

'Yuwayi,' the old man, not apparently listening, mumbles.

'When that old Jungarrayi was a boy,' Bedford says, 'a little boy – wita-pardu – he bin running through here. He run away with his father, mother, cousins. Running and running. All the way – Yurrkurru to Wave Hill. Six hundred mile. They running from Murray – that policeman bin killing all the people.'

'Yuwayi,' the old doctor repeats, happy enough with the potted biography so far.

Bedford aims north-west with his lips. 'Gurindji country. That way. One, two week walk. Those men all line up. Warlpiri.

Gurindji. Chuck spears at each other. Meeting business, eh? Dodge them spears. By and by the Gurindji take 'em in, look after 'em. Till Murray stop killing them blackfellers down south.'

Doctor Jerry turns to me, startling nicotine-yellow eyes in an ash-grey face. 'True story, Japaljarri.'

So it is official, my skin, at last – if awarded only with offhand ceremony.

'We need to stop, Bedford,' Lucy interrupts.

'By and by, Sister.'

'No. We need to stop now. For the night. Felix has had enough.'

No argument this time from Felix, struggling for breath. Still in no particular hurry, Bedford steers the Toyota in several widening circles before the two old men agree on a campsite. Felix slides immediately out of the cabin and slumps in the sand, bent forward, chest heaving. Lucy reaches into the rear compartment for her bag of doctor tools.

'Turn the . . . oxygen . . . up,' he gasps.

'It's already at six litres.'

He pulls his T-shirt over his head and reaches out a hand, snapping his fingers impatiently. 'Stethoscope.' Hunched forward, he listens intently to his own naked chest, gulping huge mouthfuls of air. At length he takes a felt-tip pen from the bag and marks a cross on his chest wall, in one of the long furrows between his heaving ribs.

'Need . . . a pleural . . . tap.' He looks up at Lucy. 'Any . . . volunteers?'

Alarm in her face. 'I haven't done one for years.'

'Martin hasn't . . . for decades.'

Even in these urgent circumstances I feel the slight sting of his rebuff; why wouldn't he ask his oldest friend? The absurd hare of emotion, as always, leaving logic plodding in its wake.

'I don't even remember where to put the needle.'

'X marks . . . the spot. No . . . big deal. Talk you . . . through it.'

'I'll do it,' I say.

'No . . . Lucy.'

I unwrap a sterile dressing tray and spill a little purple anti-septic into the small plastic dish. Lucy pulls on a pair of rubber gloves with a reassuringly professional snap. 'Local anaesthetic?'

'Quicker . . . without.'

'Shouldn't you lie down?' I ask.

Lucy's knowledge is more up-to-date after all. 'Sitting posture,' she reminds me.

Felix's eyes catch mine. Even through the strain of his breath-ing, he manages a gasped chuckle. 'Stick to . . . psychiatry . . . Prof.' His rib cage threatens to burst out through the tight-stretched skin with each inhalation. 'Keep close . . . to the top rib. Don't want . . . to hit . . . the artery.'

Lucy, gloved and masked, inserts a thick-bore needle cautiously. 'Further!'

She pushes in up to the hilt, then pulls back on the plunger. A first-time hit: the large chamber fills easily with clear, straw-coloured pleural fluid. With one hand holding the needle in place, she detaches the syringe and hands it to me for emptying, blood-warm and heavy. I step away and squirt the liquid out

282

into the sand, then return the empty chamber to Lucy for re-attachment. We repeat the procedure – and again, several times. Damp patches everywhere about us now, perhaps a litre of fluid has been sucked down into the thirsty sand.

The old men watch this sterile medical spearing from the corners of their eyes, brushing away flies; I reach across Lucy and likewise shoo the flies that are already attracted to the puncture site.

'They're getting a taste for me,' Felix mutters.

One last extraction, a half-chamber only, then a flinch from Felix as a hair-thin jet of blood spurts out and unravels in the clearer yellow fluid. I remember enough basic surgery to know that the job is done; the sharp tip of the needle has come to rest against the outer lining of the lung. I unpeel an adhesive plaster and press it to the puncture site as Felix sits cross-legged, hunched forward, a cold sweat on his brow, but breathing more easily.

'Thank you,' he says. 'Both of you.'

The whole world blood-red now, the sun sinking lower, the temperature dropping rapidly. No time to rest. Lucy fetches Felix's swag; I collect bark scraps, brittle twigs and branches. The old doctor sits buddha-fashion on a comfortable pillow of dust, waiting for dinner. Soon he has his mug of tea, and soon thereafter a plate of grilled steaks and bread.

Exhausted by the day's ordeal, Felix falls asleep as I cook. I leave his plate of food wedged in the fork of a bush, out of immediate ant-reach. Bedford places a smouldering branch beneath to keep away the last of the flies.

The sun creeps from the sky unnoticed as Lucy and I wash

dishes in a shallow ration of water. Doctor Jerry is singing again, repeating the same lines over and over, taking them a little further each time, as if trying to conjure the song up from memory. Bedford repeats phrases in chorus. Two chunky wooden clapsticks have appeared from his kitbag; one sits on his belly and he strikes it with the other in time with the older man's chanting: a sharp, short *clack-clack-clack*.

The noise wakes Felix. He rolls onto his side, watching and listening through half-closed eyes.

Lucy hands him a mug of tea. 'Can you follow it?'

'Bits and pieces. The Dreamtime budgie rested near here for a while on his travels. There seem to be a couple of women involved.' A twist of his mouth. 'Root of all evil, as usual.'

The chanting and beating of sticks suddenly stops, the doctor mutters, 'Nyurru' – 'I am finished,' Felix translates – and both men rise and walk away from the camp. After crouching at the very edge of darkness, they return and roll themselves in their swags without speaking again. Do they deliberately choose to sleep on the same side of the fire – south-west – as the night before? Or is my mind seeking patterns where none belong?

The hooting of a mopoke reaches us, far off but bell-clear. *Boobook. Boobook.* The owl might be a kilometre distant or fifty; the still night air carries the faint sound uninterrupted across the flat desert floor. *Boobook.* I am taken back to the night, weeks before, when I hid in the trees behind Felix's farmhouse, spying. *Ninox furtivus.*

'Kurrkurrpa,' Felix says, interrupting my reverie.

'Sorry?'

'That's what they call them out here, Prof.'

He repeats the word in a soft owl-hoot, and then again, seeking the origins of the bird's name in the noise it makes. Lucy and I join in, and for a time the desert resounds with a hooted chorus of *boobook*, *mopoke* and *kurrkurrpa* that ends in a paroxysm of coughing from Felix. Exhausted, he slumps forward, his head sunk between his bony shoulders.

No sound now from the mopoke, astonished into silence.

'You need to eat,' Lucy tells him.

'I need to piss,' he says.

She immediately rises and walks to the Toyota, returning with a stainless-steel bottle which he slips inside the swag. A muffled trickling, and soon I am walking out twenty metres to irrigate the roots of a bloodwood with the dark, strong-smelling urine. More body fluids, more scent patches leaving a trail across the desert. Feather-footed Death, surely only a few days distant, will have no trouble tracking him down.

Lucy has stirred more wood scraps into the fire when I return; Felix is propped on one elbow, rolling his first cigarette for some time, perhaps for the day. Faint snoring from the far side of the fire, silence on our side as we stare into the glowing coals, losing ourselves in this most ancient of meditations, a mindless visual *om*.

Mindless on my part. Felix has remained in the here and now, for when he speaks it is as if we have been talking all along, or at least privy to each other's thoughts.

'What I don't understand is this: what exactly are we afraid of? Why should the void after we die terrify us more than the void before we are born?' He coughs, recovers. 'Both are of the same length – endless. Both must feel the same.'

'You've been reading Plato,' I say.

'Not since Waldo.'

It's left to Lucy to state the obvious. 'Surely it's not death itself we fear. It's the life we miss out on.'

'Then we must discover what we can do without,' he says, quoting Waldo again. Waldo quoting Plato quoting Socrates.

Waldo denied himself nothing, I want to remind him. But again he is racked by coughing, and clearly in pain.

'You need morphine,' Lucy says. 'Or a stronger patch.'

A bent grin. 'Am I talking too much?'

'Of course not. I want you to talk.'

He lies back on his swag and inhales deeply from his cigarette. 'It seemed a good idea at the time,' he says eventually.

'What did?'

'Coming out here. Seeing what I could live without.'

'Sounds very Buddhist,' I say.

'A rehearsal for death, in a way.' Another cough. 'Life stripped back to the basics – food, water. No bullshit.'

'Budgerigar Dreaming?' I remind him.

A cheap point, but the spasm that wrenches his face is purely physical pain. He looks across at me. 'You think the jukurrpa is bullshit?'

'I think all religious belief is bullshit. Which doesn't mean it can't offer consolation.'

'You haven't been paying attention, Professor.'

'What do you mean?'

'You diminish the Dreaming songs if you think they are mere consolations. Entertainment, yes – but pragmatic entertainment. Entertainment that is also a survival kit, a way of remembering information. Maps of the desert. Sites of water, ochre, good hunting –'

'Surely *you* diminish them,' Lucy interrupts, and then, as if surprised by herself, continues more cautiously. 'You refuse to allow a whole world of spiritual nourishment. You just have to look at the old men's faces when they are singing to know it's more than that.'

'You want to believe in the tooth fairy, feel free. Whatever gets you through the night.' He shivers briefly, convulsively. 'Admittedly the nights are pretty cold out here.' He grimaces, as if the shivering itself has caused pain. 'I'll have that morphine now.'

Ask nicely, I want to say, but hold my tongue as Lucy fits needle to syringe, snaps the waist of a glass phial. I say instead, 'They've got Toyotas and satellite navigation now. They don't need song maps. Yet they still sing.'

'And we still celebrate a virgin birth,' Lucy says.

'Speak for yourself,' he mutters, then falls silent as she eases the drug smoothly into his veins. He closes his eyes, takes a deep, slow breath, returns to the world. 'Where were we?'

'You were deciding what you could do without.'

He glances at his elbow as Lucy tapes a bandaid to the puncture site. 'Point taken, Prof.' And then turns away and begins to retch, loudly and forcefully. What is coming up in all that liquid splashing? Bile? He has eaten nothing.

When he turns back he is shivering again; he pulls his swag more tightly about himself. 'I could do without the side effects.'

The stink of vomit in the air. I push myself to my feet to search for the camp shovel. As I move towards the Toyota, Lucy's voice drops to a whisper and I must strain to hear what is clearly not intended for my ears.

'What about love? Can we do without love?'

I stand frozen. What is she telling him?

'You getting sentimental on me, Frau Doktor?'

Silence. They are in their own small world, a cabin for two. I take a slow step backwards, then another.

'Aren't we allowed to be sentimental?' she is asking.

'Not if it's a fake orgasm.'

'What do you mean?'

'Not if the emotion is out of proportion to the cause.'

'You're dying,' she says more loudly, exasperated. 'What emotion could possibly be out of proportion to that?' She turns, startled by her own outburst, to catch me watching from the shadows.

She keeps her face averted as I fold the vomit into the sand, although more to hide her tears than to avoid the smell. By the time I have finished, the morphine has also done its work and Felix is asleep.

'I should never have agreed to this trip,' she says.

I spill a little billy-water over my hands, dry them against the glowing coals. 'It's too late for regrets. Let's just do the best we can.'

'He's so difficult.'

'He's fucking impossible,' I say, and she gives a tear-muffled laugh.

'What are we *doing* here, Marty? I don't know how we got here. I think back and each step seems logical. Necessary. Except the end point.'

I kneel behind her, wrap my arms about her; she nestles back into me. 'It won't be much longer.'

'I'm sorry, Marty.' Her body trembles slightly, a muffled sob.

Her late-model swag is larger than my antique roll; we remove our boots and jeans and crawl into it together, lying face to face. T-shirts and underclothes between us still; we remove them awkwardly and toss them out onto the sand, less for any sexual purpose than to lie together more closely, to amplify body warmth, to breathe sleep into each other.

Some of us can't do without love, I want to tell her. Instead I close my eyes and let the to-and-fro of her warm breath gently stroke my face.

How long do we sleep? A faint, rhythmic clattering rouses us, a knocking at some dream-door. Clapsticks? Wrong side of the fire. Lucy props herself on an elbow and shines a pencil-torch in Felix's direction. He is still asleep but trembling violently, his teeth chattering. She eases out of the swag and kneels at his side, naked in the freezing night air.

'I need to sleep with Felix.'

What can I say? Over my dead body? Over *his*?

'It's the only way to keep him warm, Marty.'

'If you must, you must.'

She glares at me through narrowed eyes. Unfamiliar eyes, utterly disconcerting. 'You just can't resist, can you?'

'What do you mean?'

A hissed whisper: 'You can't help yourself. You never miss an opportunity to make me feel guilty.'

'It's not easy for me, Lucy.'

'You think it's easy for *me*? You're as bad as he is. Worse. He has an excuse for acting like a two-year-old!'

I lie stunned, as silent as a two-year-old rebuked for the first time. Eventually: 'I'll build the fire up.'

I pull on T-shirt and jeans, push my feet into unlaced boots, and clump out into the scrub to gather wood. When I return she has unzipped Felix's swag and dragged her own next to it. Pungent ammonia fills my nostrils; he has wet himself. As I refuel the fire she slips off his jeans, balls them into a makeshift towel and rubs his groin dry.

'Help me, Marty.'

I fetch paper towels from the Toyota, warm water from the billy, and sponge his groin and thighs. I leave his penis till last, a limp split-sausage, incapable of harm. Together we log-roll him from his sodden swag onto the downy lining of hers, still warm from our two bodies. Two-dog warm. I fold over the canvas cover and zip it shut, valise-fashion. His teeth chatter on but he fails to wake, even as Lucy eases herself in next to him, naked.

I carry his swag to the Toyota and drape it, fleece out, across the roof-rack to dry. More spoor for the feather-footed.

Lucy's voice behind me, murmuring in his ear. Can he hear her words? I think, trivially, He will wake and think himself dead already, gone to heaven. Except that he has been to this particular heaven already, and more times than I want to think about. A surge of two-year-old feelings again, jealous id-feelings, which even now, at this end-stage, have the power to consume me.

Consume me, and shame me.

My own swag waits, as cold and empty as the desert floor. I drag it to the far side of the fire, the sunset side, Ngarlpa side, where the old men lie bundled in their rough blanket-rolls.

Boobook, boobook, far-off and faint, amplified by the vast sounding-board of the desert floor. *Boobook, boobook*, plaintively hopeful, as if the callers are wanting to hear again from our tribe of strange, hilarious owls.

A mutter from Doctor Jerry. 'Yampirriwanu.'

Bedford chuckles his deep, well-smoked chuckle. 'He say you in the bachelor's camp now, Mardin.'

How long have they been lying awake, watching and listening? The owl is silent again, Felix's teeth have at last ceased their chatter. Not even the snore of a bachelor disturbs the quiet. Do I imagine the muffled gasp that carries from the married man's camp across the fire – the sound of Lucy's pleasure that I know only too well? Obsessive jealousy? Hallucinations expanding to fill the available silence. Felix is beyond sexual activity, surely. Surely! Although the textbooks do talk of the last, fierce priapism of the dying, their desperate clutching at a sensual world that is about to be lost forever.

'Maybe Pillage bust him prick, Mardin,' Bedford whispers, returning from a piss, and in my numbed, obsessive state I cannot tell whether this is meant as joke or consolation, or – better still – a curse.

22

'Rain-snake bin over this country, Mardin.'

Midday, several hours further into the flat, trackless wilderness. No standing water can be seen, but the ochre-reds and whites of the desert's surface are patching over now with various greens, a thinly smeared jam of grasses and low buckbush among the mulga and feathertop spinifex.

Feather-topped cirrus cloud, also, high to the north-west; a steady breeze from that quarter.

'More rain coming?' I say.

'Fur cloud, Mardin. No rain in him.'

Felix sits wedged in his corner of the cabin, sleeping on and off. He has not eaten breakfast, but sucks occasionally at a straw in a bottle of water. His skin is stretched even tighter on his gaunt bones, his colour is sallow-yellow. He is dying, beyond question, but no longer in pain. Lucy has taped a butterfly needle beneath the skin of his chest; from time to time she squeezes in a little morphine via a syringe. The ammonia smell of urine is omnipresent; twice she has replaced the pad wedged inside the front of his jeans, but the powerful pungency remains.

'Should we stop and sponge him?'

'Not while he's sleeping.'

Doctor Jerry sits quietly in the front as we jolt along, studying the distant scrub-lines, subtly aiming his chin from time to time to indicate a change in direction to Bedford. No reason or purpose in this to my untrained eye. The desert is greener, but to me, still, it is a featureless green. The flat horizon lacks landmarks. Is he still following the birds? Birds everywhere now: zebra finches, spinifex birds, grey-headed honeyeaters. That little tonsil-bird, jintipirri, twitching its flick-knife tail. No budgerigars sighted since yesterday, but pairs and quartets of larger parrots nose the grass for seeds. Pink-dusted galahs, white corellas. And always, every few kilometres, a lone hawk or wedgetail hanging in the blue, a single brown flag flying over its tribal territory.

We grind on. More flowering shrubs, more birds. More names, English, Latin, desert-Latin. And more lizards: a pair of young, snake-thin goannas scatter away across a salt-lick at our noisy approach. Alert, bright-gilled dragons watch from vantage rocks, fat blue-tongues warm their bellies on the hot claypans. No stopping to hunt for reptile meat today; the old men are intent on a larger purpose.

'Green grass country,' Bedford mutters. And a variant: 'Green grass time. Wajirrkinyi.' He speaks the phrase less for us than as a chant to himself, a reminder of the pleasure of this time of year, its fertilities. It might even be the first line of another song, a ceremony.

Lucy, concerned as always for Felix: 'Can we stop for lunch soon, Bedford?'

'Nearly there, Sister. By and by.'

Flood-out country. Dry, crazy-paved waterways; smooth clay-pans and sand beds spreading out among thick quilts of scrub. Khaki-leafed mulga, bonsai ti-tree claws, groundcover the colour of burnt sugar. More birds: diamond doves, black-faced woodswallows. *Geopelia cuneata. Artamus cinereus.* We might be a ship, at last nearing shore among birds. Doctor Jerry is singing again, more clearly and forcefully, snatches of the Ngatijirri Jukurrpa, whole phrases now recognisable to me, made mem-orable by rhythm and repetition. Bedford sings with him, sitting hunched forward over the steering wheel, peering out through the dusty windscreen.

A sense of extra anticipation in the front seat; a sudden change in direction. We jolt on towards a dense stand of ghost gums, the first I have seen for days, until the Toyota can push no further through the rising scrub. The old man now as alert as I have seen him, his face thrust through the side window. No sign of joy on that dense, compacted face, but his wide nostrils flare as if he can smell his childhood home.

'Ngawa,' he orders, and the Toyota immediately brakes.

'This place, Mardin,' Bedford announces. 'The little green bird go in here. That hole in the ground.'

Our dust trail overtakes us, envelopes us and keeps moving,

travelling on without us to the south. The old men are already out of the Toyota and pushing through the scrub towards the trees. I climb down and find myself in a rough desert garden, of sorts. Small, yellow-flowered wattles – dead finish – sit among the larger trees. Tiny pink desert roses and yellow burr-daisies cover the ground, and even the tumbleweed – mulla-mulla? – is covered with a fine white floral embroidery.

Felix, surprisingly, accepts my help down. Unsteady on his feet, too weak to weight-bear, he nevertheless insists on immediately following the old men into the scrub. Lucy and I each take an arm around our necks.

'Watch out for snake,' Bedford calls back. 'That cheeky snake, panungkurla. This his father country too. His camp along this hole, eh?'

Which hole? Where? I can see no hole. We push on through the knee-high grass towards the smooth, white-skinned trees. There must be water, given the size of the ghost gums. Expecting some sort of modest creek-soak or rockhole, I am stunned as we step through the line of trees and the ground abruptly vanishes. I step back; a gaping hole has opened almost at our feet, a wide doorway down into the earth, perhaps twenty metres across and almost as deep. A sinkhole, certainly, although its steep sides are not the limestone I might have expected, but red sandstone. Those eroded walls and the fringe of surrounding bush are splashed with a thick whitewash of birdshit. The far wall has collapsed inwards, taking with it a small gum that now lies upside down on its own canopy, half submerged in a pond of water below. The depth of the pond – an opaque, dirty milk – is impossible to guess. Rainwater or seepage? I cannot tell.

'Billycan full of soup, eh Mardin?'

Meat soup. Carrion soup. Bedford's words echo inside the vast sandstone cistern and provoke a flurry of movement and rustling: scavenger lizards, perhaps the odd cheeky snake. Clouds of midges swirl in the air, criss-crossed by the shuttle of iridescent dragonflies. The breeze at our backs falters momentarily and the stink rises out of the cistern with full force – a dog's breath, a carnivore's breath, feral and thickly meaty. *Halitus ditis*, the breath of hell.

'Big daddy kangaroo jump in for drink,' Bedford says. 'Can't jump out.'

The rotted hide of a kangaroo lies shrink-wrapped around the cage of its own bones on the steep slope below; countless smaller bones and feathers litter the edges of the pool and the half-submerged rocks. The legendary oasis of the budgerigar? The sinkhole is an oasis of kinds – a focus of survival – but it is mostly a deathtrap.

Something rustles in the grass behind us. I tug Felix to one side; that cheeky snake cannot be too far away.

Propped on my arm, he stares impassively down into the filthy broth. '*Anus mundi*,' he mutters, and laughs weakly. And laughs again, and the feeble laugh strengthens into a cough, a paroxysm that bends him double.

Staring into the cesspit I wonder if he has planned this all along, as a last black joke. We have travelled as far from the high paradise of the Adelaide Hills as it is possible to travel. To the mouth of hell? One of the mouths of hell. One of the arseholes of the world. Are human bones also scattered down there? The rankness fills my nostrils, but is more stale than unpleasant. Less brimstone than blood and bone. And where are the birds? Another line from Virgil on the tip of my tongue: Book VI, Aeneas entering Avernus, the birdless place, the mouth of hell, its halitosis so foul no bird can fly above it.

'Don't stand so close to the edge,' Lucy cautions.

Felix can no longer stand anywhere. Exhausted as much by his coughing as by the short walk, he sinks to his knees and lies immediately on his side in the grass, much as I have seen the old doctor do. But still grinning faintly, as if at some tremendous joke.

'Bit of an anticlimax, eh Prof?'

'I didn't expect the Hanging Gardens of Babylon.'

Doctor Jerry seems to have expected more; he makes no move to sit. Is he disappointed? I still cannot read his face, those features crowded together upon it as if from more than one face, more than one lifetime.

'Make camp by that Toyota, eh? Too much fly this side.' He sniffs at the air, but clinically, without distaste. 'Bad air. Make Pillage sick.'

The insects are pestilent, midges and mites swarming above and frantic ants beneath. Felix slips one arm over my shoulders, one over Lucy's, and allows us to raise him again to his feet.

'We'll come back at nightfall,' he says.

How light he is, a cage of bones and skin himself, half rotted away inside. The feral rankness of the cesspit has faded behind us; now there is a different stink. The effort of walking has squeezed a little liquid shit from him, soiling his jeans. I light a fire and fill the billy as Lucy tugs off his clothes. We change his pad, sponge his groin and thighs and shrunken scrotum.

An odd thought: we might be changing a child's nappy, our child, our only child.

Lucy fits a condom urine-collector to his penis, clinically. The limp slug of his cock, surprisingly small, smaller than I remember it at fifteen, can surely not be the larger-than-life instrument I imagined in a jealous trance the night before, and countless other nights before that.

Sponged, dressed in clean, dry clothes, fed a little thickly sugared tea, Felix seems to gain in strength, although he is breathing with difficulty again.

'You need another pleural tap,' Lucy says.

'No more taps.' His voice might be weak but his words are emphatic.

'Then some more morphine at least.'

'Business before pleasure,' he whispers, but even this starts him coughing again. 'About the funeral . . . arrangements,' he says, recovering. 'The old men are . . . in charge. But afterwards they'll want to . . . hang about. Sorry business lasts . . . for days, but you . . . might want to talk them . . . out of it. Things will get . . . a bit, ah, biodegradable.'

On cue, the parched croaking of a crow. Two short syllables, *ka*, *ka*, and the long dying fall of a third. *Kaaaa*. One bird, at least, survives in the birdless place.

'I believe they start with the eyeballs.'

His words as sharp and jabbing as a crow-beak themselves. Lucy flinches and screws her eyes shut, as if this might also keep out his words. There is still pleasure to be had from talking tough, it seems, or at least a little shock value.

'You really want to go through with that?'

'When in Rome.'

Ka, again from the trees. *Kaaaa*.

'Quoth the raven. You speak Crow, Herr Professor? What's he saying?'

A desire to strike back at him, or at least to match his hard talk with my own, grows in me. 'Big feast tomorrow, boys.'

A gratified laugh. He looks down at his shrunken body. 'More an appetiser, I think.'

Lucy is on her feet. 'Can we not talk about this?' She walks away towards the Toyota, her face averted from us. I rise immediately, regretting my words, wanting to follow.

'Leave her be,' Felix wheezes. 'She can take it. She's not made of . . . fucking china.'

'We're *all* made of china.'

'You make . . . a religion . . . of her. Give her . . . some room to breathe.' The words are squeezed out between his own laboured breaths. His eyes find mine; amusement still lurks behind the pain and gasping respirations.

'Besides, I wanted to . . . talk to you . . . alone.'

'Then you'll have to wait your turn.'

I walk away. She is lying curled on the back seat of the Toyota, eyes closed. She might be asleep, but I know otherwise. The doors are locked. I tap on the window; she opens her eyes and looks at me through the glass.

'You okay?'

'Just needed a break.'

'You sure?'

'I'm fine. You stay with Felix.'

She closes her eyes again, dismissing me. Brief psychotherapy on my part, outcome uncertain; I walk reluctantly back to the campfire. Another crow, more distant, answers the first. Come and get it?

'Kaarnka, they call him . . . out here.' Felix caws the word, crow-fashion. '*Ka-arn-ka-a.*' He pauses, regains his breath. 'Wouldn't mind . . . coming back . . . as a crow. Honest sort . . . of life. Always plenty . . . to eat. And nothing much . . . wants to eat you.'

The shade of the coolibah has moved, his face is now in full sun. He is half-crow already, I think. Crow's-feet walking all over the gaunt face, that sharp tongue jab-jabbing. I drag his swag sideways, and him with it, following the movement of the shade. I turn up his oxygen feed again, from four litres to six. How many cylinders left?

His lips are dry, he is panting a little. The tortoise of pity ventures out of its shell. 'You want some water?'

'A better . . . idea,' he says, and props himself on an elbow and gropes in his canvas carry-bag. He pulls out an unopened bottle of Scotch. Glenfiddich, triple malt. 'While the cat's . . . away,' he says.

Can he mean Lucy? He reads my mind, grins crookedly. 'The old doctor. It would have . . . gone out . . . the window. He hates . . . the stuff. Wrecks the . . . communities.'

'Should *you* be drinking it? With your liver?'

'I'm sure I'll regret it . . . for the rest . . . of my life.'

He passes me the bottle, too weak to open it himself, too breathless even to laugh at his own joke. I spill a few thick thumbs of whisky into two enamel mugs. The slight effort of propping himself up has been too much; he falls back again. I cradle his head in my hand and tilt the mug to his lips; perhaps he manages to swallow a few drops.

'Good medicine for sick,' I say, and he smiles faintly.

'Would a . . . cigarette be . . . pushing my luck?'

He turns his head to watch as I twiddle the paper and tobacco together, pained amusement overlaying genuine pain. But I am back in practice now, crafting a cylinder of fine symmetry. I turn off the oxygen, light the cigarette, jam it between his lips and roll another for myself.

'It's probably time for . . . the big deathbed . . . reconciliation scene,' he says, exhaling. 'But I'm afraid . . . I've shat myself again.'

'I'll clean you up.'

In fact there is minimal cleaning to be done – the changing of the pad, the wiping of the soiled parts with a wet cloth. Strong whisky fumes in my nose and throat help. I take another sip before carrying away the refuse for burial. A crow wheezes out its call again, some distance away. Nearer at hand, grass wrens in the bushes. *Swe-et, swe-et.*

And sour, I mutter as I dig. And sour.

He is on his back again when I return, smoking, but clearly needing the oxygen. 'So where . . . were we?' he pants.

'Deathbed reconciliations.'

He takes another pull at the cigarette, but for once the smoke seems less medicinal than irritant, making things worse. A coughing fit nearly chokes him. I pluck the cigarette from his fingers, toss it away, and reconnect the oxygen.

Some minutes pass before he is able to speak again, but his words, barely audible, are as abrupt and shocking as the choking fit. 'I'm leaving you . . . the farm.'

What to make of this? Another joke? I search his face for clues. 'I'm sorry?'

'You heard . . . me.'

I heard, but I need thinking time, processing time. 'I couldn't possibly accept.'

'You don't have . . . a choice. The will is set . . . in concrete. John Fisk has . . . the paperwork.'

A swirl of confused thoughts in my head. 'Is this some sort of pay-off?'

'Payback? I hadn't thought . . . of that.' The thought seems to amuse him. 'No, it just seems . . . obvious. It's always meant more . . . to you than to me.'

I am speechless.

'Someone needs . . . to look after it, Japaljarri. That's your . . . spirit country, longa there.' His wheezy chuckle ends in another fit of coughing. 'Your dirt.'

'You expect us to live up there?'

The faintest of smiles. 'Not necessarily . . . both of you.'

Anger, never far from the surface of late, flares instantly inside me, erupts through my mouth. 'I don't want it, Felix. I don't want *any*thing from you. Anything that makes me remember you.'

Invigorated a little by the oxygen, he musters enough energy to prop himself on an elbow again and pour another shot of whisky. 'Come on, Marty. Let's not spoil . . . these last few precious moments . . . together.' A wry smile, and he raises his mug. 'To deathbed . . . reconciliations.'

I am still seething. 'You're asking my forgiveness?'

'I think we both . . . need to do . . . a little asking.'

'What do you mean?'

'I mean if Lucy . . . can't forgive you . . . you'll need a place . . . in the hills.'

His words stop my anger in its tracks. What can he mean? Lucy forgive *me*? For what? He peers up out of that drug-softened face, through drug-tightened pupils. Can he see anything through those pinpoints? *Swe-et*, *swe-et*, again, piercingly, from the near scrub, the wren offering words of calming advice, words of wise counsel. But I am not willing to let him off so lightly.

'I remember the first time I fell in love,' I say. 'I must have been all of seven or eight years old.'

303

'This was . . . last year?' His face has relaxed further, evidence of some extra leakage of narcotic or whisky into his bloodstream.

'I used to walk her home from school. I loved being with her. Near her. But I couldn't tell her. I didn't have the words. I used to *do* things instead.'

'You carried her bag?'

'I threw her bag over fences. Punched her on the arm, jerked her ponytail. Shoved her into hedges.'

'You must have . . . loved her . . . very much,' he says, and his own words silence him. He lies back, shading his eyes with a hand so emaciated that the sun must surely shine clear through it. 'Looks like . . . you've finally got me . . . on the couch . . . Herr Professor.'

If so, I am no longer sure I want him there. For months I have sought to unmask him, to extract some sort of straight talk from his bent mouth, but here, now, such talk might be as painful for me to hear as it is for him to utter.

'You want the truth?' he asks. 'Okay. One more time . . . with feeling.' He takes another fortifying sip of his Scotch, then several catch-up breaths. 'I couldn't get her . . . out of my head. From that first day . . . you brought her to the farm. You didn't help. Parading her around . . . like some trophy. Look at me! Look what I've got!'

'I just wanted you to like her.'

Silence. No sound but the soft snake-hiss of oxygen, the regular gasp and wheeze of his lungs.

'I liked her . . . very much.' The words are barely audible. He averts his face. A jintipirri dances on a nearby rock, twitching its tonsil-tail. 'I thought I had it . . . all sorted out. I was going to look Death . . . in the eye . . . all the way down. Stare back and say . . .' The shallow bellows of his lungs working overtime. 'Fuck you.' His rib cage in, out, in, out. 'Death was a pushover . . . compared to Lucy. In the end I thought, The only way . . . to get her out of my head . . . is to have her. Then I can get back to the real game.' A short, self-mocking laugh. 'Another . . . good idea at the time.'

He lifts his mug of whisky. 'To forgiveness, Prof?'

A lump grows in my throat. He mistakes my inability to speak for reluctance.

'To forgetfulness, then – the poor man's forgiveness.'

Chipped enamel clunks against chipped enamel, but he can barely sacrifice the breath space to allow a sip.

'You really need another tap,' I say.

He ignores me. 'One other thing. The Toyota goes . . . to Bedford.'

'Does he know?'

'Better not tell him . . . before you get back . . . to civilisation. Otherwise you might . . . be walking.' A splutter of laughter; he can still manage to amuse himself. 'There's a lot of work to be done out here. They'll need to bring some young men out. Fix the country up. Clean the hole.'

'Should I be helping?'

'Not during sorry business.' A cough. 'I'd like to talk . . . to Lucy now.'

'You *need* a pleural tap.'

He waves me away. 'Later.'

I wait, but he offers no further eye contact. I push myself reluctantly to my feet, walk to the Toyota and knock again on the window.

'Your shift.'

I reach in for the binoculars and Warlpiri dictionary and set out for the sinkhole, seeking now-familiar distractions. Noon-time, snake-time, all the lights on in the larger world and the thermostat turned high. Sunday? Possibly. The thickly grassed understorey of the scrub rustles here and there, but I tread carelessly on.

I emerge at the crumbling northern edge of the crater. On the far side the two old men are standing under a gum sapling, hats tilted back, staring intently upwards. Bedford has one hand on the slender white trunk as if to shake it; his other grasps his hatchet, reversed, club-fashion. The sapling sways, a taut bow bent by the weight of the goanna that clings precariously to its topmost reach.

More lizard meat for dinner? Belly fat for medicine?

I lift my binoculars to my eyes, willing to be entertained by a little bush theatre. The lizard is more than a metre long, its belly thick as a man's arm, its tail a thinning whip wrapped around a whipstock branch. I watch for some minutes, but the hunters seem in no hurry to dislodge their dinner. Which is what? Gould's monitor? Perentie? I open the dictionary and close it almost immediately. There seem so many desert words for lizards that each might have its own given name, a pet name. Native bees sizzle about me in the scrub; heavier things rustle in the undergrowth. Panungkurla in the grass? A sense of weird disembodiment overcomes me, a lightness of the head just this side of giddiness. My best friend is dying in the dust a spear's throw away, my wife is comforting him. There is not a hospital within five hundred kilometres, or a hospice within a thousand. We are running short of oxygen, but not of cigarettes. The oasis is a sink-hole of carrion, a stinking oubliette, a doorway into hell. Ngarlpa, the place of the budgerigar; or Avernus, the birdless place? Head-spinning puzzlements, more of which follow. How did we come to be here? What are we *doing* here? I have no answer, but like Lucy, I know that each step of the journey, each footfall of our descent, has been separately questioned, and found acceptable. A series of small, good ideas at the time? Good enough ideas. *Noctet atque dies patet atri ianua Ditis.* Night and day the dark door of hell stands open. But the mind can only take so much of hell.

The slight pressure of the strap of my binoculars on my neck reminds me of another purpose, tugs me back like a familiar, friendly arm. Settled between bushes a few feet from the northern lip of the crater, I find myself in a natural hide. Crows wheeze, wrens chirrup – how birdless can the place be?

Ka-ka-kaaaa.

Kaarnka. Is it the Australian crow or the larger raven? *Corvus orru* or *Corvus coronoides*? I lift the binoculars again to my eyes, needing to check the colouring. Trivial pursuits? Even death, last of the non-trivial pursuits, has lost a little of its substance as I settle down on my belly to watch and wait.

And almost instantly fall asleep.

23

Defence mechanisms have become coping styles in the new, softer *DSM*-speak. *Automatic psychological processes that protect the individual against anxiety or from the awareness of internal or external dangers . . .*

Soft snake-hiss in my ear. Panungkurla? Too smooth, too steady. Where am I? Cool air on my skin, eucalyptus smoke sharp in my nostrils. Bird twitter. The world begins to reassemble itself. I still seem to be lying in my grass hide, but my head now finds itself, mysteriously, on a pillow. I open my eyes.

'Back from . . . the dead . . . Herr Professor?'

Felix's whisper, close at hand. How long have I slept? The sun has gone but the sky is still bright enough to force a squint. Felix lies on his swag within arm's reach, his head in Lucy's lap. His chest rises with each intake of breath, he is sucking deeply for air – but he seems oddly calm, unpanicked by his breathlessness. Narcotic calm?

I prop myself upright. 'How did you get here?'

'With . . . difficulty.'

More of the strange world reaches me. A small fire smoking at the edge of the big sandstone crater, a blackened saucepan and billy to one side.

'We kept you some food,' Lucy says.

'Lizard meat?'

'None left. The last of the steaks. And some yams the doctor brought. Felix couldn't stomach them.'

The yams are charred and cold and inedible, the steak

charred and cold and delicious. I have woken famished and eat hungrily, half turned away from Felix, trying not to flaunt my appetite. The rumble of Doctor Jerry's singing and the sharp strike of clapsticks carries to me. The two old men are sitting before another small fire, a stone's throw to the right, halfway around the lip of the great hole. The sun has set but everything is more sharply defined, even, shadowless in the light.

'I thought the old men didn't want to camp near the waterhole.'

'Bedford says the budgerigars are going to come in,' Lucy says.

'Won't the fires keep them away?'

'They have to drink.'

Even from the mouth of Avernus. The breeze has dropped, but the stale breath of the hole, so pungent at high noon, reaches us only faintly through the colder, denser air of evening. Or else we have grown used to it. More pungent is the smell of burning eucalypt leaves – a sharp, aromatic sting. Or is that insect repellant? Reading my mind, Lucy passes a small roll-stick across.

'Should we join the old men?'

'I think I'm stuck . . . here.' Another faint twist of the lips. 'For the . . . duration.'

Gallows humour. Coping style 'high adaptive level', in *DSM-IV* nomenclature. The Glenfiddich bottle, almost empty, sits to one side. Low adaptive level, and getting lower. Lucy tilts a mug to his lips but only water dribbles down his chin. A dry tongue-tip darts out, lizard-like, to lick at his lips.

'Should we run in some saline?' I suggest.

A dismissive wave of a bony hand. 'Let's not . . . prolong the . . . agony.'

My eyes meet Lucy's. She wears no makeup, but there is no emotion to be seen in her unmasked face, only a sun-reddened weariness.

The screech of parrots provides a welcome distraction. A flock of white corellas, perhaps a dozen strong, flaps overhead. As if disorientated by the twin campfires, the birds circle several times before descending into the great mouth.

'Latin . . . name . . . Prof?' Teasing all the way to the grave.

'*Cacatua sanguinea.*'

The cheerful cockatoo. The hopeful cockatoo. The birds settle hopefully enough on the branches of the inverted gum, glowing like soft lamps in the deepening shadows of the hole. In twos and threes those soft-wattage lamps drop to the water's edge to drink, then rise again.

More screeching from above, harsher, more penetrating. An answering din erupts upwards from the sinkhole. Half a dozen Major Mitchells are now descending; the alarm of the corellas is amplified deafeningly, resonant, inside the wide echo chamber.

'Better . . . put . . . a . . . stone . . . on . . . to . . . boil.' Single words gasped between breaths, the shards of a last joke.

Harried by their larger cousins, the corellas flee upwards and away. Pinkish fruit clustered on the branches now, squabbling among themselves until, with the last light nearly gone, they also flap, screeching, up out of the mouth of the hole and vanish into the twilight.

Still no sign of the ngatijirri. The percussive *clap-clap* of Bedford's sticks begins to bounce about the walls of the crater. No danger now of scaring away that little green bird. With night upon us the budgerigars are surely tucked safely in tree-holes all across the desert. In cosy, feather-lined bird swags. The doctor is singing more loudly, long flowing lines which begin high and descend in pitch to a repetitive monotone, not unlike a race-caller's chant, before rising again for the next variation.

Felix's mouth is open, the mouth of a beached fish gasping for air, but his eyes have closed, as if lulled by the music. Drugged disconnections: peaceful eyes, tortured mouth, labouring chest, as if the morphine is a kind of guillotine, separating mind and body. Lucy's eyes have also closed, her head nodding forward as she sits cradling his own on her lap.

Abruptly the doctor's singing stops; Lucy wakes with a jerk, as if startled by the silence.

'You should sleep, Luce.'

'How can I?'

'You'll be more help to him if you sleep. Please. I'm fresh – I'll take the first shift.'

She eases his head from her lap and slips my pillow beneath it. 'Wake me at midnight,' she says. Then, as an afterthought, avoiding my eyes, 'Or before. If . . .'

'Of course.'

She slides into her swag, fully clothed. 'You'll need to keep the morphine topped up. And he'll need another oxygen cylinder in half an hour or so.'

'I can manage.'

For a time there is nothing to manage but the fire. Silence all about, a deepening coldness as the stored warmth of day radiates from the earth into the cloudless, uninsulated sky. The campfire on the far side of the hole has been doused, there is no sign now of the old men in the darkness. I presume they are sleeping back at the Toyota.

Have I nodded off myself when the hiss of oxygen begins to die? Felix's gasping alerts me, a new level of desperation. I unscrew the valve from the slender cylinder and attach it to another – the last in the box. Soon that plastic snake beneath his nose begins hissing again, his gasps reduce to wheezes. I check his plastic urine bag, holding it against the glow of the fire. The scant liquid inside is as thickly opaque as orange marmalade. Is his fluid intake adequate? Half-forgotten textbook definitions crowd back into my head. Anuria, oliguria, acute renal failure. I hold the chipped mug to his lips and tilt; water spills uselessly down his chin. He is beyond drinking now. I search Lucy's bag of tricks by torchlight, locate some cotton-buds and glycerine and brush a little of the oily fluid over his parched tongue and the dry lining of his mouth. Does he feel this? Does he feel anything? At least these simple nursing routines give me something to do, offer as much comfort to the living as to the dying.

Time passes. I draw up a syringe of morphine but leave it capped. He seems in no pain. Beyond pain, perhaps. Floating on his bed of natural opiates. He shivers a little, I rearrange his covering. A faint whiff of whisky on his breath. A line from Virgil:

Entombed in sleep and wine. I check the incontinence pad between his thighs and am almost disappointed to find it unsoiled. Wiping his arse – changing his nappy – would keep me occupied, even if he is beyond noticing.

Years have passed since I last watched someone die. Its stages, its Stations of the Cross – its timetable – have become unfamiliar. Has he passed the point of no return? Will he regain consciousness?

'Felix.'

No answer. I agitate his shoulder gently. 'Felix, can you hear me?' I pinch a fold of loose cheek-skin, sharply, between thumb-nail and fingernail. Still no response. What next? Eyeball pressure? Testicle squeeze? The degrees of pain response, the depth-of-coma measurements have also become unfamiliar.

I take his index finger and pinch the nail-bed, hard. This time, a faint moan of complaint. I feel a sudden urge to squeeze harder, to hurt him. Instantly the urge becomes something else, a hair-triggered avalanche of stored rage that tumbles uncontrollably through me, an overwhelming need to do him terrible harm.

I drop his bird-claw and roll away, trembling. For an instant, even if no more than a millisecond, I have wanted to kill him. Worse – I have known that I am capable of killing him.

I lie on my back, keeping safely out of reach. My reach, his safety. Cold sweat on my brow, trembling in my limbs. As quickly as it has come, the rush of murderous rage recedes, as if it were something that came from elsewhere, forced upon me and then taken away.

But if so, taken where? I find it difficult to accept this feeling as mine, or even as my share of some hard-wired male id. Psychiatrist, heal thyself? Watching the stars shiver in the deep darkness above, I tell myself this wave of alien rage might just as well have come from outer space. Low adaptive coping?

The hiss of oxygen nearby, the rasp of Felix's breath. Sharp, gulping intakes; slow, struggling exhalations, as if against great resistance. And a now familiar sound, the chattering of his teeth.

I rise and follow my torchbeam back through the scrub to the Toyota. Two blanket bundles lie near a faint glow of coals; two old men snoring, oblivious to the feather-footed murderer in their midst. I quietly tug open the rear door; the interior light flicks on. Shivering myself, I pull on a thick fleece jacket. I take two blankets, retrace my steps to the sinkhole and shake them out over Felix and Lucy's swags, tablecloth-fashion. I am too restless to sit. The night is cold, a penetrating bone-cold; I am still shivering despite my jacket. I head back into the scrub and gather an armful of firewood by torchlight. Nothing feather-footed about this, trampling through the undergrowth, tearing limbs from mulga and ti-tree bushes.

I stoke up the fire, slide the blackened billy in among the flames, then sit, finally, with my face to the warmth. I empty the last of the Glenfiddich into a mug, toss it down. Hugely warming, helpfully calming. Felix's tobacco pouch lies to one side of his swag; I roll and light a cigarette, suck down the fragrant, itchy smoke, its mix of nicotine and tar so soothing and scouring at the same time.

Felix: open-mouthed; breath see-sawing in, out; utterly help-less. Utterly – a slight kick of adrenaline at the thought – in my power. I brush another capful of glycerine around his chapped lips and the dry cave of his mouth, but the work seems pointless. A sudden, weird idea. I fill my lungs with smoke and kneel and bend my mouth close to his, exhale exactly as he inhales. Then take another deep suck at my cigarette and repeat the process. The notion would amuse him, I think, were he not unrousable. A last cigarette, by proxy. Passive smoking, mouth to mouth. Then I remember the oxygen and, alarmed, fling the lighted butt out into the sinkhole, a bright ember glowing, glowing, gone.

I could extinguish his life as easily. In the space of seconds. Before Lucy wakes. Before – important, this – he need bother her again. The necessary materials are at hand, packed in her doctor's bag.

And the thought erupts, fully formed, for the first time. Not just the desire to help Felix on his way, but the intent, premedi-tated. If oddly passionless, for I am too exhausted for passion. And in the absence of passion, debate becomes possible. Justifications crowd my mind. He is beyond help anyway. His suffering has gone on long enough. *She* is suffering . . .

More steps in the descent? I search through Lucy's bag for the box of morphine ampoules. I spread a towel on the sand at Felix's side and lay out my tools: large-volume syringe, tourni-quet, alcohol swab. Spear-tip.

I stare at them. I rearrange them more neatly.

All the while thinking. How merciful if he died in his sleep.

Even better, if he died in Lucy's sleep, if she didn't have to witness his last agony. Compassionate thoughts? Of a kind, but an easy compassion; an oily, slippery substance that sits on the surface of things, stilling the turbulence beneath.

I roll away out of reach again, keeping at a safe distance from that towel and its array of death-tools, lest it tempt me too easily. The eastern sky is beginning to lighten, a horizontal band of cold whiteness. Dew like a shower of tears on the ground all about, reflecting the first pale light.

Felix's breathing is noisier now, wet and gurgling, as if his lungs are also coated with dew, or have answered the moisture of the morning by producing their own. But even as he gasps desperately for each breath, his face has relaxed further into a mild, fixed smile, a smile more passive than active, a last muscular exhalation as the brain releases its hold. I lie on my side watching him. What is going on in there? Is it happening as he predicted? The best kept till last? Death coming like a rush of narcotic? The brain enjoying its own dissolution as its cells place their last margin-calls, the oxygen deficit mounts, and the mind shrinks back on itself, sacrificing body for brain, then outer brain for inner, until only a narrow tunnel of consciousness remains, lit at one end by the incandescent firing of its own dying vision cells.

The thought of so much bliss in there enrages me. What about Lucy? I want to shout at him. What about those left behind? What about *me*? My exhaustion is forgotten as I snap the neck of the first ampoule and draw up the viscous drug. And snap open the second ampoule, and the third. Martin-lore fails me as I snap the last few phials – what is the lethal dose of morphine?

Lucy turns in her sleep, moans softly. Panic: she might wake at any moment. I toss the emptied glass phials and their snapped caps far out into the sinkhole, slip the tourniquet about Felix's arm and tighten the toggle, gently. Do I tell myself I am doing this out of mercy? I tell myself nothing, but take particular care not to pinch his skin with the tourniquet. I raise a thick vein in the crook of his elbow and slip a needle into the vein. A small kickback of blood unravels in the morphine solution; the needle-tip is positioned.

'Martin?'

A gurgled question, barely audible; a head half raised, eyes groping to find me.

'Morphine for the pain,' I tell him.

The eyes find mine, hold them in a long moment of scrutiny. 'No pain.' A slight smile, as he labours for breath. 'Et tu?'

The words might as well have stabbed me in turn; tears start instantly into my eyes. 'Too much pain,' I say.

'Then . . . you must . . . relieve it.' And his head falls back and his eyes close again, and his breathing labours on.

Inevitable that I have come to this? The events of the last months seem suddenly focused on this place, this time, this exact moment of decision, as if by some great burning lens. Of course I am here. I feel as if I have always been here, been trapped here. I stare down at his arm through a blur of tears, at the needle taped in place, the syringe loaded and cocked. Inevitable, certainly, what must follow, yet for the moment my

317

own arm refuses to act. How lengthy that arm – my arm – seems, how far away its hand, as if the distance is too great for volition to travel, its bone and gristle too thick an impediment between thought and deed.

Thought has been left far behind by the time that long arm stirs and its fingers reach out and ease the plunger down casually, necessarily, inevitably. Then turn off the hissing oxygen.

I lie next to my friend, waiting.

Somewhere, still unseen, the chirrup of early birds. Honey-eaters, scrub-wrens. That little tonsil-wagging bird. *Sweet pretty creature, jintipirri creature*. Time passes, measured out in gurgled, sucking respirations. The campfire on the far side of the sinkhole is alive again; the old men have returned, unnoticed, and are sitting silently, cross-legged – two dark, flame-reddened faces staring out across the mouth.

From which the stink is beginning to rise.

Felix's breathing stops. Several long seconds pass and I think, At last, enough, and at the same time, Not yet, breathe again, please. Please! As if confused himself, he breathes – just when I think there can be no coming back, a last reflex kicks in and he takes a long, shuddering suck at the air. And gurgles on.

Lucy's panicky voice in my ear, startling me: 'Why didn't you wake me?'

'There was no need.'

'But it's nearly morning.'

'Is it?'

She is kneeling at Felix's shoulder now, as if at the shoulder of a highway, checking road-kill. 'Felix. Can you hear me?' Turning to me. 'You've turned the oxygen off!'

'He didn't need it. I gave him a shot. He's been in no pain.'

No pain, but worsening respiratory distress. Each breath is watery, wet, congested; each gap between those shuddering inspirations longer.

'He needs sucking out, Marty.'

'With what?'

She twists on the oxygen valve to maximum. Paradoxically his breathing ceases again. She slips his head onto her lap and begins to murmur to him, her head bent close, her hair brushing his face. 'We're here, Felix. We love you . . .'

Dew of a kind on her cheeks also as the long seconds drag by. This time he has taken his last breath, surely – taken his last breath *again*. But again he rises from the dead to take another deep, spasmic gasp, his lungs surviving on their own muscle reflexes now, flapping in and out as feebly as a pair of headless chickens.

He wants to live, I think. Despite all that he has said, all that he has done, he wants desperately to live.

'Can't we do something, Felix? We *must* do something.'

But I have already done it. I move closer in, holding her as she cradles him.

'It won't be long, Felix,' she whispers.

A shout from the far side of the hole. The old men are on their feet, staring out towards the south-west. A dense, fast-moving cloud of what I at first take to be insects is wheeling and banking above the plain, silhouetted against the whitening sky. Locusts?

No, a flock of birds, although I have never seen birds in these numbers. A shoal of fish perhaps, turning this way and that in unison; a school of dense-packed flying fish, hundreds of thousands strong. Waterbirds? Their noise reaches us now, a faint tidal rustling, a sea sound, although we are more than a thousand kilometres from any sea. The cloud moves overhead at speed, high up, and is suddenly, brilliantly illuminated by the first rays of sunlight: a flying carpet of luminous greens and yellows.

Ngatijirri by the hundreds of thousands, perhaps by the million.

'Lucy.' I gesture with my chin. She glances up, briefly distracted, then turns back to Felix, rocking his head gently in her lap. 'Time to let go, Felix. Time to let go, my darling.'

But now he has let go, surely. Or perhaps not. Too much is happening for me to think straight. A second flock of birds can be seen wheeling in the sky to the west as the first cloud arrives overhead and begins descending. The din of their noise reaches us ahead of the birds, the white noise of countless beating wings, countless tiny, chattering voices. And the upturned ghost gum is alive again with leaves, a green canopy rustling in a breeze of its own making. The second flock descends, rimming the edge of the sinkhole, and now we are surrounded by birds, buried in birds. The steep cliff-sides shiver with budgerigars struggling for claw-hold; the surrounding shrubs and groundcover are alive with their quivering greenery. From the thickly clustered branches of the gum they fall continuously to the water to drink, then bounce into the air, to whatever perch can be reclaimed.

Lucy, disorientated by the size and suddenness of this visitation, glances agitatedly from Felix to the seething sinkhole and back. And Felix himself? Does he take any of this in? Do the drug-narrowed pupils of those staring eyes allow one last image to enter?

This image perhaps: the birds beginning to rise. Out of the mouth of Avernus, the birdless place, the cesspit of blood and bone, the little green birds are now rising. And rising and rising, an upflowing torrent, the breeze of their million beating wings stirring the coals of our fire to fresh life.

The peaceful birds, the joyous birds, ascending.

Is this improbable synchronicity – this sign – beyond Felix? He has taken no breath for some minutes now, and those minutes are surely too deep a hole for his headless lungs to flap up from.

And inside the head itself? Few clues on the outside. No sign of pain, certainly, and no sign of mockery – *Corrugator supercilii* has dropped its guard for the last time – but his expression is more calm than ecstatic. And the eyes, pupils pin-pointed, narcotic-tightened? In a rush of benevolence, the benevolence of the executioner, I wish his eyes a last gasp also, a last gulping inhalation of the extraordinary sight around us, the unending geyser of little green birds, the peaceful birds.

I have taken his life, but perhaps no more than a few hours of his allotted years; perhaps, I tell myself, no more than a few minutes. In the aftermath this is the slick I spill onto my own inner turbulence, stilling the guilt, quietening it. My last wish for him is almost loving: that those final seconds before brain death, those final microseconds before time stops, might be the finest, most expanded moments of his life.

Less an endless sermon than an unending hymn, flooded with light and joy.

The sun is up. The budgerigars have gone.

Silence.

Then in the silence, a harsh croak. *Ka-ka-kaaaa*. Lest we be carried away, carried too high on the backs of those rising birds. *Ka-ka-kaaaa*.

I think: For every flock of peaceful, squid-beaked ngatijirri, there is a patient crow. Its sharp eye, the jag-jag of its remorseless stiletto. Again, that echoing *ka-ka-kaaaa*. Come and get it? Big feast today? And I also think, If Felix belongs to any skin, any feathered totem, it is not the ngatijirri.

This is his true Dreaming. Kaarnka Jukurrpa.

The wail of a hoarse human voice carries from across the mouth of the sinkhole. Like the crows, the old men know that it is over. They should still be celebrating the return of the budgies; instead, as I watch, each takes a stone in his right hand and strikes at his forehead, sharply, repeatedly.

The force of each blow is loud enough to carry across the mouth of the sinkhole, a dull thud, each trailing an after-clap of sharper echoes, as if those stones are striking an even harder substance.

'What on earth . . . ?' Lucy on her feet, alarmed.

But almost as soon as they have begun, they stop. These are old men, after all. Desert men, pragmatic men, thrifty with all resources, including grief.

Felix would require nothing more.

Now Bedford is ambling off into the scrub, and soon the

322

sharp wood-strike of his hatchet carries to us, each *thock* trailing a new type of echo.

The comfort of doing things, of keeping busy? I leave Lucy cradling Felix's lifeless head in her lap and follow Bedford, wanting to help. Needing to help, and knowing that I am needed. There is no way he can fashion a tree-bier to support Felix alone.

'Mardin,' he says. 'He go in, eh? Walku-jarrijalku.'

Runnels of blood streak his cheeks like tears, in place of tears perhaps, but the streaks have already dried.

'Yuwayi,' I say.

'We build that Japaljarri a proper bird-nest, eh?' And he grins and waves away the first sluggish flies gathering at his wounds, and if there were tears among the blood on his cheeks, they too have dried.

Homo sanguinea. Cheerful man. Lizard fat in his belly, the yellow fat of the morning sun basting his head and shoulders. Working away with his hatchet, working up a sweat, on a morning to die for.

PART V   Tortoise Dreaming

24

Forsan et haec olim meminisse iuvabit. Virgil: Perhaps one day we shall be glad to remember even these things.

Adelaide Hills, early winter. Sunday? Possibly. Probably. Unimportantly. It is, simply, today. The here and now, *this* here and now.

I sit at a table perched on the edge of a terrace above a valley. Felix's table, still. Felix's terrace, Felix's valley, even now, months after his death. Despite sworn affidavits from two medically qualified witnesses to that death, the certificate has not yet been issued, the will has not yet been executed.

Pending a coroner's inquest. Pending a decision as to the validity of those witnesses, given that they are named as beneficiaries. Pending also a decision on the adequacy of the records kept of drugs proscribed under the Narcotics Act – drugs which were administered to the deceased by the aforementioned beneficiaries. And perhaps – the longest legal bow – even pending the recovery of the remains of the deceased, without which the will might not be executed for a statutory seven years.

But if I am not yet permitted to inherit this half-acre of paradise, I can at least rent it, at commercial rates, from the deceased estate. As I am renting the Toyota, likewise, for Bedford. With the written permission of John Fisk, executor.

So. Today. Paradise, three months on and thirty degrees

colder. All night rain has washed the valley; now a feeble winter sun edges upwards into a cloudless sky. The frigid air bites at my face; the mere sight of the rain-sodden world below – its wet pastures and glinting farm ponds – seems to provoke an answering moisture from my eyes.

I roll a cigarette, apply a match, and drink down the smoke deeply, savouring its tickle and rapture, that now-familiar feeling of being flushed clean by filth and tar. No seven-year wait on *this* bequest. What Fisk doesn't know about Felix's tobacco stash needn't concern him.

I inhale again, immersing myself in the simple, vegetable pleasure of tobacco. Unhappiness comes from the human world, I have come to believe. The animal world. Happiness comes from the non-human – the vegetable world, the mineral world. I am alone on the terrace, sole animal in an all-vegetable, all-mineral kingdom whose simple elements – light, water, leaf – have the power to gladden me directly, instinctively, entering unexamined through eye and ear.

And lung. In, out, and another cloud of smoke dissolves in the cold air.

The sun, biggest mineral of all, a single mineral cloud, creeps further above the tree-line. The ponds and puddles and farm dams of the valley glitter like shards of a shattered bowl. Shards of bird-speak reflect up from the valley also: the screech of a parrot, the broken laughter of a kookaburra. *Dacelo gigas.* Laughing kingfisher. The desert Latin eludes me. Kookaburra is a blackfeller word, certainly, another song-mimicry – but this is a kingfisher of the forests, not a snakefisher of the dunes. His camp belongs here, not there.

And mine? I have taken six weeks' bereavement leave. One week is standard, occasionally two – but who would dispute the due dimensions of bereavement with an associate professor of psychiatry? In fact, six may be nowhere near enough. There is much still to do. The evenings I spend setting Felix's things in order. Boxing, labelling, storing. Packing up, putting away. Last week, the cellar. This week, the study. The books, the dot-paintings, the artefacts. The shelves of cassette tapes. The letters. The notebooks.

A priceless discovery, these. Translations from the Warlpiri, mostly, or transcriptions of Aboriginal English, scrawled in Felix's barely legible surgeon's hand. Songs, Dreamings, oral history. First-contact stories, massacre stories, army-time stories, bullock-droving stories. Wife-stealing stories, ambush stories, revenge stories, hand-to-hand combat stories – all the usual human narratives, the usual downloads from fifty thousand years of human id. Much of it could as easily be translated from the Greek of Homer as from the desert Latin of Doctor Jerry Jungarrayi. Has any of it seen the light of English before? I have barely scratched the surface. I'm not even sure, adopted Japaljarri skin or not, if I am allowed to read it.

When he came to that place,
That place he went into,
The place they call Ngarlpa,
The place of the water,

The camp of the birds,
Of those small green birds,
The small peaceful birds,
They covered that place,
They covered that dirt
Like grass after raintime . . .

The small hours after midnight I spend on my own writings. Boxing, labelling, storing? Of a kind. Packing things away, certainly, even if much of it might as well also be in Greek.

The days I spend sleeping. And waiting.

Expecto, expectavi. I wait. I have waited. But for what? Grief? That tortoise is still somewhere beyond the horizon, although here in the valley that horizon is no more than a stone's throw, a spear's throw, away. For forgetfulness, then? The innocence of amnesia? But have I the capacity to forget? I who remember everything, who *must* remember everything?

Dear Felix . . .

I found the sheaf of letters among his notebooks last night. I had slept little – I was exhausted, barely concentrating – but the familiar handwriting shocked me fully awake.

I can write this more easily than I can say it to your face,
if only because your first impulse would be to mock me.
Reading it, you will have to spend time digesting it.

330

Sorry to begin an apology with a sermon! But this is an apology. I'm sorry I have been so obtuse – sorry I failed to grasp your plight . . .

Undated, but placing itself instantly – written after that second mercy dash to the hills, the night of the revelation of his cancer. Written, surely, while I slept.

I cannot even imagine what you have been through, and I will not pass judgement. I know you don't want pity but perhaps it's impossible to separate pity from what I am feeling. I hope it is more than pity, if less than whatever it is you seem to want from me, even if you don't recognise what you want yourself. I think we need to talk about this . . .

Lucy stopping at road-kill? My heart pounds; I read on, but slowly, apprehensively.

A 'night with the Frau Doktor' might be out of the question, but a meal with a friend?
*   Yours, in friendship . . .*

A small, belated revelation: no wonder he rang with his invitation to dinner a few nights later. Larger shocks no doubt await me: the stack sitting on the table is ten or fifteen letters thick. When did she find time to write them? During working hours? *Where* did she write them? In the pain clinic, between clients?

I roll another cigarette, taking my time before unfolding the next. Occupational therapy, craft therapy.

My darling Felix . . .

A small shiver climbs the nape of my neck, rung by bony rung, raising hairs and goosebumps. The same handwriting, but changed, loosened, scribbled across the full width of each page as if under some great pressure of feeling.

. . . Your tenderness last night surprised me – shocked me in many ways . . .

No palliative love this. No mercy fuck. And on the back of this realisation comes a wilder, paranoid realisation: Felix *intended* me to find the letters. This was his true bequest; the farmhouse was nothing more than a means, a mailbox, a brick-and-mortar envelope addressed to me. But if so, to what purpose? Payback? Last laugh? To grant me my most driven, most obsessive wish – to watch, to eavesdrop, as my wife makes love to him?

. . . I do not understand my feelings for you, but I know now that I can love you for these last weeks. Love you and hate myself . . .

Beyond words, O queen, the grief you would make me remember. I want desperately to read more, to understand more, but for the moment I cannot. Tears prick at my eyes and still I tell myself they are nothing more than the reflections of a cold world. I screw my eyes shut but that world will not be shut out. I hear it in the rain-swollen creek, warbling over its bed of smooth stones. I hear it in the language of the magpies above that creek, their bevelled magpie-Slavic spoken as if through a mouthful of those creek stones, spoken as if in imitation of the warbling of the water.

Reflections of running water in air, running water in sky.

My darling Felix . . . Perhaps one day I shall be glad to remember even this. I hoisted the body of my wife's lover onto my shoulders that last day at the sinkhole. I carried him around the rim and out through the bush to the chosen funeral tree, a desert oak. I carried him effortlessly, his wasted body as weightless as a bird and perhaps at last as capable of flight. Bedford and Lucy followed behind, a single-file cortège through dense scrub. Music brought up our rear: the chanting of the old doctor, the clap and echoing after-clap of his rhythm sticks as he shuffled out of his sorry camp.

I found my feet involuntarily falling in time with the beat of that rapid funeral march. Several times I broke my step, slowing into something more whitefeller-stately, only to accelerate again, also involuntarily.

Mixed tempos, mixed cultures, mixed-up sorry business.

Ka-ka-kaaaa.

Too cold still for flies, but the crows were settling heavily into the nearby trees, talking their tough talk. *Come and get it. Big feast today*. With Bedford's help I heaved the body up onto the rough, shoulder-height platform of boughs. The thin branches gave a little, one or two snapped, the corpse sank more deeply into the tree, limbs awkwardly askew, head lolling alarmingly back. The bent smile had gone now; the upside-down face – white, cold, gaunt, expressionless – seemed as inscrutable in death as it had been in life.

He looked, above all, bored. Affectless, in *DSM*-speak.

I didn't begrudge him an ecstatic death, had wished it in fact, but wondered – a last, mean thought – if perhaps he might reveal a hint of that final inner ecstasy to us, if only to justify the pain of getting there. My pain, Lucy's pain, the old men's pain – the surviving pains. As I lifted his head and wedged it gently into the fork of a branch, I felt an urge to shake some feeling into it.

More hare-footed emotions? Hare-brained, certainly.

And something else from the last, moving pages of the *Phaedo* came back to me. Crito asking Socrates how his friends should bury him. The condemned man's joking reply: *Any way you like – if you can hold on to me. If I don't slip through your grasp.*

Ka-ka-kaaaa. Whatever remained of Felix would not slip through the grasp of the waiting crows.

The old doctor arrived, puffing, lacking the breath to sing more. But the moment demanded some sort of further ritual, or at least some music other than the stark chorus of the crows. Lucy, moist-eyed, gnawed at her flautist's upper lip, as if wanting to play but having no instrument.

'Ngulajukurna wangkaja,' the old doctor wheezed, settling himself cross-legged and stern-faced in the shade of a stunted coolibah. 'Nyurru.'

Bedford interpreted. 'He sing all he need to, Mardin. He finish up. He done.'

What now? A bird in the next tree was quoting Crow again – *For what we are about to receive* – as Bedford carefully placed a broken branch across the body.

'Hungry one, that one, Mardin.' He reached down for another snapped branch. 'We cover up Pillage good. Make that one wait. We build that Pillage a proper bird-nest, eh Mardin?'

I stepped forward to help, placing branch after branch across the body until only the face remained exposed, and Lucy took the last frond of leaves from my hand. Stretching on tiptoe, she kissed the dead man on the lips and rested her cheek against his for a long moment. Then placed the leaves across his face, as gently as if drawing a quilt across a sleeping lover.

My darling Felix . . . I screw my eyes more tightly shut, less against the sharpness of the cold than other sharpnesses. Felix and I are students again, two pimple-faced boys staring at each other across a stainless-steel bench. On that bench is something we cannot yet bring into clear focus, something stinking of formalin and cold pork, an oblong thing with four stiff limbs and two shrunken, opaque eyes whose dead-fish gaze we cannot quite meet.

I have a notion, incompletely thought through, that the tribe of medical initiates is permanently scarred by that first corpse – the first noisy sawing open of the skull, the first penetration of greasy body cavities by gloved fingers. The process of skin-thickening – skin-kinship – that is needed to survive our trade surely begins there. The defence mechanisms – humour, denial, projection – quickly become fixed and immovable; coping style becomes lifestyle.

Monday morning, twenty years past. Summer. We stand around our assigned corpse that first day, nervous and edgy. As we clutch our gleaming dissecting tools, armoured in white starched ceremonial dress, our true vocations will soon be clear to us.

Defence mechanics. Coping stylists.

Within those vocations are sub-specialties. Stella Robinson, clever, methodical Stella, unsheathes her scalpel and begins to slice open the cadaver's foot as if it's so much white shoe-leather. Frank Boyd, fez-less but still three-quarters drunk from some all-night party, reeks so much of booze and its morning-after, glue-sniffer metabolites – acetone, methyl alcohol – that he surely can't even smell the cold pork, let alone focus his bloodshot eyes or steady the tools in his hands.

I sit to one side, nose buried in *Gray's Anatomy*, memorising the names of muscles and nerves, chanting their liturgy in my head. *Flexor pollicis longus. Extensor carpi radialis brevis* . . .

And Felix? When do I glance up from my Latin and notice that he has slipped from the room? After ten minutes? An hour? I rise from my stool and walk out into an empty corridor, then on into the locker-room. His locker stands open, his white coat lies discarded on the floor. Retching sounds beyond another door: alarmed, I push through to find him on his knees in front of a toilet bowl. His face is deathly white, as white as the corpse inside, but he pushes away the paper cup of water I offer and rises to his feet.

'Missed breakfast,' he says. And then, 'A cold pork sandwich might hit the spot.'

A small laugh stirs inside me, jolts me back into the present. I open my eyes, blink away the wetness. The chitter of wrens in a nearby bush, finch-flutter in a corner of my eye. The vegetable and mineral worlds are filling with animals again. A wagtail hopscotches across the flagstones on the far side of the terrace, cocking its head, flicking its tail. *Sweet pretty creature, jintipirri creature.*

The sound of passing cars carries to me faintly from beyond the ridge, each of them sketching a rough sound-shape of the freeway, none of them turning off into the valley. From further away comes the chutter of a helicopter. *Pinta-pinta. Pinta-pinta.*

Tree-moth. Butterfly.

Expecto, expectabo. I am still waiting. Perhaps for forgiveness? One thing is clear to me: forgiveness is more than forgetting. Forgiveness is the opposite of forgetting. Forgiveness is another kind of remembering, a special case of remembering.

Am I waiting for blame, then? Desert justice? Kunka?

Match-strike, inhalation, exhalation. The smoke hangs in the still air, a roughly head-sized cloud, holding its shape and size, rotating slightly as if turning to look back at me. Felix's smoky

337

ghost? I am tempted to speak to it, but what else is there to say? Sorry? Shit happens? *Death* happens?

'No such thing as death from natural causes in the desert,' he often told me during that last trip. Told *us* – aiming his tough talk more at Lucy, wanting to jolt her, provoke her, to move her somehow. Anyhow. 'Someone is always to blame, Frau Doktor. An enemy. A sorcerer.'

I close my eyes and am sitting with him again on that first day in the desert, reluctantly chewing grilled lizard rubber, trying to take in as little by ear as I take in by mouth.

'The old doctor can read a decomposing corpse like a book.'

'Do we have to talk about this now?'

His chest is heaving a little, filling slowly with the fluid that will drown him, but he can't, or won't, stop himself hectoring us, relishing the black details. 'I thought you'd be interested. It's very forensic. They'll find clues – the direction of maggot-strike, or the leakage of body juices – to locate the murderer.' His gaze lighting on me as he speaks the word: murderer.

'What are you trying to tell me?' I ask.

The bent smile, the hooded but hair-raisingly clairvoyant gaze. 'I'm telling you that you'd better look after me, Featherfoot.'

Today. Here and now. Another small laugh, a laugh no larger than a hiccup, surprises me. *We build that Pillage a proper bird-nest, eh Mardin?* I have built him a bird's nest of words, have conducted my own sorry-business inquest. I have struck my head against these pages, these memories, these foot-and-a-half-long words, repeatedly. But to what end? To prove that my crime was less than murder? More than murder? To prove that Lucy's love for Felix was less or more than love? To prove my innocence – our innocence, all of us, all three of us – more or less?

I do not understand my feelings . . . I have spent my working life trying to understand the confusions of others, their confused thoughts, their even more confused feelings. I have spent my life trying to explain confused actions, to make them plausible, explicable. Forgivable? This is the blanket forgiveness that psychiatry offers all comers – a forgiveness that is a comprehensive remembering.

We are all innocent till proven innocent.

The old men's inquest was brief, its verdict mere inches long – an inch and a half at most. Bedford and the doctor put their scarred, pragmatic heads together and came up with this: 'He kill him properly, that one, Mardin.'

'He killed *himself* ?'

'Yuwayi.'

'I'm sorry – you're saying he was responsible for his own death?'

'Yuwayi. He kill himself dead, that one.'

Pragmatic sorry business. Face-saving all round. *We cover him up good, Mardin.*

Myself, also, with fronds of words. The sun slips behind a cloud and a breeze shivers the treetops, a breeze with icy edges. A south wind, a fish breath, a polar breath. More rain is on the way. A swirl of air now through the terrace and the topmost letter lifts from the table and takes flight, briefly, before settling on the flagstones a few steps away. I quickly pin the others with the palm of my hand. I have barely scratched the surface of Lucy's letters. Inexplicable, still, her actions to me – or less her actions than the feelings that drove them. Actions speak less than feelings? *I don't know who you are any more.*

And an odd thought strikes me: These letters piled on the table are a kind of test. No, more than a test: a trial. A test of nerve. A mad thought, a magical thought, but once it's taken hold, it's impossible to dislodge, and quickly gains powerful focus.

If I refuse to read any further, Lucy will be returned to me. If I refuse to look back into the mouth of hell, she will return herself to me. She will follow me home.

Dreamtime magic, or Pascal's wager? *You have nothing to lose by believing in magic, Herr Professor, and everything to gain.*

Nothing to lose, either, by breaking with the thinking habits of a lifetime – all those relentless case studies and fact-findings and exhaustive human histories. By breaking, in short, with the need to know.

I have tried to tell this story as it happened, in the living, breathing present. Without – Waldo again, one last time – getting too previous. Of course I have failed, but I have only failed up to this particular moment in the present. I have only failed *so far.*

And as I sit here stuck in that moment – the here and now, the only moment that counts, finally, ever – another hiccup of laughter surprises me. And then another, slightly larger. And another, following closely, the splutter of a cold engine coming to life. And with the laughter come tears. Not many tears – a frugal desert quota – but true tears this time. Eye tears.

Tears, and pragmatic magic: I remove my hand from the stack of letters and the top sheet takes wing. *Bury me any way you like, dear Crito – if I don't slip through your grasp.* Another swirl and the next page follows, then the next, as if by some invisible copying machine. The pages rustle and tumble across the terrace, one sheet sliding ahead, then another, walking left and right away from me as lightly as feather slippers.

The wagtail also takes to the air, alarmed, as the breeze dies and the first heavy drops of rain splatter onto the paving. By the end of the day the letters will be pulp, and whatever explanations or understandings they might offer – sweet nothings or dirty talk, mea culpas or confessions, tender blandishments or celebrations of myth-swollen cock – will be writ in water.

I wait. I have waited. *Expectabo*: I will wait. For how much longer, I have no idea. Perhaps sometime soon, an hour hence, a week, a month, a small red car will detach from the freeway and crawl up over the far ridge and down into the town below. And on through the town and up the creek road, as slowly and steadily as a tortoise.

A tortoise that carries an entire world on its broad back, a whole sweet and sorry world.

Forsan et haec olim meminisse iuvabit. Perhaps, for now, I have remembered enough. As the tears dry in my eyes and the laughter stops jumping about like a jintipirri in my throat, the blunter desert Latin is enough.

He went in.

Yes, he died. Yuwayi, walku-jarrijalku.

That is all. Ngulajuku. That is all I need to say. Nyurru. I am done.

Nyurru. *Expectabo*.

I am done. Yet still I wait.

ACKNOWLEDGEMENTS

I owe an enormous debt to Tommy Driver Jupurrula that can never be repaid now that he has gone in. I am indebted also to the late Engineer Jack Japaljarri and Charlie Charles Jakamarra for generously sharing their time and country with me; these debts also can never be repaid. Thanks also to David Nash for his immense tact, knowledge and language skills.

Lee Cataldi, Jane Simpson and Robin Japanangka Granites provided further invaluable commentary and help. They can in no way be held responsible for the resulting monster. Among extensive background reading, I should make special mention of Meggitt's classic *Desert People: A Study of the Walbiri Aborigines of Central Australia*; Diane Bell's more recent *Daughters of the Dreaming*; and *Warlpiri Dreamings and Histories*, collected and translated by Peggy Rockman Napaljarri and Lee Cataldi.

My partner Lisa Temple offered often painful criticisms, sentence by sentence; my daughter Anna provided her usual close critical reading and advice; my son Daniel discovered numerous non-sequiturs; my daughter Alexandra provided a useful overview. From Alexander McFarlane came the necessary psychiatric perspective. My brother Jeffrey offered some useful legal-process advice. Clare Forster and Christopher Pearson gave editorial advice on early versions of the manuscript; Meredith Rose had the final, crucial hand in the book's editing. Several lines were filched from conversations with Les Murray and Christopher Pearson.

The detour of the Budgerigar Dreaming described in this novel is entirely fictional, as are the Dreaming site Ngarlpa and the community named Widjuri. All characters, whitefeller and black, are likewise fictional, or life-based composites in the manner of most fiction writing. As Engineer Jack Japaljarri once remarked of another story I told him, 'That your Dreaming, Peter.'

ALSO FROM PENGUIN

THE LIST OF ALL ANSWERS: COLLECTED STORIES
Peter Goldsworthy

Ranging from the early comic sketches to the disturbing brilliance of his recent stories, this outstanding collection reinforces Peter Goldsworthy's reputation as a modern master of short fiction. Simultaneously light and dark, unsettling and amusing, his stories leave indelible traces in the memory. A writer's writer, he is also never less than compellingly readable.

'These stories are tinged with irony and delectable wit, running the gamut of emotions from envy to despair. Goldsworthy's ear for dialogue is as exceptional as his inner eye for character is exquisite.'

Ali Lavau, *Who Weekly*

'In some ways Goldsworthy is the Chekhov of his time and place . . . poised, controlled, acute, funny, mean, miserable.'

Heather Falkner, *The Australian*

'A subtle hook draws the reader in at the beginning . . . Once the lure is taken, you're drawn effortlessly to the end.'

Barry Oakley, *The Weekend Australian*

NAVEL GAZING
Peter Goldsworthy

Funny, wise, idiosyncratic and original, these occasional essays chart a course through the genres of fiction, science fiction, poetry, opera and film. Spiced with often hilarious personal anecdotes and references to the wide-ranging reading of a self-confessed 'hick autodidact', this book is at once a writing manual for various literary disciplines and an exploration of Goldsworthy's key themes and obsessions: death, humour, the limits of language, the relationship of biology to thought and culture, and the role and responsibilities of art. And first love also gets a look in . . .

'A rare intelligence, combining a scientific and poetic appreciation of life, each expressed with great elegance and love of language.'

The Sunday Age

THE PHILOSOPHER'S DOLL
Amanda Lohrey

What happens when one partner in a relationship wants to have a child and the other doesn't? Lindsay Eynon, a philosophy lecturer, isn't ready to start a family yet; he has other plans. But Kirsten's biological clock is ticking and she sees the world differently. As their arguments intensify, so does the probability of the unexpected . . .

The Philosopher's Doll is a highly unusual, constantly surprising novel about the perennial conflict between the head and the heart. Thought-provoking and compellingly readable, it reverberates with the dilemmas of contemporary life. In a culture of affluence, what do we need in order to be happy? And just how much control do we really have over our lives?

'Lohrey is about the finest fiction writer currently working in Australia. You emerge from the novel newly thoughtful. And that's only one of the myriad satisfying aspects of this complex, subtle and often very funny novel.'

Limelight Magazine